Jewish Latin America

Jewish Latin America
Ilan Stavans, series editor

Moacyr Scliar: Collected Stories is the eighth volume of the
University of New Mexico Press series Jewish Latin America.
It was made possible thanks to a generous grant
from the Lucius N. Littauer Foundation.

 *The Collected Stories of Moacyr Scliar*

The Collected Stories of Moacyr Scliar

Translated by Eloah F. Giacomelli
Introduction by Ilan Stavans

University of New Mexico Press
Albuquerque

*Other titles available in the University of New Mexico Press
Jewish Latin America series:*

The Jewish Gauchos of the Pampas by Alberto Gerchunoff

Cláper: A Novel by Alicia Freilich

The Book of Memories by Ana María Shua

The Prophet and Other Stories by Samuel Rawet

The Fragmented Life of Don Jacobo Lerner by Isaac Goldemberg

Passion, Memory, and Identity: Twentieth-Century Latin American
    Jewish Women Writers, edited by Marjorie Agosín

King David's Harp: Autobiographical Essays by Jewish Latin Ameri-
    can Writers, edited by Stephen A. Sadow

Library of Congress Cataloging-in-Publication Data

Scliar, Moacyr
    The collected stories of Moacyr Scliar / translated by Eloah F. Giacomelli ;
introduction by Ilan Stavans. — 1st ed.
        p.   cm. — (Jewish Latin America ; 7)
    Contents: The carnival of animals — The ballad of the false messiah —
The tremulous earth — The dwarf in the television set — The enigmatic
eye — Van Gogh's Ear.
    ISBN 0-8263-1911-4 (cloth : alk. paper). — ISBN 0-8263-1912-2
(paper : alk. paper)
    1. Scliar, Moacyr—Translations into English.   I. Giacomelli, Eloah F.
II. Title.   III. Series.
PQ9698.29.C54A24   1999   99-32298
869.3—dc21   CIP

For Ilan Stavans—
writer, friend

 *Contents*

Introduction by Ilan Stavans xv

The Carnival of the Animals [1968]

The Lions 3

The She-Bears 4

Rabbits 7

The Cow 10

The Dog 13

Shazam 16

The Fishing Tournament 20

We Gunmen Mustn't Feel Pity 22

Blind Man and Amigo Gedeão
   Alongside the Highway 24

The Pause 27

Of Cannibals 30

The Aging Marx 32

Leo 40

A House 42

The Phantom Train 46

The Day When We Killed James Cagney 47

Vegetable Kingdom 50

Navigation Chart 52

Ecology 56

Before Making the Investment 58

Communication 62

Hello! Hello! 63

Dr. Shylock 64

The Ballad of the False Messiah [1976]

The Ballad of the False Messiah   69

Don't Release the Cataracts   76

New Year, New Life   79

The Scalp   82

The Spider   86

Agenda of Executive Jorge T. Flacks
    for Judgment Day   88

Eating Paper   90

The Evidence   92

The Offerings of Dalila Store   100

The Short-Story Writers   104

The Tremulous Earth [1977]

Quick, Quick   151

The Price of the Living Steer   163

Youth Is an Eternal Treasure   165

Grand Prize   167

Friends   171

It's Time to Fall   173

The Thief   178

Requiem   180

Images   183

The Picnic   185

Rest in Peace   190

Festive Dawn   194

Skinny Enough to Become a Kite   196

Profile of the Hen of the Golden Eggs
    as She Lay Dying   199

Capital Punishment   206

The Last One   209

The Riddle   210

The Dream   211

The Shadow   212

Stories of the Tremulous Earth   214

The Dwarf in the Television Set [1979]

The Prophets of Benjamin Bok   225

Ah, Mommy Dear   235

Good Night, Love   239

The Apex of the Pyramid   245

A Porto Alegre Story   249

The Noises in the Attic   253

At the Figtree Retreat   257

The Secret Tourists   261

Milton and His Competitor   263

The Soothsayer   264

A Vacancy   266

In a State of Coma   269

The Dwarf in the Television Set   284

The Memoirs of a Researcher   288

The Loves of a Ventriloquist   297

The Peal of Bells at Christmas   302

The Phantom Ship   306

The Enigmatic Eye [1986]

The Enigmatic Eye   311

Inside My Dirty Head–The Holocaust   314

Five Anarchists   318

Among the Wise Men   321

The Conspiracy   322

The Prodigal Uncle   325

Root Canal Treatment   328

The Interpreter   338

Atlas   342

A Brief History of Capitalism   346

A Public Act   350

Burning Angels   352

Free Topics   353

The Password   355

The Emissary   361

The Candidate   362

General Delivery   365

In the Submarine Restaurant   367

Peace and War   369

The Blank   372

Many Many Meters Above Good and Evil   374

Prognoses   377

Real Estate Transactions   379

Life and Death of a Terrorist   381

Resurrection   383

Genesis   385

Van Gogh's Ear [1989]

The Plagues   389

Don't Think About It, Jorge   404

Van Gogh's Ear   405

The Fragment   408

The Decision Tree   409

Jigsaw Puzzles   410

The March of the Sun
   in the Temperate Regions   411

The Diary of a Lentil Eater   428

Misereor   432

The Calligraphers' Union   437

French Current Events   444

A Job for the Angel of Death   447

The Right Time   449

The Public Enemy   451

The Message   454

Unpublished Works   454
A Minute of Silence   458
The Prince   459
The Problem   460
In the World of Letters   461
Sensitive Skin   462
The Surprise   464
The Winner: An Alternative View   465
Memoirs of an Anorexic   466

Epilogue

In the Tribe of the Short-Story Writers:
   A Deposition   471

Introduction

ILAN STAVANS

*The pen is apt to leap across middle ground
and see itself as designer of a universe.*

V.S. Pritchett

In 1986 I took a long trip to Brazil. I had just finished a graduate degree and my first novel and wanted to come to terms with my literary roots. While my objective was to wander around, I specifically planned to visit Moacyr Scliar, the Brazilian-Jewish master, in his native Porto Alegre. I had encountered his astonishing stories in magazines and had read his novel *The Centaur in the Garden* in English. A mutual friend, Thomas Colchie, had given me his address a month prior. I had sent Scliar a letter announcing my arrival but had left before his reply had come back. So I wasn't sure our encounter would occur, although I prayed that it would, for I knew, the moment I put the final word to *Talia in Heaven*, that Scliar was my true forebear. Through his work—and through that of Alberto Gerchunoff and Isaac Goldemberg—I sensed a feeling of belonging to a tradition not unlike that of Yiddish letters.

In his introduction to *A Treasury of Yiddish Stories*, a path-making anthology I had fallen in love with around that time, Irving Howe called attention to I. L. Peretz's marked ambiguity toward tradition and modernity, an either/or at the heart of Diaspora Jewish literature. What attracted Howe to the Polish writer responsible for "Monish" and *Impressions of a Journey Through the Tomaszow Region*, among other major works, was the way he struggled, at times in total despair, to balance his admiration for Hasidism on the one hand with his outright refusal to endorse orthodox religion on the other. This ambivalence, of course, is also present in the best of Kafka and Isaac Babel, but in Howe's eyes, Peretz had been the first to articulate it. To Howe, a Socialist in 1950s America, one who hoped to find in ideology and literature the panacea to the human condition, it was the key to the divided Jewish self. "[Peretz] had abandoned strict faith," he wrote,

> yet it must be remembered—this is perhaps the single over-
> riding fact in the experience of Yiddish writers at the end of
> the nineteenth-century—that faith abandoned could still be a
> far more imperious presence than new creeds adopted. Like
> such Western writers as George Eliot and Thomas Hardy, he
> found himself enabled to draw upon traditional faith and feel-
> ings precisely through the act of denying them intellectually;
> indeed, the greatest influence on the work of such writers is
> the rich entanglement of images, symbols, language, and cere-
> monies associated with a discarded belief.

Born in 1937, more than twenty years after Peretz's death, Scliar (in English, his name is pronounced *Mwa seer Skleer*) is a different sort of literary animal—on the surface, at least. He belongs to a genera-tion further removed from orthodoxy and the ghetto than that of Peretz or his immediate successors in the Yiddish literary tradition. His readership, at least at home, comprises equally Jew and non-Jews, and his objective is to explain, in a racially hybrid country marked by its amorphous Catholicism, what his Jewish ancestry is about. His challenge, then, is unique: if Peretz sought to ease the transition of his people from isolation into modernity, Scliar's audi-ence is already all too modern, but marginal nonetheless. He, too, struggles to explain today's Jewish angst in the light of our abandonment of faith: faith in ideology, faith in religion. His task is to make compatible the incompatible: to explain the clash between Jewish and Brazilian values and to build a universe out of that clash. After obsessively embracing all sorts of orthodoxies (Communism, Socialism, Zionism, nationalism, religious doctrine), his characters are forced to realize, inevitably, that our modern condition is one of perpetual chaos and anxiety, and that no cure can truly redeem us from it.

But he isn't a pessimist; rather, he approaches our condition not as an end but as a beginning. That, more than anything else, makes me see him as my precursor and vanguard. Raised in a self-enclosed, secular Jewish neighborhood—Bom Fim—in Porto Alegre, Scliar came of age in the late forties and early fifties, in youth organizations such as *Habonim* and *Hashomer Hatzair*. Two forces colored his up-bringing: ideology and culture—and the two emanated from a single source: his Jewishness. "I have lived my life among Jews," Scliar told me, "and my Jewish world view circumscribes everything I do, for I am the child of Eastern European immigrants. Socialism was their principle and Yiddish their first tongue." For his generation at least, Yiddish would become a conduit for nostalgia. He added: "My parents spoke Portuguese quite well, but reverted to Yiddish only when the topic was judged too dangerous for the kids. Thus, I heard it only sporadically, and it was music to my ears. It is a lullaby, a very emotional tongue. Among the things I lament the most today is not to be fluent in Yiddish. . . . I could have learned it, since my grandmother almost solely spoke Yiddish to me. But my parents thought that the sooner I became a full-fledged Brazilian, the better, and so, regrettably, they never insisted on me speaking Yiddish." Hebrew, instead, was the language of dogma, for in Zionism he foresaw the road to Socialism: it led to Israel, to a land where Judaism and politics are forever married.

Adulthood surprised Scliar with forking paths wherein he could link the forces shaping his identity. He became a writer and public-health physician. In 1955 he enrolled in the Facultade de Medicina da Universidade Federal, a starting point in a career marked by expertise and compassion. Decades later, he would be named Rio Grande do Sul's head of the Department of Public Health. His first book, *Histórias de um médico em Formação*, released in 1962, even if Scliar would later reject it as unworthy, marks the point where both paths meet. It also announces a theme that permeates his vast oeuvre: medicine not as a mere enhancer of Western civilization and a repository of modernity, but as a way to mend the world. His talent to invent a cast of pathetic characters, always in search of some cure for the miseries of society, is astounding. His creatures are radicals from Europe seeking to establish an egalitarian Promised Land in the Brazilian pampa, Jews involved in voodoo, disoriented false messiahs, mythical figures (Van Gogh, Shakespeare's Shylock, Marx, James Cagney, Freud, Sabbethai Zevi), doctors who view Judaism and activism as synonyms. None of them ever finds redemption in these faiths, and the acts of embracing and then renouncing them are equally appealing to Scliar. Salvation, he knows, is only a subterfuge, a lie we like repeating to ourselves. Their Jewishness is a condition they cannot escape, a condition of alienation, but one that carries within itself the strength to combat it.

Linking Scliar to Peretz is risky, for his talents have more in common with Sholem Aleichem. In fact, when I settled into a cheap downtown hotel and called him, I felt, curiously, as if I had made a date to meet a Brazilian reincarnation of the author of *Tevye the Dairyman*, whom Scliar, by the way, resembles not only in his *joie de vivre* but physically too, even though he is considerably taller. To friends I would describe him as "a Jewish Mark Twain," a master whose spirit becomes flesh through anecdotes and whose florid imagination brought Kasrilevke to life in Rio Grande do Sul. To me, his self-proclaimed successor, Scliar personified the father of Jewish-

Latin American literary tradition, with Gerchunoff, author of *The Jewish Gauchos of the Pampas*, the magisterial grandfatherly figure. But as soon as we began to talk, I realized how tricky the act of comparing him to Sholem Aleichem could be. Our conversation made the differences revelatory. Portuguese is not Yiddish, of course; it isn't a "Jewish tongue" per se. Actually, it is a most gentile tongue, and not a genteel one at that, at least as far as Jews are concerned. It has been since 1496, when King Manuel decreed they convert to Christianity or else be expelled from Portugal, much as they had been from the rest of the Iberian peninsula six years prior. And the comparison might be ineffectual for another reason: the search for literary fathers suggests a genealogical tree; its different branches denote a sense of transmission, of continuity, of commitment to the permanence of knowledge and beliefs from one generation to the next. But Brazil's Jews, as Scliar made clear to me, have not really been aware of their counterparts in Argentina and Mexico—not, that is, until quite recently. I don't mean to say that in general, they are unacquainted with the fact that Jews have been a permanent fixture in the Americas since Columbus arrived, and that Yiddish-speaking Eastern European immigrants settled not only in São Paulo and Rio de Janeiro but in almost every major city this side of the Atlantic. The awareness, nevertheless, has been minimal, and certainly doesn't amount to a full-fledged cultural tradition. Scliar, for instance, is far more familiar with the work of Philip Roth than with that of Gerchunoff.

Has the time come to reconsider? Well, not exactly—and therein lies the *real* connection between him and Sholem Aleichem, one I hereby repeat, as I did in my introduction to *Tropical Synagogues*.[+] The particular tradition Scliar belongs to manifests itself not in a writer's influences, but in the overall stimuli that nurture him—his

[+]Holmes and Meier, 1994.

milieu, in which Jews are and are not full, unequivocal partners. In 1888, in the preface to his first Yiddish novel, *Stempenyu*, when Sholom Aleichem described S. Y. Ambramovitch as "the grandfather of our literature," the feeling of self-enclosure within Yiddish letters, which would last until the Holocaust, was already apparent. In spite of the spread of the Pale, writers in Vilnius and Warsaw, among other cultural capitals, knew each other. They ate in the same restaurants, read the same magazines, frequented each other's offices, and even slept with the same partners. Yiddish, *die mame-losh*, served as the glue. The Portuguese- and Spanish-speaking Americas are altogether different: to begin with, the geographical spread is enormous; Brazil alone, the largest nation in the hemisphere, is eight times the size of Poland before World War II. Language isn't a unifier: in spite of its size, and as a result of its verbal otherness, Brazil often feels like an island within a continent, a ghetto of 160 million people. But while the sense of community might be lost, the *conditions* a Jewish writer in a country like Brazil are, in essence, similar—though not identical—to those of his counterparts in Buenos Aires and Ciudad de México, all habitats colored by a peculiar mix, to various degrees, of aboriginal, Catholic, and African religions, and all politically fragile and socially explosive landscapes where modernity arrived haphazardly, *in medias res*. That explains why Gerchunoff's *Jewish Gauchos*, bucolic in style, naive in its endorsement of Argentina's democratic future, feels so close to Scliar's phantasmagorical cosmos. That, too, reveals why I felt—and still feel—the urge to seek his guidance by traveling to his homeland: separated by time and tongue, we are all responses to the same existential dilemma.

This approach to Jewish-Latin American literature must suffice, for even within Brazil a sense of tradition in Jewish letters is difficult to trace. When Scliar began his writing career, the country didn't already have well-established Jewish writers. Not that the stage was empty. Yiddish stories were written in Brazil. In 1973, in

Musteverke, published by YIVO in Buenos Aires, Shmuel Rodzansky included a volume, entitled *Antpologie Brasilianish*, with tales by Moyshe Lockietsh, Meir Kutshinsky, Pinye Polotnik, and Itzjak Guterman. But Scliar knew nothing about them, for their readership was a minuscule group of old immigrants. Sure, Porto Alegre had an excellent library of Yiddish classics, frequented by Yiddish-speaking intellectuals, but, again, not by him. Only when, decades later, Jacó Guinzburg, the father of nonreligious Jewish culture in Brazil, translated these and countless other Jewish stories and books from Yiddish into Portuguese (he is one of the editors of *Jóias do Conto Idish*), did Scliar feel as if the ground under his feet was less shaky.

His reading about Jews in Brazil was minimal. The only writer he was acquainted with was Marcos Lolovitch, a lawyer whose memoir, *Numa Clara Manha De Abril*, is a valuable, if undistinguished chronicle of immigration. Also the extraordinary Clarice Lispector, of Jewish descent, author of *Family Ties* and other famous novels, known as "Brazil's Virginia Woolf," already had a solid following. But her Jewish themes are so eclipsed, so buried in their allegorical fantasies that it takes heavy critical tools to unearth them. Not finding role models at home, Scliar read Jewish writers from Europe and the United States, among them Peretz's parables (he acknowledged to me that he has reread "If Not Higher . . . " at least a hundred times) and Sholem Aleichem, but also Michael Gold. Humor, he quickly learned, is the most efficient Jewish response to catastrophe, and, like Sholem Aleichem, he makes his characters laugh constantly at themselves and their circumstance. But he is darker, more dismal in his approach to life, and so, his true idols are Kafka and Babel, whom he trusts to be indisputable literary geniuses. "[Babel's] portrait of childhood remains unparalleled," he told me. "I could easily see myself reflected in his Odessa. Kafka, of course, is an ambivalent figure, but so is Babel. His ambivalence toward the Jews and his idolatry of the Cossacks. . . . His Jews are ugly, even monstrous, whereas the

Cossacks are imposing and muscular. One could even go so far as to suggest a certain dose of anti-Semitism in *Red Chivalry*." This ambivalence, with roots in Peretz, is what typifies Scliar's work: his animosity is toward the ghetto Jew, but it is tarnished by nostalgia. His characters are stereotypes aware of their cartoonish predicament.

More than anyone else, Scliar has *re-Judaized* the Portuguese tongue, making it more akin to Jewishness. He is responsible for building a sizable Jewish readership in Brazil. His books invariably become huge best-sellers and are reprinted numerous times. Brazilians perceive him not only as an entertainer, but as an educator too. A large segment of the nation is curious about the mysterious Jewish immigrant and his progeny, and Scliar knows how to both enlighten and enthrall them. To an extent, his fame is due to the reality he invents in his novels, in particular to those novels in which alienation, one way or another, is at center stage. His most famous title might well be *The Centaur in the Garden*, a delightful meditation "so powerful, so enchanting," claims Alberto Manguel, "that it succeeds in imposing its own magic on skeptical readers, convincing us that [the] centaur's world is ours, unfathomable and overwhelming." Scliar's centaur forces the reader to reformulate his understanding of what alienation is about. He examines assimilation and disfigurement . . . and ugliness. Released in 1980, this book—translated into German, French, Spanish, and Swedish—is probably the single most important novel by a Jew in Brazil, and perhaps in all of Latin America. Its main character is, well, a centaur, one born of Russian immigrants: not only is he half human, he is Jewish too. Alienation, then, comes to him from different angles, but he rises above his handicap by turning his defects into the substance of his triumph. Equally distinguished is *A Majestade do Xingu*, published in 1996, in which he follows the path of a legendary doctor in Rio Grande do Sul known during the Getulio Vargas dictatorship for fleeing his private practice and moving to the Amazon jungle to help its Indian population.

As he took me back to my hotel, I confessed a stronger passion for his allegorical stories, gems where, I dared to say, his artistic genius shines the brightest and where, yet again, he is, in my eyes, closer to Peretz. (See especially his enchanting deposition "In the Tribe of the Short-Story Writers," the epilogue to this volume.) Scliar's delight was spontaneous. He, too, enjoyed this genre more than any other, and felt it justified him.

Scliar has produced over a hundred and twenty stories, most of them falling in the category that Irving Howe called "short shorts." Three collections, written in Portuguese between 1968 and 1986, have been available in English: *The Carnival of the Animals*, *The Ballad of the False Messiah*, and *The Enigmatic Eye*. They form the bulk of this volume, along with *The Tremulous Earth*, *The Dwarf in the Television Set*, and *Van Gogh's Ear*, hereby translated for the first time. In 1995, the São Paulo publishing house Companhia das Letras brought out most of Scliar's published tales, plus some uncollected ones, in *Contos reunidos*. The present book follows a different format: unlike its Brazilian counterpart, it does not follow a thematic pattern; instead, it is structured chronologically by the date of publication of each collection. The effect, to a large extent, is the same: Scliar gives us the impossible: a varied bestiary, a masonry of obituary writers, a midget trapped in a TV, a blind painter, a suicidal club, a slow-moving mailman, the memoirs of an aphasiac and anorexic patients, as well as an endless gallery of necrophiles. Not since Kafka's "A Report to an Academy" and Borges's *Book of Imaginary Beings* has a writer so bluntly competed with God's creations, inventing his own parallel universe, filled with a cavalcade of bizarre types. "Inventing a secret," Cynthia Ozick wrote once, "then revealing it in the drama of entanglement—that is what ignites the will to write stories," and the definition suits Scliar to the finger. His stories aren't cerebral but anecdotal; they are generally about the secrets of inheritance, about the ways ideology and culture shape our life.

I left the restaurant and returned from my journey to Brazil with a clearer mind. I had arrived in search of origins and in the process found my mission. *Res ipsa loquitur.*

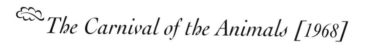*The Carnival of the Animals* [1968]

The Lions

NOT NOWADAYS, BUT YEARS AGO, lions posed a threat. Thousands, nay, millions of them used to roam Africa, making the jungle quiver with their roars. It was feared that they would invade Europe and America. Wright, Friedman, Mason, and others warned against this possible danger. Consequently, it was decided to wipe out the frightful feline beasts. Their destruction was carried out in the following manner:

A great mass of them, gathered near Lake Chad, was destroyed by one single atom device of medium explosive force dropped from a bomber one summer day. After the characteristic mushroom cloud disappeared, it was ascertained by means of photographs that the nucleus of the leonine mass had been completely disintegrated, and was now surrounded by a two kilometer–wide band that was strewn with chunks of bloody flesh, fragments of bone, and bloodstained manes. Dying lions lay on its periphery.

The authorities in charge described the operation as "satisfactory." However, as always happens in undertakings of this scope, the residual problems became in turn a source of concern. There was, for instance, the matter of the radioactive lions that had survived the blast and were now roaming the forests. True, about 20 percent of them were killed by the Zulus during the two weeks following the explosion. However, the proportion of casualties among the natives (two for each lion) discouraged even the most optimistic among the experts.

It became necessary to resort to more elaborate methods. For this purpose, a laboratory was set up to train gazelles; the lab's primary goal was to free the animals from their normal instincts. It would be too tiresome to go into the details of this project, which was, incidentally, quite refined; suffice it to say that the method employed—a kind of brainwashing technique adapted to animals—was one devised by Walsh and his assistants. After obtaining a considerable number of these prepared gazelles, they injected them with a powerful dose of a toxic with delayed action. The gazelles then searched out the lions, and let themselves be killed and eaten by them; the beasts of prey, after eating the poisoned flesh, died painlessly within a few days.

The solution seemed ideal; however, there was one race of lions (fortunately, not many of them) that seemed to be resistant to this and other powerful poisons. The task of killing them was assigned to hunters equipped with sophisticated and ultrasecret weapons. This time, only one specimen survived, a female that was captured and quartered near Brazzaville. In the uterus of this lioness, they found a viable fetus: Showing no signs of radioactivity, the tiny animal was raised in an incubator. It was hoped that in this way the exotic fauna would be kept from extinction.

Later the cub was taken to the London Zoo, where despite the tight security, it was killed by a fanatic. The death of the small beast was greeted enthusiastically by large segments of the population. "The lions are dead!" a drunken soldier kept shouting. "From now on everybody will be happy!"

On the following day the Korean War broke out.

The She-Bears

PROPHET ELISHA IS ON HIS WAY TO BETHEL. It is a hot day. Insects are buzzing in the thicket. The prophet is marching at fast pace. He has an important mission in Bethel.

Suddenly, a large number of children begin to give chase, shouting: "Let's see you levitate, baldy! Come on, levitate!"

Elisha turns around and curses them in the name of the Lord a moment later, two big she-bears come out of the thicket and devour forty-two kids: The smaller bear devours twelve; the bigger one, thirty.

The little bear has active digestion; the children that fall into its stomach are attacked by powerful acids, made soluble, and reduced to small particles. They vanish.

The other thirty children meet with a different fate. Going down the great bear's esophagus, they land in its huge stomach. There they remain. At first, numbed by fear, they cling to one another, barely able to breathe; then the younger kids start to cry and wail, and their cries echo dismally in the large space. "Woe to us! Woe to us!"

Finally, the oldest child turns on a light and they find themselves in a place resembling a cavern, from whose sinuous walls a viscous fluid oozes. The ground is strewn with the half-rotten residue of former prey: babies' skulls, little girls' legs. "Woe to us!" they wail. "We'll die!"

Time goes by, and seeing that they haven't died, they take heart. They chat, laugh, play, romp about, throw debris and remains of food at one another.

When tired out, they sit down and talk in earnest. They organize themselves and outline a plan of action.

Time goes by. They grow up, but not much; the confined space doesn't allow for much growth. They are turned into a strange race of dwarfs, with short limbs and large heads on which glow beacon-like eyes that endlessly scrutinize the darkness of the entrails. And there they build their minitown, with pretty whitewashed mini-houses. The minischool.

The minitown hall. The minihospital. And they are happy.

They have now forgotten the past. Vague memories still remain, memories that acquire mystic configurations as time goes by.

They pray: "Great Bears who art in heaven . . . " They appoint a priest-the Great Prophet, a man with a shaved head and fright-ful eyes; once a year he scourges the inhabitants with the Sacred Whip. He demands faith and hard work. The people, diligent work-ers, don't fail him. The ministorehouses overflow with foodstuffs; the minifactories manufacture thousands of beautiful minithings.

Time goes by. A new generation emerges. After years of happi-ness, the inhabitants are now worried: Due to some strange atavism, the children are born with long arms and legs, well—proportioned heads, and gentle brown eyes. Each birth brings renewed uneasiness. People begin to grumble: "If they grow much taller, there won't be room for US." Birth control measures are under consideration. The minigovernment considers consulting the Great Prophet about the desirability of executing babies as soon as they are born. Endless dis-cussions follow.

Time goes by. The children have grown up and they look power-ful as they move about in groups. Much bigger than their parents, it's impossible to restrain them. They take over the minimovie theaters, the minichurches, the miniclubs. They show no respect for the po-lice. They roam the minihighways.

One day the Great Prophet is on his way to his minimansion when the youngsters catch sight of him. Immediately they give chase, shouting: "Let's see you levitate, baldy! Come on, levitate!

The prophet turns around and curses them in the name of the Lord.

Soon afterward two she-bears appear and devour the children— all forty-two of them.

Twelve are swallowed by the little bear and destroyed. But thirty go down the esophagus of the great bear and land in its stomach—a great hollow where the blackest darkness prevails. And there they remain, crying and wailing: "Woe to us!"

Finally, they turn on a light.

Rabbits

THE RABBIT IS AN ANIMAL that is quick at copulating. Alice opened her eyes. She recalled a story her husband used to tell: about a he-rabbit, who after having relations with a she-rabbit, said to her: "It is very good, my darling—wasn't it?"

She yawned and jumped out of bed. "What's the day today? Wednesday? No, yesterday was Wednesday. . . . It's the day when we play cards. But did we play cards yesterday? Yes, we did.

"I remember Gilda saying to me—you're lucky—and I was. Wait now, that was Wednesday last week. Or last month?"

She sat down at the dressing table and began to brush her hair. "I'm now brushing my hair. Just as I did yesterday." She looked closely at herself. "My face, always the same. I'm thirty-two years old. I could be twenty-two. Or twelve?" "My little girl." She turned around. There was nobody in the room. However, she had heard her husband's deep voice quite distinctly. She looked at the watch: seven-thirty. At this hour he would be on the highway. He was the manager of a cannery located thirty kilometers outside the city. He owned a big car; an old black Dodge. She would tease him: "Nobody else has such an old car!" "I know, my darling. But the manager of a cannery has to be conservative. "The laughter, short and coarse. She winced and turned around again. The wind was stirring the curtains gently. She rose to her feet and walked to the window.

They lived on the top of a bleak, rocky hill on the outskirts of the city. It was a beautiful, spacious house, built of solid white stone and dark wood. The church towers could be seen from there. "But it's so isolated," she had complained to her husband. "I know, my darling." A strong man, with thick black eyebrows and powerful teeth.

A lonely wolf. He would hold her tight in his hairy arms. They spent the winter evenings sitting before the fireplace. He would gaze at her in silence. Suddenly, he would say: "The rabbit, my darling, is an animal that is quick at copulating . . . " He would laugh, hugging her.

She winced.

She drew the curtains aside. A mist, like a white sea, covered everything. Not even the church towers were visible. The house floated, half submerged in the fog. A chilly breeze gave her goose bumps. She closed the window. "How cold it is! I'll put on the white woolen dress."

She went to the closet and opened the heavy doors, made of dark cedar. She looked at herself in the mirror. "I'm quite pretty," she murmured. She was thirty-two years old; she could be twenty.

Always well-dressed: In a white . . .

She was startled: She already had the dress on. "I must be very absentminded. I got dressed without realizing I was doing so." Her husband liked the white dress. "You look twelve years old." They would sit face to face before the fireplace, where a fire burned. Spellbound, she would sit staring at his teeth, which glinted in the light of the fire. He would break into his short, coarse laughter. "The rabbit . . . " She would blush. "Why?" he would ask. "It's this loneliness. I don't like this house, so secluded . . . " Saying nothing, he would gaze at her.

But one evening they got into the car, the big black Dodge. "It's a surprise," he said, laughing. And so it was: They were going to visit her husband's partner. "Let me introduce you to my partner, my darling. Rabbit, meet my wife." Rabbit! She laughed. Everybody was laughing. They played cards on Wednesdays. The two of them, Rabbit and Gilda.

It felt good to be together . . . "The rabbit is an animal that is quick at copulating . . . " She would say and they laughed. It felt good throughout those sweet winter mornings. "You are an animal that is quick at copulating." Rabbit would laugh. "White becomes you, it really does."

Fully dressed, she walked down the grand stairway. She called the maid: "Julia!" There was no reply. She frowned. Then she remembered: "Today's Thursday. She must have gone to the market." She was startled: "But is today Thursday? Yes, it must be. We played cards yesterday, I know! I remember Gilda telling me . . . But was it yesterday . . . ? It was: I turned thirty-two on Tuesday. Or was it twenty-two?" Her husband had promised her a present.

The big table had been set—for one person. She always had coffee by herself in the huge dining room. It displeased her greatly—this solitude. She sat down.

"I'm going to the hairdresser . . . But is this the day when I always have an appointment with the hairdresser?" She took the coffeepot, then checked herself: Her cup was already filled with coffee. "Who poured it? Did I? Strange, isn't it—wasn't it?"

She put the coffeepot down, and stood motionless, absolutely still.

It was only a few minutes later that she saw the white rabbit.

Her hand reached out abruptly, overturning the cup.

A black coffee stain spread over the white tablecloth. Behind the coffeepot, a white plush bunny.

"For my second birthday my father gave me a white plush bunny." Alice and her white rabbit, he said laughing. The white teeth, the bushy eyebrows. "When I was two years old. Or when I was twelve?" She was crying. She rose from the table. "But today's Thursday! We're getting together at eight o'clock!" Sweet winter mornings. Sweet kisses. She was laughing.

She dashed out to the garage and took out the small white car, a present from her husband. On the front seat—a white plush rabbit.

Her eyes were blurred with tears as she began to go down the narrow, gravely road. "It's late! It's late!" The fog was getting denser and denser.

"Wait for me, Rabbit!" She was running. "The rabbit is an animal . . . " Her husband was laughing.

It was then that she saw the big black Dodge looming large before her. Her husband, his fingers gripping the steering wheel, was laughing—baring his powerful teeth, which were white, very white. Shards of glass piercing her throat, a mass of metal crushing her chest.

Everything is much too quick—wasn't it? she murmured and closed her eyes.

The Cow

DURING A STORMY NIGHT there was a shipwreck off the African coast. The ship split in half and sank in less than a minute. Passengers and crew died instantly. There was one survivor, a sailor who had been hurled far away when the disaster occurred. Almost drowning—for he wasn't a good swimmer—the sailor was praying and saying farewell to life, when he saw Carola, the cow, swimming quickly and vigorously next to him.

Carola, the cow, had been loaded in Amsterdam.

A superb breeder, her destination had been a farm in South America.

Holding on to the cow's horn, the sailor let her lead him; and so, at daybreak they reached a sandy islet, where the cow deposited the unfortunate young man, and she kept licking his face until he woke up.

Realizing that he was on a deserted island, the sailor burst into tears. "Woe to me! This island isn't on any sea route! I'll never see another human being again." Throwing himself upon the sand, he cried for a long time, while Carola, the cow, stood gazing at him with her big brown eyes.

Finally, the young man wiped his tears and rose to his feet.

He looked around him: There was nothing on the island except for sharp rocks and a few rickety-looking trees. He felt hungry; he called the cow: "Come here, Carola!" He milked her and drank the good, warm, foamy milk. Then he felt better; he sat down and stood staring at the ocean. "Woe to me!" he would wail at times, but now without much conviction: The milk had done him good.

That night he slept snuggled against the cow. He had a good night's sleep, full of refreshing dreams, and when he woke up, there within his reach was the udder with its abundant milk.

The days went by and the young man grew more and more attached to the cow. "Come here, Carola!" She would obey him.

He would slice off a piece of her tender meat—he was quite partial to tongue—and would eat it raw while still warm, the blood dribbling down his chin. The cow didn't even moo. She merely licked her wounds. The sailor was careful not to injure her vital organs; if he removed a lung, he'd leave the other one in place; he ate the spleen but not the heart, and so on.

With scraps of her skin the sailor made clothes and shoes and a tent to shelter him from the sun and the rain. He cut off Carola's tail and used it to drive the flies away.

When the meat began to get scarce, he hitched the cow to a plow crudely made of tree branches, and then tilled the plot of land lying between the trees, where the soil was more fertile.

He used the animal's excrement for manure. As there wasn't much of it, he ground a few of her bones to powder so that he could use them as fertilizer.

Then he sowed the few grains of corn that had remained stuck in the cavities of Carola's teeth. Soon, seedlings began to sprout and the young man's hopes rekindled.

The Carnival of the Animals [1968] 11

He celebrated St. John's Day by eating *canjica*, the traditional grated corn pudding.

Spring arrived. At night, from far-off regions, a gentle breeze brought subtle aromas.

Gazing at the stars, the sailor would sigh. One night he plucked out one of Carola's eyes, mixed it with seawater and then swallowed this light concoction. He had voluptuous visions, never before experienced by a human being. . . . Overcome by desire, he went up to the cow. And in this matter too, Carola was ready to oblige.

A long time went by, and one day the sailor spotted a ship on the horizon. Wild with joy, he began to yell at the top of his voice, but he got no reply: The vessel was much too far away. The sailor plucked out one of Carola's horns and used it as a makeshift trumpet. The powerful sound roared through the air, but even so he failed to make himself heard.

The young man grew desperate: Night was falling and the ship was sailing farther away from the island. At last, the young man set Carola on the ground and threw a lit match into her ulcerated womb, where a scrap of fat still remained.

The cow caught fire quickly. From amid the black smoke, her one remaining eye looked steadily at the sailor. The young man started; he thought he had detected a tear. But it was just an impression.

The huge flash of light called the attention of the captain of the ship; a motorboat came to pick up the sailor. They were about to leave, taking advantage of the tide, when the young man shouted: "Just a minute!" He went back to the island, and from the smoldering pile he took a handful of ashes and put it in his leather vest. "Farewell, Carola," he murmured. The crew of the motorboat exchanged glances. "Sunstricken," one of them said.

The sailor arrived in his native country. He resigned from the sea and became a wealthy and respected farmer who owned a dairy farm with hundreds of cows.

But even so he led a lonely, unhappy life, and he had frightening nightmares every night until he was forty years old. When he turned forty, he traveled to Europe by boat.

One night, unable to sleep, he left his luxurious stateroom and went up to the quarterdeck, which was bathed in moonlight. He lit a cigarette, leaned on the ship's rail, and stood gazing at the sea. Suddenly he stretched his neck eagerly. He had spotted an islet on the horizon.

"Hi, there!" said someone next to him.

He turned. She was a beautiful blonde with brown eyes and a luxuriant bust.

"My name is Carola," she said.

The Dog

"LOOK WHAT I'VE BROUGHT back from my trip," Senhor Armando said to his friend Heitor, taking something out of his pocket. They were sitting in the pleasant front garden of Senhor Heitor's house.

It was a dog; a tiny dog, perhaps the smallest dog in the world. Senhor Armando placed it on the table, where the tiny creature stood throbbing. It was smaller than a whiskey glass.

"What is it?" asked Senhor Heitor.

"It's a Japanese dog. As you know, the Japanese are experts in miniature art. This dog is a typical example. For several generations now they've been crossbreeding ever smaller specimens until they've come up with this tiny creature. And mind you, they started with the wild dog, which is the wolf's next of kin.

"It has retained the ferocity of the wolf," Senhor Armando went on, "now allied with the attributes of the watchdog. In addition, it has undergone several technical improvements. Its teeth have been capped with platinum; they are hard and extremely sharp. In its ears, as you can see, an acoustic device has been implanted to improve its hearing. Over its eyes there are contact lenses that have been specially treated to enable it to see in the dark. And the conditioning! Ah, the conditioning! For twelve years . . . "

"Is this animal twelve years old?"

"Twelve, yes. Twelve years of continuous conditioning. It's able to smell out derelicts who are still miles away. It hates their guts. Let me tell you, I feel much more relaxed now that I have this treasure at home with me."

He leaned back in the armchair and took a sip of whiskey.

Just then somebody knocked at the gate. It was a man; a beggar dressed in rags, leaning on a crutch.

"What do you want?" shouted Senhor Heitor.

"A little something for the love of God . . . "

"Adolfo!" Senhor Heitor was calling his manservant. "Come here! "

"Just a moment, Heitor," said Senhor Armando, his eyes sparkling. "How would you like to see my little dog in action?"

And without waiting for a reply, he whispered into the dog's ear: "Go, Bilbo, go! Bring him here!" And to his friend, "It's the first time he'll be working here in Brazil."

In the meantime, Bilbo had jumped off the table and was darting across the lawn. A moment later, the beggar was walking through the gate as if he were being hauled in by a tractor.

"Did you see that?" Senhor Armando cried out excitedly. And the beggar already stood in front of them, with Bilbo's platinum teeth sunk into the man's only leg.

"What do you want?" demanded Senhor Heitor in a hard tone of voice.

"A little something for the love of . . . " the beggar began, his face contorted with pain.

"And why aren't you working, my good man?"

"I can't . . . I have only one leg . . . "

"There are plenty of jobs which people can do even without a leg."

"I can make more money by begging than by having a job."

"You're a bum!" shouted Senhor Heitor, incensed. "A derelict! The scum of society! Get out of my sight before I punish you."

"Just a moment, Heitor," said Senhor Armando. "Bilbo is pointing out the right course of action to us. Why let this man go free? So that tomorrow he can break into my house, or into yours? "

"But . . . " Senhor Heitor began to say.

Let's leave this matter for Bilbo to handle. Go, Bilbo, go!"

With a skillful maneuver of its tiny head, Bilbo threw its prey upon the ground Then, starting with the leg into which its teeth were already sunk, Bilbo began to chew methodically. First, it ate the lower limb; then the stump of the leg; from there it proceeded to the abdomen, the thorax, and the head. Everything happened in a twinkling; simultaneously, the dog sucked up the blood so as not to let it stain the green grass. Finally, the beggar's last remaining part—his right eye—disappeared, still glowing with terror, into the tiny dog's mouth. To finish everything off, Bilbo ate up the crutch that had been left leaning against the table.

"Did you see that?" said Senhor Armando, pleased. "Even the wood."

"Very ingenious," remarked Senhor Heitor, taking a sip of whiskey. I'll accept it."

"What do you mean?" Senhor Armando was astonished.

"In exchange for the money you owe me."

"No way, Heitor!" shouted Senhor Armando indignantly. He rose to his feet, picked up the tiny dog and placed it in his pocket. "A debt is a debt. You'll get your money when it is due. You can't put a money value on this dog. Your attitude surprises me. I never suspected a gentleman could act in such a way. Good-bye! "

He headed for the gate.

"You derelict!" shouted Senhor Heitor. "You thief!"

Senhor Armando turned around. He was about to say something but instead let out a howl. Senhor Heitor, whose eyesight was poor, was looking for his glasses; meanwhile, he could indistinctly see the figure of Senior Armando disintegrating by the gate. When he finally succeeded in locating his glasses, he saw Bilbo before him, barking joyfully. There were no traces of Senhor Armando

"Great!" murmured Senhor Heitor, draining off the glass of whiskey.

"Heitor!" It was his wife, who had just appeared at the door. Senhor Heitor quickly put Bilbo in his pocket. "What's that you've got there?"

"It's a . . . a tiny dog," replied Senhor Heitor.

"Well, really, Heitor!" His wife was furious. "How many times have I told you I don't want any animals in this house? Where did you get this dog?"

"From Armando, it was his. He . . . he gave it to me."

"That's a lie! Armando would never give anything to anyone You stole it from him." The woman's eyes were glowing. "You thief! You derelict!"

Senhor Heitor stood smiling. Suddenly, he let out a howl and vanished. As for the woman, she could see nothing but a tiny dog, its tongue hanging out.

Shazam

COMIC STRIPS ARE BEING REAPPRAISED; there has been a lot of talk about the strength of the heroes, yet what is there to be said about their sorrows?

The Invisible Man suffered from a deep feeling of depersonalization. "I keep touching myself all the time to make sure that I'm really present in the world right now," he wrote in his journal. The

Rubber Man would buy a suit on one day only to find on the following day that it no longer fit him. He, not the suit, had either shrunk or stretched. Prince Sub-Mariner grieved over the pollution of the sea. And what a temptation, those savory baits! Luckily, he knew fishermen and fishhooks quite well. The Human Torch was constantly being persecuted by sadists carrying fire extinguishers as well as constantly harassed by the fire insurance companies (woe to him if he was caught anywhere near a fire!). The Shadow, who knew all about the evil that lurks in the hearts of men, was vexed by hypochondriacs obsessed about heart diseases. Zorro kept receiving indecent propositions from a fetishist with a fixation on objects beginning with the letter Z.

Lothar was accused of conspiring against the government of one of the fledgling African republics. It was impossible for anyone to give Superman a shot in the arm; the needles would break against his steel skin. "One day I'll die because of this," he would complain but nobody paid any attention to what he said; it has been proved that heroes are impervious to the ravages of time.

—A. Napp, *The Heroes Revisited*

Crime having been eliminated from the world, Captain Marvel was invited to a special session of the American Congress. There he was greeted by Lester Brainerd, a Louisiana senator, and awarded the Military Merit Medal and a life pension. Deeply moved, Captain Marvel expressed his thanks and stated his desire to live peacefully forever—writing his memoirs, perhaps.

FOR HIS RETREAT, Captain Marvel selected the city of Pôrto Alegre in Brazil, where he rented a room in a picturesque residential hotel in the Alto da Bronze area.

At first, his life was far from peaceful; whenever he was on the street, crowds of kids would run after him: "Fly! Fly!" They would throw stones and make faces at him. Annoyed, Captain Marvel considered moving to Nepal. As time went by, however, people gradually took less notice of him. He started by giving up his eye-catching attire and now wore ordinary clothes, a gray Tergal suit. Then, when television started to show a new movie series, the young people were taken up with the new heroes that had replaced him. There was a brief moment of glory when his memoirs were launched at an autograph party attended by dozens of people. The event received a great deal of attention and critics saw in his book unexpected values ("A new outlook on the world," somebody said), but afterward Captain Marvel was once more forgotten. He spent the days in his room, leafing through old comic books and nostalgically remembering the evil Silvana, who had died of cancer many years before. Sometimes Captain Marvel worked in his garden. He had succeeded in persuading his landlady to let him use the yard beyond the kitchen, and there he grew roses. He wanted to produce a hybrid variety.

In the evenings Captain Marvel watched television or went to the movies. With melancholy contempt he watched the modern heroes, unable to fly, vulnerable to bullets, and even so, incredibly violent. He used to spend Saturdays at a bar near the residential hotel, drinking rum with passion fruit juice and chatting with ex-boxers, who had gotten used to his heavy accent.

On one of those evenings Captain Marvel was feeling particularly depressed. He had already had eleven drinks and was thinking of going to bed, when a woman came to the bar, sat down at the counter, and asked for a beer.

Silently, Captain Marvel looked her over. He had never paid much attention to women; the fight against crime had always been an engrossing task. But now, being retired, Captain Marvel could afford to think of himself. His peeling mirror revealed that he still cut a splendidly virile figure, and he couldn't help being aware of the fact.

As for the woman, she wasn't pretty. Fortyish, short, and fat, she smacked her lips every time she took a gulp of beer. But she was the only woman at the bar that Saturday night. Besides, she not only returned the captain's gaze, but also got up, walked over, and sat down next to him.

Captain Marvel introduced himself, saying his name was Jose Silva, a car salesman. He did so feeling ill at ease: Unlike the modern heroes, he wasn't used to dissembling, scheming, disguising himself.

"Shall we go to my room, honey?" the woman whispered at three o'clock in the morning.

They went. It was on the fourth floor of an old building on Rua Duque de Caxias. The wooden steps creaked under their weight. The woman was panting and had to stop at each landing. "It's my blood pressure." Uneasy, Captain Marvel felt like taking her in his arms and flying up; but he didn't want to reveal his identity. Finally, they got there.

The women opened the door. It was a filthy little room, decorated with paper flowers and religious statues. In the corner, a bed covered with a red spread.

The woman drew closer. She turned to Captain Marvel and smiled: "Kiss me, darling." They kissed for a long time, took off their clothes, and got into bed. "How cold you are, honey," the woman complained. It was his steel skin—the invulnerable shell that had so often protected Captain Marvel and that was now getting somewhat rusty under the armpits. Captain Marvel thought of rubbing his chest with his hands, but he was afraid that this would create sparks and cause a fire. So he confined himself to saying: "It'll be better soon."

"It's all right. Come now," the woman murmured, her eyes glowing in the dark. Captain Marvel threw himself upon her.

A howl of pain shook the room.

"You've killed me! You've killed me! How it hurts!"

Scared, Captain Marvel turned on the light. The bed was soaked with blood.

"You've stuck a sword into me, you bastard, you devil!"

Hurriedly, Captain Marvel put on his pants. The woman was screaming for help. Not knowing what to do, Captain Marvel opened the window. Lights began to go on in the nearby houses. He jumped.

For a moment he was going down like a stone, but he quickly gained control and glided gently. He flew aimlessly over the city, which was still lying asleep. At times he sobbed; he remembered the days when he was just Billy Batson, a simple radio announcer.

There was one word that could have taken him back to those days; however, Captain Marvel no longer remembered it.

The Fishing Tournament

AN EXTREMELY UNPLEASANT INCIDENT took place during the last fishing tournament on Joy Beach.

Outstanding individuals participated in that popular sport.

Among others, the following were present: Miller, Saraiva, Zeca, Judge of the Court of Appeal Otavio, Brunneleschi, and Senhora Santos.

The weather was wonderful. The water abounded in fish.

All one had to do was throw in a fishhook in order to catch a beautiful specimen.

Contentment was widespread. In an atmosphere of goodwill, people congratulated the luckiest among them.

On the third day of the tournament a strange vehicle arrived. It was a large, gaudily painted wagon, pulled by ridiculous-looking jades. Amid a great rumpus, a big clan made up of father, mother, and many children alighted.

As one might have expected, the people already there felt very ill at ease. The newcomers were filthy, rude, and undesirable companions.

The man was especially unpleasant: short, with bronze-colored skin, evil black eyes, a thick-lipped mouth displaying gold-capped teeth. And a vicious tongue: He wouldn't walk past a woman, whether married or single, without uttering a coarse joke.

Had the intruders remained in the empty lot they had chosen for their stopping place, their insolence would have been bearable.

However, on the following morning the man—his name was Antonio—shows up on the beach, and without asking for permission, becomes absorbed in the following activities: He rolls his trouser legs up to his knees. He enters the water, marching right in among the sportsmen's fishing lines. He dips his arms into the water up to his elbows. He utters some words in a low voice. And when he removes his arms, they are filled with fish!

Such violation of the rules caused great uneasiness. The tournament participants complained to the president of the fishing club, who—together with a committee—headed for the parking lot where the weird individuals were camped.

The family was eating lunch. They picked up the fish—some still alive—and put them in their mouths, chewing ravenously. The president alleged that it was against the law to eat the little creatures before they had been weighed and properly registered.

"Know do you what? Want you do what?" Antonio yelled at them in his twisted manner of speech, a morsel of fish intestines hanging out of his lecherous-looking mouth. And with great disrespect, the whole tribe burst out laughing. The president and his committee left, ready to report the affair to the proper authority. However, when the judge of the Court of Appeal heard about the case, he said: "Gentlemen, please leave the matter in my hands."

It was obvious that he was overcome by righteous indignation.

Judge of the Court of Appeal Otavio took action that very night. He was a tall, agile, vigorous man.

On the following morning he announced to his peers: "Gentlemen, soon you'll see the results of a punitive expedition."

And they all headed for the river.

Around nine o'clock Antonio showed up. From the distance it could be seen that his upper limbs were tied with blood-drenched rags.

"I cut his arms off at the elbows," the judge of the Court of Appeal explained. "My reliable fish knife hasn't failed me."

Then the grotesque creature drew closer. He was moaning softly. Just as he had done on the previous day, he entered the river. He tried to thrust his amputated stumps into the water But the cold made him howl with pain.

Widespread laughter.

Next, the stranger proceeded to intone a monotonous singsong, his face turned up to the sky. Then he got out of the water and walked past the sportsmen without looking at them.

Later on, people saw the wagon drive away and disappear northward.

Those waters have since not yielded a single fish. There have been no more fishing tournaments at Joy Beach.

We Gunmen Mustn't Feel Pity

WE'RE A FEARFUL GUNMAN. We're in a saloon in a small town in Texas. The year is 1880. We're sipping whiskey. There's a doleful expression in our eyes. There are countless deaths in our past. We're filled with remorse. That's why we're drinking.

The door opens. In walks a Chicano named Alonso. He addresses us disrespectfully. He calls us gringo, laughs loudly, makes his spurs clink. We act as if he weren't there. We keep on sipping whiskey. The Chicano walks up to us. He insults us. He gives us a slap on the cheek. Our heart contracts in anguish. We don't feel like killing anyone anymore. But we'll have to make an exception for Alonso, this Chicano dog.

We arrange a duel for the following morning at sunrise. Alonso slaps us on the cheek once more and then leaves. We stand lost in thought, sipping the whiskey. Finally, we toss a gold coin on the counter and leave.

We walk slowly to our hotel. The townsfolk are watching us. They know we are a fearful gunman. Poor Chicano, poor Alonso. We enter the hotel, climb the stairs to our room, and lie down fully dressed and with our boots on. We lie staring at the ceiling as we smoke. We heave a sigh. We are filled with remorse.

And it is already dawn. We get up. We set our wide belt in place. We submit the gun to the usual inspection. We walk down the stairs. The street is deserted, but we sense the townsfolk watching us from behind closed curtains. The wind blows, raising small swirls of dust. Ah, this wind! This wind! How many times has it watched us walking slowly, our back turned to the rising sun?

At the end of the street Alonso is already waiting for us. This Chicano really wants to die.

We position ourselves in front of him. He sees a gunman with a doleful expression in his eyes. The grin on his face fades. In our eyes he sees countless deaths. That's what he sees.

We see a Chicano. Poor devil. Soon he won't be eating any more tortillas. His widow and her six kids will bury him at the foot of the hill. They'll lock up their shack and head for Veracruz. The oldest daughter will become a prostitute. The youngest son, a thief.

Our eyes become blurry. Poor Alonso. He shouldn't have slapped us. Now he's terrified. His rotten teeth are chattering. What a pitiful sight.

A tear drops to the dusty ground. It's ours. We place our hand on the holster. But we don't draw the gun. The Chicano does. We see the gun in his hand, we hear the shot, the bullet flies toward our chest, it nestles in our heart. We feel a piercing pain and we slump to the ground.

We die as Alonso, the Chicano, laughs.

We, the gunman, shouldn't have felt pity.

Blind Man and Amigo Gedeão Alongside the Highway

"THE ONE THAT JUST WENT BY was a 1962 Volkswagen, wasn't it, amigo Gedeão?"

"No, Blind Man. It was a Simca Typhoon."

"A Simca Typhoon . . . ? Ah, yes, that's right. Powerful, the Simca. And very economical. I can tell a Simca Typhoon from a great distance. I can tell any car by the noise of its engine.

"Now this one that just went by was a Ford, wasn't it?"

"No, Blind Man. It was a Mercedes truck"

"A Mercedes truck? You don't say! We haven't had a Mercedes go by in a long time. I can tell a Mercedes from a great distance . . . I can tell one car from another. Do you have any idea how long I've been sitting here alongside this highway, listening to all these engines, amigo Gedeão? Twelve years, amigo Gedeão. For twelve years.

"That's an awful long time, amigo Gedeão, wouldn't you say so? Long enough for me to have learned a lot. About cars, I mean. Wasn't this one that just went by a Gordini Willfulness."

No, Blind Man. That was a motor scooter."

"A motor scooter . . . well, well, they can really deceive a person, those motor scooters. 'Specially when the exhaust doesn't have a muffler.

"But as I was saying, if there's one thing I can do, it's to tell one car from another by the way the engines sound. Which is not surprising, really, considering all these years I've spent listening and listening!

"It's an ability that served me well once when . . . This one that just went by was another Mercedes wasn't it?"

"No, Blind Man. It was a bus."

"That's what I figured. You'd never get two Mercedes in a row. I said Mercedes just for the heck of it. But where was I? Ah, yes.

"This ability of mine came in quite handy one time. Would you care to hear about it, friend Gedeão? Yes? In that case I'll tell you about it. It'll help while the hours away, right? Thus the day will end sooner. I like evenings much better: They're much cooler at this time of the year. But as I was saying, several years ago a man was killed about two kilometers from here. A very wealthy farmer, he was. They put fifteen bullets into him. Wasn't this one that just went by a Galaxy?"

"No. It was a 1964 Volkswagen."

"Ah, a Volkswagen . . . Great car. Very economical. The transmission's very good. Well, so they killed this farmer. Haven't you heard about the case? It was much talked about. Fifteen gunshots. And they got away with all the money the farmer had on him. In those days I was already in the habit of sitting here by the highway and I heard about the crime. It happened on a Sunday. On Friday I heard it on the radio that the police still didn't have the slightest clue. Wasn't this one that just went by a Candango."

"No, Blind Man, it wasn't a Candango."

"I was dead sure it was a Candango. . . . But as I was saying, it was Friday and they still didn't have a clue.

"I happened to be sitting right here, on this very chair, cudgeling my brain . . . Mulling things over, you know. Until I reached a con-

The Carnival of the Animals [1968] 25

clusion. I decided I should help the police. I asked my neighbor to tell the district chief of police that I had some information for them. Sure, this one must have been a Candango."

"No, Blind Man. It was a Gordini Willfulness."

"I could have sworn it was a Candango. The district chief of police wasn't in any big hurry to see me. He probably thought, 'A blind man? What could a blind man have seen?' Or something like that, sheer bunk, of course, you know the things they say, amigo Gedeão. Anyway, he ended up coming here because the police were at a loss and willing to interview even a rock. So, the district chief of police, he came here and sat down where you're sitting now, amigo Gedeão. Was this one now the bus?"

"No, Blind Man. That was a pickup, a Chevrolet Peacock."

"A good pickup, too, old but good. Where was I? Ah, yes. The district chief of police came to see me. I asked him: 'What time was it, sir, when the crime was committed?'"

"About three in the afternoon, Blind Man."

"In that case,' I said, "you should try to locate a 1927 Oldsmobile. The muffler of this car has got a hole in it."

"And there is a defective spark plug. A very fat man was sitting in the front of the car. In the back, I'm sure, there were possibly two or three people. The district chief of police was flabbergasted. 'How do you know, friend?' was all he kept asking. Wasn't this one that just went by a DKW?"

"No, Blind Man. It was a Volkswagen."

"Yes. The district chief of police was flabbergasted. 'How come you know all this?' 'Well, chief,' I replied, "it so happens that for years now I've been sitting here next to this highway, listening to the cars go by. I can tell one car from another. And that's not all: I can tell if the engine is in poor shape, if there's too much weight in the front, if there are people on the back seat. It was two-forty-five when this car drove in that direction, and it was three-fifteen when it headed back to the city.' 'How come you knew about the time?' the district chief of police wanted to know. 'Well, Chief,' I replied, 'if there's one thing I can do—aside from being able to tell cars apart by listening to the sound of their engines—it is to tell the time of the day by the position of the sun in the sky.' Although skeptical, the district chief of police went to . . . That was an Willys Aero, wasn't it?"

"No, Blind Man. It was a Chevrolet."

"The district chief of police succeeded in locating the 1927 Oldsmobile with the entire gang inside. They were so flabbergasted that they gave themselves up without putting up any resistance. The district chief of police recovered all the money they'd stolen from the farmer, and his family gave me quite a bundle of a reward. Wasn't the one that went by a Toyota?" "No, Blind Man. It was a 1956 Ford."

The Pause

AT SEVEN O'CLOCK the alarm clock went off. Samuel jumped out of bed, dashed into the bathroom, shaved, washed up.

He got dressed quickly and noiselessly. He was in the kitchen making sandwiches when his wife appeared, yawning.

"Going out again, Samuel?"

He nodded in reply. Although young, his hair had already receded from his forehead, but his eyebrows were thick, and even though he had just shaved, his beard had left a bluish shadow on his face. The effect was that of a dark mask.

"You leave so early on Sundays," the woman remarked peevishly.

"There's a backlog of work to get through at the office."

She looked at the sandwiches.

"Why don't you come home for lunch?"

"I've already told you: We have a backlog of work. There's no time. I'm taking something for lunch."

The woman stood scratching her left armpit. Before she had a chance to resume her nagging, Samuel grabbed his hat: "I'll be back this evening."

The streets were still damp with fog. Samuel got the car out of the garage. He was driving slowly past the waterfront, looking at the idle derricks, at the large barges tied up at the docks.

He parked on a quiet side street. Carrying the bag of sandwiches under his arm, he walked hurriedly for two blocks. He stopped at the entrance of a small grubby hotel. He glanced around, then walked in stealthily. He tapped the car keys on the counter, waking up a small man who sat asleep in an armchair with a torn slipcover. He was the manager. Rubbing his eyes, he rose to his feet: "Ah, it's you, Senhor Isidoro! You're earlier than usual today. Nippy outside, isn't it? People—"

"I'm in a hurry, Senhor Raul," Samuel said, cutting him short.

"Okay, I won't keep you." He held out a key. "It's the usual one."

Samuel climbed four flights up a rickety stairway.

When he reached the top floor, two fat women wearing housecoats with a floral design looked at him curiously: "Over here, sweetie!" said one of them. The other laughed.

Gasping for breath, Samuel went into the room and locked the door behind him. It was a small room: a double bed, a pine wardrobe; in a corner, a basin filled with water rested on a tripod. Samuel drew the tattered curtains, took a travel alarm clock out of his pocket, wound it, and placed it on the small bedside table.

He pulled aside the bedspread and examined the sheets, frowning; sighing, he took off his jacket and his shoes, and loosened his tie. Seated on the bed, he ate four sandwiches ravenously. He wiped his fingers on the wrapping paper, lay down, and closed his eyes.

To sleep.

A moment later, he was asleep. Naked, he was running across an immense plain, pursued by an Indian on horseback. The galloping echoed in the stuffy room. Over the highlands of the forehead, down the hills of the belly, in the valley between the legs, they kept running, the pursuer and the quarry.

Samuel tossed about, muttering. At two-thirty in the afternoon he felt a piercing pain in his back. He sat up in bed, his eyes bulging: The Indian had just pierced him with his spear. Bleeding to death, soaked with sweat, Samuel sank slowly to the ground; he heard the gloomy whistle of a steamboat. Then there was silence.

At seven o'clock the alarm clock went off. Samuel jumped out of bed, dashed to the washbasin, and washed up. He got dressed quickly and left.

Seated in the armchair, the hotel manager was reading a magazine.

"Checking out already, Senhor?"

"Yeah," said Samuel, handing over the key. He paid and counted his change in silence.

"See you next Sunday, Senhor Isidoro," said the manager.

"Don't know if I'll be back," replied Samuel, looking out the door; night was falling.

"That's what you keep saying, sir, but you always come back," remarked the man, laughing.

Samuel went out.

He drove slowly along the waterfront. He stopped briefly to look at the derricks silhouetted against a reddish sky. Then he drove home.

Of Cannibals

IN 1950 TWO YOUNG WOMEN were flying over the desolate table-lands of Bolivia. The plane, a Piper, was being piloted by Barbara, a beautiful woman, tall and blonde, married to a wealthy Mato Grosso rancher. Her companion, Angelina, was slender, dark-complexioned, and had big startled eyes. They were foster sisters.

The sun was sinking below the horizon when the aircraft engine stalled. After some desperate maneuvering, Barbara managed to crash-land on a plateau. The airplane was completely demolished, and the two women found themselves all alone, hundreds of kilometers from the nearest village.

Fortunately (and perhaps having anticipated such a contingency), Barbara had brought a big case containing assorted delicacies: anchovies, Brazil nuts, caviar from the Black Sea, strawberries, broiled kidneys, pineapple compote, soft cheese from Minas, and even bottles of vitamin pills. The case was intact.

The following morning Angelina was hungry, and she asked Barbara for something to eat. Barbara, however, made it very clear that it was impossible for her to comply with Angelina's request, for the food belonged to Barbara, not to Angelina. Resigning herself to this situation, Angelina went off in search of fruits and roots. She found nothing, for the area was completely barren. So she had nothing to eat that day.

Nor did she have anything to eat on the next three days. Barbara on the other hand, was quite noticeably putting on weight, maybe due to her idleness: She spent the time lying down, eating and waiting for someone to come and rescue them. Angelina kept pacing to and fro, weeping and bemoaning her fate—which merely increased her need for calories.

On the fourth day, while Barbara was eating lunch, Angelina approached her, holding a knife in her hand. Intrigued, Barbara stopped munching—it was a chicken thigh—and stood watching the other woman, who was standing absolutely still. Suddenly, Angelina placed her left hand on a rock, and with a single blow, cut off her ring finger. Blood spouted. Angelina then brought her hand to her mouth and sucked at her own blood.

Since the bleeding wouldn't stop, Barbara made a tourniquet around the stump of her sister's finger. In a few minutes the bleeding stopped. Angelina then took the finger, which had been lying on the ground, wiped it off, and picked the little bones clean. She discarded only the fingernail.

Barbara watched in silence. When Angelina finished eating, Barbara asked her for the bone; then she broke it and used a sliver to pick her teeth. Then the two of them stood talking, reminiscing about childhood events, and so forth and so on.

On the following day Angelina ate the remainder of her fingers, and then her toes. The legs and the thighs followed next.

Barbara helped her prepare the meals, tightened tourniquets whenever necessary, offered advice on how to make the best of the bone marrow, and so forth.

On the fifteenth day, Angelina had to resort to opening up her stomach. The first organ that she removed was the liver. As she was quite hungry, she devoured it raw, although her sister had advised her to fry it first. Consequently Angelina was still hungry when she finished her meal. She asked for a piece of bread to soak up the tiny amount of gravy.

Barbara refused her sister's request with the well-reasoned statement she had previously made.

After the spleen and the ovaries, it was the turn of the uterus, which gave Angelina an unpleasant surprise, for she found a large tumor in that organ. Barbara remarked that it must have been the reason why she hadn't been feeling well for months. Angelina agreed adding, "What a pity I didn't find out about it until now." Then she asked Barbara if it would be harmful to eat the cancer. Barbara advised her to discard that part, which was already showing signs of decay.

On the twentieth clay, Angelina passed away, and on the following day a rescue team reached the crash site. On seeing the mangled corpse, they asked Barbara what had happened; and the young woman, bent on preserving her sister's reputation, lied for the first time in her life. "It was the Indians."

The newspapers reported the existence of cannibalistic Indians in Bolivia—which is completely groundless.

The Aging Marx

BY THE END OF THE LAST CENTURY Karl Marx was feeling rather tired. The political battles were draining him of his energies. His health was poor and he lacked faith in his own future as leader of the international working men's movement. He had already accomplished everything he had set out to do. *Das Kapital* had been published and was in circulation; his articles were being studiously read. And yet Marx continued to be ill, poor, and frustrated.

"That's enough," said Marx. "I don't have too many years of life left. I'm going to spend these remaining years incognito, yet comfortably."

It was a painful decision, which brings to mind the story about a man who believed himself to be superior to everybody else because he happened to have six toes on his left foot. He kept mentioning this fact until one day a friend wanted to have a look at those six toes of his. The man then takes off his shoe and sock, and when he looks, he sees that he has five toes, just like everybody else. Widespread laughter. The man goes home, and feeling somewhat disappointed, he goes to bed. He takes off his shoe again: There are four toes on his left foot.

Marx was tired out. "I want to enjoy the rest of my life." Marx made an empirical estimation: He subtracted his age from the life expectancy for those days and was overcome with anxiety; it looked as if he didn't have much longer to live. What should he do? Abandon himself to some playful adventure? But would it be right to trade austerity for frivolity? To squander in laughter, as the Rosicrucians would say, years of life?

Marx had several daughters. He hoped they would have a better future, a more comfortable life. But how?

Far better than anyone else, Marx understood the foundations upon which rising capitalism was based. He had aptly diagnosed all the errors made by the new industrial society. "I'm in the best possible position to profit from these very errors," he thought. Wealth was within his reach.

And yet he hesitated, unable to make a decision. He let the days slip by, making excuses to his wife: "I've been studying the best way." . . . "I'll have to make some calculations." . . . "I haven't been up to it lately." Irresponsible. Marx was plainly irresponsible.

His wife and daughters, however, wouldn't be able to bear their predicament much longer. They had hardly any clothes to wear. They were down to one meal a day, and that consisted mostly of potatoes and stale bread.

So, Marx had no other choice but to make up his mind. He decided to test his theories about easy profits in a new country. He chose Brazil.

One winter morning at the turn of the century Marx arrived in Pôrto Alegre. The ship tied up at the fog-shrouded wharf. Marx and his daughters looked at the barges loaded with oranges. The girls, hungry, cried for food. An old gaucho gave one of them a piece of sausage. The girl devoured it and laughed, happy.

"Now look at that. A hungry little girl!" said the gaucho, amazed.

"I'll have to do some research on the role of the proletariat in underdeveloped countries," Marx was thinking, but soon remembered that he was there to make money, not to formulate theories.

"Let's go!" he said to his family.

They settled at a boarding house located on the old-fashioned Rua Pantaleão Telles. Soon after their arrival there, another tragedy struck the family: The youngest child, Punzi, who had eaten the sausage, became ill with cramps and diarrhea. Marx, who couldn't afford to send for a doctor, took her to a public charity hospital, where she died that same night.

"If you had brought her sooner. . . " said the intern on duty.

In her grief, Marx's wife turned against her husband. "It's your fault, you damned revolutionary! You're incapable of loving anyone. You know nothing except how to sow hatred everywhere. You enjoy class warfare, but you're unconcerned about what happens to your own family!"

Feeling contrite, Marx bore with the torrent of abuse.

The following day he went in search of work.

He found a job at a furniture factory on Avenida Cauduro. It was a small place, dark and dusty; the net income was barely enough to support the owner, an old bearded Jew. However, the owner was philosophical about life: "The food that feeds one person can easily feed two, three, even four people. Especially if this person is a Jew; even if he happens to be German too."

Besides Marx, two other people worked in the factory: Quirino, a Negro, and Iossel, a bespectacled youth with a pimply face. Quirino was skillful at handling the drill, the plane, the gouge, the chisel, the hammer. He also knew how to use the sanding machine, and whenever necessary, he worked as the polisher, too. There was nobody who could handle the band saw as well as he.

Iossel would lend them a hand occasionally. He spoke to Marx one day: "Would you like to join us? I belong to a group of good Jewish youths. We take turns meeting at one another's houses and discuss a variety of subjects. We intend to marry good girls and have families of our own. We want to improve the quality of life in our community. Would you like to participate in our meetings, Karl Marx?"

Marx declined the invitation for two reasons: First, after having written "On the Jewish Question," he believed he had nothing new to say about the Jewish people; second, his goal was to make money, not to fraternize.

"I can't join you, Iossel. My objective is to succeed in life. I advise you to put illusions aside. Turn your energies to something serious before it's too late. Your health is already suffering. You'll end up dying of tuberculosis."

Indeed, although tuberculosis is rare among the Jews, Iossel began to cough up blood and he died without having started a family of his own. The old man, Marx, and the Negro Quirino attended the burial. Some young men with frightened expressions on their faces showed up at the cemetery. Marx supposed that they were members of the discussion group. He was right: Marx was hardly ever wrong nowadays.

Before going to bed one night, Marx looked at his left foot. "Five toes!" he said aloud. "Four previously; six someday!"

"What?" asked his wife sleepily.

"Go back to sleep, woman," he replied.

Marx followed the economic predicament carefully. He read everything he could lay his hands on: newspapers, magazines, books. He listened to the radio, to what people were talking about on the street corners. He gathered data. He examined trends.

The factory owner was getting on in years. One day he called Marx into his office: "I'm an old man. I need a partner. How would you like to become my partner?"

"But I have nothing."

"That's all right. I trust your Jewish integrity, even though you're a German too."

Marx accepted the offer. There were two of them now to boss the Negro Quirino about. Quirino didn't mind, though: He would rush from the sanding machine to the band saw, from the band saw to the wood polisher, and in between, he would nail down a slat, always crooning "My Precious Darling."

Slowly at first, but like an engine gradually picking up speed, Marx worked. Before his arrival, the factory operated on a simple system: A customer would come to the factory, order, say, a wardrobe—giving his own specifications for size and shape—and even stipulate the price.

After the contract was sealed with a handshake, everybody—boss and employees—set to work. Marx put an end to this disorganized way of doing things. He announced that an assembly line would be instituted. But first he fired the Negro Quirino.

"But why?" protested the old man. "Such a good employee! He can do everything."

"Precisely for that reason," replied Marx. "I want people who are capable of doing just one thing: specialists, do you follow me? People who are able to handle the gouge, the plane, the band saw equally well, people who are skillful at everything—well, I have no use for them!"

"But you don't know a thing about furniture!" The old man was desolate.

"But I do know about economics. Why don't you go to bed, partner?"

World War II was just beginning. Marx, who had already shaved off his beard, raised the Brazilian flag at the factory. He spoke perfect Portuguese; nobody would have guessed that he was a European. However, he was smart enough to take precautions. He had just entered into a contract with the army to manufacture furniture and he didn't want his foreign status to jeopardize his business.

The old man spent his days at the synagogue.

There was horrifying news from Europe. Concentration camps. Gas chambers . . . One day while they were sitting drinking coffee, Marx's wife said: "You were right about saying that there's a line of blood running across the history of mankind," and she helped herself to some butter.

Churchill was offering blood, sweat, and tears to the Englishmen. Marx had a loudspeaker system installed at the factory in order to broadcast patriotic anthems as well as requests for increased productivity on the part of the workers. "London has been suffering bombings! And what about you, what have you been doing?" He was one of the very first entrepreneurs to invest in an advertising campaign. Thanks to his vision and other qualities, he made a lot of money.

True, there was no continuity or smoothness in his method. The floods of 1941 were a major setback. Thousands of hardwood planks floated away in the muddy waters. Marx accepted this blow with resignation. "Man has turned himself into a giant by controlling the forces of nature," he thought.

On the other hand, at the time of the floods, the old man came down with pneumonia and died. Marx was relieved: He just couldn't stand his partner's admonitions anymore. However, Marx had the old man's portrait hung in the office and he made a touching speech on the occasion.

He was still to suffer through a major moral crisis. It happened toward the end of the war: The Russian troops were marching across Europe, leaving tumult in their wake. Red flags were being raised in various capitals.

"Could I have been right after all?" Marx wondered, alarmed. "Will the proletariat gain power after all? Will the capitalists he crushed? Will the guts of the last landowner be used to hang the last financier?"

He decided to put his old theories to the test. If they proved to be wrong, he would acknowledge his mistake and help the proletariat win the class war.

In one of his factories, there was an apprentice named Quirininho. He was the Negro Quirino's son. Marx decided to use him as a guinea pig.

Marx called him.

"Quirininho."

"Yes, sir?"

"Clean my shoes." Smiling, Quirininho cleaned Marx's shoes.

"Quirininho."

"Yes, sir?"

"You're an idiot."

"Yes, sir."

"Don't you realize that everything here belongs to you? These machines are yours, the furniture that you've made is yours, the mansion where I live is yours. You could become the lover of one of my daughters if you wanted to. The future belongs to you."

"Yes, sir."

"Don't you want to own this factory?"

"You're pulling my leg, Senhor Marx!" the Brazilian-born Negro said, grinning widely.

"I'm not pulling your leg, you idiot!" Marx was shouting him. "Take over this factory! It belongs to you. Go on strike! Set up barricades!"

Quirininho remained silent, staring at the floor.

"What is it that you want most in life?"

"To own a small house in Vila Jardim. To go to a soccer game every Sunday. To drink rum with my friends on Saturday nights. To get married. To be happy."

Every night Marx counted his toes.

"Are there six now?" his wife would ask, mocking him.

She, too, died. Marx set up a special fund in her memory.

Now that he was getting on in years, Marx became embittered. One of his daughters got married to the owner of an airline company. He didn't go to the wedding. Another daughter eloped with the company's accountant. He didn't care.

What was Marx's secret? He was always riding the crest of the wave. He noticed trends. "There's bound to be a housing shortage, what with all these people emigrating from the rural areas in search of the attractions of the big cities." And he rushed headlong into investing in real estate. He made use of psychology: He offered things like Security, with a capital S. He made friends with everyone in the financial world; lines of credit were always open to him. In times of recession, he offered financing at high interest rates.

Now that he was getting on in years, Marx became embittered. He drank unsweetened maté, which he had always abhorred. Gloomily sucking up the bitter liquid through a straw, he grumbled about the modern entrepreneurs. ("Bums. Bums and idiots. Don't know a thing about economics. Can't function at all without a computer. They lack vision. I've always been able to predict a crisis with the precision of a stopwatch without ever having to resort to a computer.") He grumbled about the communist countries. ("They quarrel among themselves like a bunch of gossips. And all they can think of is expenditure.") He complained about the maté. ("It's cold, stone cold!")

Quirininho was mortally injured in an accident at the factory. Before he died he wanted to see his boss, whom he asked humbly for his blessing.

Marx was deeply impressed. Three days later Marx was hospitalized and his left foot had to be amputated. He insisted on having it embalmed and buried, with a solemn funeral ceremony. Representatives from the upper echelons were present at the burial; ill at ease, they exchanged glances.

Marx died many years ago.

During some antileftist demonstrations, the foot was exhumed by an infuriated crowd. Before they burned it, someone observed that it had six toes.

Leo

LEO, THE JEWISH BOY: In the liquid brown eyes, the remains of small villages in Poland. The smile, rare and sorrowful.

Leo's father was a tall, strong cabinetmaker who worked hard and didn't make much money. At times he suffered from headaches and would moan softly. Leo's mother cooked the meals and intoned sad songs in Yiddish. On Fridays she sacrificed a fish from the sea. The family sat around the table covered with a white tablecloth. By the light of the candles, they apportioned the food. The father was given the head; he ate it slowly. Then he sucked at the bones of the flattened skull.

They lived in a frame house located on a side street. At the far end of the big backyard there was a wooden shed, kept padlocked, and inside which Leo had never been.

It was winter. . . . Every morning, dark-complexioned boys took their fishing rods and went fishing in the river.

Leo stood at the window, watching the street. He couldn't go fishing. He looked after the house while his father worked at the furniture factory and his mother shopped at the open-air market. Leo couldn't go out.

Once it rained for days on end. One morning Leo went to the kitchen door and looked out: The backyard was flooded. He got dressed, said good-bye to his mother, and started to row. He hoisted his flag up the mast and sounded the vastness of the waters.

The boat sailed the waters dauntlessly. The nights went by, star-studded. From the crow's nest, Leo watched and thought of all the magnificent adventurers: John, the Englishman, who had climbed the Himalayas with one of his hands tied behind his back; Fred, who had set off on a journey inside a barrel launched in the Gulf of Mexico and had been picked up off Pintada Island a year later; Boris, the blood brother of a Comanche chief.

Leo lived on fish and algae; he wrote entries in his logbook and gazed at the islands. The natives watched him sail by—a morose man, keeping himself aloof from the waters, aloof from the skies. Once there was a storm. But it didn't defeat him, it didn't!

And what about the monsters? What is there to say about them since nobody has ever seen them?

"Leo, come in and have lunch!" his mother shouted.

Leo was sailing afar; off the coast of Africa.

One day he came back. From then on, he was never again free.

A winter afternoon. The pale sun was sliding across the sky. At the furniture factory, his father worked with the sanding machine, his head white with dust. He stacked up cupboard doors amid heaps of sawdust. The boss would come and yell at him in Yiddish.

His mother baked a fish for the approaching night, the holy Sabbath night. She was pregnant and moved about with difficulty. In the cold, rarefied air, pigeons fluttered about sluggishly, looking furtive. At the far end of the backyard, there was the padlocked shed.

They ate dinner in silence. His parents went to bed. In the kitchen sink, a stack of dishes, still with the remains of fish. The cupboard doors made snapping sounds.

Leo couldn't sleep; he was running a temperature. He was crying softly, his damp hands holding his treasure: a fishing line and a fishhook. Everything was enveloped in darkness. In this darkness Leo got up and began to walk. He walked across the narrow hall, across the kitchen, toward the backyard. It was past eleven o'clock, it was past midnight.

Leo stepped out into the chilly night. He walked, at first leaning against the slimy wall, then without propping himself up.

The Carnival of the Animals [1968] 41

Left behind were the house, his father and his mother.

He reached the shed. He bent down, inserted the fishing line and the fishhook under the big door, and stood waiting. Motionless beneath the sky, confined by the wall, Leo stood waiting. Inside him, something was growing and throbbing.

He stood waiting. Suddenly, he felt the fishing line quiver. A signal? He didn't dare pull it. He was afraid. He wanted to let go and flee. But he controlled himself; he waited; and there he stood, peaceful and very quiet, ready for the long vigil. And when the fishing line quivered again, he pulled it with all his strength.

Something jumped up into the air and fell into his arms.

It was a fish, a pitiful animal, a wretched creature of the water. Surely it must have lived in the deepest depths, for it was eyeless. Leo had plucked it from the depths and now he was holding it in his lap. He examined the fish, its bruised skin, its grotesque fins. He examined its twisted mouth, which at times emitted a faint moan. Leo stroked its absurd head.

He was crying softly; he was running a temperature. In Poland, the villages lay asleep.

A House

A CERTAIN MAN still didn't have a house of his own when he suffered a heart attack. The pain was quite severe and, as usual under such circumstances, he felt close to death. He asked the doctor who examined him how much longer he would live.

"Who knows?" replied the doctor. "Maybe one day, maybe ten years."

The man was deeply impressed, something he hadn't experienced in a long time. He led a peaceful life. He was retired. Every day he got up, read the newspaper (limiting himself to the entertainment and leisure sections), walked as far as Alfândega Square, talked to his friends there, had his shoes shined. Then he would have lunch, take a nap, and listen to the radio in the afternoons. In the evenings he watched television. All these things lulled his soul soothingly, without making any great demands on him. Since he was single and his parents were dead, he was free from care; he lived in a room in a boardinghouse, and his landlady—a kindly woman—looked after everything.

But then the man sees his life draining away. While washing up, he watches the water in the washbasin flowing down the drain. "That's how it is." He wipes his face dry; he combs his hair carefully. "At least a home." Any kind: A cottage, a tiny apartment, even a basement would do. But to die in his own house. At home.

He looks for a real estate agency. The real estate agent shows him house designs and photographs. The man looks at them, perplexed. He's unable to choose. He doesn't know if he needs two bedrooms or three. There's one house with air-conditioning, but will he live until the summer?

Suddenly, he finds it: "This one. I'll buy it." The photograph shows an old wooden bungalow, with colonial-style eaves and faded paintwork. "This one is on the market just for the lot," explains the real estate agent. "The house itself is falling apart." "It doesn't matter." The real estate agent tries to reason with him: "It's quite far away . . . " Far away! The man smiles. He signs the papers, gets the keys, jots down the address, and leaves.

The day is drawing in and the man moves among people in the streets, feeling elated. He is about to move into his own house! In a square near his boardinghouse some draymen stand waiting for a customer. The man talks to one of them and hires his services.

It takes the drayman just a few minutes to place the baggage on his cart, but it's dark night when they start out. The man is silent throughout the trip. He hasn't said good-bye to his landlady. After giving the address to the drayman, he hasn't uttered a single word.

The cart moves slowly along the deserted streets. Lulled by the movement, the man dozes off—and he has dreams, visions or recollections: old songs; his mother calling him in at coffee time; the sound of the school bell.

"Here we are," says the drayman. The man opens his eyes: It's the same house he saw in the photograph. Impulsively, the man grabs the drayman's hand, thanking him and wishing all the best. The man feels like inviting the other in: "Come in and have tea with me." But there is no tea. The drayman takes his money and leaves, coughing.

The man carries his belongings indoors, shuts the door, and double-locks it. He lights a candle. He looks about: at the floor strewn with dead insects and shreds of paper, at the dirty wall. He feels very tired. He spreads a blanket on the floor and lies down, wrapping his overcoat around him.

The floorboards creak and he can hear whispers; the voices sound familiar: Father, Mother, Aunt Rafaela; they are all here—even Grandfather, with his ironic feigned laughter.

No, the man is not afraid. His heart—a piece of dried-out leather, as he imagines it to be—keeps beating in the usual rhythm. He falls asleep, life goes out, and it is already morning.

It's morning; but the sun hasn't risen. The man gets up and opens the window; a cold gray light seeps into the room. It's neither sunlight nor moonlight. And by this light he sees the street that runs along in front of the house. A fragment of street, emerging from the fog and ending in it. There are no other houses; or, if there are, he can't see them. The bungalow looks out on an empty lot where, half-covered by vegetation, lies the rusty skeleton of an old Packard.

An animal jumps out of the empty lot into the road. It's an outlandish creature: It looks like a rat but is almost as big as a donkey. "What kind of animal could it be?" wonders the man. In high school

he used to like zoology quite a lot; he had studied the ornithorhynchus and the zebra in detail, and the rodent as well. He had
wanted to become a zoologist, but friends showing good judgment
had dissuaded him from pursuing a career which, according to them,
didn't exist—unless proven otherwise. Nevertheless, seeing this
strange specimen has jolted him. And the man has barely recovered
from this jolt when he hears someone whistling.

Out of the mists steps a man. A snort, dark-complexioned man
who looks like an Indian. He walks slowly, tapping on the stones
with a shepherd's staff, and he keeps on whistling.

"Good morning!"

The aborigine doesn't reply. He stops walking, then stands smiling and staring.

Somewhat perplexed, the man persists: "Do you live around
here?"

Still smiling, the wanderer murmurs a few words in some exotic
language and disappears.

"It's an exotic language," the man thinks. So, he must be in some
distant country. The real estate agent had certainly warned him. But
that was a long time ago.

Disoriented, the man decides to go to the top floor, from where
he hopes to find his bearings. He runs toward the stairway, climbs up
the steps two at a time ("and there's no sign of angina!"), reaches
what looks like a turret, and opens its tiny windows. The fog has
lifted and he is able to see. And what does he see?

Rivers scintillating along prairies, that's what he sees; lakes
abounding in fish, huge forests, snow-covered peaks, volcanoes. He
spots the sea in the distance, and in the harbors, caravels lie at an-
chor. He can even see sailors climbing the mast and letting down
the canvas.

"Yes, it's another country," the man concludes. "And I'll have to
start from scratch."

The Carnival of the Animals [1968]   45

It could be about ten in the morning—that is, if hours still counted—and the temperature might be said to be pleasant.

The man starts off by removing his overcoat.

The Phantom Train

FINALLY, IT WAS CONFIRMED: Matias's disease was indeed leukemia, and his mother sent for me. In tears, she told me that Matias's greatest wish had always been to take a ride on the Phantom Train; she would like to grant him this wish now, and she counted on me. Matias was nine years old. I was ten. I scratched my head.

It would be impossible to take him to the park where the Phantom Train was. We would have to improvise something in his house, an old mansion in Moinhos Velhos, full of dark furniture and wine-colored velvet curtains. Matias's mother gave me some money; I went to the park and took a ride on the Phantom Train. I did so several times. And wrote everything down on a sheet of paper, just as I'm doing now. I also drew a diagram. Having this data on hand, we set up our own Phantom Train.

The event took place at 9:00 P.M. on July 3, 1956. The cold winter wind from the southwest was hissing through the trees, but the house was quiet. We woke up Matias. He was shivering with cold; his mother wrapped him in blankets. Taking the utmost care, we placed him in a baby carriage. He was so withered now that he fit inside. I took him to the entrance hall of the old mansion and there we stood waiting on the marble floor.

The lights went out. It was the signal. Pushing the baby carriage, I dashed headlong, running at full speed down the long hall. The drawing room door opened; I went in. There stood Matias's mother, dressed up like a witch (her face plastered with red makeup; her painted eyes, wide open; black apparel; on her shoulder, a stuffed owl; she was invoking evil spirits).

I went around the drawing room twice, always pursued by the woman. Matias shrieked with fright and pleasure. I returned to the hall.

Another door opened—into the bathroom, an old-fashioned bathroom full of potted ferns and faucets of burnished bronze. Dangling from the shower head was Matias's father: a hanged man, his tongue protruding, his face a purplish blue.

After leaving the bathroom, I entered a bedroom where Matias's brother was lying—he was a skeleton (on his thin thorax, the ribs had been painted with phosphorescent paint; in his hands, a rusty chain).

In the den we found Matias's two sisters, who'd been stabbed (the knives buried in their breasts; their faces smeared with chicken blood; from one of them, the sound of the death rattle).

That was what the Phantom Train was like in 1956.

Matias was exhausted. His brother lifted him out of the baby carriage and, with the utmost care, laid him on his bed.

His parents were crying softly. His mother wanted to give me some money. I didn't take it. I ran home.

Matias died a few weeks later. To the best of my recollection, I have never taken a ride on the Phantom Train since then.

The Day When We Killed James Cagney

ONE DAY WE WENT to the Apollo movie theater.

Since it was a Sunday matinee, we expected to see a good movie, with the hero being the winner. We ate coffee candy and kept hitting each other on the head with our comic books. When the lights were turned off, we cheered and whistled, but soon after the opening scenes, we began to have some misgivings . . .

The hero, whose name was James Cagney, was quite short and he didn't hit anybody. Quite the opposite: Every time he ran into the bad guy—a tall fellow called Sam—this guy, who sported a large mustache, would beat the living daylights out of him. There were punches and blows and a monkey wrench, and even kicks aimed at his belly. James Cagney was beaten to a pulp—he was a bloody mess, with a swollen eye—and he didn't fight back.

At first we just grumbled, but soon we were stomping our feet. It was impossible for us to respect or hold in high regard such a despicable milksop.

James Cagney had led a wretched life. He had to earn a living when he was still quite young. He used to sell newspapers on the street corner. Street kids were always trying to steal money from him, but he had always defended himself bravely. And now look at what had become of his promising career! Yes, we booed him and called him all kinds of names.

James Cagney began to show signs that he was afraid of us. He would slip away, flattening himself against walls. He looked at us sideways. Dastardly dog, scoundrel, traitor!

Three months later into the movie, Sam gives him another whopping thrashing and he is left sprawled on the floor, bleeding like a pig. We had just about given up on him. Quite frankly, we felt so disgusted with him that, as far as we were concerned, he could just die there once and for all—such was the degree of our revulsion.

But then one of us noticed a faint twitching in the fingers of his left hand and a discreet tightening of his lips.

In a man lying beaten up on the ground, such signs could be considered encouraging.

We decided that in spite of everything, it would be worthwhile to root for James Cagney. We began to cheer, moderately but resolutely.

James Cagney rose to his feet. We clapped our hands somewhat more loudly—not too clamorously, however, just enough to keep him on his feet. We made him walk a few steps. When he comes to a mirror, he should take a good look at himself, that's what we are hoping for at that moment.

James Cagney looked at himself in the mirror. We stood in silence as he watched his shame surfacing on his battered face.

"Get your revenge on him!" somebody shouted. It was quite unnecessary, though: To the wise, our silence was sufficient, and James Cagney had already learned enough from us that Sunday afternoon there in the Apollo movie theater.

Slowly he began to pull open a drawer in the dresser, and then he took out his father's old gun. He examined it: It was a .45 revolver. We were now whistling and clapping our hands wildly. James Cagney put on his hat and made a dash for his car. His hands gripped the steering wheel firmly; his face showed determination. We had made a new man of James Cagney. We let him know that we approved of the self-confident expression in his eyes.

He found Sam in a third-rate hotel. He climbed the stairs slowly. We punctuated his footsteps by rhythmically stamping our lace-up boots on the floor. When he opened the bedroom door, we broke into some deafening screaming.

Sam was sitting on the bed. He rose to his feet. He was a giant of a man. James Cagney looked at the bad guy, then he looked at us. We had to admit it: He was afraid. All our hard work, all our efforts during all those weeks proved to be in vain. James Cagney continued to be James Cagney. The bad guy grabbed the .45 away from him and shot him right in the middle of his forehead: He fell to the ground without a moan.

"It serves him right," muttered Pedro, when the lights were turned on. "He richly deserved it"

It was our first crime. We have committed many others since then.

Vegetable Kingdom

IN THE VEGETABLE KINGDOM. That's what Gloria says: We live in the vegetable kingdom, amid giant ferns, maidenhair, rubber trees, boa constrictors, green tumid growing things unfolding their leaves throughout the house. It's Marina who looks after them, as well as after everything else. Marina cooks, Gloria spruces herself up. Marina sews, Gloria makes bantering remarks. Gloria sleeps, Marina keeps vigil. Marina does needlework and cleans and polishes. She makes buttonholes and covers for the buttons; she embroiders and she knits. Proficient in the domestic arts, people say about her. She makes and sells artificial flowers. The income that she gets from this work makes up a substantial amount of her domestic budget and even provides her with enough reserve funds for a rainy day. Hardworking as an ant, that's what Marina is like. As for Gloria, she sings before the mirror, makes up her face, examines the skin on her face anxiously. But after all—wonder the neighbors—which one is the mother, which one is the daughter?

Gloria is the mother. She was born earlier. She got married, conceived Marina and became a widow. She mourned the death of her husband, but not overly so; then she forgot him. She's got her daughter, who brightens her days, but only with a dim light. However, the light is bright enough to chase away the shadows that rise from the dead corners of the house and from amid the ferns.

Marina looks after her mother and their house, moving about silently in the kitchen. After lunch, while Gloria lies snoring, she sits down by the stove, lights a cigarette and with a scowl (she cultivates wrinkles, says Gloria) stares at the cracks in the walls.

And it's three in the afternoon. Soon a sunbeam ("the witch's little horse," says Marina) will seep into the bedroom through a slit in the venetian blind. Marina will sit down on the bed, place Gloria's head in her lap, and wake her gently. "Mummy, mummy," Gloria, still half-asleep, will murmur. "Can I have some chocolate?" "Yes, my little daughter," Marina will say, kissing her rosy cheeks. She'll help Gloria get dressed; she'll let her go for a walk in the main square, but she'll ask her to be home by five, when a strong breeze starts to blow in the square.

Alone in the empty house, Marina will think a little about her own childhood, about the doll with the blond hair. She'll compress her lips, pushing these memories aside with a small gesture, and she'll water the boa constrictor, which grows luxuriantly, displaying a mass of strong sinews, before her admiring eyes. There was a time when Marina was afraid that this plant might be carnivorous, then a time when she laughed at such fears, but now she neither fears nor laughs: She merely tightens her lips and proceeds to get dinner ready.

Gloria returns, her face aglow, and announces that she has a secret to tell.

"Do tell me," says Marina, her eyes blank. But now Gloria doesn't want to: "After dinner . . . " Marina serves her soup; she places a napkin around Gloria's neck so that she won't soil her new blouse. "Tell me now," she insists. Gloria laughs, claps her hands: She's being naughty; she won't tell. And on top of that, she slurps her soup, knowing that Marina can't stand it. Marina doesn't like noises.

After dinner they'll sit on the sofa. Marina will light a cigarette, Gloria will rest her head on Marina's shoulder and will talk about the man who keeps following her in the square. "He's tall, with a dark complexion. His face is grave . . . " She would like to become his girlfriend. "Will you let me?"

Marina will hesitate, and she won't have to reply because by then Gloria will already be dozing off. A moonbeam—the witch's little mule—slides over the wooden floor of the living room. The vine begins to unfurl its long, thin stems. A thousand eyes glitter from amid the leaves of the ferns. They are drops of water, Marina believes.

Navigation Chart

THE TIME: 7:30. Distance from the island: about 800 meters. Distance from the bank of the river: zero (note—boat run aground). Depth of the water: 20 centimeters at most. Facial expression: normal (big brown eyes, wide open; mouth, half-open). Normal.

THE ISLAND WAS THERE, eight hundred meters from the bank: We didn't dare reach it by swimming. We were small boys; besides, our parents had warned us about the dangers of the Guaíba—a treacherous river, full of currents.

But the island was there, a small stretch of land covered with thick, wild vegetation. During the floods only the top leafage of the trees stood visible, and there the corpses of animals floating down the river got entangled. Caught in the branches, the carcasses would slowly decay, and then when the waters receded, the skeletons were left bleaching in the branches.

Nowadays we know this. However, in those days, when we looked through the binoculars (whose binoculars were they?) and saw the bulls' skulls on the treetops, we wanted to find out who had placed them there. Indians?

Then we discovered the boat. An old canoe run aground amid the sedge. It was filled with greenish water; as we came closer, a small snake slithered away from it and disappeared into the vegetation.

That greenish water—it would delight Rogério nowadays; he is a biologist. Ah, the things he would notice today in that water. Paramecia, amoebas, tiny worms, various larvae—all of them living in a stagnant world, but a stagnant world seething with creatures moving about frantically in search of things, of food—and in their search constantly colliding with one another. Today Rogério knows. We turned the boat over and drained out the putrid water, which then vanished into the hot, coarse sand, leaving tiny creatures flitting about in the air; later, they grew quiet. Egg shells. A pack of Continental cigarettes. Assorted bits and pieces.

The boat returned to its normal position and it was ready to sail.

Then we turned to him and said: Climb in.

THE TIME: 8:05. Distance to the island: the same. Distance from the bank: the same. Depth of the water: the same. Facial expression: surprise; mild apprehension, noticeable only in a slight frown.

YES, YOU, WE INSISTED.

He was the youngest and the lightest among us.

But those weren't the only reasons. There were others: He could be silent when it was time to be silent; when he was supposed to look, he looked, and when he was supposed to listen, he listened, his mouth half open, his big brown eyes wide open. . . . And when he was supposed to speak, he spoke; he'd tell us everything, his dreams, other people's dreams, his brothers' . . .

But where in the world does he hear—we wondered, intrigued—all these things? (Lies, all these lies, we were about to say, but didn't, for after all how could we know for sure whether they were lies? What if they were indeed the truth?)

Now he was refusing to go. I'm afraid, he said; and we prodded him on. Come on, don't be such a drag; you're dying to go. For how could we know whether he was telling us the truth? Wasn't it possible that he was just whining? (This happened in the early fifties, when there were plenty of coy people around; Plenty of people who jawed away; plenty of drivelers.) Cut it out and climb in, we told him.

And we began to push him—but not roughly, because then he would just go to pieces. We jostled him gently, playfully, even tenderly; he kept resisting, but without much conviction, without the inflexibility of someone refusing to budge another inch, or of someone who would rather die than give in. Maybe he was simply unable to offer any resistance, for he was rather frail. Anyway, when he found himself hemmed in by the boat behind him and by us closing in on him—with our laughter, our hands, our fingernails, our eyes, our freckles, our hair—it was with an almost automatic gesture that he raised a leg over the side of the boat. Then he realized that he was halfway in it, and he still could have taken his leg out again—but did he want to, did he? Anyway, he didn't take his leg out; he hesitated for a while, then moved the other leg inside the boat. Was it an automatic gesture? Was it an inner voice that commanded him to do so? Was it a conscious decision, a prudent act of submission?

Then we looked, and he looked, and all of us realized that he was in the boat.

THE TIME: 8:35. Distance to the island: the same. Distance from the bank: the same. Depth of the water: the same. Facial expression: changeable according to each individual onlooker: artful connivance (Rui, nowadays a merchant); calm despair (Alberto, nowadays a priest); sheer terror (Jorge, nowadays a journalist).

FROM THEN ON he did whatever we told him to do. Sit down in the boat, we said, and he sat down. Take the paddle and he took the paddle, which was a board taken from a packing case. When you reach the island, we told him, beach the boat, tie it securely, get off the boat, walk around, go into the bushes and look around very carefully; but if there are any Indians, hide yourself; steal a skull . . .

Frozen still, he sat listening to us in silence.

He was staring at us; We stared back. We kept consulting among ourselves, exchanging glances: What if there's a house there, should he go in? Should he speak to anyone he finds there?

And we began to push the boat into the water, into the river.

Push! we shouted at each other. Push! The boat was heavy. Push! We managed to move it a few centimeters, then a few more—
Then we realized that it was floating away.
Start rowing! we shouted. Row!
But he didn't row. He sat staring at us.

THE TIME: 8:40. Distance to the island: about 750 meters. Distance from the bank: 50 meters (note—boat moving). Depth of the water: 4 to 5 meters. Facial expression: (nobody noticed).

START ROWING! Come on, row! we shouted anxiously.

THE TIME: 8:55. Distance to the island: about 600 meters. Distance from the bank 200 meters (note: boat moving rapidly). Depth of the water: 20 to 30 meters. Facial expression: impossible to describe; kept facing the island.

THIS FOG, the fog that enveloped everything at that moment isn't—wasn't—unusual. . . . No, it isn't. For a couple of hours it was impossible to see a thing. We shouted, but got no reply.

When the fog lifted, there was no sign of the boat. The island was there, and so were the trees and the skulls, but the boat wasn't.

And we didn't even know where he lived. We didn't even know his full name.

THE TIME: 10:15. Distance to the island: about 500 meters. Distance from the bank 300 meters. Depth of the water: 20 to 30 meters. Facial expressions (ours): peaceful, generally speaking.

WE COME HERE SOMETIMES. The entire old gang, now aboard Rui's boat (almost as big as a yacht).

We don't talk about the island, but we glance at it.

The Carnival of the Animals [1968] 55

There's now a bridge connecting it to the bank—to the other bank, not ours. The trees are still there but the bulls' skulls are gone. And there's some construction work going on there—a factory, it seems. The concrete uprights loom off-white against the dark green of the vegetation. And there are smokestacks.

Who owns it? I ask, but get no reply. The time is 10:30, the distance from the island is four hundred meters, and the facial expressions—of the ones I can see—show calm indifference.

Ecology

THERE WAS A TIME when this entire area was quite pastoral, you know. The meadow, the birds, the breeze, the brook. Very peaceful, it used to be around here.

Not so anymore. Now, things happen. For example, the two dots that have just appeared on the horizon. They advance slowly; finally, they take form. It's a couple. He, a fat, elderly man wearing a white suit, a red tie, and a Panama hat; he wipes his sweaty face with a large handkerchief. (I recognize the linen in the white suit: the fibers from the plants that used to grow in a meadow similar to this one. Poor fibers; poor plants.)

The woman is also fat and dumpy. She is sweaty, too, but she doesn't wipe her face; she keeps muttering. (I recognize the silk in the woman's dress: a substance extracted from a larva's cocoon, and then made into thread, and then dyed, and then cut up, and then sewn. Poor larvae; poor substance.)

They are approaching. They come nearer. Now they are three meters away, at most. They raise their eyes, then hug each other and burst into tears. That's right: They're crying. And they cry and cry . . . Finally, the man wipes his tears with the handkerchief. (I recognize the cotton in it. Poor cotton.) He takes a step forward, keeping his eyes raised all the time, and says in a tearful voice: "Come down, daughter. Come down and speak to your parents." He cuts a sorry figure, this tearful old man. "We had a hard time finding you, my daughter. We took a plane, then a bus. . . . And we had to cover this final stretch of country on foot because there are no roads here. . . . Ah, my daughter, we're dead tired, daughter. Come down and talk to us."

Silence.

A lie: There's never absolute silence here because of the breeze, of the birds; but they are nature's sounds. Whereas these sobs, his puffing and panting. . . . No. They are not nature's. They are something revolting.

"Come down, my daughter." The old man has resumed his litany. "Did you ever see anyone living in a treetop like that? What are you, an animal? No, of course you're not an animal, my daughter. Come down now, come down and embrace your parents. Come down, will you? We'll forgive you everything."

There's no reply.

"Don't you realize you're killing your mother?"

Ah, this sounds like an outrage. The effrontery!

"Come down, my daughter. Come down, for God's sake!"

Now it is the old woman's turn to shout in her shrill voice. Take a good look at your face! Just look at your hair. It looks like chaff."

Chaff. Yeah, I know. It's what remains of the wheat, of the hay, after they thresh them, after they . . . But I'd rather not talk about it. The brutes. Poor plants, poor chaff.

"Daughter, listen!" (It's the old woman again.) "I've brought you some apples, my daughter. Come down, and eat with us, daughter. Apples, look! You like them so much."

Apples! Now, that's the limit. So they dared pluck apples from a tree. And now they have the gall to offer them to me. But what kind of people are they? The two of them would be perfectly capable of roasting a child and then offer him to his mother.

"Come down, daughter!"

Never.

"Come down!"

Let them shout to their hearts' content.

Time goes by. We know for a fact that time does go by here. We have, as we know, the days and the nights, the rain and the sunshine, the heat, the cold, the heat. Right now, for example, night is falling. There's logic and certainty in this fact. But they, the old couple, don't know that night falls here. They are startled, look around them, and exchange words in a low voice. What are they afraid of? Animals? Poor animals!

They make a hasty departure. The old man turns around once: "We'll be back tomorrow, my daughter."

Let them come back. It's no concern of mine. You know: *I am the tree.*

Before Making the Investment

WE DIDN'T HAVE MONEY for a bus ticket to the next city, therefore my friend suggested that we board a freight train—the transportation system used by shrewd people. As soon as night began to fall, we made a dash for one of the empty boxcars, where he hid ourselves. Panting, we slid the heavy door shut and then lay down on the floor. We were tired and hungry.

Then I smelled something.

"Amigo, do you detect something strange in here?"

He didn't reply. I ignored the smell. Then I noticed that we were lying on a thin layer of straw. Much too thin, as a matter of fact—yet we seemed quite far away from the real floor of the boxcar.

"Not much straw in here, is there?"

In the dark, I could hear him panting. He heaved a sigh and said:

"Amigo, you ask too many questions. Why don't you shut up and try to get some sleep? We have a lot to do tomorrow."

My friend dislikes unnecessary questions. I, however, have an inborn curiosity. My father used to say that I would be a scientist. God has already forgiven him his mistake and he rests in peace.

I kept thinking and asking myself questions while my fingers explored the straw. However, I didn't want my friend to notice that I was carrying on my investigation; he could take offense at what I was doing. I asked him casually: "Amigo, what's the name of this city?"

"You know it, amigo," he muttered.

"Yeah," I admitted, and went on, "doesn't it strike you as a strange city, amigo?"

He was definitely annoyed now.

"Strange? Nonsense, amigo. To you everything is strange. You'll never succeed in life if you persist in thinking like this. You've got to know people and cities like the back of your hand so that you can exploit their weaknesses and take advantage of the opportunities. See what I mean? Now, why don't you try to get some sleep, amigo. We have a lot to do tomorrow. We'll strike oil, you'll see, amigo."

At that moment I discovered something in the straw.

I touched him on the shoulder.

"Amigo."

"What's the matter now, old buddy?"

"What do you think this could be? It's three or four centimeters long, roughly cylindrical in shape but thicker at the ends, and it's hard, smooth, and dry."

He didn't reply.

I persisted: "What do you think it is, amigo?"

"What I do think is that I won't be able to get any sleep."

I ignored his rudeness, "Couldn't it be a terminal phalanx, amigo?"

"What's a terminal phalanx?"

"A finger bone. The bone is quite dry, and fleshless."

He was silent. But he wasn't asleep; my guess was that he had become quite concerned.

"Here, hold it, amigo."

He hesitated, but then took the phalanx.

"So? What do you think?"

He didn't reply. I'll tell a few things about my friend: He's a young man; cool, thoughtful, shrewd. He believes he'll make a fortune by entering into some bold business deals.

He hasn't achieved his goal yet, but I think he's getting pretty close. We met by chance, for I'm a mere vagabond who is overcome by curiosity. We've been wandering from city to city: I look for food, old clothes, a woman once in a while; he sniffs out profitable deals. He believes that the right moment has finally arrived.

"No. Looks like a piece of bamboo to me. That's what it is, a small piece of bamboo." We've already found out about the bamboo groves around that city and we know that the construction of the huge bamboo-furniture factory is due to begin pretty soon. The construction of this factory is still a secret, but somehow he has managed to find out about it. A sharpie, that's my friend. "Throw this piece of rubbish away."

It seems to me that if bamboo is indeed so valuable, it's not fair to refer to it as rubbish. But my friend knows best and I discard the bone.

"What's the matter with this train, won't it ever pull out?" he asked.

My friend is getting impatient. He would like to set out on this trip right away: We'll be making our fortune in the next city. His plan of action is quite simple: The municipal government of the city where the bamboo grows has just issued public bonds. So far these bonds are worth nothing. But with the construction of the bamboo-furniture factory their value will rise tremendously.

Nobody in the next city knows about this factory yet: We'll buy the bonds there for peanuts and later resell them for ten times as much.

I'm still exploring the straw. "Friend . . . "

"Yeah, what is it now?"

"Something long, smooth, and hard, with what feels like a head at the end . . . what could it be?" He hesitates and then breaks into laughter. "I've heard that gag somewhere before, but I can't think of a suitable repartee. . ."

"It's not a gag, friend. It's something I'm holding in my hand."

"Ha, ha, ha!"

I fail to see what's so funny. "Couldn't it be a femur, friend? A human femur."

Now he's no longer laughing. "Let me see it."

I hand him the femur. He is silent for a while.

"No. It looks like bamboo to me. Notice the strength and the hardness of the bamboo that they grow in this city."

It is indeed quite surprising that nobody had thought before of using this material to make furniture.

I still think it's a femur, but I say nothing to avoid getting into an argument. I decide to change the subject. "Friend, wasn't this train supposed to have left at nightfall? I find it strange that it hasn't."

He rises to his feet: "It's really impossible to get any sleep here. Okay, so the train hasn't left. So what? It's been delayed, that's it. Don't trains often run behind schedule? To you everything is strange. The bamboo is strange, this city is strange."

"I've heard stories about this city, amigo . . . "

"Stories, indeed, come on now!"

"I've heard that workers from all over the country are brought here to work. They don't get paid for months."

"So? Don't they complain?"

"No, they disappear."

The Carnival of the Animals [1968]   61

"Disappear? Only someone like you would believe something like that. How in the world could a worker disappear just like that?" I stood thinking about an explanation, but my friend prevented me from replying: "Besides, we're investors; we're not interested in money, not in its sources. Tomorrow we'll buy those bonds . . . "

I was about to ask where we would get the capital to buy them, but thought better of it: My friend is shrewd and must know what he's doing. I was now amusing myself with something vaguely reminiscent of a container with two cavities similar to eye sockets. Interesting: I have never come across any bamboo shaped like this

"If this train leaves now, we'll be there at ten o'clock."

The train didn't leave. Suddenly, the door of the boxcar was opened: There stood the police.

It looks as if we'll take this trip later on: Underneath the straw.

Communication

ROBERTO GETS A PHONE CALL from his brother Marcelo, who sounds distressed. The telephone connection is bad, and the only thing he can understand is the word *died*.

"Who died? Who did you say died?" Roberto shouts. He is overcome with anxiety. Stammering, he repeats the same words.

The telephone connection, however, remains bad. Shouting, they tell each other to hang up and try again. Roberto puts the receiver down and waits impatiently for the phone to ring. Seconds, then minutes go by and the phone remains silent. It occurs to him that maybe he is expected to ring first.

"But what if I do," he says aloud to himself, "and Marcelo also thinks that he should ring first, and then if he does ring first, he'll get a busy signal. I'd better wait."

He keeps waiting. The telephone doesn't ring. More time goes by.

Then on the spur of the moment, he picks up the receiver and dials Marcelo's number; and just as he feared, he gets a busy signal. He hangs up. He waits for a while, smoking and pacing back and forth. Although he is convinced that he shouldn't dial again, he can't refrain himself from doing so. He hears the busy signal.

Let's suppose that it takes a person one second to pick up the receiver; eight seconds to dial; two seconds to realize that the line at the other end is busy; fifteen to forty seconds to wait anxiously before dialing again. Let's figure out how long it will take Roberto to find Marcelo's phone free. And in addition let's try to guess who has died.

Hello! Hello!

IRMA, A DEEPLY RELIGIOUS WOMAN, falls in love with her coworker Teófilo, who is an atheist. Knowing that she will never be able to marry a man from whom she is kept apart by the barriers of her faith, she decides to move away from him, without ever letting him in on her feelings. She resigns from her job, moves to a distant neighborhood, and begins to lead a life of self-denial.

Periods of fasting and penance take place.

Her love, however, does not die, and Irma is tormented by yearnings. Every night she phones Teófilo.

"Hello!" he says.

Irma remains silent.

"Yes! Hello!"

Hearing the beloved voice, Irma quivers with pain and pleasure.

"Hello! Who's that? Answer me, will you?"

Irma cups her hand over the mouthpiece and quietly kisses her knuckles.

"Why don't you say something, you animal? Identify yourself."

Irma stifles a sob while abusive language pours out of the telephone. Finally, she hangs up.

This same routine goes on each night. Teófilo is beside himself with anger. He is so angry that he can't eat or sleep; he feels helpless.

On his friends' advice, he asks the police for help. An investigation reveals that the phone calls originate from Irma's telephone. Teófilo is asked to inform the police as soon as he gets the next mysterious call.

He does as he is told.

The policemen break into Irma's apartment and catch her still on the phone, as she is kissing the back of her thin hand. Moved by despair, she jumps out the window. Luckily, the building is not high and except for some abrasions, she is not injured. After receiving medical attention, she is taken to the police station.

Teófilo is called in.

He is shocked when he sees Irma surrounded by policemen. And to everybody's surprise, he shouts: "But I loved you, Irma! I loved you!"

"Be gone, Satan," she replies, weeping.

The newsmen present at the scene understand her pain.

Dr. Shylock

IT IS SAID THAT IN FORMER DAYS, Dr. Shylock used to be a notorious usurer. It is said that he lent a certain sum of money to a young man, demanding a pound of the debtor's own flesh as the only collateral. The debtor, sure that he would be able to repay the debt on time, acquiesced. However, it turned out that he was unable to do so, and Shylock, insensitive to the pleas from people of goodwill, demanded that the agreement between them be fulfilled.

Fortunately, the young man got a skillful lawyer to defend him.

The lawyer pointed out to the court that the agreement clearly specified the word *flesh*, and not *blood*. The usurer could cut out a piece of flesh as long as he did not shed *blood*, not a drop of it. After this clever reasoning, there was nothing Shylock could do but beat a retreat amid widespread laughter.

This event took place a long time ago. Today Dr. Shylock is a famous surgeon.

True, he does have some idiosyncrasies. For instance, he demands that every single organ and tumor that he cuts out be carefully weighed: If the scales show that it weighs one pound, he laughs and claps his hands; if it weighs more, or less, he walks away dejectedly.

Nobody pays attention to this eccentricity of his. However, what everybody—professionals and laymen—does remark upon is Dr. Shylock's extraordinary skills: He has the ability to perform even the most complex operations without shedding a single drop of blood.

The Ballad of the False Messiah [1976]

The Ballad of the False Messiah

HE'S ABOUT TO POUR THE WINE into the glass. His hands are now wrinkled and unsteady. And yet, those big, strong hands of his still deeply affect me. I compare them with my own hands with their stubby fingers and I admit that I've never understood him and never will.

I first met him on board the *Zemlia*. We were Jews leaving Russia in that old ship; we feared the pogroms. Enticed by the promises of America, we were now journeying toward our destination, crammed into the third class. We wept and were seasick in that year of 1906.

They were already aboard the ship when we embarked. Shabtai Zvi and Natan de Gaza. We shunned them. We knew that they were Jews, but we from Russia are wary of strangers. We dislike anyone who looks more Oriental than we do. And Shabtai Zvi was from Smirna, in Asia Minor—one could tell by his swarthy complexion and dark eyes. The captain told us that he was from a very wealthy family. As a matter of fact, he and Natan de Gaza occupied the only decent stateroom in the ship. What made them leave for America? What were they escaping from? Questions with no answers.

Natan de Gaza, in particular—a short, dark complexioned man— roused our curiosity. Until then we had never seen a Jew from Palestine, from Eretz Israel—a land which to many of us existed only in dreams. Natan, an eloquent public speaker, would tell an attentive audience about the rolling hills of Galilee, about beautiful Lake Kineret, about the historical city of Gaza, where he had been born, and whose gates Samson had wrenched off their hinges. When drunk, however, he would curse his native land: "Nothing but rocks and sand, camels, larcenous Arabs . . . " When we were off the Canary Islands, Shabtai Zvi caught him execrating Eretz Israel. He beat Natan up, until he collapsed on the floor, where he lay bleeding; when Natan dared to protest, Shabtai knocked him out with one final kick.

After this incident he spent days shut up in his stateroom, speaking to no one. As we walked past his door, we could hear moans . . . and sighs . . . and melodious songs.

One day at dawn we were awakened by the shouts of the seamen. We rushed to the deck and saw Shabtai Zvi swimming in the icy sea. A lifeboat was lowered and with great difficulty he was pulled out of the water. Stark naked as he was, he walked past us, without a glance in our direction, his head held high—and he went straight to his stateroom, where he shut himself up. Natan de Gaza said that the bathing in the sea had been an act of penance, but our own conclusion was quite different: "He's crazy, this Turk."

We arrived at Ilha das Flores in Rio de Janeiro, and from there we traveled to Erexim, from where we proceeded in covered wagons to our new homes in the settlement called Barão Franck, named for the Austrian philanthropist who had sponsored our coming. We felt very grateful to this man, whom, incidentally, we never met. It was rumored that later a railroad would be built across the lands where we were being settled, and that the baron was interested in the valuation of the shares of stock in the railroad company. I don't believe this rumor was true. I do think that he was a generous man, that's all. He gave each family a plot of land, a wooden house, agricultural tools, livestock.

Shabtai Zvi and Natan de Gaza stayed with us. They were given a house, too, although the baron's representative wasn't pleased with the idea of having two men living together under the same roof.

"We need families," he stated incisively—"not fairies."
Shabtai Zvi stared at him. It was such a powerful gaze that it froze us.

The baron's agent shuddered, bid us farewell, and left hastily. We threw ourselves wholeheartedly into our work.

How hard country life was! Felling trees. Plowing the fields. Sowing . . . Our hands were covered with bleeding blisters.

We hadn't seen Shabtai Zvi for months. He had shut himself up in his house. Apparently he had run out of money because Natan de Gaza began to wander about the village, asking for clothes and food. He would tell us that Shabtai Zvi would reappear in the near future to bring good tidings to the entire population.

"But what has he been doing?" we would ask.

What has he been doing? Studying. He has been studying the Cabalah, the masterpiece work of Jewish mysticism: The Book of Creation, the Book of Brightness, the Book of Splendor. The occult sciences. Metempsychosis. Demonology. The power of names (names can exorcise demons; a person well versed in the power of names can walk on the water without getting his feet wet; and there is also the power of the secret, ineffable, unpronounceable name of God). The mysterious science of letters and numbers (letters are numbers and numbers are letters; numbers have magical powers; as for letters, they are the steps leading to wisdom).

It is around that time that the outlaw Chico Devil puts in an appearance at Barão Franck for the first time. A fugitive from the law, he comes from the frontier, he and his band of desperados. While fleeing from the "Stetsons," he finds a hideout near our settlement. And he plunders and he destroys and he sneers. Laughing, he kills our bulls, wrenches out their testicles, then eats them slightly roasted. And he threatens to kill every one of us if we denounce him to the authorities. As if this misfortune weren't enough, we are struck by hail, which destroys our fields of wheat.

We are plunged into the deepest despair when Shabtai Zvi reappears.

He is transformed. Fasting has ravaged his once robust body, his shoulders stoop. His beard, oddly turned grey, now reaches down to his chest. Sainthood enfolds him like a mantle and it glows in his eyes.

Slowly he walks toward the end of the main street . . . We drop our tools, we leave our houses, we follow him. Then, standing on a mound of earth, Shabtai Zvi addresses us.

"Divine punishment will befall you!"

He was referring to Chico Devil and to the hail. We had attracted God's wrath. And what could we do to expiate our sins?

"We will abandon everything: the houses; the cultivated fields; the school; the synagogue; with our own hands we will build a boat—the timber of our houses will be made up into the hull, and our talliths will be made up into sails. Then we will cross the ocean. We will arrive in Palestine, in Eretz Israel; and there, in the ancient, holy city of Sfat, we will build a large temple."

"And will we await the coming of the Messiah there?" somebody asked in a trembling voice.

"The Messiah has already come!" shouted Natan de Gaza. "The Messiah is right here! The Messiah is our own Shabtai Zvi!"

Shabtai Zvi opened the mantle which enveloped him. We stepped back, horrified. What we saw was a naked body covered with scars; circling his belly was a wide belt studded with spikes that penetrated his flesh.

That day we stopped working. Let the hail destroy the cultivated fields. Let Chico Devil steal our livestock; we no longer cared, because we were leaving soon. Jubilant, we tore down our houses. The women sewed pieces of cloth together to make sails for the boat. The children gathered wild berries to make jam. Natan de Gaza collected money, which was needed, he said, to buy off the Turkish potentates that ruled over the Holy Land.

"What's been going on in the Jewish settlement?" wondered the settlers in the neighboring areas. They were so intrigued that they sent Father Batistella over to find out. The priest came to see us; he was aware of our plight and willing to help us.

"We don't need anything, Father," we replied with great earnestness. "Our Messiah has come; he's going to set us free and make us happy."

"The Messiah?" The priest was astonished. "But the Messiah has already been here on earth. He was our Lord Jesus Christ, who changed water into wine and who died on the cross because of our sins."

"Shut up, Father!" shouted Sarita. "The Messiah is Shabtai Zvi!"

Sarita, the adopted daughter of fat Leib Rubin, had lost her parents in a pogrom. Ever since, she had been mentally unbalanced. She would follow Shabtai Zvi everywhere, convinced that she was destined to become the wife of the Anointed of the Lord. And to our surprise, Shabtai Zvi accepted her: they were married on the day when we finished the hull of the boat. As for the vessel itself, it was quite good; we planned to transport it to the sea on a big oxcart, the way Bento Gonçalves had transported his own boat.

There weren't many oxen left. Chico Devil was now showing up once a week, each time stealing a couple of them. Some of us began talking about confronting the bandits. Shabtai Zvi disapproved of this idea. "Our kingdom lies overseas. And God is protecting us. He will provide for us."

Indeed: Chico Devil disappeared. For two weeks we worked in peace, putting the finishing touches to the preparations for our departure. Then on a Saturday morning, a horseman galloped into the village. It was Gumercindo, Chico Devil's lieutenant.

"Chico Devil is ill!" he shouted without dismounting from his horse. "He's seriously ill. The doctor doesn't seem to be able to come up with the right treatment. Chico Devil has asked me to bring your saint over so that he can cure him."

We surrounded him in silence.

"And if he refuses to come with me," Gumercindo went on, "then I have orders to set the whole village on fire. Did you hear?"

"I'll go," thundered a strong voice.

It was Shabtai Zvi. We made way for him. Slowly he drew closer, his eyes fastened on the outlaw.

"Get down from the horse."

Gumercindo dismounted. Shabtai Zvi mounted the horse.

"You go in front of me, running."

The three of them set off: Gumercindo, running ahead; then Shabtai Zvi, on horseback; and bringing up the rear, Natan de Gaza, riding on a donkey. Sarita wanted to go with them, but Leib Rubin didn't let her.

We were assembled in the school building all day long. We were far too anxious to speak. When night fell, we heard a horse's trotting. We ran to the door. It was Natan de Gaza, gasping for breath.

"When we got there," he said, "we found Chico Devil lying on the floor. Beside him, a witch doctor was performing his sorcery. Shabtai Zvi sat down by the bandit. He didn't say a word, he didn't do a thing, he never touched the man—the just sat there watching. Then Chico Devil raised his head, looked at Shabtai Zvi, let out a yell, and died. The witch doctor, he was killed right then and there. I don't know what happened to Shabtai Zvi. I came over to warn you: Cut and run!"

We got into our wagons and fled from Erexim. Sarita had to be taken forcibly.

On the following day, Leib Rubin called us to a meeting.

"I don't know about the rest of you," he said, "but I've had enough of the whole shebang: Barão Franck, Palestine, Sfat . . . I've made up my mind to go to Porto Alegre. Do you want to come with me?"

"And what about Shabtai Zvi?" asked Natan de Gaza in a shaky voice (was he feeling remorse?).

"The hell with him. He's nuts!" yelled Leib Rubin. "He has caused us nothing but misfortunes."

"Don't speak like that, Father!" shouted Sarita. "He is the Messiah!"

"The Messiah, my foot! Enough of this story—it's the kind of thing that might well provoke the Jew-haters. Didn't you hear what the priest said? The Messiah has already come, didn't you hear? He changed water into wine, among other things. And we're leaving. That husband of yours, if he's still alive—and if he has gotten his head together—can join us later. It's my duty to look after you—which I'm going to do, husband or no husband!"

We traveled to Porto Alegre. Kindly Jews took us in. And to our surprise, Shabtai Zvi showed up a few days later. The "Stetsons," who had arrested Chico Devil's gang, brought him to us.

One of the soldiers told us that they had found Shabtai Zvi sitting on a stone, his eyes fixed on the body of Chico Devil. And throughout the floor—the bandits, dead drunk, lay snoring. There were quartered oxen scattered everywhere. And wine. "I've never seen so much wine! Every single container previously filled with water was now filled with wine! Bottles, flasks, buckets, basins, barrels. The waters of a nearby marsh were red. I don't know if it was the blood of the oxen or if it was wine. But I think it was wine."

With the help of a wealthy relative, Leib Rubin set up shop: first he ran a store that sold fabrics. Then he moved on to furniture, and eventually he established a brokerage firm, and ended up amassing a great fortune. Shabtai Zvi worked in one of his companies, where I was also an employee. Natan de Gaza, after getting mixed up in some smuggling activities, had to flee the country and was never heard of again.

After Sarita's death, Shabtai Zvi and I got into the habit of getting together in a bar to drink wine. That's where we spend our evenings. He doesn't say much, and neither do I; he pours the wine and we drink in silence. Just before midnight he closes his eyes, lays his hands over the glass and murmurs some words in Hebrew (or in Aramaic, or in Ladino). The wine is changed into water. The bar owner thinks it is just a trick. As for myself, I'm not so sure.

Don't Release the Cataracts

I AM A GOD OF JUSTICE. Even from the inside I can look and see: A bus runs across the hollow of the night. The lakes reflect the pale Moon. Men murmur.

It is fair: The lakes have been placed there so that they can reflect the pale Moon and so that men, touched by the sight, can murmur: "The lakes reflect the pale Moon." Everything has been planned from the beginning in the fairest possible way. Many remain unaware of such eternal designs: They open highways, and set buses to run on them. Where are they going in such a hurry? I know. They don't. Yet they keep running.

The passengers are asleep. All except for one. A short, thin man; he is forty years old, has worn a mustache for twenty years and bifocals for ten years.

He boarded the bus in Porto Alegre. He said good-bye to his wife and children; he was quitting his dull job; he was flying the coop. He thought that nobody knew about it. I know.

"In Florianopolis I'll have dinner at Aurora Restaurant. In Florianopolis I'll make new friends. In Florianopolis I'll have a mistress." He was chuckling to himself. They are funny. They come up with phrases, then they laugh. The little man laughed a great deal. But time went by. And now he sits wriggling. It's funny. He wriggles like an earthworm. And he screws up his face. He is no longer laughing.

Three times already has he reached out for the buzzer. But he hasn't pressed the button. Because he knows that pressing it would be useless.

There are men who can cut short the course of events by merely pressing a button. He is not such a man: The bus driver has already told him that he can't stop. There is a pregnant woman on the bus, he has to reach Florianopolis without delay so that the child can be born on terra firma. Clever, this bus driver. He knows that the baby will be a leader and that the little forty-year-old man is already in the death throes—already rotten, maggoty. He stinks. He has some kind of disease, and he stinks of ammonia.

The passenger, however, thinks otherwise. "It's not fair the way I'm being treated," he whimpers. It is fair, yes: I am a god of justice. "I've paid for my bus ticket, I have rights . . . " There are no rights, my dear fellow; only concessions. The owner of this bus line has a concession: He has been granted the right to put buses without toilets on the Porto Alegre–Florianopolis run. You have a different one: You've been granted the right to whimper. Until the moment of the ultimate silence.

He suffers, this man, bloated up that he is, like a pregnant woman. Suffering takes the joy away from this trip; he even feels half-dead . . . What does he expect me to do? Let him find support in recollecting his friends, his mistress, Aurora Restaurant. (Ineffective crutches, aren't they, my cripple?)

"Why? But why?"

So much anxiety. Well, I'll reply then. In the beginning, a hollow seed was sown in his lower belly. It was named bladder. Centuries and hours have gone by, and the bladder fills up: It's a pouch—elastic, true, but only up to a point. It contains lukewarm urine. In a moment the man will have the Sun in his belly. "How it burns!" However, as it is said in the psalm, neither the Moon at night nor the Sun in the daytime should burn him—far less so this Sun of the night.

Sweet memories come to the man's mind: "How good we felt in that public urinal! All of us, citizens of Porto Alegre. Some would chat, others would whistle, many would compare sizes. We would watch the yellow rivulets run along the little white-tiled canals, heading toward the bigger river."

And where do you think the bigger river flowed, my friend?

Nothing escapes my control. Nothing. Every one of those men who stood chatting or whistling or comparing sizes will have to account for everything. For every single droplet of urine.

The man is anguished, afraid he's going to die. He looks at his watch: I see that his time hasn't come yet. Therefore, I take pity on him. And I decide to come to his rescue: I allow him to notice an empty bottle on the seat next to him.

He looks at the bottle. Listlessly, at first, stupefied as he is by suffering. Gradually he begins to show an interest in the bottle. Then he sets his brains to work. Zoom . . . the bus runs. The man thinks and thinks. In a scientific way: hypotheses, calculations. He imagines that he is plotting his own fate. That's all right. He has my permission to think in this way.

Even from the inside I can look and see. I see him unzip his fly, I see him relieve his bladder. The urine pours out into the bottle. Aaaah . . . such a beautiful song.

This orgasmic act lasts a few seconds, and then is over. And as soon as it is over, the man has already forgotten the past suffering, it's completely out of his mind! He sticks his head out of the window, sees lights in the landscape of Santa Catarina state, and feels cheerful: "I've been born again!" It's a lie. He was born only once, forty years ago. And he will die at the age of forty. Only once. I am a god of justice. Each person gets one chance.

He presses the bottle of urine, still warm, against his chest. Quite understandable it is, this tenderness surfacing in the middle of the night: After all, it is his own urine. Nothing could be more his in this world. A moment of tenderness . . . But so fleeting. He is already rejecting his own liquid: Filled with disgust, he opens the window and hurls the bottle up into the sky; the bottle turns a somersault in the air. For a moment the drops sparkle in the moonlight. Then they are swallowed by the black earth.

The bus runs on.

But the seeds have been sown. In that place, in that earth, poisonous mushrooms will sprout, the kind of mushrooms that incurably poison the kidney. Mushrooms. Which a farmer will pick, then sell to the manager of Aurora Restaurant.

And who will eat them? Hm, who will eat them?

I am tired. In Florianopolis I will take a long, long rest. It is only fair: I am a god of justice. My name is Kidney.

New Year, New Life

LIFE IS PAIN, and I wake up with a toothache. It's a gorgeous day, a summer sun invades the shack; as for myself, I'm crying with pain. I'm crying for other reasons as well, but mostly, I'm crying with pain.

Life is a fight. It's no use lying down. I get up and start exercising. While flexing my torso, I notice Francisca's note lying on the chair.

Writing is one of Francisca's latest achievements; with great sacrifice, she attends a literacy course in the evenings. Her handwriting has been improving by the day, as I verify when I unfold her message, which unfortunately doesn't give me any further reason to feel pleased: Francisca has just left me for a longshoreman—as a matter of fact, her choice matches her lack of sensitivity perfectly well, but it also creates problems for myself: Who's going to do the cooking? Who's going to tidy up the shack? Who's going to get me money for the movies? Alas, life is worries.

But life is also joy. The Sun shines, the physical exercises do me good, and if Francisca ditched me, well, there are plenty of other women for the asking. Actually, I bear Francisca no grudge. She has never measured up to me. Because, if nowadays I live in a shack, it's by choice: I was raised by a rich uncle, I never lacked the necessities of life, but I suffered from boredom. It was boredom that turned me into a hippie. Later I decided to turn professional and I became a genuine destitute man. That's what brought me to this shack, where I lived by myself at first; later Francisca, at the time a domestic servant who didn't know how to read or write, moved in with me. And now she has ditched me. Ah well, it doesn't matter; onward, I say, tomorrow will be another day.

The toothache, momentarily eased, is back with a vengeance. I'll have to see a dentist, I conclude. White rum with tobacco won't do me any good, especially because—in this case—there isn't any white rum or tobacco around. In times like these I rather regret having left my uncle's house. At least, I shouldn't have discarded the credit card that he had given me.

I decide to go to the dentist at the village's benevolent association—he treats the poor free. The dentist turns out to be a nice fellow, chubby and likable; after a quick examination, he decides it's a case of extraction. I have a choice, he informs me: either extraction with anesthesia (which will cost me a modest sum of money), or without. I opt for the latter, and I howl when the tooth is pulled out. The dentist thinks that I scream with pain, but he's wrong: it's a howl of satisfaction with having saved money. To spend money to make me insensitive? How absurd. Life is suffering; to suffer is to swig life down, I explain to the dentist when I take my leave, my mouth full of blood.

Spitting out globules of blood upon the dusty roads of the village, I head for the city center with the intention of having some coffee, since I didn't have any morning coffee, might as well have some afternoon coffee: it's almost three o'clock.

I am surprised by the hustle and bustle downtown. Large crowds of people in the streets, in the stores. Suddenly it dawns on me: It's December 31. The last day of the year!

Life is emotion. I recall how my uncle and I used to celebrate the end of the year: with cakes and champagne aplenty. Uncle, I forgot to mention, was an importer of fine wines, so the champagne was always of the best quality, but even so it was rather difficult for me to get stoned with him. The night of December 31 was a night of dreams and hopes. Remembering this, I sit down on the curb of the sidewalk and cry and cry . . .

Hunger stings me. I stand up, ready to battle with life. Life is a battle.

I devise a plan: I set forth clearly defined—and ambitious— objectives: I'll manage to get hold of some money, I'll buy champagne and cakes, I'll celebrate New Year's fittingly. My uncle would have no cause to feel ashamed of me.

But what about money? Where can I get it? Not knowing very well what to do next, I begin to stroll along Rua da Praia, hoping that something will turn up. Something does turn up: At the corner of Rua da Praia and Rua Uruguai I run into the dentist. I accost him, and ask this compassionate man for a loan. Much to my surprise, he refuses; he pushes me aside, he wants to be on his way. Desperate as I am, I grab him.

"Keep your hands off me, you bum! Why don't you get a job, you good-for-nothing!"

He extricates himself free and walks away, muttering. I let him go: His wallet is already in my hand.

Chortling, I step into a dark recess and examine the fruit of my labor. In addition to a credit card, I find a one-hundred-cruzado bill. Happy New Year!

I enter a confectioner's shop to buy cakes. As I'm taking the wallet out of my pocket—a blow on my hand! A purse-snatcher! I've been robbed!

I leave the store in hot pursuit of him: *Thief! Thief!* During the chase we run past the dentist, now also following hot on our heels: *Thief! Thief!* I keep running, hoping that the dentist is with me, not against me.

Finally, a policeman cuts short the race of the pickpocket. I thank the cop and ask for the wallet back. Unfortunately, the dentist has now caught up with us and is also demanding the return of the wallet. The credit card settles the matter. If only I hadn't discarded mine ...

My mouth starts bleeding again, which is unpleasant, but it gives me an idea: I head for a hospital with the intention of giving blood. I've heard that they pay well.

The doorkeeper won't let me in.

"I've come here to give blood," I explain.

"You?" He laughs. "You look as if you badly need a transfusion yourself."

Night has already fallen when I return to my shack: with no cakes, with no champagne, with nothing. Life is wretchedness.

Seated on the bed, I weep. And then I recall the dentist's advice, and I start the New Year with a resolution: I'll work.

I'll plant a grapevine. All I need is one grape, one single grape from which to take out the seed. In a few years I'll have a vineyard and then I'll be able to make my own champagne. New year, new life: tomorrow I'll get hold of one grape.

The Scalp

A FAMILY—FATHER, MOTHER, DAUGHTER—was traveling by car through the hinterland. The father, still young, was an engineer; he was driving in a bad mood because it was hot; besides, the generator was malfunctioning. His wife, who was pregnant, was fanning herself with a paper fan. His daughter—a five-year-old girl—was lying asleep on the back seat. Throughout the preceding kilometers she had been acting up, crying, and biting her mother. Now she was asleep.

The car, an old Ford, advanced with difficulty along the muddy road, which was flanked with steep banks of red earth rising on either side. The engine was groaning, the water in the radiator was boiling. The engineer was beset with anxiety. Night was beginning to fall and he was afraid that the engine might conk out. Cursing under his breath, he kept pressing down the accelerator.

All of a sudden the woman let out a cry: "Look, over there!" Startled, he braked the car. "What is it?" "Over there," she said, "right in front of us." A young woman was walking along the road. Tall, with a beautiful body. Her naked feet were kneading the mud of the road. "But what's the matter?" asked the husband, puzzled. "Her hair," murmured the wife, "how beautiful her hair is!"

Slowly they drove past the young woman, who turned around; smiling, she stood staring at them for a long time.

The wife sighed, and fidgeted on the seat. "Stop the car," she groaned. The engineer slowed down: "Aren't you feeling well? Do you want to throw up?" She lowered her eyes: "No, I don't want to throw up; it's something else, but I'm not telling you because I know you won't do it . . ." "What is it?" asked the engineer. She, tearfully: "It's no use telling you, you won't oblige me . . ." "But what is it that you want?" Worried, the husband glanced at his watch. "Out with it, for heaven's sake!" She blew her nose: "That woman . . ." "Yes," said the engineer, "that woman; what about her?" "Have you noticed her hair?" The wife was no longer crying; her eyes were now glistening. "What about her hair?" groaned the engineer. "Come on, tell me, what about her hair?" "Black," replied the wife, "black like mine, but much longer, far more beautiful." "Yes," said the husband, "so what? What's the problem?"

"Nothing," said the woman, lowering her head. A large teardrop gathered on the tip of her nose.

The engineer stared at her, bewildered. "So, shall we press on?" he asked. "Wait," she murmured, and noisily blew her nose. "But can't you see," he shouted, "that it's getting late, that we still have another sixty kilometers of this dreadful road ahead of us? Do I drive on or not?" She raised her head, took a deep breath, and said angrily: "All right, drive on, let's go. And let's drop the subject, okay?"

He stepped on the brake pedal, turned off the engine. "No, now you've got me worried, I want you to tell me what's the matter with you." The wife, silent. The young woman with the black hair came into sight, overtook them, smiled again, and walked on.

"Her hair," said the woman. "But for God's sake, what about her hair?" shouted the engineer. "People buy it," the wife shouted back. "People buy it—didn't you know? People buy it! To make wigs! It costs a fortune in the city. Here, you can get it cheap."

The engineer was staring at the young woman, who then disappeared around a bend of the road. "I gather that you want to buy her hair," he said in a low voice. "No," said the wife with a smile, "I want *you* to buy it. It's going to be a gift from you."

"No way," muttered the husband, turning on the engine. With a beseeching smile, she rested a hand on his arm: "Please, darling."

"Okay," he sighed. He drove off.

They overtook the young woman. The car came to a halt and the engineer got out.

"Good afternoon, young lady," he said with a forced smile. "Good afternoon," she replied; gorgeous, she was; her teeth were in pretty bad shape, but her eyes were beautiful, and such hair! Long, black, falling over her naked shoulders. The young woman looked at him, waiting.

He explained: He would like to buy her hair to give it to his wife, many girls sold their hair, didn't she know? Yes, she did, the young woman knew about it but she couldn't sell her hair. She had promised her dying mother: She would only cut her hair when she had her own man. "Whoever gets my hair gets me as well," she said, crossing herself. The engineer still tried to persuade her to change her mind; seeing that it was pointless to persist, he thanked her and went back to the car. "She won't sell it," he said to his wife.

"That's a lie," shouted the wife, her eyes glittering with anger, "she'll sell it all right, they all do, she's just trying to raise her price." "Maybe," said the husband, turning on the engine, "but we're driving on." "No!" shouted the woman, her face distorted by pain. "Please!"

The engineer—*oh God, I sure got out of bed on the wrong side today*—turned off the engine and got out of the car.

The young woman had left the road and was now walking along an uphill trail. He followed her.

She walked at a brisk pace. He was trying to overtake her, he got scratched in the shrubs. He was panting. Insects buzzed . . .

He overtook her in a glade, where she had stopped to take a rest. "Young lady," he murmured.

She turned around. She didn't seem surprised. She was smiling.

"Young lady, see, it's like this: My wife is pregnant, she mustn't get upset, you understand, don't you? Do sell me your hair, young lady," he said.

"It's impossible," she was saying with a smile, "I've already told you I can't sell my hair." She stood up and disappeared amid the trees. He hesitated for a moment, then cursing, went in pursuit of her. His boots sank into the damp earth, sweat ran down his neck. He overtook her once more. "Young lady," he groaned. She stared at him, saying nothing.

HE CUT OFF HER HAIR while still lying on top of her. In a rage, he cut it off with his knife, a fistful at a time. She didn't make a single gesture, didn't say a single word. She kept staring at the treetops.

HE RAN BACK TO THE CAR, stumbling over roots. He opened the car door, flung the strands of muddy hair at his wife: "There you are, hold on to them." "How disgusting," protested the woman, "you've dropped the hair, haven't you?" "Yeah," he said, and drove off. "It's all right, I'll have it washed," she said after considering the matter. She carefully placed the hair into a plastic bag.

KILOMETERS FARTHER DOWN THE ROAD, the engineer touched his shirt pocket with his hand: He had lost his documents. But I'm not going back there, he said to himself, nothing in the world will make me. The child woke up: "What's that, Mother?" "It's a wig for Mummy," the mother intoned. "Give it to me," whimpered the girl. "Shut up," the father yelled. Both mother and daughter shut up.

THE WIG WAS MADE, months went by, a child was born—a boy.

One Sunday afternoon the engineer was relaxing at home, reading a magazine. He was alone. His wife and children had gone out for the day.

The bell rang. He got up with a groan and went to the door.

It was the young woman. Her hair hadn't grown back yet; her smile was the same.

"Remember me?" she said, and stepped in.

The Spider

MOTIONLESS ON THE WHITE WALL—the spider. The legs, eight of them, are articulated to her black body. The spider has been there for a long time. Waiting: the male will soon be there.

At the moment, he is away on a hunting expedition. He is after flies; pouncing upon them, he kills them, then draws nourishment from their delicious juices. Soon he'll forget their depleted carcasses.

He'll return to the female. The killing has roused him: He wants to copulate.

Their legs entangled, they make love. Then they disengage themselves. While he lies, lethargic, she moves away a little. Then suddenly she is back, energized—with a quick, accurate maneuver she pulls out one of his legs. And then devours it with pleasure: it has the taste of a dry, velvety cracker. The male, gripped by a sudden dread, wants to flee but can't: deprived of the support of his limb, he heels over, out of control. On the white wall, the female makes periodic raids on the male and dexterously extracts leg after leg.

Finally, all that is left of him is his trunk, from which every outgrowth has been excised—and yet, fits of spasm still ruffle his coat. What is left of him is so small that the she-spider—with only a minor effort—could gulp it down in its entirety. Which she does. Then she remains motionless on the white wall of the spacious bedroom: she and Alice.

Lying in bed, Alice only noticed the spider at the moment when she stretched her long, brown leg. Alice had been gazing at herself; it wasn't until her eyes roamed beyond herself that she caught sight of the spider. Her first impulse was to squash it to death. But she didn't want to soil the wall. She lay staring at the spider.

Alice was waiting for Antonio. Soon he would be there after leaving the grocery store; late, as usual, he would come huffing and puffing: "I'm much too fat to be climbing these stairs!" To make up for it: rings, earrings, cold cash. And a fur coat, too: "How do you like this beast?" He would notice the spider on the wall: "An insect!" A blow with the flat of his huge hand—and there: A black smudge on the wall. He would wipe his hands on his pants, and then would lie down on the wide bed.

For the time being, the spider remained alive. And motionless. She didn't even stir when the key turned in the lock, or when the voice thundered: "I'm much too fat to be climbing these stairs!" He was huffing and puffing, Antonio was. With a smile, he held out a package wrapped in newspaper. "A surprise! Made them myself. A recipe from the old country!" Alice opened the package: dry crackers. Made in various shapes: snakes, lizards. Alice took a cracker out of the package. "A spider!" shouted Antonio. Alice bit into a leg: dry, velvety. Slowly, she crunched it. Dark crumbs fell upon the white bedspread, but she wasn't looking at them.

She was looking at Antonio. Naked, he was slowly drawing near the wall, his raised hand splayed.

Alice slid down to the floor. On all fours on the carpet, she advanced noiselessly and more quickly than the man. Antonio came to a halt, ready to deliver the blow. As for Alice, she saw a hairy leg in front of her. She bit into it. Caught unawares, the man let out a yell. Alice bit again. The leg wasn't dry: it was fleshy, it bled.

With a kick, Antonio shoved her away. He was swearing at her loudly while he put on his clothes. Finally, the door slammed shut. Silence fell upon the bedroom.

Alice smiled. And she stood staring at the spider, motionless on the white surface.

Agenda of Executive Jorge T. Flacks for Judgment Day

SEVEN A.M.

Get up (earlier, today). Don't think. Don't lie motionless in an attempt to recapture fleeting images; let dreams trickle away, jump out of bed.

From the terrace: watch the Sunrise—with dry eyes, without thinking of the millions, billions of years throughout which this poignant light, and so on and so forth. Nothing of the kind. A bath, soon afterward.

Breakfast: orange juice, toast, eggs. Eat with appetite, chew vigorously and swiftly; don't ruminate, don't mix food with bitter thoughts. Don't! Coffee. Very strong, with sugar today, just today, never again (from now on, avoid expressions such as "never again"). Finish off the meal with a glass of ice-cold water, sipping it slowly. Pay special attention to the ice cubes tinkling against the glass. Joyful sound.

EIGHT A.M.

Wake up the wife. Make love. And why not? She's been the companion of so many years. Wife, mother. Make love, yes, a quick act of love, but with the utmost tenderness. Let her go back to sleep afterward. Let her roam through the country of dreams as much as she wants; let her say farewell to her monsters, to her demons, to her fairies, to her princesses, to her godparents.

EIGHT-THIRTY A.M.

Gymnastics. Brisk, fierce movements. Afterward, feel the arms tingling, the head throbbing, splitting, almost: life.

NINE A.M.

Take the car out of the garage. Drive downtown. Take advantage of the time spent driving to do some thinking. Try to clarify certain doubts once and for all; maybe stop off at the rabbi's place. Maybe talk to a priest as well. Maybe bring priest and rabbi together?

TEN A.M.

At the office. Render decisions on the latest documents. Tidy up the desk. Clean out drawers, throw away gewgaws. Set pen to paper. Write a letter, a poem, anything. Write.

The Ballad of the False Messiah [1976]   89

Luncheon. Friends. Salad, cold cuts. Wine. Gab away, talk drivel. Laugh. Observe the faces. Memorize the details of the faces. Hug the friends. Hug them deeply touched. But tearless. No tears at all.

Phone Dr. Francisco. Ask if there's anything that can be done (quite unlikely); but say no to tranquilizers.

Return home. Get the family together, including the baby of the family. Mention they'll be taken for a drive, and get the station wagon out of the garage. Head for the outskirts of the city. Find a spot on an elevation with a panoramic view. Park. Have everybody get out of the car. In a low, quiet voice, explain what is about to happen: the earth, which will open up (explain: as if it were parched), the bones, which will appear—the bones only, white, clean—bones that will then be covered with flesh, with hair, with eyes, with finger and toenails: men, women, laughing, crying.

Conclude with: It's about to begin, children. It's about to begin. Up to now, everything has been a lark.

Eating Paper

I WORK FOR AN INSURANCE COMPANY. One day the manager sends for me.

I'd like you to meet Senhor Álvaro," he says introducing me to a thin young man with gloomy yes. "He's going to work for us and I'd like you to show him the ropes."

Stealthily he thrusts a small piece of paper into my pocket. While escorting Senhor Álvaro, I linger behind him for a moment and read the note: "Watch out. He's the Director's son." I wad the paper into a tiny ball and swallow it nonchalantly. It hasn't been the first time.

I show our files to Senhor Álvaro.

"As you can see," I say to him, "we insure some bigwigs."

He shows interest, writes down names.

I take him to my office, where a little fat man sits waiting.

"I'd like to introduce you to a client who has come to us to buy life insurance . . .

"Leave him to me." He addresses the man:

"Very well. So you would like to take out life insurance. And when do you intend to die?"

"I . . . " mumbles the man, perplexed.

"You didn't understand my question," shouts Senhor Álvaro. "When do you intend to die?"

Startled, the man recoils in his chair. Senhor Álvaro turns to me:

"He doesn't know. They're a bunch of idiots, generally speaking. I'll try cause of death and see if it'll get me somewhere. So then, my friend, what are you planning to die of?"

The client gets up and makes a bolt for the door.

"Maybe that's not a very good technique," I suggest cautiously. I explain a few things about life insurance. A certain degree of optimism is necessary, I tell him. He heaves a sigh, seems to agree.

With satisfaction he informs the next client:

"There's no need to worry, my friend! Very few people have died recently."

The client looks at me and says he'll be back some other day.

I escort Senhor Álvaro back to the manager, and thrust a note into his pocket: "Impossible!" He swallows the paper with ease and leaves the room to get hold of the Director, who walks in with him shortly after. The Director asks us to leave him alone with Senhor Álvaro.

We pace back and forth in the corridor outside. From within come muffled outcries. Finally the door opens, Senhor Álvaro appears and looks straight at us with an ironic expression:

"So you think I'm not suitable. Very well. But you'll be hearing about my performance one of these days."

Lately, the Company has been on the brink of bankruptcy. Our most important clients have been dying mysteriously, one after the other. We've been swallowing notes from the Director without any letup. The manager is upset. As for myself, I think I have an idea as to the cause of these deaths.

The Evidence

BEFORE THE ACCIDENT I used to sell vacuum cleaners and write poems. Sometimes I composed verses during work hours. Once, as I was crossing the street absentmindedly, I was run over by Senhor Alexandre's luxury car.

> One day when I have enough money
> I'll win over the love of my sweet.
> Then proudly I'll walk down the street
> And—

And what? I don't know. I've forgotten. And whose love did I want to win over? I don't know. All I know is that I was well treated; my legs had to be amputated, true, but Alexandre (out of guilt? out of fear of being implicated?) took me in. There were only the two of us and the servants in the big house. We talked a great deal; the blithe, friendly kind of conversation about trivialities. But invisible currents of hatred, of repressed hostility would flow in the moments of silence. For this reason we kept talking, and we talked on and on. Until Alexandre suffered a stroke that struck him dumb. And now here we are, the two of us, in Alexandre's bedroom, facing each other in silence.

The doctor comes in. He's a bespectacled man, melancholic but very efficient. He comes every day, and even twice a day.

Medicine is dedication
with no breaks or vacation.

When Alexandre still spoke, he would insist that the doctor examine me, too; and on such occasions he would inquire about leg transplants, artificial limbs, and so on. Alexandre was concerned. It's not his fault that I am physically disabled. And thanks to him, the doctor continues to follow up my case. However, I do get short shrift.

"How are you doing? Fine? That's great, young man. See you later."

His real concern is for Alexandre.

"Feeling any better, Senhor Alexandre?"

Alexandre does his best to answer; his face becomes congested; the veins in his neck dilate. And finally:

"Ga-ga-ga-ga . . . "

That's his answer. The doctor produces a smile.

"Very good, Senhor Alexandre! Your speech is improving!"

The doctor examines him for a long time, then he sighs. Alexandre's eyes meet mine. That's how we carry on a conversation nowadays.

"Did you hear? He says I'm better," his eyes say.

"A lie," I reply. "He said that your speech has improved. Which is not true either."

I'm angry because the physician didn't examine me properly, he didn't even take my blood pressure. However, I can now vent my anger on Alexandre, even if it's only with my eyes. Misfortune has equalized us.

We've done away with the oppressor,
now nobody feels oppressed,
now nobody feels abased,
now nobody feels insulted.

In comes blond Ester, Alexandre's niece.

"How is he, doctor?"

"So-so."

"Is he any better?"

"Neither better nor worse."

"And his heart?"

"So-so . . . He doesn't tolerate digitalis very well . . . "

Digitalis. Alexandre gets a shot of it for his heart. At first they gave him pills, but he choked on them. The doctor then prescribed injections. "Why don't they grind the pills into powder? Why don't they give him the medicine in liquid form?" I wondered. I just wondered, without saying anything. After all, the doctor knows best about Alexandre's heart.

Blond Ester draws the doctor aside. We prick our ears, Alexandre and I.

"How much longer, doctor?" asks the niece in a low voice, not too low, though; just low enough so that she sounds sad to the doctor, but not too low, sure as she is that Alexandre can't hear, and whether I can, well, she doesn't give a damn.

"How long? . . . " The doctor sighs. "Who knows? It could be a week. A month. A year . . . "

Blond Ester's face looks afflicted.

"Sometimes I think, doctor . . . All this struggle, all this suffering . . . Wouldn't it be better if we stopped giving him medication so as to put an end to this poor man's suffering?"

Oh, no! I say to myself. And what about me, what's going to happen to me then? You can barely wait for the old man to die so that you can kick me out! You're heartless! Let the old guy live! It might be for just one week, but it might also be for another month or year. Let nature run its course. Nature is wise, it knows what it is doing. That's what I think. But I don't voice my thoughts.

"Besides," the niece goes on, "what kind of life is this? Can we call it life? There's more life in a head of lettuce than in my uncle, doctor!"

"My young lady . . . " The doctor is ill at ease.

Ester leans toward the doctor. She has beautiful breasts, I notice—I'm handicapped but not comatose. The expression on her face changes, and so does her voice, which is now full of tenderness.

"Think of the little children, doctor. Thousands of starving little children everywhere. Have you thought how many little children could be fed with the money we've been spending to keep my uncle alive? A man with a foot in the grave, a man whose heart no longer tolerates digitalis?"

I look at Alexandre. I feel sorry for him. But I feel sorry for the young woman, too. She sounds sincere. And a poet can't help feeling touched before such helpless altruism.

This beautiful young woman
such pain she's been through:
being unable to help the poor
makes her feel oh-so-blue.
And yet all that is needed
for her dream to come true
is rich uncle in a coffin
if only this were true.

The doctor takes his leave. The young woman lingers for a while longer and then she too leaves.

The young woman departs at last,
night is falling fast,
another day in the past.

The following afternoon the doctor is examining Alexandre. In comes Gregório, Alexandre's brother-in-law and the manager of one of Alexandre's factories. "How is he, doctor?"

"So-so."

"Is he any better?"

"Neither better nor worse."

"And his heart?"

"So-so . . . He doesn't tolerate digitalis very well . . . "

Gregório sits down. His hands are wringing his gloves. He wants to ask something—this strong, tall man with an anguished face. He hesitates; finally, he sets up and draws the doctor aside.

"How much longer is this going to last, doctor?"

"Who knows? It could be a week. A month . . . year . . . "

"A year!"

Gregório is nervously striking the gloves against his hand. "A year!"

He walks up to the window and stands staring at the cypresses in the garden. And it is from the window that he says in a low, expressionless voice:

"I'm going to tell you something, doctor. I think that very few people would be saddened by his death."

"What are you saying?" The doctor is indignant. "What about the family members? And the servants, to whom he has been a veritable father?"

"A father!" Gregório laughs with bitterness. "You have no idea, sir! A cruel man, that's what he is. He made them work for peanuts, he was always abusing everybody in sight, and punishing people left and right!"

Alexandre doesn't even blink. It's my eyes that brim with tears. My heart is anguished. I can't bear to watch this scene.

This scene is unbearable
tears roll down my face
when I see such a disgrace
—the powerful man treated like a dog!

The doctor doesn't say a word. Gregório takes his leave.

Gregório departs at last
night is falling fast,
another day in the past.

The following afternoon the doctor is examining Alexandre when Maria, the patient's sister, comes in. And how is he, doctor, so-so, is he any better, neither better nor worse, and his heart, and so on and so forth—she draws the doctor aside and goes straight to the point.

"If we were to get the inheritance now, doctor . . . I have a son who's about to enter the university . . . "

Just then, in walks an attractive young man; he greets the doctor, is apprised of the matter under discussion, and corroborates his mother's words:

"My mother is right, doctor. My greatest dream is to attend the school of medicine. But it's going to be difficult . . . My father is dead . . . I need money to pay for the college preparatory course, to buy books. Doctor, help me! You're the model I want to emulate. Show your solidarity to a future colleague!"

The doctor, horrified:

"Vultures! Get out!"

Vultures, Get out,
shouted the doctor,

it's time no doubt

for some compassion.

All three have left. Alexandre and I look at each other.

"I can't believe it," he says with his eyes.

"Well, Alexandre. They're upset. But deep in their hearts they want your welfare."

"Do they?"

"Sure, you'll see."

A nurse comes in (there are two of them, the day and the night nurse) and begins to prepare an injection of digitalis. The door opens and in comes Ester, her eyes brimming with tears.

"Dear uncle, I'm so sorry! Is there anything I can do for you?"

"Excuse me," says the nurse, holding the hypodermic.

"Leave it to me, nurse," shouts Ester. "Leave it to me, I'll give my uncle the injection."

"This is my job," says the woman dryly. "Will you please get out of my way."

Ester snatches the hypodermic away.

"You stupid woman! Witch! No wonder my uncle is so ill, looked after by viragos like you. Get out, now!"

Offended, the nurse walks away. Ester gives her uncle a shot, tucks him in, and kisses him good-bye on the forehead.

Soon afterward, Gregório comes in.

"I'm so sorry!"

He's both sorry and outraged. He has run into the nurse at the gate. "There's no way I'll ever give that old man another injection, I won't lift a finger anymore," the woman had allegedly said. Gregório was indignant.

"The idiot! She didn't look after you! But from now on things will be different. I'll personally take care of everything. Including the injections!"

He takes a sterilized hypodermic and prepares an injection of digitalis.

"Ga-ga-ga-ga . . . "Alexandre, terrified, attempts to extricate his arm.

"He would rather have the shot in his buttocks," says Gregório, commiserating with him. "Poor man! His arms must be quite sore after the shots given by that virago."

"It's that . . . " I say timidly.

"Shut up, parasite!" yells Gregório. "I'll reckon with you later."

If he wants me to shut up, then I shut up. In silence I watch Gregório give Alexandre a shot of digitalis, after which he leaves. Still in silence, I watch Maria come in. She lives nearby.

"From my window I saw the nurse bolting. What a hussy!"

She gives him another injection and leaves. Soon after in comes the future doctor, who has been making passes at the nurse, an activity related to his interest in medicine.

"Dear Uncle, I've heard that the nurse didn't give you an injection and that she won't be working here anymore. Don't worry. She was incompetent. Besides, she was frigid, too. So, I'll be looking after you. As you'll see, I'm already experienced."

He is. It takes him one minute to give his uncle an injection of digitalis and leave the room. The night nurse arrives, looks at the notes written by her colleague:

"That tart didn't give him an injection!"

Alexandre no longer offered any resistance.

As for myself, I've always been a man of few words; I'd much rather write poems. But out of consideration for the old man, I said something to the nurse. It's cold here, that's what I mumbled, but she didn't hear me, or if she did, she chose to ignore me. Too bad.

It's cold in here.

Alexandre will die.

The Ballad of the False Messiah [1976]   99

Both the hill and the river weep
as they watch a man die.

There was no ministration
of either liquid or powder medication.
And they wouldn't listen to
anything I said.
Thus, Alexandre dies
from too many injections.
He'll live on in my recollections
and in our big heart, too.

The Offerings of the Dalila Store

EVERYTHING IS FINE in São Paulo, I'm happy with my job manag-
ing a store chain—a good house, two cars, a trip to the Caribbean
already booked, everything—when all of a sudden I get a phone call
from my mother in Porto Alegre. My old man is sick, she finds herself unable to cope with looking after the house and running their
business.

I'm an only son. I fly out on the first flight available.

I find my father much better. However, since I'm here, I decide I
might as well straighten out their business affairs; they own a small
men's clothing store in Mont'Serrat. They could make ends meet
when it was the only such store in the area, patronized by a loyal
clientele consisting mostly of civil servants and small businessmen.
Thanks to the store, I was able to go to college and graduate. That's
the reason why nowadays my diploma in accounting hangs behind
the cash register, together with the business license and the picture
of my grandfather, the founder of this commercial establishment.

Now, however, I see that there's another store on this street, right
across from ours—the Dalila Store. Small and untidy like ours, and

yet business is much livelier there. Why? I wonder, looking at the owner, an old woman with bleached hair and painted eyes who stares at me defiantly from her door. She has no idea whom she is up against.

I get to work on this problem. A preliminary investigation reveals the fact that a substantial number of our customers now patronize the Dalila Store. And I soon find out why: the receipts issued by the store entitle the customers to attend certain movie sessions held in the back of the Dalila Store on Friday nights. I get hold of some of these receipts. And I book a seat on a plane flying out on Saturday. I intend to solve this matter in my own way: quickly, efficiently, quietly.

Wearing dark glasses and a false mustache, I ring the doorbell at the Dalila Store at 9 P.M. on Friday. The door opens; the painted face of the old woman appears. I produce my proof of purchase, step in, and am taken to a poorly lit room in the back of the store. There, amid the smiling mannequins and boxes of merchandise, I find the other members of the audience. As it turns out, I'm not the only one wearing dark glasses. I sit down on a rustic wooden bench, light a cigarette, and wait.

Dona Dalila is nervous. She runs about the room, straightens the torn screen, looks at her watch; finally she announces in a hoarse voice that the movie is about to start. She switches off the light and turns on the old, noisy movie projector.

A caption appears on the screen: THE ADVENTURES OF DALILA. Even before the movie starts I guess what it is: one of those wretched pornographic movies, old, dark, silent—the woman with the dog, the woman with two men, the woman with another woman. And indeed, the first scene already depicts a bed; and from amid the furs and the feathers emerges the face of the debauchee: eyes painted black, heart-shaped mouth—beautiful, this slut, despite everything.

The Ballad of the False Messiah [1976] 101

In comes the dog; then the two men; then another woman. The audience laughs and applauds; some even moan with excitement.

The movie is over. The light is turned on. Mutterings; somebody wants more. No, says the old woman, that's all for today. There's more next Friday. And don't forget to bring your receipts.

Half-hidden behind a mannequin, I wait until everybody is gone. The old woman is rewinding the film. I leave my hiding place; she's startled to see me.

"What is it?" she yells, enraged. "It's over! Scram! Out with you, it's late and I still have lots to do."

I remove the mustache and the glasses. Surprised, she steps back: "But it's Dona Cecilia's son!"

"That's right," I say, adding: "the son of your competitors. I am here to put an end to this circus."

Incredulous, she laughs. "Put an end, how? Why?"

"Because it's an unfair competition," I say. "That's the only reason."

"Your parents can do the same in their store," she remarks with sarcasm.

"Shut up!" I yell (but mine is a calculated fury). "My parents are not trash like you, you bitch. They're honest people."

She is frightened. "There's no need to shout, I'm not deaf; besides, what's wrong with showing a few movies?"

"It's a dirty trick," I shout, "to attract customers by such means."

She sighs. "All right," she says. "I won't show movies anymore." She begins to remove the film reel from the projector.

"Give it to me," I tell her.

"What for?" Her voice is tremulous, and there's genuine terror in her eyes. Ah!

"Give it to me!" I say again.

She tries to escape through the back door. I grab her and snatch the reel away. She tries to fight back. I placate her with a good punch.

"I'm going to burn this filth," I say, still puffing. "Right here and right now."

"Wait a moment!" The tone of voice is entreating and her mouth is bleeding. "Do me just one favor, will you? Let me watch this movie for one last time.'

"Why?"

"Let me show the movie, will you? Then I'll explain."

I look at my watch. I still have time; besides, I didn't see the movie right.

"Okay."

She puts the reel in the projector, turns off the light. I sit down on the bench and light a cigarette. She sits down next to me. We look at the face on the screen—at the painted eyes, at the heart-shaped mouth.

"Do you know who she is?" she murmurs in my ear. "That's me."

"You're lying."

I'm not, honest. That's me, in Europe. I was very famous . . . The beautiful Dalila."

I look at her. Indeed, I seem to recognize in her fat face the features of the woman on the screen.

"Let's look at the movie again."

There's no doubt about it: the same eyes, the same mouth.

"That's me all right," she whispers, and laughs.

We sank to the floor, amid the mannequins.

On Saturday morning I'm in an airplane heading for São Paulo. I've already persuaded my parents to sell their store to Dalila; I've already arranged for a monthly allowance, which I'll send them from São Paulo; and I've already made up my mind that I won't be returning to the Mont'Serrat district in Porto Alegre in the foreseeable future.

The Short-Story Writers

EVERYBODY WENT TO RAMIRO'S AFTERNOON of autographs. Every single one of the forty or fifty short-story writers. I was one of the first to arrive: I didn't want to miss the hot dogs. I was out of luck. I was only the tenth person to have arrived there but all I could see was half a sausage and adulterated whiskey. Which didn't prevent me from hugging Ramiro effusively. What's the matter, man, he asked, and I said, Nothing, there's nothing the matter, Ramiro, nothing, really. And I added: Congratulations on your book, Ramiro, I haven't gotten around to reading it yet but I understand it's very good; as a matter of fact, I've always thought of you as a guy who has made it. One of the very few. (I was getting maudlin, an afternoon of autographs affects me in this way.) Thank you, said Ramiro, we try to do what we can. What about you, he asked, what have you been up to? Nothing, I said, except working my ass off at the newspaper, that's all.

"Writing anything?"

Yes, indeed, I was. I was writing a short story called "The Short-Story Writers."

Ramiro laughed and excused himself; he had to autograph a book for an elderly aunt of his who lived in a rest home and had come especially for the occasion.

There was no sign of hot dogs but more people were coming. Orlando approached me; he was about to ask me to lend him money; by the look on my face he saw it would be no use. So he asked me what I was writing. A short story called "The Short-Story Writers," I replied. That's the way, man, let 'em have it, the short story in the state of Santa Catarina has been waiting for someone to rejuvenate it. I'm not from Santa Catarina, I said, but he had already moved on. Poor Orlando, always in such a muddle.

I've heard he has cancer, whispered Marisa. And what's worse, she went on, he doesn't seek treatment, he can't afford to go to the hospital, he doesn't contribute toward the social security. Besides, she concluded, he's a jerk. I agreed, watching the back door, through which, for some reason, I expected a man to come in with hot dogs.

And what about you, asked Marisa, what are you writing? A short story called "The Short-Story Writers," I said. You're a jerk too, Marisa was laughing. She never missed an afternoon of autographs, not Marisa, and she was always laughing. I was laughing, too: That's right, Marisa, I'm a jerk. She laughed and laughed; she was looking at me and I was looking at her, thinking what a knockout she was. One of these days I'll have to talk with her; not now, though, now I'm dying for a hot dog. And a drink.

Standing beside me, short-story writer Nathan was saying that we short-story writers moan and grind our teeth as we produce our short stories. Meanwhile, the short-story writer went on, we ignore the radio programs, the television soap operas, the gossip columns in the newspapers, the Technicolor movies, the weekly magazines, the politicians, the civil servants, the gossip column writers, the new rich, the bourgeoisie, the demagogues, the socially committed writers, the platitudes, the sonnets, such words as *despair, tenderness, fate, twilight, heart, soul* . . . And painstakingly, Nathan went on, we plod away at our short stories. Our characters are nameless; they are just he. "He lit a cigarette and lay staring at the ceiling." The sharpest among our readers, remarked Nathan, realize that we are referring to ourselves; that we are engaging ourselves in a dialogue with our own personal demons; that from the bottom of our souls we are pouring out a clear, lukewarm liquid that turns cold and turbid when exposed to the raw light of the world, and what's more: This liquid solidifies and is turned into a hard gemstone whose nature is unknown but whose value can only be appreciated by a few rare connoisseurs, really admirable creatures. A gemstone resembling opal. While we wait for recognition, continued Nathan, who was waxing excited, we lie on our dirty beds, we light up cigarettes and stare at the ceiling. We suffer the pangs imposed by a dull, amorphous world. We think we could swallow this world as if it were a tiny pill. Why don't we? Is it out of pity—or is it out of fear that we might find out that this particle is indeed larger than our gullets? Idiots, shouted Nathan, we're such idiots! Let's admit it! Like everybody else, we eat, we fuck, we breathe but we are half dead, we're zombies. We only begin to live and at this point Nathan was really bellowing—when we painfully give birth to our sad sentences, which lie forgotten on bookshelves, pages and pages, letter after letter—but these letters don't touch each other, waiting as they are for the intellectual adventurer, for the consumer, an entity entirely dependent upon the laws of the marketplace. Supply and demand! concluded short-story writer Nathan.

After listening to this rant of his, I sneaked away. I joined a group: Milton, Capaverde, and Afonso. A photographer came up to us and took a picture. Then he wanted to charge us for it. I got raving mad; I had thought he was someone from my newspaper. I'm not paying you anything, I yelled, I should be charging you instead for having posed. The photographer swore at us and left the bookstore. Good riddance, I bellowed after him.

Ramiro was busy autographing books for this one here, for that one there. Poy was watching and saying to me: This book of his is not going to sell, it's much too entangled, much too hermetic. People want simple stuff, bread and cheese kind of thing. This reminded me of the hot dogs and I glanced around: plenty of short-story writers but no food in sight.

"And what about you," asked Poy, "what are you writing?"

A short story called "The Short-Story Writers," I replied. It's hopeless, Poy assured me, we should be writing for radio, for television. Books are expensive, books are difficult, there's no future in books, it's even worse with fiction. I've given up on books, Poy was saying; I'm trying to get into a different line of work, I have this brother-in-law who works for television, he'll see if he can land me a job. My eyes were searching for Marisa, or hot dogs, but all I could see was short-story writers.

"Some short-story writers," it was Nathan speaking again, "refuse to take part in any kind of activity. They don't eat, they don't drink, they write. They're bogged down by apathy, waiting for someone to tell them: Wake up, lucid prophets!"

I caught sight of short-story writer Lúcio, who wrote only after going through a meticulous ritual: he closed the windows, lit candles, put on a tuxedo, then sat down at a jacaranda table made in Bahia. I caught sight of short-story writer Armando, who always wrote with a fountain pen. I caught sight of short-story writer Celomar, who went to the seaside to write; and of short-story writer Guerra, who went to the mountains. I caught sight of short-story writer Jerônimo, who wrote first the end, then the beginning, then the middle.

I caught sight of short-story writer Volmir. Whenever short-story writer Volmir wanted to write, he would closet himself in his study for two or more days. When he reappeared, he was changed but happy. He would invite his wife and daughters into his study, where they would stand around the desk upon which lay the typed pages held together with a brand-new paper clip. Full of jubilant respect, they would stare at the short story for several minutes. "What's the title?" the wife would ask, and when the short-story writer disclosed it, they would hug one another, overcome by joy.

Short-story writer Murtinho organized the production of his short stories in accordance with the assembly-line principles: outlines in the top drawer, half-finished short stories in the second drawer, finished short stories in the third drawer.

Short-story writer Manduca, quite soused, hugs me whimpering: "I can only write under the influence of bennies and lately they haven't had any effect . . . I've been taking the weirdest things, I've even tried deodorant . . . "

"I'm writing a short story called 'The Short-Story Writers.' I'll keep in mind what you've told me."

I don't remember exactly when I began to write. It must have been something that sneaked up on me. When I became aware, I was already working with paper and pencil. I would watch people, animals, and things, and would imagine how they would look under the form of words. And so I began to shape my sentences, at first with great difficulty; after a period of time, all I had to do was to let my hand slide across the sheet of paper and observe how the words looked on the page; at the dawn of my life I would appraise my own work by taking into account the length of the sentences, the slant of each letter, the number of smears on the page: when a short story was good, it also looked neat. I would hold it at a distance, admire it for a while—and it was time for me to write another short story. Rain or shine, sleet or fog—there I was, keeping at it!

Short-story writer Katz selected ten famous short-story writers. From each one he picked five short stories at random. He found out the average number of words in each sentence, the words most frequently used, and other such parameters. With the data collected, he composed a short story—which he considered perfect. Not everybody shared his opinion.

Short-story writer Almeirindo insisted that his book be printed in lower-case letters only and in very fine print. It's going to be rather hard to read, warned the owner of the print shop. It doesn't matter, said short-story writer Almeirindo, I'm paying, I can have the book printed any way I want. In sharp contrast with him, short-story writer Cabrão had written an entire chapter in which each word took up a full page.

Short-story writer Almir misplaced the last page of his short story "The Glory." He spent two days rummaging the house in search of it.

Suddenly realizing that the short story was really much better just the way it was, he gave up the search.

I've once written a short story in two minutes, but on another occasion it took me six months to write one. In one single drawer I counted twenty-seven short stories; under my bed I found a briefcase with sixteen short stories, whose existence I had entirely forgotten. At that time I had been writing a short story called "The Short-Story Writers" and I had been looking for a young woman called Marisa, or was it a drink? The whiskey turned up first, brought in by a sullen–looking waiter.

The dream of short-story writer Reinaldo was a short story that would write itself: given the theme, or the first word at the most—all the other words would inevitably follow. The short-story writer visualized a pen set to paper, wires connected to a machine, some feedback gadget to correct possible stylistic or other deviations. Short-story writer Damasceno had in mind a multiple-choice kind of short story, written in the second-person singular: "It was a summer afternoon. You were: a) home; b) at the movies; c) in a bookstore. If (a) is true . . . " Short-story writer Auro was thinking of impregnating the pages of his books with hallucinogenic substances. By licking the paper, the reader would have erratic visions.

I caught sight of Marisa. She was sitting in her car in front of the bookstore. The car door was open, exposing her legs. Hell, how can anyone be such a knockout, I groaned. I really needed a car. If I had a car, Marisa would now be sitting next to me, with my hand constantly sliding down the gear-shift onto her thigh. But I didn't have a car; on foot I moved among the short-story writers.

Short-story writers. Their origin is lost in the darkness of time.

"Waiter!" I called out, rather loudly. The short-story writers turn around to stare. "Waiter!" I say again, lowering my voice. "Whiskey, waiter!"

There is some information available on a mysterious tribe of storytellers in Central Asia, who used to roam from region to region to tell their stories. Nobody knows anything concrete about those mysterious storytellers, who allegedly were decimated by hostile peoples . . . Masterpieces of the short story can be found in the Bible . . . The Persian storytellers believed that certain seeds sown on a night of full moon would bring forth trees that yielded hollow fruit, inside which were very brief short stories with one, or at the most, two characters each . . . Storyteller Scheherazade told the sultan more than a thousand stories, thereby ensuring her survival. In his first book, short-story writer Hebel depicted Nazi Germany accurately; and he did it again in his second and third book. Uneasy, people would wonder: When will he stop depicting Nazi Germany so accurately?

Short-story writers are ubiquitous. In the book *The Family of Man* there is a photograph taken by Nat Farbman (*Life*) in what was formerly Bechuanaland; it shows an African narrating something to his fellow Africans. There is no explanatory caption, but one can be sure that the man is telling a story; and his audience, albeit small, is attentive.

In the Middle Ages some storytellers accused of witchcraft were burned alive. In certain regions of Italy, their ashes are kept in small bottles; shortly before exam time, students go on a pilgrimage to such regions to venerate the remains of those storytellers.

What is a short story? People have been arguing about it. Let's rephrase the question more appropriately: What characterizes the short story? For short-story-writer Poe—Poe hm!—brevity, a demand of modern life. I agree, says short-story writer Jones, adding: Let's not forget the role of the subway, which demands stories short enough for commuters to read at one sitting. According to Jones, the concept of teamwork—an outcome of the Industrial Revolution—fostered the appearance of short-story anthologies.

The short story reached its peak during the nineteenth century (with Poe, Chekhov, Maupassant). Nowadays it doesn't enjoy the same prestige it once had, according to short-story writer Eulálio. Short-story writer Poy blames television for the decline of the short story, whereas short-story writer Tomás thinks that the cause of the decline lies in the disappearance of the wood-burning stove, around which the family used to gather to listen to short stories being read aloud.

I think that from the beginning I enjoyed listening to stories. Sitting on the curb of the sidewalk, I'd listen to the other kids that lived on my street tell about the woman who had decapitated her husband, about the airplane pilot who had shot down twelve enemy planes, about the movie that they had watched on Sunday. As a matter of fact, I too had gone to the movie theater, where amid the deafening screams of the audience I had looked at the figures moving on the screen . . . And yet, it was only after listening to my friends tell the story line of the movie that everything became clear to me; the action made sense, the climax was revealed through the appropriate tone of voice of the narrator; and only then would I feel the authentic emotion that had eluded me in the movie theater although I had paid for my admission ticket.

My friends had a knack for telling a story. Today they are businessmen or professionals in various fields . . . Not one of them is a writer. I think that the idea of writing simply never occurred to them. If only they had tried, if only they had scribbled just a few words. In the end, I was the one who decided to get entangled with words and lies.

Young short-story writer Afonso is now approaching. A chubby fellow, he minces up to me and gives me a short story to read. It's called "The Eye Within the Eye." Interesting. Afonso skillfully depicts the life of Hermes, a loner who works for a big company. We follow Hermes from the moment when he wakes up in a modest house in the suburbs; we see him making coffee according to a routine established years before (Hermes is in his forties, Afonso informs me); we see him on the bus on his way to work; later we see him sitting at his desk, typing away the company letters. He eats lunch—by himself—in a cafeteria and returns to the office, picking his teeth with a toothpick.

Afonso writes well and he started just a short while ago.

But back to the story: After leaving the office at the end of the day, Hermes strolls about the city center, looks into the store windows, and ogles at the women. Sometimes he returns home with someone he picked up, says Afonso; more often, however, he buries himself in a movie theater. He rather enjoys comedies.

Sitting in the nearly empty theater, indifferent to the fleas, Hermes gets all worked up over the movie: he laughs, talks to himself:

"Look at Fatso! Such a numbskull, this roly-poly fool! Hey, Fatso!"

At this point Afonso turns the lights on. We see Hermes blushing as he casts glances around him. We see him leave slowly, his head lowered. What is he going to do next? Some foolishness?

No: Afonso has him in the men's room. There he stays while the minutes trickle away. The next movie has just begun and—look! Hermes is leaving the men's room. He looks around for a good seat, sits down and:

"Hey, look at Fatso!"

SHORT-STORY WRITER LEVINO leaves the theater deeply impressed by the movie about a short-story writer. He is going to do exactly what the leading character in the movie did. He strides back and forth in his bedroom, his lips compressed, his eyes fixed upon the floor; suddenly, he sits down at the typewriter, inserts a sheet of paper and, just like the short-story writer in the movie, takes a deep breath, then starts typing at a fast pace, keeping at it for a full five minutes; he lights up a cigarette, takes a long pull at it, holds the sheet of paper up by the upper left-hand corner, reads what he has written so far; he types away for another five minutes, reads again. Just like the short-story writer in the movie, he rips the paper off the typewriter, crumples the paper up and angrily tosses it into the wastebasket. As in the movie, it was a crummy short story.

Short-story writer Guilherme, a former seminarian, arrives.

"Am I late?"

"I'm afraid so," I say, already slurring my words.

"Too bad. I've almost finished my book of short stories, I don't have time for anything else. What have you been doing?"

"Writing a short story called 'The Short-Story Writers.' "

"Are you going to portray us?"

I WRITE. The writer writes. He has to cover page after page with writing.

At first I only aspired to do what my friends did with such liveliness as they sat on the curb of the sidewalk: to tell a story. However, the truth of the matter is that I became fascinated by the possibility of reducing my friend Lelo, today an engineer, to "a diminutive fellow." Poor Lelo: there he was, all of a sudden, motionless, frozen, reduced to a miniature. Headhunters must experience some such similar sensation. Still not satisfied, I then compared his nose with a parrot's beak. Actually, years later he came down with a disease called psittacosis, which is apparently transmitted by parrots. The curse of the short-story writer?

It could be. Hatred inspired short-story writer José Homero; after being evicted from his apartment, he wrote a bitter short story about tenancy. The landlord oppresses the tenant, takes away his money, his furniture, his wife. The oppressed tenant ends up machine-gunning the oppressor. A poignant sentence describes the lease agreement lying on the floor, spattered with blood. At the end of the story, the tenant opens the window and sees the rising sun heralding a new day. To satirize his enemies, short-story writer Catarino depicted them as animals. When he ran out of well-known animals, he resorted to the exotic fauna—the ornithorhynchus, the koala; to prehistoric creatures—the brontosaur, the dinosaur; and to mythological animals—the unicorn. In an index as thick as a phone book he listed the names of his enemies and their corresponding animals.

BACK IN MY HOMETOWN I once had a short story of mine called "A Family of the Interior" published in the Sunday supplement of a newspaper. Very well. On Monday night I was alone at home, peacefully reading a short story when there was a knock on the door. As soon as I opened it I was greeted with a violent shove that sent me rolling on the floor. When I got to my feet, I was face to face with my neighbor, Senhor Antonio. A big mustachioed man—well, nothing wrong with that—but he was holding a gun and it was loaded.

"Very well, you son of a bitch," he said, "I know that your parents aren't home, so the two of us can have a nice quiet chat. Be very careful about what you're going to say because your life will depend on this conversation of ours."

"What have I done, Senhor Antonio?" I stuttered.

"What have you done?" he shouted. The man sounded really mad. "What have you done? So, you don't know? What about this here?"

He took a newspaper clipping out of his pocket. It was my short story.

"What do you take me for? An idiot? Do you think that I don't know who you are referring to? 'A fat man,' you say here. Who is this fat man? Who else in this neighborhood weighs over one hundred kilograms? 'The fat man owned a bar,' you wrote. It so happens that I'm fat and that I own a grocery store. Bar, grocery store—pretty similar, wouldn't you say?"

He pressed the gun against my chest. Even in this dire predicament of mine, the writer in me showed through! "His beady, blood-shot eyes were filled with rage," I observed.

"You're rather smart, kid. But not as smart as you may think. You want to describe my life as being a dull routine: 'Every day after dinner, they would sit down and listen to the radio . . . ' " Now, listening to the radio might be dull to you. But is it for everybody else? Can you imagine what a joy it is when we succeed in turning in to a foreign radio station? 'On Sundays they ate chicken.' So what? Are all chickens alike? Are all Sundays alike?"

He stopped, took a deep breath.

"But worst of all," he went on in a strangled voice, "is the way you end the short story, saying that I kill my wife, that I dissolve her body in acid so as to leave no traces . . . What do you mean? Acid doesn't leave any traces?"

At that moment we heard noises at the front door. Senhor Antonio, fat but nimble, fled through the back door and I ran to my bedroom. Quickly I jotted down what I had seen in the man's eyes: "Genuine interest, anxious expectancy . . . "

Antonio died before his wife: He suffered an infarct when he caught his wife in bed with a neighbor (it wasn't me, some other neighbor). "I was up to here with that routine," she said at the funeral.

It wasn't always, however, that my short stories had this kind of outcome. For instance, I never succeeded in upsetting alderman Ximenes, a venal politician whom I particularly abhorred. I satirized him by depicting him as the rotten apple that clings to the branch even after the death of the apple tree ("Autumn Is Over"); as the tick that poisons his fellow ticks with DDT so that he can have the bull all for himself ("One for All"); as the king who steals his own crown and then accuses his enemies ("To Arms, Citizens!"). My friends would praise these stories, although admitting that they couldn't make head or tail of them. As for the alderman, he was my greatest admirer. At a city council meeting he made a motion that a literary prize be established as an incentive to the city's short-story writers; he told me confidentially that he had me in mind when he wrote the draft bill: "I'm sure you'll win the prize. And if I can use my clout with the selection committee, you've got the prize in the bag. No need to thank me, I like people with a flair for writing, with a talent for literature." He himself was a short-story writer of sorts, who wrote but sporadically.

In order to castigate the likes of him I needed power. I had it and wielded it, I can assure you. Autumn would come and go, I would write and presto! three months were thus subtracted from the life of a protagonist. In my short stories the protagonist went from the cradle to the grave hopping like a grasshopper on the sand, leaving his faint imprints upon it.

Gradually I became less and less interested in the hopping itself and began to focus my attention on the imprints, which I would describe to the best of my abilities. Finally I set the imprints aside, too, and was left only with the words: I no longer concerned myself with the characters and their stories. Of course, my short stories became unintelligible. What did I care? Let the readers brace themselves for the crossing of this region of dense bushes and quicksands. Great discoveries would lie in store for those brave enough to set out on this intellectual adventure. The small number of my readers didn't surprise me: many are called, few are chosen, was my belief.

Suddenly I was assailed by doubts. I began to mistrust the demons inside me, the demons that kept manufacturing and sending to the surface sentences that I was to imprint on paper. Did they really know what they were talking about? And if they didn't, what was to be done with the growing stack of short stories? I took to drinking.

Which merely worsened matters because during my lucid moments my fate became crystal clear. Nobody would ever read my work. The thousands of kindred spirits who supposedly would flock into my bedroom demanding short stories would never materialize. And I was more lonely than ever. Not even the passionate glances of Senhor Antonio's widow were enough to comfort me. That is what the crisis in the life of the short-story writer is like, a terrible episode.

Short-story writer César, while rereading his first short stories, exclaimed:

"But I was a much better writer then!"

Afterward he went years without writing.

"What wouldn't I give to be able to experience anti-gravity," short-story writer W., who wrote science fiction, would say with longing. "Me? I don't talk to anybody. If anybody wants to find out about me, they should read my short stories," stated short-story writer Ordovaz, who lived in a cottage in the suburbs and subsisted on lettuce and canned food.

I WAS BORN in a small town in the interior. I've been writing ever since I was a child. My first short story was called "The Notary Public's Wife." At the age of nineteen, I came to the big city, bringing with me a suit, two shirts, and a blue briefcase with many short stories. None of these short stories ever got published but I succeeded in getting a job working for a newspaper. And I met many short-story writers: I met them at social gatherings, at birthday parties, in movie theaters, at university student organizations. "We sprout like mushrooms!" said short-story writer Michel.

"I'll kill myself if my book isn't sold out!" said short-story writer Osmar. "A warning to the public." When the book didn't sell out, short-story writer Osmar shot himself in the chest. He was seriously but not fatally wounded; he was left with an ugly scar. On the beach, short-story writer Osmar had to wear a T-shirt.

Short-story writer Odair wrote quietly for twelve years. Nothing he wrote ever got published. He kept his work in big manila envelopes and never mentioned his writing to anyone. One day he looked at the stack of envelopes—eighty centimeters high—and despairing, he cried out:

"What's the use?"

He threw the short stories into the fire. Changing his mind before it was too late, he took them out of the flames, burning himself a little. However, some of his best short stories—"Despair," for instance—were lost forever. Others were severely damaged.

After returning home drunk from an evening of autographs, I threw seventy-three short stories up into the air; the pages were scattered throughout my bedroom. On the following day, the owner of the boarding house where I lived threw away the mass of paper, which was soiled with vomit. When I woke up, I ran to the garbage can, but it was too late; the garbage truck had already been there. I found the beginning of a short story lying in the gutter. It described some very personal suffering. I left it right there, hoping that a curious passerby would read it.

Short-story writer Otaviano wrote his short stories in public toilets, where they appeared in the form of graffiti on the walls. Whenever he was in the middle of a short story, someone would invariably start knocking on the door, asking him to hurry up; short-story writer Otaviano was then forced to finish the story in another stall. Fragments of his short stories are to be found scattered throughout the public toilets of the city.

Short-story writer Pascoal threw a party at his house; he invited his friends, secretly taped their conversations, then used actual quotes to write a short story. He showed it to his friends, who weren't amused.

"What's the world coming to," wondered Pascoal, anguished, "when people don't like what they say?"

AFTER A WHILE I was overcome by the urge to write again. My job at the newspaper was exhausting, but even so I still had time left for literature. What I lacked were certain conditions, such as the right props. For instance, I didn't have a good typewriter. Without further delay, I bought an electric one, which was perfect; however, it didn't work when there was a power failure—at the very moment when I was hit by inspiration. I also bought a desk, a swivel armchair, a pair of lined slippers. In addition, with the intention of promoting my short stories, I began to coordinate my public relations activities: I got a good supply of liquor, I made off with the address book of a literary critic, I cultivated the friendship of a gossip columnist, etc.

Such things took up a lot of my time, and what's worse, they cost me a bundle. The salary from the newspaper was no longer enough. I had to moonlight as an instructor in a typing course (I had to lend them my own typewriter); I was now working day and night. That's all right, I would say to myself, it's only until I can lay the groundwork for my literary production; afterward, I'll have plenty of time for writing. But I got tired of waiting. Then in one single night I quit my evening job, threw away the address book, and quarreled with the gossip columnist.

Problems. Short-story writer Caio can produce one short story every two hours. Knowing that 50 percent of these short stories are bad, 25 percent are so-so, and 25 percent are good, how many short stories can short-story writer Caio produce in one day, and how many of them will be good, how many so-so, and how many bad? Answer: Short-story writer Caio can produce twelve short stories per day, six of which are bad, three so-so, and three (hurray!) good.

But things don't work out in such a mathematical way with short-story writer Caio . . . He needs eight hours of sleep per day. He has tried to get by with less sleep, but he can't: he becomes irritable and gets a headache. Therefore, he is left with sixteen hours, during which the short-story writer could write eight short stories, four of which would be bad, two so-so, and two good.

However, short-story writer Caio has to *eat* as well. He has already tried to live on nothing but sandwiches so that he wouldn't waste time with regular meals, but he lost weight, became undernourished, and even lost interest in writing. Nowadays he is more careful and sets aside two hours for meals, knowing that he still has another fourteen hours, during which he could write seven short stories, three-and-a-half of which would be bad, one-and-three-quarters good, and one-and-three-quarters so-so (luckily, short-story writer Caio knows his fractions well, common or otherwise).

But . . . short-story writer Caio has to earn a living, too. He has already tried to live off literature but found it impossible. The best he could do was to get a job working six hours a day, which left him an additional eight hours, during which he could write four short stories: two bad, one so-so, one good.

Furthermore, he has to read: books, newspapers, magazines. Otherwise he wouldn't be up-to-date, would lose contact with the world, and would deprive himself of the influence of various other writers (some good, some so-so, some bad—yet, one should experience everything). And then there is television, too—not all programs are good, but at least the *medium* deserves scrutiny; and there are movies, plays, concerts; and jazz records—a foible of the short-story writer, an indulgence without which he would run the risk of becoming narrow-minded. Such activities take up two hours on the average; the remaining six hours could be the equivalent of three bad short stories, one-and-a-half so-so short stories, and one-and-a-half good short stories.

Short-story writer Caio has a family. Wife and two kids, a normal family. Naturally, the short-story writer plays with his children—and tells them stories (which he could count as part of his output but doesn't because they are not properly recorded—unless one were to consider the children's unconscious a book, as some people claim it is. The short-story writer would rather not count on this possibility).

As for his wife, she's beautiful . . . Well-versed in the art of seductive smiles to lure the short-story writer. He gives in and is rewarded with immense pleasure. Sometimes he feels guilty and thinks that only priests have the ideal conditions to become short-story writers. But he can't ignore the urges of his own body; besides, how could he describe love scenes if he didn't make love?

Consequently, the short-story writer devotes half an hour a day to his wife. There's this, that, and the other, a caress and other things like that . . . The short-story writer is a refined, sensitive man. Could a short-story writer be otherwise?

Well then. Such activities with the family take up two hours a day; there are four hours left, which means two short stories, one bad and one-half so-so, one-half good.

There are also other things that eat into whatever time is left. The short-story writer suffers from constipation and spends half an hour a day in the bathroom. He has already tried to write there, but without success; it seems that the two activities are mutually exclusive. Incidentally, the short-story writer also enjoys a game of cards with his friends (friends: source of inspiration, potential readers, help in time of need, and so on. Quite indispensable, friends are. And so are recreational activities; as a matter of fact, the short-story writer does some gardening every day to promote mental health. If it weren't for this hobby of his, the emotional stress would be unbearable!).

As it turns out after all this calculation, short-story writer Caio is left with two hours per day. He could, therefore, produce one short story per day. And herein lies the *problem*: Will half of this short story be bad, one-quarter so-so, and one-quarter good? Or will he produce, perhaps, one good short story every four days? In this case, could the days of the bad short stories be spent on something else—on meditation, for instance?

So, that's the problem. The short-story writer spends at least two hours a day turning this matter over in his mind.

Short-story writer Valfredo, a taxi driver, installed a tape recorder in his taxi. While driving, he would dictate short stories. Some of the passengers were frightened and wanted to get out of the car; others listened with interest, and some even made suggestions: "Make the woman kill the son!" Short-story writer Valfredo had problems of his own, too. A rival short-story writer, a traffic cop, fined him several times for driving recklessly. As a matter of fact, short-story writer Valfredo had been involved in accidents but according to him, they were caused by the car itself (brakes in poor condition) rather than by literature. Whatever the reason, the insurance agents wouldn't have anything to do with him and it was only through sheer perseverance that short-story writer Valfredo kept writing.

"You're a frustrated short-story writer!" Guilherme was yelling at me. "You lack form, you lack content, you lack everything!"

Me? And what about short-story writer Sílvio, who would tear up a short story as soon as he was halfway through and start a new one? Rumor had it that he didn't even know how to end a short story; I, however, being far less spiteful than Guilherme, would spread among the short-story writers the information that Sílvio certainly knew how to end a short story but he was very clever—by leaving it unfinished, he could always experience the joy of new things. Short-story writer Matias, not knowing what to write about, produced a short story consisting of incoherent sentences. It was rejected by all publishers. "It's stream of consciousness," Matias would say, indignant. "Why is Joyce's stream of consciousness considered good, but mine isn't? What's the difference? Is it because I'm Brazilian?" The short-story writers wouldn't reply to his questions; embarrassed, they averted their eyes.

At the age of eight, short-story writer Miguel wrote about nymphomaniacs. Short-story writer Rosenberg gave his sentences a special cadence, reminiscent of waltzes or tangos, as the case may be. Short-story writer Augusto, very involved in political concerns, went to a students' convention, where he watched the young people and took notes. The students, suspecting his motives, beat him up.

Short-story writer Vasco would take words from Guimarães Rosa's work and reshape them. Critic Valdo uncovered the following about short-story writer Marco: all his characters always had five-letter names, the second letter was always A, the last one always O, with the stress falling on the first syllable: Marco, Tarso, Lauro. Short-story writer Paulo wrote only in the morning, when he merely transcribed the dreams of the night before.

Short-story writer Norberto and short-story writer Geraldo stood chatting on the street when they witnessed the following scene: A lady was crossing the street with a child in her arms. A car driving at high speed appears. The driver tries to brake the car, without success. The lady manages to throw the child on the sidewalk, but she herself is struck down and crushed by the car.

"Write a short story about it," said short-story writer Norberto.

Short-story writer Geraldo wrote the following:

"Short-story writer Norberto and short-story writer Geraldo stood chatting on the street when they witnessed the following scene: A lady is crossing the street with a child in her arms. A car driving at high speed appears. The driver tries to brake the car, without success. The lady manages to throw the child on the sidewalk, but she herself is struck down and crushed by the car."

"Are you trying to pull my leg?" asked short-story writer Norberto when he finished reading.

"Yeah," said short-story writer Geraldo.

They laughed but soon fell silent and parted company without saying a word.

Imaginary news items. "The life of a short-story writer can be filled with fun. Here at this moment some short-story writers are showing us the pleasant intimacy of an afternoon of autographs . . ."

Descriptions. Short-story writer Vasco, tall and thin. Short-story writer Simão, short and fat. Short-story writer Jan, tall and fat. Short-story writer Aurélio, thin (at the age of eighteen) and fat (at the age of twenty-nine). Details: Lalo's hooked nose. My mustache. My eyeglasses. The gait of some people, the clothes of others, the laughter of this one here, the hair of that one there.

Short-story writer Antonio has native Indian blood. He wrote tragicomic stories about the aborigines. A tribal chief came to see him: "Why do you ridicule us? Haven't we had enough suffering already? Isn't it enough that our lands have been taken away from us? That we are stricken with tuberculosis? Do you still feel the need to make everybody laugh at us?" The tribal chief misunderstood my work, said short-story writer Antonio, chagrined. The Indians I talk about are not real, they are the Indians we have inside us. In our hearts we all wear ornamental feathers and G-strings.

Short-story writer Ramón wrote a series of stories about an imaginary country in Central America, called Cuenca. It had a dictator, large feudal landowners, a rising middle class, a national liberation front whose members were arrested and tortured. Short-story writer Ramón, who lived in the United States, succeeded in having his book published. It sold well. A crafty entrepreneur made a bundle by raising money for Cuencan refugees.

Short-story writer Rômulo satirized his hometown in his writing. A mayor once kicked him out of town, but his successor requested that the writer return and then awarded him the Medal of Tourist Merit.

Short-story writer Sidney never used swear words in his short stories. He was afraid he might offend his aunt, an old nun.

Short-story writer Humberto, an algebra teacher, conceived the short story as a mathematical model. Short-story writer Ramião transcribed his own extrasensorial experiences.

Short-story writer John Sullivan wrote a series of stories published under the title *1997, After the Atomic War*. One hundred copies were placed in a radiation-proof shelter.

Short-story writer Ramsés said that there was more to a short story than just words; it should also include evidence of the circumstances under which it had been generated. To his book he affixed bus tickets of the buses in which he had shaped his short stories while traveling; movie tickets; bits and pieces of clothes; and even scraps of food. "I'm a wretched tailor," said short-story writer Newton, "but in my short stories I destroy villages and towns."

"It has just occurred to me that that tree in my short story is actually me," short-story writer Mecário said to his lover at two o'clock in the morning. "What tree? What short story?" she muttered. She, too, was a short-story writer, but she suffered from insomnia, had difficulty falling asleep, and hated being wakened.

"I've been thinking a great deal about the meaning of my short stories," wrote elderly short-story writer Douglas in his journal, a notebook bound in leather. He always kept it under his pillow; if he were to die in his sleep, it wouldn't be hard for someone to find it and have it published.

GUILHERME WAS GRABBING AT ME, I was ready to pick a fight with him. Ramiro came over to restrain me. He seized the opportunity to inform me that thirty-eight copies of his book had already been sold, and his wife's relatives weren't even there yet: "It'll go as high as eighty, you'll see! Eighty!"

ONE DAY I TOOK IT into my head that short-story writers aren't writers at all: they are characters. I started thinking about a short story called "The Short-Story Writers." It would be my last one, I promised myself. But it wouldn't remain unpublished, oh no, it wouldn't; I'd see to it that it got published.

Every short story is a plea for help, short-story writer Nicolau used to say. A resident of Green Island, he would stuff the most an-guished of his short stories into bottles, which he would then hurl into the river. "Maybe the fishermen will understand me, he would say to his wife.

Short-story writer Wenceslau said to his wife, a beautiful bru-nette: "I'm sure that if you were to have a talk with the editor, he would publish my book, Morena. I'm sure he would, Morena."

Short-story writer Olívio, who worked with me at the newspaper, was responsible for the trivia column. Surreptitiously he began to introduce his short stories into the column: "Did you know that . . . Adelaide, married to a French language teacher and the lover of short-story writer Milton, has a dream in which she sees the moon, split into two parts, fall off the sky?" He was also considering the possibility of writing short stories in the form of crossword puzzles.

Short-story writer Benjamin, a civil servant, would report on a file of papers in a case by writing a short story: "João M. Guimarães urgently requests the overdue payments for the year 1965. I can imagine João M. Guimarães in his small wooden house . . . " He was severely admonished by his boss, also a short-story writer, who how-ever, never fiddled away the hours when at work.

The inventive short-story writer Jane was contemplating the pos-sibility of transmitting her short stories via the telephone: "Hello! I'm short-story writer Jane. I'm now going to read you one of my short stories."

Short-story writer Misael intended to write brief short stories in smoke up in the sky, using a squadron of airplanes for this purpose.

Short-story writer Reginaldo had an inspiration: He would write a short story in the form of an epitaph. He started to scrutinize his friends, trying to detect in them signs of some serious disease.

Seeing that her book *Efflorescence* wasn't selling, short-story writer Bárbara had a boy steal it from the bookstores for a sum of money. Over forty copies were stolen in a month and *Efflorescence* became third on the Best Sellers List.

Short-story writer Pedroso introduced the notion of efficiency into his literary production. His short stories were systematically rejected by newspapers and magazines; so, he had *Leviathan* published at his own expense and then hired the services of a specialized firm to conduct a public opinion poll. "How much has *Leviathan* changed your life?" was one of the questions posed to groups A, B, and C, to both men and women, to both blacks and whites. He intended to prove that his short stories were effective and that editors had a grudge against him. Unfortunately, the results of the poll were inconclusive.

Short-story writer Luís Ernesto would mimeograph his short stories, which he would then hand out at the gates of soccer stadiums; short-story writer Múcio painted short stories on Chinese vases.

Short-story writer Teodoro had his youngest son write to the program "The Little Box of Knowledge" requesting information on short-story writer Teodoro and the short stories he had written. The boy didn't get a reply because he had failed to enclose a Moko label with his letter.

Short-story writer Sezefredo lifted the prescription pad of his friend, Doctor Raul; then he forged a certificate stating that he suffered from an incurable disease. With this piece of paper in hand, he went from editor to editor, trying to get his book published: It's my last wish, he would say.

Short-story writer Rafael (Rafa). During the day he worked as a sales representative for a small appliances company; at night he wrote. Unable to find an editor willing to publish his book, he turned to his job with a vengeance. He ended up rich. Then he bought a publishing house, a printing shop, and had his book printed. He also bought several bookstores, whose store windows displayed dozens of copies of his book. Even so, the book didn't sell

. . . Short-story writer Rafa then began to give out free copies of his book to the schools; and he awarded scholarships to any student who learned his book by heart.

THERE WAS QUITE A HULLABALOO in the bookstore. A salesclerk was accusing short-story writer Rodolfo of stealing a book.

"Me? Why would I want to steal a book?" Rodolfo was shouting. "And a book written by short-story writer Afranio at that! Everybody knows that Afranio and I are sworn enemies. Ramiro! Hey, Ramiro! Come over here, man! Tell this ass of a salesclerk what I think of Afranio's short stories. Come on, Ramiro! You can tell him that I . . . Come on, man, say it! I'll back you up! I will, Ramiro! You know me!"

Rodolfo was led away. While being dragged out of the store, he shouted:

"You bastards, you've torn my leather jacket! You accuse me of theft and on top of it you tear my jacket!"

It was true, his jacket had been torn. And Rodolfo was proud of that jacket of his, which made him feel, it was said, a Hemingway, a García Marquez.

This incident upset the short-story writers. Groups of them clustered together in the corners of the bookstore, where they stood whispering. Every so often, a short-story writer would detach himself from a group and walk over to another group, smoking and gesticulating.

On the whole, the short-story writers present there were young. Many had big brown eyes. On their faces one could see: anguish, despair, a need for greater participation, concern for social tensions, acute awareness of existential problems. Money was being discussed, and what is money? wondered one of them, while another smiled. I began looking for Marisa, in real earnest this time, but all I could see were books, short-story writers, and problems.

PROBLEMS. Short-story writer Arnulfo, married, the father of five children, found it impossible to get a moment of peace and quiet at home. It occurred to him that he should build a studio of sorts at the far end of his backyard. It took short-story writer Arnulfo, working Saturdays and Sundays, three years to finish the job. Then his oldest son asked him permission to use the place as a repair shop where he could fix home appliances. After giving much thought to his son's request, he finally gave his consent. My son is young, and I'm old, he would explain to his fellow short-story writers. Besides, the future of electronics is bright . . . As for the short story, who knows?

Problems. Short-story writer Fischer wrote in a trancelike condition, when he scrawled away in big letters. His secretary (Fischer was the director of a publicity agency) typed out the originals. Fischer suspected that she added passages of her own but he had no proof that she actually did so.

Short-story writer Nepocumeno's problem was quite different. Not knowing how to type, he hired an excellent typist on a monthly basis at a high salary. She typed his work quickly. The short-story writer's output wasn't enough to keep her busy; the young woman was idle for long periods of time. Seeing his money draining away, he fired her. She went to the Ministry of Labor, brought an action against him, and the court ruled in her favor.

Short-story writer Plínio had an interesting problem, too. Once when he was alone at home, he was struck by a bright idea for a short story. Just then there was a power failure. There was no flashlight, nor candles, nor matches, nothing. Groping about, short-story writer Plínio managed to find a pen and a sheet of paper and he began to write a short story in the dark. He never succeeded (unlike short-story writer Fischer) in deciphering what he had written but he still has this sheet of paper, which he has saved with great care.

Whatever this piece of writing is all about, one thing is sure: it is *not* a short story called "The Short-Story Writers."

Problems. Short-story writer Amílcar was kidnapped by five individuals who got out of a black car. He was taken to an empty house and for a week he was forced to write two short stories a day. Afterward, Amílcar saw those short stories published, under different names, in magazines and literary supplements.

As part of a development plan for the town of Ibirituiçá, its mayor, Macario, invited various short-story writers to take up residence there. He thought it would be a good way of promoting the town. However, when the few tourists who got there saw the short-story writers strolling in the main public square or sitting in the verandahs of old houses, where they were busy typing or writing in longhand, they were disappointed. The mayor, too, was disappointed and after taking legal action to have the short-story writers evicted, he repossessed the houses that had been granted to them.

Another problem. Short-story writer David wrote a series of historical short stories about the Italian settlements. For months he researched the subject in the libraries of the hinterland, wrote down testimonies, took pictures. "In your short stories," he was asked, "which parts are real, and which parts are fictional?" He didn't know, as he had lost the briefcase containing all the evidence he had gathered. Short-story writer Ofélia had to have sex with her husband soon after finishing a short story. When he happened to be away traveling, she found it impossible to write and considered being unfaithful to him. Short-story writer Gervásio wrote obscure short stories, which he showed to his girlfriends, promising to marry the one who understood them. None of them did. Short stories and women kept accumulating in the life of Gervásio.

Short-story writer Pereira . . . Now, that's a good one! Short-story writer Pereira once stopped writing when he was halfway through a short story. He couldn't come up with the right word. His wife suggested that he flip through the dictionary: I'm sure, she said, that when you chance upon the word you've been trying to find, it'll hit you like a seizure, you'll be thrilled, you'll be on cloud nine. The short-story writer rejected her suggestion. He thought it wouldn't be fair. It would be like a surgeon who had to look up things in a book in order to perform surgery, he explained.

She went ahead and bought a dictionary and started some re-search of her own. She would write down the more suggestive words on pieces of paper, which she would put in the bathroom, or on the coffee table. Pereira would tear them up without reading. When she reached the end of the dictionary, she left him.

THE WAITER WALKS BY with a tray of empty glasses.

"Waiter," I say, "I've got plenty of problems."

He smiles at me, sympathetic. I feel encouraged.

"Waiter, let's see if you're smart enough to know the answer to this: If a short-story writer consumes eight hundred and twenty cubic centimeters of whiskey, how many cubic centimeters would twenty-eight short-story writers consume?"

The man eyes me suspiciously and wants to get away. I grab him by the arm:

"If eight short-story writers weigh five hundred and seventy kilo-grams, how many kilograms does one short-story writer weigh? And if you add two hundred and seventy-one short-story writers to four hundred and twenty-nine short-story writers, how much does it amount to?"

I've offended the waiter. I can see I have. I'll make it up to him by befriending him.

"Waiter . . ." I whisper in his ear. "This girl . . . this Marisa . . . what a body she has, out of this world . . . "

Then a sudden misgiving:

"What if she writes short stories, too?"

IN ONE OF HIS SHORT STORIES, short-story writer Leandro compares the face of a young woman to a cloud; in another, he compares a cloud to the face of a young woman.

Short-story writer Frederico, believing that his short stories should have something practical about them, refused to use metaphors; instead, his writing was interspersed with the proverbs of La Rochefoucauld. He used to say that any idiot could write a short story using the first person narrator.

"I'll have to avoid this kind of mistake in 'The Short-Story Writers,'" I mumble.

All of a sudden, I'm all fired up. "The Short Story—Writers"! What a short story! It will consist of a succession of cameos, there will be a multitude of characters revealed by quick flashes—a Woodstock of the short story! A short story of a book! Bound to have repercussions, no doubt about it. Will it?

AFTER THE PUBLICATION OF HER BOOK, short-story writer Malvina sent anonymous letters to every newspaper. "Malvina has invigorated literature," she stated in one of the letters. "She is dynamic," she wrote in another, "gentle," in yet another.

Short-story writer Victor put together an anthology of unknown short-story writers. The collection was well received by the critics. Many years later, short-story writer Victor revealed that he was the author of every single short story in it.

And now for the tricks!

Short-story writer Manoel wrote letters, such as the following, to American writers:

Dear Mr. Roth,

Below is a list of my most recently written short stories, and at the prices quoted, they are available to you for immediate delivery.

"The Discovery" (US$15.00). Gilberto and Paulo, old friends, find out that they are homosexual. A great shock to both of them. Three dramatic, yet exciting, situations, each one a paragraph long.

"Specks" (US$13.80). Alberto knows that painting is his vocation, but he has to look after his father's farm. A violent conflict: the father, hemiplegic but domineering. A detailed account of the problem of the arts in an underdeveloped country. The sinister figure of a *marchand de tableaux*.

Untitled (US$9.90). A long story, but with an impressive unity of time: one single night. A group of intellectuals discusses national and world issues. Intoxicants are present. Deep introspection.

In addition to the short stories listed above, there are also four others in various stages of completion.

Yours truly, etc., etc.

SHORT-STORY WRITER ZEFERINO was very afraid of baring his soul in his short stories. And yet he was terribly autobiographical. He solved the problem, at least in part, by using a simple trick: He narrated the events in the life of his mother as if they had happened to his father; and the things that had actually happened to the writer himself, he would ascribe to his sister.

THE WAITER WALKS BY, this time the glasses are full. I run after him. Short-story writer Mateus accosts me:

"Have you met my daughter?"

A beautiful girl, blond, with green eyes.

"Are you going to be a short-story writer too, my child?" I ask.

"She's into writing already," informs her mother proudly.

"Writing must run in the family," I remark.

"What about you, what are you writing?" asks Mateus.

"A short story called 'The Short-Story Writers.' "

"Ah," says Mateus. He gathers his family round him and hurries away.

Meanwhile, the waiter has disappeared. I loiter about, watching the other short-story writers. They chat, tell stories, narrate the extraordinary adventures they have been through.

Short-story writer Ronny rips the cover from each book of short stories that he reads; he plasters the walls of his bedroom with them; however, the book covers are not properly glued and they flutter with a soft rustling sound in the evening breeze that comes in through the window. Short-story writer Ronny claims that in this faint noise he can hear the voices of the short-story writers mumbling their short stories but nobody believes him, they laugh at this nonsense.

Whenever short-story writer Aderbal got home, he would phone his editor to ask him how many copies of his book had been sold that day. Not one, the answer invariably was. Uttering a swear word, the short-story writer would hang up. He would then ask the housemaid if there were any messages. Yes, one—requesting him to go to a certain address to do a special job. With a sigh, the short-story writer would pick up a small black suitcase; taking a taxi, he would go to the given address. A beautiful house. He would ring the bell and a man, fat and diffident, would open the door.

"You can call me Alberto," the man would say. "Follow me this way, please."

He would lead the short-story writer to a bedroom, where a blond, middle-aged woman, not very attractive, would be lying in bed. She would be wearing a pink nightgown and would smile shyly. The short-story writer would look at her carefully, then would open the small suitcase from which he would take out a transmitter, earphones, and microphones.

"Where should I stay?" the man would ask.

"As far away as possible, Alberto. In the large hall, for instance."

Alberto would fit a set of headphones over his ears, clutch one of the microphones, and disappear. Short-story writer Aderbal would wait for a while and then begin to test the sound equipment:

"Testing, testing. Hello, Alberto."

"Hello," would reply the voice at the other end of the line. A voice that almost cracked.

"Okay, Alberto."

Then, lying down alongside the woman, his eyes fixed on her, the short-story writer would begin to speak into the microphone:

"Her eyes are as blue as the lakes in the Alps."

The woman would draw closer to him.

"Her hair is like silk."

"And her arms?" The man's voice would echo anxiously in the headphones.

"Take it easy, Alberto. Her arms . . . Her arms are nicely shaped, perfect. Like alabaster."

"Like what?"

"Alabaster, Alberto. Alabaster. It's used in chandeliers. "

"Ah. "

"Alabaster skin, with delicate blue veins."

"Oh, my God," Alberto would moan "I never . . . And her legs?"

"Like two fish moving about in tepid waters, two elongated fish."

"Ah, you don't say! And tell me now: her small boobs?"

"Just a moment. "

After a pause:

"Like two little fawns."

"But isn't this from the *Song of Songs?*" Alberto would ask, suspicious.

"So what? Just because something has been said before doesn't make it invalid."

Another pause.

"And her belly?" Alberto would ask.

There would be no reply.

And her belly? Hello. Hello! And her belly?"

"One moment . . . Just a moment, one short moment . . . "

"And her belly? What about her belly?"

"Ah . . . "

"Hello?"

"Yes. Her belly. Now yes. Her belly is like a sea of placid waters . . . "

"Oh . . . "

Another pause.

"Wait for three minutes, then you can come in," Aderbal would announce in a neutral tone of voice.

The man would come in, look first at the woman, who would be facing the wall, then at the short-story writer, who would be putting the equipment back into the small suitcase.

"I'll be darned . . . Gosh . . . Imagine . . . I never . . . How much do I owe you?"

"Three hundred."

"Money well spent," the man would say, writing out a check. "You know, I also dabble at writing short stories. Would you care to . . . ?"

"Sorry," Aderbal would say. "Not my specialty. Get a literary critic. Good-bye."

Once out in the street, he would run toward the first phone booth that he saw, then dial the editor's number: Had any copies of his book been sold yet? Nope. Aderbal would return home.

SHORT-STORY WRITERS might be aggressive, but they are harmless. In World War I a battalion of short-story writers was decimated; an inspection of their rifles revealed that not a single bullet had been fired. Short-story writers are hard to digest. A tribe of cannibals once devoured an entire expedition of short-story writers; the cannibals became sick and suffered from hallucinations during which they kept telling endless stories.

From Stockholm, a friend of short-story writer Emilio once sent him the following telegram written in Swedish: "We inform you that you've been selected for the Nobel prize for literature. Be in Stockholm on the tenth." When somebody translated the telegram for him, short-story writer Emilio laughed his head off, but later he was torn by nagging doubts. And on the night between the ninth and the tenth, he didn't get a wink of sleep. On the following morning, the winner of the Nobel prize was announced, and it wasn't short-story writer Emilio. It's a literary clique, he said, piqued.

Castaway on a deserted island, short-story writer Carmosino had nothing but his manuscripts; however, it was thanks to them that he managed to survive.

He attracted the fish to the shore by throwing scraps of paper into the water; he caught the fish with fishhooks made from the paper clips that had held the short stories together. The bait? Paper pellets. For some reason, the fish went for them.

Using a few sheets of paper, the short-story writer would start a fire with the help of the sun shining through the lenses of his eyeglasses. He ate broiled fish.

He also built a paper shed and with the only blank sheet of paper he made a small flag that, hoisted up a tall pole, proved to be his salvation: He was seen and rescued. While on board the ship, he asked for paper and pen and immediately hurled himself into the task of reconstructing his short stories.

Short-story writer Morton, a missionary, lived for many years in Africa, among the Pygmies. He wrote a great deal, but there was nobody to whom he could show his short stories: the barbarians didn't like him. As Morton related in his memoirs: "I would ask God to send me a person willing to read one of my short stories. Just one single short story would do. And he wouldn't have to express an opinion, just read it. One single reader is enough to save a short-story writer."

Short-story writer Efraim became a hippie, built a tree house on top of a fig tree, and there he spent his days writing short stories. The tree had to be cut down to save him from starving himself to death.

Short-story writer Franz regarded himself as a man who hadn't had much life experience (his short stories were purely introspective). Bent on seeing the world, he boarded a Norwegian freighter. Eight years later, he was one of the best stokers in the Atlantic. He still wrote, but only letters to his family. The characters created by short-story writer Helena, a manicurist, were fingernails: "I write about what I know," she would say.

And what about closet short-story writers?

A young acquaintance of mine is apprenticed to a printer.

Although intelligent and hard-working, he hasn't been successful in his effort to master the craft. Throughout the day he has a run of bad luck: he bumps into the machines, spills ink, overturns the galleys. He is the laughingstock of his fellow workers. And the owner of the print shop, a grouchy man, is always taking him to task.

I know this print shop, which is located in a distant neighborhood. It's in an old house, dismal-looking and isolated: All the neighboring houses are being torn down to make room for a wide tree-lined street.

I can imagine this area at night. The moon shines upon what is left of the walls. The street, covered with potholes, is deserted.

It is then that the printer's devil appears. Wrapped up in an old cape, he walks fast. He arrives at the print shop; he glances around him to make sure he is alone; he inserts something resembling a hook into the keyhole. There is some maneuvering, a click, the door opens, and zap! He is inside, puffing. He lights a candle—just one. He doesn't dare have more light, even though he knows he is alone.

Taking off his cape, he gets down to work: He turns on the machines, he melts down the lead. And he turns his full attention to the linotype.

Hours of strenuous work.

What does the apprentice write as he practices his craft? Well, things that pop into his head, phrases, stories . . .

Short stories.

Short stories! He writes short stories. Are these short stories any good? What if they are very good? What if the printer's devil happens to be the best short-story writer in the country?

I would like to see his writing revealed to the world. Unfortunately there's nothing I can do about this.

While I stand pondering the matter, the printer's devil toils on. Before his supervisor he is slow, but the solitude of dawn endues unsuspected deftness. Sentences sprout quickly in his brain, but his fingers, even swifter, involuntarily devise protagonists, situations.

And if I were to have a word with the owner of the print shop? I'm not sure . . . I don't know him; besides, I'm afraid I'm no good at persuading a pragmatic, inflexible man.

Maybe with the help of the authorities . . . An anonymous letter to the police. "Suspicious activities have been observed in print shop X in the small hours." The authorities would go to the place, catch the apprentice red-handed, confiscate his short stories. And if the youth is indeed as good a short-story writer as I suspect he is, his short stories would surely make an impression on some police clerk or newspaperman, who would then take it upon themselves to show the short stories to an editor brave enough to take a chance on them. As for the legal complications rising from the act of breaking into the print shop, from the work done after hours—well, who would bother with such things if the book became a success?

While I formulate hypotheses, the printer's devil makes haste. He doesn't want to be caught there by the rising sun! With brazenness, he now works at full tilt.

Finally the book is finished. It is a beautiful volume of two hundred and twenty pages, containing five long short stories and twenty-two short short stories. It doesn't have a title; it's an experimental piece of work.

The printer's devil stands up, stretches, rubs his congested eyes. Listlessly, he leafs through the book. Yawning, he opens the furnace—and hurls it into the flames!

The next half hour is spent tidying up. He cleans and sweeps up until everything is orderly. When he is finished, the print shop looks exactly as he found it. After casting one last glance around him, he snuffs out the candle and leaves. He goes home. Where does he live? I don't know.

What I do know, however, is that tomorrow he'll write another book. That's what short-story writers are like.

Short-story writer Herman carried out two kinds of experiments: One involved a singer who emitted a high note capable of shattering a crystal glass; the other involved newly formed words. About the singer, he found out that the shattering of the crystal was caused by the particular vowel she had chosen rather than by the highness and intensity of the sound—and this vowel happened to be Herman's favorite. As for the newly formed words, Herman found out that when these words were combined with that particular vowel, the vibrations they emitted were so powerful that they rocked the very foundations of buildings and bridges.

"My God!" murmured Herman in his study. "Such is the power of words!"

Despite his friends' insistence, he refused to reveal these words. His friends kept bugging him so much that he finally promised to utter the words after he retired; but he died before his retirement.

Sitting on the floor, I notice a sausage under a bookcase; I'm going to pick it up; however, I think better of it. "The cockroaches need it more than I do," I mumble disdainfully. Short-story writer Kafka, now there's a guy who liked cockroaches.

I found myself unable to get to my feet. What the devil, I muttered.

The devil? The devil.

Rumor has it that the devil had an appointment with mediocre short-story writer Neto; they were to meet at the city's cemetery. There, at midnight, the evil one presented the following option to the short-story writer: another forty years of life and bad literature— or one single outstanding short story, the best ever written, to be followed by death one minute after the completion of the last sentence. Without the slightest hesitation, short-story writer Neto opted for the second alternative. The contract was signed in blood, etc., and the devil told him to go home and start writing; his hand would be guided throughout the composition of the precious lines.

However, as he was leaving the cemetery, the short-story writer was killed after being run over by a hearse. Afterward the devil disclaimed responsibility for the accident; the hearse belonged to the local parish and was therefore in the service of God.

"THE SHORT-STORY WRITERS." What a short story! I dispensed with all kinds of rituals—short-story writer Lucio's ritual or anyone else's. I didn't have to fortify myself with a drink before I started working, neither was there any need for me to crease my brow as I sat down at the typewriter. As a matter of fact, I wrote "The Short-Story Writers" as I lay down, motionless; my eyes would follow the words that appeared on the ceiling of my bedroom (that's how the short-story writer produced a very abbreviated short story on the wall of Nebuchadnezzar's palace for his reader Daniel). At first the words emerged one by one; soon they came in sentences and paragraphs flashing by so swiftly that I could follow them only by speed reading. I was open-mouthed with astonishment. The short story was in the process of being written!

STRUGGLING SHORT-STORY WRITERS. Short-story writer Lauro went hungry and yet he lent money to short-story writer Antonio so that he could have a book of his published. Short-story writers Rudimar, Heráclito, and Costa were thinking of starting up a writers' cooperative. Short-story writer Breno dreamed of a farm where all short-story writers would live a communal life, milking cows and plowing fields in the morning and writing in the afternoon. He even considered setting up a print shop where the writers themselves would do all the work. The profits would go to a common fund. Short-story writer Paulo and his brother, a photographer, worked in a park. The photographer blew up photographs to poster size and the short-story writer wrote a two-page short story about the person in the photograph. Short-story writers João, Lino, and Amílcar wrote a six-handed short story. Each one wrote one line. Before starting, they decided that the total number of lines would be a multiple of three.

Four short-story writers decided to beat up literary critic Arthur. One night they went to this Arthur's house. Four strong, tall young men walked abreast in silence, their footsteps echoing on the deserted street. "Just like in the Old West," murmured one of them. Five short-story writers about to part company tore a short story into five pieces. Each one of them left with one piece. Thirty short-story writers made a pact: They would read each other's short stories to the end of their lives.

"Marisa!" I shout, but the book-filled shelves muffle my voice.

Daily, upon waking up, short-story writer Firmo murmured: "I'm a short-story writer, I'm a short-story writer." And he felt better.

The bookstore emptied gradually. Outside, pedestrians carrying briefcases hurried by, wrapped in their grey overcoats. They looked at us and wondered: Who are they?

"We're short-story writers," I bellowed, and pummeled myself on the head: "Are you nuts, short-story writer?"

The mother of Absalão, the crazy short-story writer, took him to a psychologist who practiced in the neighborhood.

"Listen carefully," said the psychologist, "I'm going to say something absurd. A man was found with his feet tied up. And with his hands tied up behind his back. It is believed that he tied himself up."

Absalão remains silent.

"The man's feet," went on the psychologist, carefully watching the short-story writer, "were so huge that in order to take off his pants he had to pull them over his head."

Absalão still silent. The psychologist:

"A skull was found in an old grave in Spain. It was Christopher Columbus's, at the age of ten."

"Such marvelous stories, doctor!" shouted Absalão, amazed. Drawing out paper and pen, he proceeded to write them down.

SHORT-STORY WRITER GARCIA read his short stories to his psychiatrist. When paying for his treatment, he demanded that he be given a discount for the time he had spent reading aloud; he even thought he should receive a token payment, arguing that, if his short stories were available in books, the doctor would have to pay for them.

Short-story writer Jesualdo, a medical student, lifted case histories from textbooks and then had them published as short stories. Short-story writer Baltazar, a psychiatric nurse, read his short stories to his patients. He believed that by doing so, he improved their condition. "The more depressing the short stories are, the better the patients feel."

RAMIRO EYES ME RANCOROUSLY. I'm spoiling the best afternoon of his life. I'm a despicable bastard, I say to myself, hiccuping. What's the matter with me?

A SHORT-STORY WRITER COMPLAINED to his doctor about being unable to write. X-rays were taken but nothing abnormal was found. Short-story writer Nélio wrote incessantly. His short stories described something insignificant that grew and grew, spilling over into the house, the city; a mouse was transformed into a thirty-ton rat; excrement piled up mountain high; a person's left ear was changed into a wing two meters in diameter. While writing, short-story writer Nélio didn't pay attention to the small tumor that kept growing near his nose.

Short-story writer Bárbara tells about a short-story writer who is almost killed when a bookshelf comes crashing down upon him. The books were written by the short-story writer himself, who then gives up writing.

Short-story writer Hildebrando, a flight attendant, was on board a plane that caught fire during a crash landing. Passengers say that he acted bravely; he only stopped looking after them when the captain announced that they were about to land. Then, drawing a notebook out of his pocket, he began to write. Later, his wife read in the scorched notebook: "Idea for a short story: R., a rich banker, is on board an airplane that . . . " The sentence was unfinished. That's the way it was printed in Hildebrando's posthumous book.

Short-story writer Amélio was the subject of a photographic study. A Praktisix camera with a 180mm lens was used with an aperture opening of f/5.6, an exposure time of 1/125, and Tri-X Kodak film. Some remarkable details of these photographs: the whites of the eyes—the creased forehead—the fingers crimped over the keyboard of the typewriter—the rictus of the mouth. The untimely death of short-story writer Amélio increased the value of these photographs.

Short-story writer Miro, who suffered from cerebral arteriosclerosis, had difficulty coming up with the right words for his short stories. He would then leave blank spaces in his sentences, hoping to fill them in later when memory came to his aid. His last short stories had many blank pages.

While suffering the pains of a renal colic, short-story writer Ibrahim wrote an inspired short story . . . Short-story writer Peter broke a leg and wrote a short story on the cast . . . Short-story writer Alfredo was cross-eyed; short-story writer Elizabeth suffered from generalized lupus erythematosus. "What would you do if you had only one hour to live?" a reporter asked short-story writer Matos. "I would do what has to be done: I would write a short story." "Would it be a pessimistic short story?" "Not necessarily." "And would one hour be enough to write it?" "Maybe yes, maybe no."

In the last days of his life, short-story writer Salomão wrote effortlessly. He didn't even have to think: The phrases kept sprouting spontaneously. "I'm pure literature," he would say. He looked translucent because of the leukemia.

MARISA HAS LEFT, there's nothing else for me to do, except gymnastics. I take hold of two thick books and start doing arm lifts. They take the books away from me. They, who? The short-story writers. But death will catch up with them.

SHORT-STORY WRITER MARTIM SAID: "There are more cars for people to drive than there are pedestrians for drivers to run over, more people who write than people who read—this is the portrait of our times." Short-story writer Raimundo: "Paper has become so expensive that we can no longer afford to write long short stories." Somebody phoned this same short-story writer to find out which stores sold his book. He refused to give out the information: "You'd be better off not buying it. There are at least two hundred other books on the market far better than mine." Short-story writer Barroso, a rich heir, did nothing but write, and he wouldn't accept any form of payment for his short stories: "It's my way of paying back to mankind the money I've inequitably received," he would say. Short-story writer Limeira, from the state of Acre, used to say: "Show me an anthology that includes someone from Acre." He was a very distrustful person and finally gave up literature.

Another person who gave up literature was short-story writer Alberto. He opened a grocery store and would say: "All of us have had a father and a mother, all of us have been through childhood, we've been traumatized, we've had affairs. Why in the world should we get under everybody's skin by foisting our short stories on them? Isn't it enough to have to deal with life's daily worries, with taxes, with expenses? I sell salami, which soothes the stomach." Short-story writer Morais gave up writing to grow roses and short-story writer Ymai to become a terrorist. Short-story writer Murilo didn't give up literature entirely: He opened a correspondence school for writers. "In a month you will be able to write as well as Guimarães Rosa," the brochures guaranteed. Short-story writer Feijó systematically received rejection slips from publishers. He set his short stories aside, established himself in the grain business, and became rich. He then established the Feijó Literary Prize, whose rules stipulated that the winning short story would become the property of the Feijó Group.

When he got hold of the winning short story, Feijó would tear it up, saying: I've just saved this short-story writer from a painful career.

THERE WERE ONLY A COUPLE OF US NOW—even Ramiro had left—and the waiter had long since made himself scarce. I felt it was time for me to go. I had to finish a short story called "The Short-Story Writers."

SHORT-STORY WRITER GEORGARIOU lived in an attic and wrote at dusk. At that hour huge bats would fly in through the open window and attack him viciously. The short-story writer did his best to defend himself; but at times he became absent-minded and the bats sucked his blood. Despite being anemic, the short-story writer wrote incessantly.

Short-story writer Ronny . . . No, I've already mentioned him.

Short-story writer Aristarco: "To live? Who? Me? I live only to gather material for my short stories."

I LABORED UP THE STAIRS. Like short-story writer Hawthorne, I could say: "Here I am, in my own room. Here I have finished many short stories. It's a bewitched place, haunted by thousands and thousands of visions—some of which have now been made visible to the world. Sometimes I felt as if I were lying in a tomb, cold, motionless, bloated; sometimes I felt happy . . . Now I begin to understand why I have been imprisoned in this solitary room for so many years, and why it was impossible for me to tear down its invisible bars. Had I succeeded in escaping, I would now be insensitive and harsh and my heart would be covered with the dust of the earth . . . Truly, we are nothing but shadows."

"Shadows," I muttered. I pushed the door open with my foot, testing my unsteady balance.

Marisa was there, lying on my bed, smoking.

"I dropped in to read this short story of yours," she said." 'The Short-Story Writers,' isn't it?"

It was.

*The Tremulous Earth [1977]*

Quick, Quick

I SUFFER — SUFFERED — FROM PROGERIA, a genetic disorder that makes the body race madly toward old age and death. *Madly* is probably not the right word, but I can't think of another one, and I have no time to search for a better one in the dictionary—we, the victims of progeria, have an inordinate sense of urgency. For us, establishing priorities is a process as vital as breathing. For us, ten minutes equals one year. Here is a problem for you people with plenty of time—or who *think* you've got plenty of time—to work out. Meanwhile, I'll continue with my writing—and all I hope is to be able to finish my story. Each letter that I trace is the equivalent of entire pages written by you—another problem for you to work out. Meanwhile, in a nutshell:

08:15—I'm about to be born. I'm a first child—such rotten luck!—and it's a long, difficult childbirth. I start breathing and right away, to everybody's surprise, I begin to utter my first words (simple things, naturally: mummy, daddy). The surprise is even greater when twenty minutes after my parents placed me in my crib, I climb out and laughing, demand food. Yes, laughing! At that time

08:45—I still could laugh.

09:20—I've already been weaned, and I'm already through with my oral stage. My parents (he, the owner of a small grocery store; she, a housewife) have already accepted reality, at least in part, after the pediatrician (a specialist that is of no use to me anymore) explained both the diagnosis and the prognosis to them. And my teeth have already emerged! In the course of but a few minutes (as measured by my father's watch, let me point this out) I come down with measles, small pox, and other childhood diseases.

My parents enroll me in school, not realizing that at 10:40, when the bell rings to announce the mid-morning break, I will already be old enough to graduate from elementary school. I ride to school on my scooter, but when I get to the street corner I discard my toy, for I find it too childish. I turn around and see my parents in tears—poor folks.

10:20—I find it impossible to wait until recess time; excusing myself to the teacher, I leave the classroom to go to the bathroom. The sap of life circulates impatiently in my veins. I masturbate. My desire has a name—Mara, a girl in grade eight. For the time being, she is still several years my senior. But by eleven o'clock or so, I will be old enough to date her but by then I will no longer be attending this school. Ah, the sweet bird of youth eludes me!

11:15—Upon leaving school, I decide to go for a walk in the city, which I don't know and will never have the chance to know—what a savage, implacable disease, the one afflicting me. I walk (as measured by my biological clock) for months. I arrive at a housing project. I see wretched shacks; I see naked, dirty children. It is a shocking sight, and I cry for those poor people; I'm afraid that all Latin Americans live in this condition, and I cry for them. I cry for myself.

12:15—Lunch time, but I'm not hungry. Besides, I'm loath to eat the bread that I have not earned. Then, as I walk past a print shop, I see a sign: *Helper needed.*

I go in. The owner of the print shop is about to leave for lunch. I apply for the job; he asks me to come back before closing time—at an hour when I'll be old enough to retire, or to . . . I insist: I want to start right now. He scratches his head, undecided. He then assigns me the task of cleaning the linotype machine.

"You can start on that. I'll be back in half an hour."

And he is in fact back in half an hour, but by then I'm already fed up with the years of exploitation, the years of working for no pay. We have an argument, he tries to attack me; he is faster than I am, it takes me years to complete my movements, but even so I manage to hit him with an iron bar. He collapses to the floor. Is he dead? (Death, inevitable sooner or later—sooner in my case). No, he is not dead, he is breathing, but helping him is out of the question. I flee. I can't run the risk of being arrested. Or of being brought to trial, not even if it is a summary trial.

I flee.

13:05—I can no longer run with my former agility. I get tired more easily. It is old age creeping up on me. I find myself on a narrow, dismal street, full of old houses. When I see one with the door open, I walk in. I climb up an old wooden stairway, dimly lit, and I come upon some kind of drawing room.

Lying on sofas, seated in armchairs, or sprawled across the floor are half-naked women. I'm old enough to realize what sort of business goes on here, and since I have no time to waste—

"You!" I point to a thin and rather pretty brunette. She smiles at me. She is hot to trot. Great. At least for once time is on my side.

We go to her room. Smiling at each other, we take off our clothes. She is my first one; I feel that she will be my last one, too; and then I yield myself to her, forgetting all about the police, forgetting all about the night that will be here all too soon. I forget everything, and I kiss her and kiss her.

"What's this all about, honey?" she asks, surprised at her client's rapturous demonstrations of affection, and yet obviously moved. She praises me, regretting only that it ended too quickly. Quickly? It lasted for months.

She gets up and goes to the bathroom. I remain lying for a while. For a long while: when I get up, I'm a bald man; my hair has fallen out and now lies on the pillow. I pick it up, and not without sorrow, I throw it out of the window. The breeze carries it away.

"I didn't realize you were wearing a wig, honey," she says upon returning from the bathroom.

"Marry me," I beg her. "Marry me, and let's have a baby."

I throw myself at her feet. Thinking that I'm putting on an act, she sulks, and later says that people shouldn't make fun of such things. Alas, she doesn't believe me! But I'm in dead earnest.

A noisy commotion out on the street. I peer through the window: It's the owner of the print shop, with a policeman. He has recognized the hair borne along by the breeze as being mine. With immense grief, I say good-bye to the brunette and flee through the back door.

14:02—I walk down the street, feeling a great pain in my leg: I hurt myself while escaping through the barbed-wire fence at the back of the brunette's house. But I must keep walking.

I bump into my mother, who tells me that my father has fallen ill—he is grief-stricken, she states—and that he needs me to look after the grocery store. In reply, I say that I have to do my own thing. My mother looks at me in an odd way, as if not recognizing me. In fact, I've changed a lot in the last . . . minutes? Months, I mean.

For the first time in my life, I start complaining. I complain about my wounded leg. I hitch up my pants (which I have now outgrown) to take a look at my leg, and even I am startled by the nature of the wound. It looks terribly nasty. I'll have to do something about it right away.

"Good-bye, Mother!" I give her a hug. "I've got to see a doctor, Mother."

I rush away. On the street corner—light-years away—I stop and turn around. My mother, looking disconsolate, waves to me. A good mother, she is. Will I ever see her again?

15:08—I burst into the office of a Dr. Schuler—General Practice and Surgery. Startled, the receptionist rises to her feet and asks me to wait in the waiting room. Waiting room, indeed! I laugh. I have no use for waiting rooms, I shout and then add in a threatening way: I want to see the doctor immediately.

The receptionist takes me by the arm, with the intention of showing me out. A scuffle ensues. While scuffling with her, I can feel her breasts against my chest. *Marry me*, I whisper in her ear. But no, she is not in the mood to marry. She wants to fight.

The door opens and the doctor appears.

"What's going on here?" bleats out a timid little man. He does sound like a sheep—a German sheep. I let go of my almost bride and rush pell-mell into the consulting room, carrying the doctor along with me.

"Sorry, doctor," I start saying as I strip off, "but I suffer from progeria, and a person with this disease—and you must know this better than I do—can't waste time in waiting rooms."

Astonished, he looks at me, his eyes blinking behind thick lenses. Soon, however (undoubtedly at the sound of the word *progeria*) the sacred spirit of diagnosis takes hold of him; he draws near, and with great attention, he runs his fingers over my face:

"Yes . . . It's really progeria . . . I had never seen a case before, it's undoubtedly progeria . . . Interesting . . . "

(He rolls his r's and he mispronounces words. But I'm not going to correct him. I have only grade one education, whereas he is a doctor.)

"And what seems to be the trouble, my friend?" he asks a few minutes—months—later.

Naked as I am, I have to show him my leg. The wound, now black, emits an awfully foul smell. It is gangrene, I can tell. Although I've never heard this word, I know perfectly well that's what it is.

"Gangrene," says the doctor, stooping over my leg. "Interesting . . . Progeria, gangrene . . . "

Interesting, says the doctor, and I am furious. Interesting, is it, a combination of two diseases? And is there anything else that the son-of-a-bitch would like? What about a little cancer as well? What about a little brain hemorrhage? But I soon regret entertaining such thoughts. A doctor at my feet—and yet here I am thinking ill of him.

"What can be done, doctor?" I ask, anxious. (But not distraught, mind you. Not yet distraught. Perhaps later. For the time being, just anxious.)

"It will have to be amputated," he says, straightening himself up.

"Then do so!" I say, courteous but firm, desperate but stoic, calm but anxious—with a smile on my lips and anxiety in my eyes. "Amputate it!"

"Pardon me?" The doctor thinks he hasn't heard well; he is somewhat deaf (a misfortune I've been spared so far). "Pardon me?"

"Amputate the leg! Soon!"

"Well . . . " He is obviously reluctant. "Then we'll have to make arrangements at the hospital for tomorrow, or perhaps . . . "

"No!" I cut him short. "Amputation, now!"

(An elliptical phrase. Progeria sufferers value ellipsis.)

"Now?"

He forces me to say it again. The little man is really slow on the uptake.

"Now and here. Here and now."

"But I can't . . . It's humanly impossible."

I look around me. There is a small iron stool that will serve my purpose very well. I seize hold of it:

"If you don't amputate now, I'll kill you, old man!"

"But . . . " He is now terrified. "What about the pain?"

"Forget the pain! I'll deal with the pain!"

I go and sit on the small operation table. Muttering, he applies iodine to my leg, puts on his rubber gloves, takes the surgical instruments out of a glass cabinet, and proceeds to amputate.

At first it doesn't hurt much—he is cutting through dead tissue, tissue that died just shortly before the death of the organism to which it belonged. While watching the doctor at work, I tell jokes, I roar with laughter.

Later on, however, things start to get painful, and upon feeling the stimulating pain, I bellow with gusto. "It's so good to be alive, doctor," I say while he cauterizes the bloody wound.

When he is finished, he gets up, goes to another room, from where he soon returns with crutches.

"They're my wife's," he says. "But I think that you need them more than she does."

"Thanks, doctor," I say, moved, and I ask for the bill—just for the sake of asking, for I have no money. I haven't had enough time to save any. He says that he is not going to charge me anything, but he adds:

"If you don't mind, I'd like to keep your leg. I intend to do research on the metabolism of these tissues. . . . "

He then takes me into his confidence: My dream, he says in a tremulous voice, was to be a scientist. I still hope that one day I'll make an important discovery—like finding the causes of aging, for example. If I can find the basic genetic flaw that causes progeria, he continues, with a glitter in his eyes, humankind will finally be able to control the aging process—and behold, the Fountain of Youth!

"Do you think you'll be able to come up with something by six o'-clock?" I ask, heartened by a faint hope.

"I'm afraid not," he says, sympathetic but truthful. He cannot lie to me. He must not lie to me. "But I'll try. I promise I will. Give me a call later today, will you? And now," he looks at his watch, "why don't you get dressed . . . Make yourself comfortable."

The consultation is over, that's what he wants to tell me. I've got other things to do, you creep, so why don't you bug off?

I pick up my clothes, and with the help of the crutches I go to the adjoining room. I move about nimbly: I'm already used to my new way of walking. Amazing: what others take months to learn, I can learn in a matter of minutes. Which is only fair.

I find myself in the living room of the doctor's house. I go up to a mirror and examine my face attentively. I notice that the aging process hasn't stopped; on the contrary, it seems to have accelerated in the last few minutes—months. The wrinkles on my face are more accentuated; what little hair I have left has turned white; my eyebrows have become bristly. The line of the eyebrows coincides with the meanders of the river that flows through my head. And there, caught in those meanders, are branches of trees, feathers of wild birds, bits and pieces of wood. The back of a porcupine, the dirty back of a porcupine. (Alas, not a very good comparison. Ah, well. Any man of letters over forty would be able to come up with a better one. One day I'll solve this problem.)

"Despicable, what you've done to me, mister."

I turn around. It's the doctor's wife, in a wheelchair; and like me, she has an amputated leg. She looks at me with hatred. I know why: I've got her crutches.

"I'm sorry, ma'am," I say, trying to be friendly—but what for? She is old; we're not going to become entangled in a scuffle; besides, she is already married; she is not going to marry me. I look at her wrinkled face and shudder: It's my own face that I see. Mumbling an excuse, I leave.

16:45—Already so late in the day!

16:47—I enjoy being alive. I stop at a news stand. Beautiful women on the colorful covers of the magazines. Good to look at. I pick up a newspaper and read a news item about some sensational discoveries. American doctors . . .

What if I were to go to the United States . . . ? Maybe the doctors there could cure me . . . That would be great, but . . . how much more time have I got left? And what about the money? If I bought a lottery ticket, and if the draw were to take place right now, and if I won, and if I received the money without delay, and if I rushed to the airport, and if I chartered a private jet plane . . .

Furtively, I tear the news item out of the paper, and I walk away, headed for a place that sells lottery tickets.

"Any draws being held today?"

"One at five o'clock," the man informs me, looking at his watch. "And I've got a number ending in thirteen. Your big chance to win, don't miss it."

"Listen . . . " I lean my head toward the man, but I then change my mind. No, he wouldn't give me the ticket for free, not even if I were to tell him that I'm a progeria sufferer, not even if I were to bring up the fact that my minutes are numbered. No, he doesn't look like a person who would give out lottery tickets as freebies.

I go out into the street. It's becoming increasingly more difficult for me to walk. It's not just the amputated leg; it's also the insidious rheumatism that is taking hold of me on this foggy winter's afternoon.

I see a young woman standing before a news stand. She opens her purse and takes out a wad of paper money. Without thinking, I make a pounce—bang!—snatch the money out of her hand, then cut and run. I'm running on my crutches! Farther down the street, three heavily bearded young men seize me.

"Young men . . . " I plead.

The young woman comes running.

"Young lady!" I shout. "Help me, young lady! I'm a sick man."

A policeman grabs me by the arm, and a small crowd has already gathered around me. A crippled old geezer, and a thief to boot, remarks an old woman. Shut up, you hag, I retort, and the policeman gives me a good shove.

Gasping for breath, the young woman draws near. She isn't pretty; she wears glasses, her mouth is too big, but . . . had we met under different circumstances, I would ask her to marry me . . . Too late now. All I can do is to wait for the night to come.

The young woman looks at me.

"I must have made a mistake," she says. "I don't think he has stolen anything from me."

She opens her purse.

"That's right. None of the money is missing. I was wrong."

After some reluctance, the policeman finally lets me go, but he warns me that next time I'll be clapped into jail, no matter what. Next time . . . Poor fellow! Little does he know about the power of progeria.

The crowd disperses. The young woman just stands there, looking at me. I glance at the watch. It's

17:00—precisely. The draw for the lottery has been held, and I don't have to be a soothsayer to know that the winning ticket had that number ending in thirteen, and so I kiss goodbye to my plans, to the possibility of being cured of my disease. I sway in dizziness . . . She supports me.

"I'm sorry," I murmur. "It's that I haven't had anything to eat since I was six years old."

She looks at me, incredulous, and chooses to laugh. We both laugh; she then offers to treat me to a cup of coffee with bread and butter.

"But only if you return my money," she adds. We laugh again, and I return the money to her.

17:18—In her apartment, my clothes on a chair, the crutches on the floor, the stump of my leg resting on the edge of the bed, and me—drenched in sweat, and exerting myself—on top of her; moaning, I try and try, my whole body aches, it's not easy at my age. She looks at me. Earlier, it was with love. Now, it's still with love—but mingled with pity.

I sit on the edge of the bed.

"You can't?"

"No," I sigh.

"Perhaps if . . . ?" trying to be helpful.

I stand up, pick up the crutches, and start pacing back and forth. An idea then occurs to me:

"Where's the phone?"

"Over there," she says, surprised. "But what is it that you have in mind?"

I pick up the phone book. I'm shaking so badly that I can barely turn the pages. She has to help me. I find Dr. Schuler's number and start dialing. The line is busy. I dial again. Still busy. Oh God, will I never, not even once, strike it lucky? Finally I manage to get through.

"Hello, doctor!" I say, anguished. "Ah, doctor, I've been trying and trying to reach you, but the line was always busy . . . "

"It was my wife on the phone, ordering new crutches," says the doctor, calm as usual. "But what can I do for you, my friend? How's the amputated leg?"

"Doctor!" I shout. "Doctor, there's nothing wrong with my leg, it's me who's not well. Doctor, I'm growing old by the minute. Doctor, I'm dying. Doctor, have you made any discoveries yet?"

"Not yet, but you know . . . "

"Ah, doctor!" I say in a slough of despair.

"But you know what," he continues, "my receptionist was drinking milk here in the office—you see, she has an ulcer—and then she spilled the ulcer, I mean, the milk, on your leg, I mean, your old leg—and I think—you see—it seems to me that the leg has changed its appearance, the skin is smoother, silkier . . . "

"Milk!"

I turn to the young woman—what's her name, I don't even know her name—and I ask her anxiously:

"Have you got any milk here, love?"

"No," she replies. "Normally I don't drink coffee at home, and so I . . . "

I'm no longer listening to her. I've already put the phone down and I make a dash for the bedroom.

Trembling, I try to put on my pants. Twice I fall down. Finally, with her help, I succeed in getting dressed.

"Quick!" I shout. "Let's get some milk!"

I look at the watch; it's

SEVENTEEN HOURS AND FORTY-TWO MINUTES

and I believe—it's a deep conviction, a faith that comes from within, an age-old belief—that *eighteen hours* is the fatal deadline. I'm afraid of this number, eighteen. I'm afraid of the hands of the clock at variance with each other on the dial: one pointing upward, the other downward—one pointing heavenward, the other hell-ward. I'm afraid of the blackness of the hands of the clock and the blackness of the numbers; I yearn for the whiteness of the milk and

SEVENTEEN HOURS AND FORTY-FIVE MINUTES

and the elevator won't come!

"Let's take the stairway!" I shout.

"But you can't," she says, her eyes brimming with tears. "We're on the eighth floor, and you with your amputated leg . . . "

"Yes, I can!"

Holding me back, she points to the small panel over the elevator door. The numbers light up one after the other: *one, two, three* . . .

"Look, it's coming."

She smiles. A very nice girl, she is. She works in an office, she writes poetry. She lives alone because she wants to find her own way in life, she wants to find a man to love. And I . . .

The elevator door opens. She cries out very cheerfully: "Father! Long time no see, Dad!"

The owner of the print shop.

"You bastard!" Even though I'm old, he recognizes me. "You old bastard! And with my daughter, too, you sleazeball!"

I start to wobble. She supports me. It's too late. The cold of the night is already encroaching upon my bones. I sit down on the floor and lean my head against the wall.

"Write everything down," I ask her. "Write everything down, as if you were me."

My eyes are blurred. The last thing that I see: She, opening her purse, taking out paper and pencil, and beginning to write: *I suffer—I suffered.*

The Price of the Living Steer

ALEXANDRA WAS ENGAGED to the son of a cattle rancher—a young man who was attending law school in Porto Alegre. They were in love.

One day they went to his father's ranch to eat a *churrasco*—a Brazilian style barbecue, with meat roasted on the spit. When it was time to slaughter the calf, the rancher's son moved forward, his eyes glittering:

"I'll do it."

He snatched the cleaver from the hands of the farm hand, and then killed the animal.

Finding the sight of blood repugnant, Alexandra burst into tears. The rancher was annoyed; the son was furious.

"You cow! You don't fit in with our family. Go away!"

Alexandra picked up her handbag.

Smiling, the rancher's son approached her with a piece of raw meat in his hand.

"But first you must eat."

Alexandra turned her face away.

"No . . ."

"Eat! Eat!"

The rancher even made an attempt to intervene, but Alexandra, with an abrupt gesture, snatched the chunk of tenderloin from the

hand of her ex-fiancé and proceeded to bite into the warm meat ooz-
ing with blood. The young man had his eyes on her Adam's apple to
see if she was really swallowing the meat.

"Good. Leave now."

She left. She vowed to herself that she would never again eat the
flesh of a slaughtered animal. That she would never again go near a
man.

Her father passed away; her mother passed away; her eyes started
to grow weaker by the day, her periods became more painful and
more infrequent. She lived alone in an old house in the Menino
Deus district.

Then on a winter night she heard the mooing of the calf for the
first time. In her drowsiness, it sounded like the distant whistle of a
train. But the mooing went on and on, so she finally got out of bed.
She opened the window and tried to locate the animal. There was
no calf in sight—neither in the patio nor on the street outside.

On the following night the mooing started anew. What impressed her the most was its mournfulness. It even made her cry,
which she hadn't done in a long time.

Then on the third night, it dawned on her: the moos came from
inside her—from her chest, from her belly. From her lower belly.
And she was unable to fall asleep: the supplication of the bovine
kept her awake.

She brought home some fresh hay and put it under the blankets.
In vain. The invisible animal was now bellowing more than ever before. Thrown into a frenzy by the smell of hay?

She ate up the fodder. Little by little, with plenty of water. Her
mouth became impregnated with the scents of the meadows; even
so, she continued to hear the mooing.

"It's not hunger that makes him cry," she concluded. "It's home-
sickness."

She remembered having seen the calf on the banks of a lake, near a grove of pinetrees. She then began to drink water from the lake and to eat pine needles—at first cooked, then uncooked. The mooing persisted.

"He misses his mother, the poor thing!"

The wind kept hissing.

"If only I could set him free!"

Anxious, she began feeling about her body, trying to find a hole, a crack, through which the imprisoned calf could be set free. In vain. All her orifices were occluded. Definitively closed. Inside her, the little animal kept writhing in agony.

She jumped out of bed, took the car out of the garage, and headed for the cattle ranch, ninety kilometers from the capital city.

Leaving the car at the gates, she then ran across the field, her naked feet treading on the damp pasture. She ran past the farm house (a party was going on there—a *churrasco*?) but she didn't go in. It wasn't that scoundrel that she wanted to see.

She came to the barn where the cow was. She was panting, and her eyes were brimming with tears. But she was happy when she murmured:

"I'm here, Mother."

Youth Is an Eternal Treasure

A BANQUET IS HELD in honor of Senhor Pedro Rittner. There are two reasons for the celebration: to mark Senhor Rittner's birthday (his seventy-fifth), and to herald the opening of another store (the twentieth) of the Rittner supermarket chain. Over three hundred guests are present at the feast.

Senhor Rittner has the floor. He begins by saying that he will broach a topic very much in vogue nowadays: the generation gap.

"What I'm going to do," he says in a firm voice (his lucidity is admirable) "is to debunk the myth of youth. For this purpose I will use as an example a young man whom you know very well: Pedro Rittner."

The guests laugh and set down their forks and knives, showing interest. Retrogressing over fifty years in time, Senhor Rittner proceeds to recall the days when he was the young, newlywed owner of a grocery store.

"I see before me a strong young man. Beside him, a beautiful girl: his wife."

Moved, the guests burst into applause.

"Yes, you applaud," says Senhor Rittner, somewhat irritated. "You applaud, and that's all very nice and dandy. But who are you in fact applauding? The Pedro Rittner of today or the Pedro Rittner of yesterday?"

The applause ceases.

"There is no reason why the young should be applauded," the old man goes on. "In the young I find nothing but errors, distortions, iniquities."

He takes a sip of water, his hands shake.

"Consider the case of the young Pedro Rittner. Recently married, he and his wife went to live in a room in a boardinghouse. A beautiful couple—but in fact, they were very conservative, she in particular. Even though the room where they lived was nothing but a fetid cubicle, she wouldn't hear of moving out. She would claim that the place evoked fond memories of their happy hours there, that she really enjoyed living there. She would come up with a thousand such inane excuses not to move out just to cover up the fact that she had backward-looking notions.

And she was unprogressive as well. She persisted in using kerosene lamps even after everybody else had switched over to electricity. She found the light of a kerosene lamp romantic. Romantic, indeed! Backward, that's what it was. Reactionary, eccentric. It would never have occurred to her that one day the community would need a chain of supermarkets. She was the kind of person that would gladly spend the rest of her life behind the counter of a second-rate corner store. She just couldn't envision the advent of the consumer society."

A new round of applause.

"It was a pretty bad situation," the guest of honor went on, "because the young Pedro Rittner, like everyone else in his age group, had a one-track mind: all he thought of was sex. He was incapable of setting his mind free for other activities. And his wife was even worse. In her case, sex was a fixed idea. She really had a thing about it.

Luckily, the young Pedro Rittner reacted against this situation. He decided to put an end to that life of stagnation, even though it meant overlooking his wife's needs, even though it meant using violent methods. And on the day when he made this decision, ladies and gentlemen, he ceased to be Pedro Rittner, the youth, to become Pedro Rittner, the man! From then on, he has always unfailingly succeeded in life."

Amid a burst of applause, Senhor Rittner sits down. He is happy. He turns around to tell his wife how happy he is. But there is no wife. His wife died fifty years ago: eight months after the wedding.

Grand Prize

LET'S TALK NOW ABOUT the two friends who were in the habit of buying a lottery ticket in partnership.

Longtime friends. They worked for the same real estate company: they were the same age, they dressed in a similar fashion, and they even resembled each other physically. Every Monday morning Túlio would ask:

"Did we win anything Saturday, Marcos?"

"No, nothing at all, Túlio."

"Not even the last two numbers came up, Marcos?"

"Not even that, Túlio."

"Shit! Let's try the eighty-two again next Saturday, Marcos."

"Sure, Túlio. Give me the money, will you?"

They always split the cost equally. Longtime friends. Marcos, married, with three children. Túlio, single—a confirmed bachelor. They both sported a mustache. One of them—Túlio—always had a somewhat disturbed look on his face.

Ever since his birth, things had never turned out right for this Túlio. He had been deprived of breastfeeding; his mother had run away with a Spanish sailor, consigning him to the baby formula and the care of an irascible grandmother. As a baby, he had often had nearly fatal bouts of diarrhea, which would leave him dehydrated, with a hollowed fontanel and lusterless eyes. The compassionate neighborhood doctor would always save him.

Not so in the case of Marcos. Marcos had always had his nice and hot bowl of soup right on time.

This world is full of thieves, Túlio would say. I don't steal from anybody, I don't misappropriate any money, I don't engage in smuggling. (But he wanted to be rich one day. Thus, he kept buying lottery tickets. Or rather: he kept giving the money to Marcos, who would buy the lottery tickets. And he would say to himself: One day I'll get a pot of money. Then correcting himself: half a pot.)

He didn't have much of an appetite, Túlio didn't. He would chew the food slowly, almost with hatred. And yet, the steak that he ate invariably encountered a hostile environment in his stomach. A sour belch and bad breath were souvenirs left behind by every meal.

Not so in the case of Marcos. Marcos would wake up whistling and ask his wife: Bela, what adventures does life have in store for me today? His wife would smile and give him a kiss that tasted of honey. She was beautiful. The children, beautiful.

On Saturdays he would get dressed and go downtown—mainly to buy the lottery ticket. He would joke with the bookie, make predictions about striking it rich one day—but realist that he was, he would add that he didn't entertain any hopes of ever winning. He gambled just for fun. The same with the soccer game on Saturday afternoons: just for the sake of the sport. He wasn't one to get all worked up over such things. I've got the arteries of a six-year-old, he was in the habit of saying. Of a five-year-old, Bela would amend. Their son had won a short-story contest. Fortune has already given me what it had to give me, Marcos would say in conclusion.

Túlio thought of nothing but money. Investments: When I lay my hands on that pot of money . . . It would be just a matter of getting the ball rolling: Money attracts money.

Marcos would play the guitar. Marcos would read magazines. With the tenuous mist of his affection, Marcos would fill up the space between the television screen and the family gathered around him.

Túlio would read nothing but a brochure entitled *The Financial Supplement*, distributed free by an investment company. He invariably fell asleep before he finished reading it.

Marcos would sometimes take a slick chick to the apartment of a friend of his, a bachelor. He would leave the place whistling, bump into a friend, and slap him heartily on the back.

Túlio had frequent nightmares. From the lap of the Spanish sailor, his mother would wave at him and murmur things that he couldn't understand. Sorrowful memories.

In the summer, Marcos would go fishing. He would cast his bewitching net into a place where no fish had ever been caught—and the net would come up overbrimming with fish. Speak louder, Mother! Túlio would cry out, tossing about in bed.

One Monday Túlio came running into the office:

"We won, Marcos! We won, I've just found out! I stopped at a tobacco shop to check through the list of the winning numbers. We won!"

Marcos, who was reading the newspaper, lifted his head—and everybody saw that he was surprised.

"We won? No, we didn't, Túlio. I wish we had. But we drew a blank. Not even the last two numbers came up."

Túlio, with a somewhat incredulous smile:

"But didn't I tell you to get the thirty-five sixty one?"

"No, you didn't, Túlio . . . " Marcos kept smiling.

Túlio was getting angry.

"Yes, I did! I even told you that I'd seen my mother in a dream, and that she told me to buy a ticket with this very number."

"No, you didn't, Túlio."

Their co-workers began to gather around them.

"You didn't say anything to me. And that wasn't the number on the ticket I bought."

Túlio ripped the newspaper out of his hands.

"So, which number did you get? Where's the ticket? I want to see it."

Marcos stood up.

"Come on now, Túlio, stop this nonsense. We drew a blank. I checked, then threw the ticket away."

Túlio turned pale. He was shaking.

"So, you threw it away, did you? Did you really? Or did you stash it away somewhere in your house? Or perhaps you had someone pick up the pot of money for you?"

Marcos stepped back.

"But what pot of money, man? Are you crazy, or what?"

Túlio drew a knife. A silver knife, the kind used for carving *churrasco*. He lashed out and the knife grazed Marcos's arm. Instantaneously, the fellow workers pounced on Túlio and disarmed him.

He was badly beaten up. His co-workers disliked him with the same intensity that they liked Marcos. They broke his collarbone and two of his ribs, they burst his mouth with punches, they tore his new clothes to pieces. Marcos, who had received the knife wound, begged them to stop: in vain. It took the police to restrain them.

Túlio was imprisoned for two years. In jail, he learned that Marcos had indeed won in that lottery, but he didn't care. All he wanted now was to dream. And it wasn't even about his mother. But about the Spanish sailor: the very image of his cellmate.

Friends

THE TWO OF THEM CAME RUNNING to the corner of the street. They stopped, panting. Soon they were laughing, hugging each other, and slapping each other on the back in a friendly way. One of them:

"And that moment when I punched him in the belly? Terrific, wasn't it, friend?"

"You betcha," concurred the other. "And when I buffeted him on the neck and kneed him in the back and shoved him real good and he landed on all fours and then I gave him that final kick? Terrific, wasn't it, friend?"

"Sure was, friend. And when I delivered that punch to his kisser—look, I even cut my knuckles—and he went reeling against that lamppost and then collapsed in the middle of the street? Terrific, wasn't it, friend?"

"And that moment, friend, when I was twisting his arm and he started to bellow like a calf?"

"Ah, friend . . . And that moment, friend, when just for the hell of it, I bit him on the ear?"

"And when I tripped him up, friend, and then gave him that karate chop, friend?"

"And what about that neat maneuver of mine, friend, when I dropped on my hands and swang my legs against his and knocked him off his feet?"

"And what about that crushing blow of mine, friend?"

"And that blow of mine, friend? What about that one?"

They stood in silence for a while.

"I think . . . " The first one began.

"I think I finished him off," said the second one.

"You?" The first one, scowling. "You finished him off?"

"That's right," said the second one, speaking slowly. "That buffet on his neck was meant to kill. And that other blow . . . "

"I was the one who delivered that blow!" shouted the first one. "Don't give me this shit. That was my blow! The blow that finished him off, that was my doing!"

"The blow that finished him off? Hey, fuck off, you! No way that blow of yours could finish anybody off. I was watching you. Face it. You did a lousy job."

"I did a lousy job? Me? And what about you? Because I was watching you, too. At one moment you said something in his ear, you think I didn't notice?"

They stood confronting each other.

"And you, haven't you been talking to him on the sly for the past few days? You think I knew nothing about it? Well, I happen to know lots of things, man. Your play-acting today didn't fool me a bit. And now you want to tell me it wasn't me that demolished him with those blows?"

"Your blows?" (A snigger.) "Your blows wouldn't demolish any-thing. I've been meaning to tell you this for some time now: Your blows are nothing, you hear? Nothing. Do you know what nothing is? It's nothing. Your blows wouldn't kill a fly. One thousand of your blows aren't worth one single little slap of mine. And you know what? There's something else I'm going to tell you: I'm sure the two of you were in cahoots. I bet you were. You're a real shit heel."

With their faces almost touching:

"You're the one who's a shit heel, and you know what, you don't know how to pack a hard punch, you've never fooled me, you're a never-was, a limp dishrag—I'll show you anytime you want. Anytime. Today? Tomorrow? Anytime."

Saying nothing else, they parted company. They both knew that they would meet again. And there was only one thing they wanted to know: which of the them would be bringing the friend.

It's Time to Fall

If only the doorman were to deny me entrance, I thought as I entered the building. But he merely nodded his head—which was only to be expected from the caretaker of a high-class building: This pretext I wouldn't have. Taking a deep breath, I walked toward the elevator, with a reasonably steady gait. My finger kept missing the elevator button, but the palm of my hand did the job. I looked at myself in the mirror. I had a neat appearance. Well-dressed, a bit thin, perhaps—but nothing unusual in a newly divorced fellow. My breath smelled of mint rather than of booze, and I felt that I would be able to supply all the necessary information: *Hi, my name is Roberto, I'm an architect, and yes, I, too, dislike the Mediterranean style.* But as a matter of fact, I was feeling ill at ease standing there, in that severe entrance hall all done in marble and granite, and sparsely furnished with dark, heavy furniture. I thanked God when the elevator came, and was even more relieved when I saw that it was empty.

I pressed the number twelve, the last one, and started on the slow ascent. Slow to me; the residents of the building might perhaps regard haste as being a gross display of anxiety. Not me, though. I was eager to get the whole thing over and done with as soon as possible. I was eager to go home and sleep.

The elevator stopped. The inner door slid open, the outer door remained closed, waiting for me to push it open—and I standing there, still hesitating. Finally, I hurled myself forward at the very moment when the inner door was closing again. I collided violently with it and almost fell down in the passageway. Fortunately, there was nobody there.

I was faced with two large carved doors made of solid wood, one in front of the other. I made for the one on the left—that was where the music was coming from—and rang the door bell with the palm of my hand.

Adriana, the wife of the apartment owner, opened the door. She greeted me; nice person that she was, she made a few encouraging remarks about my appearance. Then she said: You already know everybody here, don't you? Make yourself at home. I found myself alone—but now with a drink in my hand.

I started to move about the apartment—huge, and crowded with people—greeting someone here, another one there, catching snatches of their conversation: a bearded, bespectacled young man was outraged by the abuse the Indians had to suffer; a tall, grey-haired man was defending the cost-of-living allowance; and a young woman with a very loud and shrill voice was telling funny stories about her trip to the northern state of Bahia. I decided to hide myself in the study—but there were already two people there, necking on the leather sofa. Another room was crowded with teenagers, who eyed me with suspicion. I finally came to the bedroom of the married couple.

It was dark. It took me a while to find the light switch; with some trepidation—I thought I could hear whispers—I turned on the light, but there was nobody there. I sat down on the bed, with my face turned to the door, and there I remained, drinking.

It was then that he appeared. A well-dressed man in a suit and a tie—perhaps the only one wearing a tie at that party. I had no more than a nodding acquaintance with him; I knew that his name was Siqueira, and that he was a lawyer. I greeted him. He replied with a dry *How do you do?* and proceeded to walk about the room, examining things, like a visitor to a museum. The room wasn't very big, and I began to feel uncomfortable with him prowling about. I thought perhaps I'd better leave but to go where? Besides, I was getting tired of running away. I took a long swig of my drink, and sat watching him.

It was he who finally broke the silence. *Some people think they have good taste but they don't*—he murmured as if speaking to himself but in a voice loud enough for me to hear. A sourpuss, this guy, I thought.

"Just take a look at this painting." There was no doubt that he was now addressing me. He was pointing to a landscape: a lake in the moonlight, with two or three little boats. Something very primitive.

"It could be the work of a primitive," I ventured.

"Primitive, my foot!" He was almost shouting now. "It's downright awful. Primitive! Garbage, that's what it is." He then pointed to some bibelots on the top of a chest of drawers. "Garbage. Nothing but garbage."

He fell silent and stood there, motionless.

All of a sudden he grabbed one of the bibelots and threw it out of the door that opened on to the roof terrace. Just like that. As if it had been a cigarette butt. Soon afterward he threw out another bibelot. And then another one!

I got up and went to the roof terrace. There was nothing there. The bibelots had passed over the railing and fallen all the way down, landing on a big vacant lot.

"Luckily, there are still some vacant lots left in Porto Alegre," I said. An idiotic remark, but what else could I say?

He made no reply. With the same look of disdain as before, he was now examining a statuette.

"More garbage," he muttered, and hurled the statuette away, almost hitting me in the process.

"Hey, watch it!" I protested, but he seemed not to have heard. A vase had now caught his attention; he looked at it and—*garbage, garbage*—hurled it through the door. It was followed by more vases, more statuettes, then by ashtrays and picture frames.

He then abandoned the chest of drawers—there was nothing left there to be discarded—and he made for one of the bedside tables. He opened the drawer.

"It's his," he said. "The husband's."

He examined the books lying on the table.

"Pornography! Sheer pornography! I'm very familiar with this stuff. The same kind of books that my wife reads. Sheer pornography."

He threw one of the books out of the door.

"Pornography!"

He then turned to me:

"Here, give me a hand with this, will you?"

I set my glass down and took the books—a whole stack of them—that he was reaching me. *Throw them out,* he said, and I obeyed: I ran to the terrace and started to throw the books over the railing. And you know what? I was getting a kick out of the whole thing. No kidding. I returned to the bedroom: Any more books? Yes: plenty of books, not to mention magazines, both national and foreign. I made two more trips between the night table and the terrace. Loaded down with reading stuff.

"Any more?" I asked upon returning.

He made no reply. He was now carefully examining the huge wardrobe: an ancient piece of furniture, in colonial style.

Studying it, obviously.

His hand reached out for the knob on the huge middle door of that piece of furniture, but he didn't touch it. I stood waiting.

"Look at this wardrobe," he said finally.

"What about it?" I was surprised at the way my voice sounded. Different. Strained.

"It clashes sharply with the rest of the furniture. A different style. Huge. Almost another room within this room. A cavern. A hiding place."

He drew nearer the wardrobe.

"Give me a hand with this, will you?"

"But—the wardrobe?" I asked in disbelief.

"Give me a hand with this!"

The two of us started to push the wardrobe out of the bedroom.

It wasn't difficult: We made it slide over the waxed floor. Gathering momentum, the wardrobe reached the terrace and rushed headlong over the railing.

He looked way down below. And then he laughed for the first time. He laughed softly, choking and coughing. He then signalled to me, turned off the light, and we both left the bedroom.

Most of the guests were gone. The apartment was almost empty.

Adriana came up to me: Ah, Roberto, you were here! She grabbed me by the arm, reproaching me: But you haven't had anything to eat, come over here, I'm going to help you to some food. The lawyer walked past us: hat in hand, he was hastening to the door: *Where's your wife, Siqueira?* asked the hostess. Without looking at her, the lawyer replied: *I don't know, she must have left, I'm going after her.*

"They don't get along well," Adriana confided to me, heaping cold cuts on my plate.

She paused, the big fork in the air, her forehead creased:

"Talking of which, you know what? I haven't seen my husband tonight. *Really*, I haven't seen him."

I was about to suggest a place where she could go and look for him, but I remained silent: It was now time to fall. *Really*, it was time to fall.

The Thief

IT WAS MY YOUNGER BROTHER who discovered the thief in the garage. He came running to tell us about it, but at first we wouldn't believe him because even though our house was located in a distant neighborhood, and even though it was somewhat isolated, it was after all a Thursday afternoon and we found it most unlikely that a thief would come in broad daylight to steal from us. Anyway, we all went to the garage.

We peered through a chink in the door, and indeed the thief—a skinny old man—was there, but he wasn't stealing anything, just looking at the old household articles stored in the garage (which was now used as a storage room, for we hadn't had a car for a long time). Laughing softly and communicating among ourselves through signs, we locked him in.

Mother came home from work in the evening. Tired, as usual—after Father died, she started working as a seamstress—and grumbling. What have you kids been up to? she asked, suspicious. What's all this laughing about? Nothing, Mother, replied the four of us (the oldest was only twelve years old). We're laughing about nothing in particular.

That night there was nothing we could do about the thief because Mother was a light sleeper. But we kept peeping out of our bedroom window to make sure that the garage door was still locked—and the whole thing made us seethe with excitement. We could hardly wait for the day to dawn—but finally it grew light, Mother left for work, and we had the house to ourselves.

We made a beeline for the garage. We looked through a crack in the door, and there he was, the old thief, sitting on a broken armchair and looking very dejected. Hey, you thief! we shouted. Startled, he stood up. Open the door, he asked, almost in tears, open it, let me out, I promise I'll never come back here.

Of course we weren't about to open the door, and we told him as much. Give me some food, he said. I'm very hungry, I haven't had anything to eat in the last three days. What are you giving us in return? my older brother wanted to know.

The old man remained silent for a while and then he said: I'll perform a magic trick for you kids. A magic trick! We exchanged glances among ourselves. What kind of magic trick? we asked him. He: I'll change things into anything you want.

My older brother, who was always very suspicious of everything, decided to put the case to the test. Inserting a stick through the crack in the door, he said: Change this stick into an animal. Wait a moment, said the old man in a nearly inaudible voice.

We waited. A moment later, a mouse, squeezing itself through the opening, made its appearance. It's mine, cried out my youngest brother, and he took hold of the mouse. Laughing at the kid, we went and got a few slices of bread for the old man.

On the following days, there were other transmutations—bottle caps turned into coins, a nail turned into a watch (an old watch, it didn't work), and so on. But then came the day when we knocked on the door and there was no answer. We peeped through the crack in the door and saw nobody. My older brother—you guys wait here— then opened the garage door with the utmost caution. He went in and began to search for the thief amid the old household articles:

"This old tire, that's not him . . . This torn mattress, not him.. . ."

As it turned out, my brother didn't find the old man, and we soon forgot the whole business. But I, for one, was left with this lingering doubt: the old tire, wasn't it him?

Requiem

I HAD BEEN FEELING DEPRESSED, and had been crying a lot. It's because you've got nothing to do, said my husband. In part, he was right: the children were grownup, we were well-off—what could I do to keep myself busy? Why don't you take a course in something? suggested my husband. I thought it was a good idea. After graduating from university (with a degree in psychology), I never went back to school; so, taking a course—classes, assignments, and what not—was a good idea.

I went to the university to get information about its winter courses. There were many—a real festival of courses: in languages, in business administration, in computers . . . A heading in the catalogue caught my attention: *Thanatology* (100 hours). "Nowadays death has become the subject of serious research," the catalogue explained. "There is now widespread preoccupation with an event so often kept under wraps."

It sounded fascinating. I rushed to the Admissions' Office and paid my registration fee. On that same day I got to know the instructor—a psychologist like me, but young and handsome.

"As you can see," he was saying to me later in bed (after some thirty hours into the course), "death is a field that has been opening out."

Undoubtedly, I said, and I hugged him. I could feel the melancholy in his voice; he didn't have many students—there were only about a dozen of us—and I was afraid he might cancel the course even before we were halfway through. My cuddly teddy bear of a teacher, I whispered, I'm your pet student, am I not? Yes, he said, and sighed.

He arranged for my internship in a hospital. I was to accompany the doctors and interview the patients that they indicated to me: a report on those interviews would be the final assignment for the course. So, wearing a white lab coat, I followed the doctors on their rounds.

During the first few days no patient was willing to talk to me. I was already on the verge of tears and beginning to feel depressed when I was told about a patient—a doctor—who refused any form of medical treatment. If I wanted, I could try and talk to him. By then I had completed sixty hours of the course.

I didn't go and see him right away. I spent a whole day at home, reading my class notes, preparing myself for task ahead . . . On the day of the interview, I was so excited that I woke up very early in the morning. I took the car and drove about the city. On the streets, I saw many elderly people; in the poor neighborhoods, I saw many undernourished children. Death lurks everywhere, I thought to myself; we've got to understand death, was the conclusion I reached. But even after having completed almost two-thirds of the course, I still felt that I hadn't fully mastered the subject of death. (Its biological aspects, yes; its social aspects, a little; its psychological aspects, almost nothing. I hadn't dealt with its mystical aspects yet, but I doubted that I would ever be able to grasp them.)

I finally arrived at the hospital. A fine hospital, luxurious even. In the middle of a park . . .

A nurse conducted me to the patient's room. She knocked on the door. Come in, said a hoarse voice. We went in. An unpleasant smell of ammonia. A renal case, whispered the nurse; I didn't get it—but the patient, as if guessing, muttered: "Renal. She said renal. What she means is that I have renal insufficiency—kidney malfunction. I'm a terminal patient. I refuse any treatment. I won't let anybody nurse me. Or even give me a bath. I stink, don't I?"

The patient in question—I made a mental note of the situation (scared as I was, I still did my best to follow the instructor's recommendations and I was observing everything attentively)—is a man in his mid-forties, with a sickly appearance, a sallow complexion . . . A man neither ugly nor handsome.

Neither ugly nor handsome—that's what I said to Hélio, my instructor. He looked at me: Watch out! Jealousy? Seventy hours of instruction.

I visited the doctor several times. I gained his friendship. He bared his soul to me, he told me all about himself—his illness, his unhappy marriage, everything. Finally, the inevitable happened: when I had almost completed the course (ninety hours of instruction), the man, whose days were numbered according to the nurse, this very man, tried to grab me. I had no problem extricating myself free—he was so weak—but at the same time I didn't want to hurt his feelings, that's why I said to him that I was there to help him but what he wanted wasn't help but sex, pure sex.

Panting from the exertion, he was now lying on his back, his eyes fixed on the ceiling; he then turned to me—poor fellow, his mouth all macerated—and said softly: Can I at least put my hand on your breasts? He looked so sick that I didn't have the courage to say no. I unbuttoned my blouse and he inserted his hand through the opening. A tremulous hand. A cold hand.

He began to feel my left breast . . .

It was then that he found the lump. I didn't even complete the course.

Images

I. (*Three Ways of Looking at the Photograph*
   of Private Detective Modesto A. de Oliveira

THE FIRST WAY

The detective seated at the table.

Even in this photograph, in which everything that can be seen of his body is reduced to an image no larger than four by two centimeters, even here, it is obvious that he is a big, strong man. A better photograph, perhaps a three-dimensional one, would show how his large eyes stand out. How they glitter.

His right hand wields a big knife; his left, a three-pronged fork. He has a fondness for this strange-looking set of knife and fork. He is said to have once killed a foe with it.

The sleeves, rolled up, disclose a watch on one wrist, and a silver bracelet on the other. Foppish, he is. But he wears suspenders over his striped shirt.

There are shadows on his face—but they could be from his beard which, as it is well known, grows at an incredibly fast speed. Besides, this photo—and this is worth repeating—is of poor quality.

THE SECOND WAY

To the left and to the right of the detective stand two women, and they are not smiling. The one on the right, the older of the two, is holding a tureen; the one on the left—thus the younger one—a salad bowl. There is every indication that they are about to serve him.

The women are neat in appearance, with their hair carefully combed, but they are dressed in an old-fashioned way. The woman on the right, the one with the soup, is rather hunch-backed; the one

The Tremulous Earth [1977] 183

on the left is pretty—and that's about all that can be said about them from this photograph.

But who is that figure now more clearly discernible amid the shadows in the background?

Yes, indeed, it's him alright: it's Zorro, with his ironic smile and his vengeful sword.

II. A Trick of Mirrors

Two mirrors placed at a certain angle disclose to yourself four images of your face. In the first three images, you can easily recognize yourself by the expression of intense earnestness on your face. But what about that mocking smile that appears on the fourth face?

III. The Chevalier Pero de Abreu Projects Slides

That's me, at the age of three, in the arms of the senhora my mother, Dona Ana de Abreu. Notice the determined look on my face, already denoting firmness of character.

That's me, on the occasion of my first communion. Surrounding me, countless members of the Court.

That's me, upon disembarking at the colony. I was thirty years old. By my side is the senhora my wife. Behold the natives, on their knees!

That's me, traveling on horseback across the plantations. Notice the natives working. They were rebellious at first, but I subjugated them.

That's me, in my castle. Notice that I am in my suit of armor, dressed for battle: it was during the fourth or fifth week of the siege of the natives.

That's me, lying beheaded. My head can be seen farther away; all around, the natives, dancing.

That's my tombstone. Notice the Gothic characters in my epi-taph; very beautiful. The ones looking on are the natives. And that was all.

The Picnic

AT THIS MOMENT, it is like a picnic: all of us are gathered here on the hill we call Morro da Viúva—men, women, children—eating sandwiches and drinking the cold, limpid water from the spring. Some have brought their rifles with them, although there is ab-solutely no need for such precaution—we are certain that nothing will happen to us. It is already five o'clock in the afternoon, night will be falling soon, and we will then return to our homes. The chil-dren have finished playing, the women have finished gathering flowers, the men have finished talking to each other, and only I—the absent-minded one—am still here doodling away on this piece of paper. Some look at me with an ironic smile, others with an air of deference; I don't mind. Leaning against a rock, a blade of grass be-tween my teeth, my gun thrown aside, I amuse myself by thinking of something that everybody else is trying hard not to think of: What could possibly have happened in our town on this beautiful day of April? A day that started in a normal way: the stores opened for busi-ness at eight, the dogs were barking on our main street as usual, the children were on their way to school. Suddenly—it was then nine o'clock—the church bells started to peal in a persistent way: in our small town this is a distress signal, usually to warn us of a fire. Within a few minutes, we were all assembled in front of the church, where the sheriff was already standing—a tall, strong man, rifle in hand.

He was a newcomer to our town; as a matter of fact, we had never had a sheriff before. We lived harmoniously, planting and harvesting our soybeans; the children played, we had picnics in the fields, and I had my usual epileptic seizures. Then one day we woke up to find him standing in the middle of our main street, rifle in hand; he waited until a small crowd had gathered around him before he announced that he had been appointed as the representative of the law in our region. We accepted him; at his request, we built a jail—a small but solid construction. We built it on a Sunday; with all the citizens pitching in, it took us just one Sunday, and by sunset we had already installed the roof, and then we ate the sandwiches that our wives had made and drank our good local beer.

At six o'clock in the afternoon I looked at the sheriff, who was standing in front of the jail, his face reddened by the sunset; at that moment I felt sure I had seen him before, and I was about to tell everybody about it, but instead, I let out a scream, and even before the air passed through my throat, I already knew that it would be a terrifying scream and that I would fall flat on my face on the dusty street and lie there, thrashing about; that people would walk away, afraid of touching me and of contaminating themselves with my viscous drool; and that afterward I would wake up with no recollection of anything. A confused impression of having seen the tall man somewhere would persist, and I would tell the doctor about it, but he would say that no, it couldn't have been, that it was nothing but a sensation common to epileptics. And I would be left with a soreness in my body and a numbness in my mind. After which I would head for the fields, where leaning against a rock, a blade of grass between my teeth, I would scribble or doodle. They—the superstitious people—say that I have the gift of prophecy and that everything I write after coming out from my convulsions is prophetic; however, nobody has ever been able to verify whether this is in fact so because I'm always writing and doodling, then tearing up whatever I wrote and doodled. The bits and pieces of paper are carried by the wind; eventually, they fall upon the damp earth and decompose.

Right now, as I sit here on this day of April, I fix my eyes on a scrap of yellowed paper that got caught amid the stones, and it says there " . . . in the newspaper." It's my own handwriting, I know, but when did I write that? And what did I mean? It was a long time ago, for sure, but was it before the arrival of the sheriff? Earlier today, sometime in the morning, HE HAD US ASSEMBLE IN FRONT OF THE CHURCH. From the churchyard, the tall man, rifle in hand, addressed us; he recalled the day of his arrival, not so long ago. "I've come here to protect you. . . . " And everybody standing there, motionless, silent. But I, I was seated: on a chair, on the sidewalk outside the cafe that is directly across the street from the church. And I was indulging in my usual pastime: paper and pencil. But I wasn't writing: I was drawing, something I'm also very good at. From my pencil emerged the impassive face of the tall man. *It has just come to my knowledge that a gang of bandits is heading for our town. They should arrive here within an hour. They know that there is a lot of money in our bank* . . . Which was true: the soybean crops had been sold, the farmers had made large deposits throughout the week.

It is my duty to defend you. However, I count on the help of every able-bodied citizen. . . . " Naturally, I jotted down some of his words: in them, I could feel the weight of a historical moment. Alarmed, people were whispering to each other.

Return to your homes, the tall man was saying in conclusion. *Arm yourselves and come back here within half an hour. I'll be waiting here.* The crowd dispersed, and I saw apprehensive faces, tearful children, and women whispering in their husbands' ears.

The main square became deserted. In the square, only the tall man, his face front-lit by the strong sun—and me, hidden in the shade cast by the awning of the cafe. Five minutes later, the first citizen arrived—the barber; when he emerged in the square I already knew what he was going to say: that he hoped the sheriff would excuse him, that he had many children, that he was the breadwinner for a large family; and I already knew that the sheriff would accept his excuse and advise him to take his family to the hill that we call

Morro da Viúva, where they would all be safe. Hardly had the barber left when the pharmacist came: overweight, eyes bulging out, brow drenched in sweat: he hoped the sheriff would understand . . . The sheriff showed great understanding toward him, as well as toward the bar owner and the storekeeper, who appeared next.

The last one to come was the bank manager; he still tried to persuade the law-enforcement officer to go with him, but his gesture of concern met with a polite rebuff. Before hurrying away, the bank manager shouted: *Sheriff, I've left the coffer open; if you can't frighten the robbers away, for heavens' sake, hand them the money and save your life!* The sheriff nodded in agreement, and the man was gone.

It was then that he saw me. I think that aside from the dogs that were sniffing at the gutter, we were the only creatures left in town.

For a few moments the tall man stood looking at me. Then he started to cross the street at a slow pace. The man with the rifle in his hand positioned himself in front of me.

"You haven't gotten an assistant, sir," I said, without interrupting my doodling.

"True," he said. "I've never needed one."

"But now you do."

"That's true, too."

"Well, there's me."

A faint smile.

"You're a sick person, son."

"That's precisely why," I said to him. "I want to prove that I can make myself useful."

And it is then that he sees the drawing in my hands; with a frown on his face, he advances upon me, and snatches the sheet of paper from me: *Give it to me, young man, I don't want to be remembered afterward,* he says, and I'm about to protest, about to tell him he shouldn't do this, but at this point his face is right in front of mine—

where? where?—and can I feel the scream rushing out of my chest, and everything goes blank.

Upon waking up, I find myself tied to a horse that is slowly climbing up the hill. There, on the top, amid the rocks, the entire population of the town: astounded, they untie me and help me dismount; some look at me in an ironic way; others ask me questions. Finally, they leave me in peace.

I remain seated here, listening to them talk: The telegraphist is explaining that he has tried to send a telegram to the garrison but without success. *The wires have been cut, I'm sure.*

It was then that the fire shots echoed through the hills. We all rose to our feet, and stood rigid, pricking up our ears, and a great silence fell upon the region.

"Let's go back there." I heard the voice with great surprise, for it was my own. Everybody turned to me. I remained seated, a blade of grass between my teeth.

The bank manager came up to me.

"Are you crazy? We promised not to go back until the church bells started to ring, or to wait here until six o'clock."

I make no reply. I remain silent, doodling away. The sun is beginning to set, and the church bells haven't rung yet. Everybody is cheerful, for becoming destitute is preferable to being killed. Soon we will be climbing down the hill, and everybody is eaten up with anxiety: What awaits us in our town? I amuse myself by thinking about what we will find there; I know that upon arriving there, I'll have a feeling of déjà vu (which, according to the doctor, is not unusual for people with my disease to experience): the streets deserted, the doors of the bank wide open, the coffer empty. It also seems to me that far off along the road goes a tall man on horseback, the saddlebags stuffed with money. There could be three or four of them, but it is certain that the tall man rides laughing.

Rest in Peace

I BECAME RICH SELLING PROVIDENCE BONDS. Being now thirty-five years old, a millionaire, in the pink of health, and always surrounded by women, I decided I would do something for my poor friend Bruno, a philosophy professor who lived in the squalid district of Beco da Boiada.

I asked him to come to my office. He came and as usual, he cut a sorry figure. I sighed. Bruno, I said, Bruno, I'm very rich. Bruno, I've become a millionaire selling Providence Bonds . . .

I stopped talking. He wasn't listening. He was looking out of the window, absent-minded. He was looking at the river, at the tugboat that was slowly advancing. He wasn't looking at me. Bruno: a small, ugly man sunk into the armchair; thinning hair, a red unkempt beard. A faded shirt. Blue jeans. Sandals with uppers made of thick straps.

"Bruno!"

He flinched, and looked at me, startled.

"Bruno!" I shouted. "Bruno, I'm rolling in it! Bruno, I've made a fortune selling Providence Bonds. Hey, Bruno, this humbuggery of mine has made me filthy rich. Bruno, the only reason I'm not in jail is because the buyers are swindlers just like me. Hey, Bruno, listen to me!"

He was listening; terrified, he was.

"Bruno," I went on in a more subdued way. "Bruno, I feel guilty about having made so much money without having really earned it . . . Bruno, my friend, I've decided to do something for you. Bruno, I'm going to give you a nice apartment, a decent apartment. . . . You'll be able to move out of that shack of yours. Besides, Bruno, I'm going to give you a nice monthly allowance . . . for a whole year."

That's what I said, my voice already cracking with emotion.

Bruno was looking at the river again. He seemed to have forgotten me . . . He was looking at the river and fiddling with a key—the key to his house. I rose to my feet and snatched the key from him.

"There now! You can't go to that pad of yours even if you want to."

I returned to my desk and pressed the interphone button:

"The apartment for my friend Bruno, is it ready?"

"Yes, sir," replied my secretary, an unpleasant but efficient woman.

"Then take him there, please."

The secretary came and led Bruno out of the room. Like an automaton, he allowed himself to be led.

That night I had my chauffeur drive me aimlessly all over the city. The man—a mere chauffeur, but I allowed him to take certain liberties—was concerned:

"Aren't you going to Adelaide's, sir?"

I was feeling weird. Restless. Because of Bruno. Damn him.

It started to rain. Sighing, I told the chauffeur to head for Adelaide's house.

I got out of the car and rang the doorbell. She opened the door. A gorgeous woman. Very tall, almost two meters in height, she was wearing a sexy black negligee. She extended her arms to me—but I was feeling restless and pushed her away.

"What's the matter, sweetie?" She was upset. "Have I done something wrong, sweetie?"

"Get dressed," I said.

"But . . . " She opened her eyes wide, strikingly beautiful green eyes. "Weren't we going to dine in, sweetie? I've sent out for some Japanese food . . . "

"Chinese," I said. "Get dressed."

"Chinese what?" She was really very stupid.

"The food!" I shouted. "The food you ordered is Chinese, not Japanese. Now get dressed. You're coming with me."

The Tremulous Earth [1977]   191

She got dressed and we left, she sobbing. "Shut up," I said. She became silent.

The car cruised in the rain. Alas, I wasn't feeling well at all. A kind of anguish, of nausea . . . I was perspiring.

The chauffeur turned on the cassette player. Soft music.

"Turn the fucking thing off!"

Adelaide started, the chauffeur turned the tape player off. Bruno's visit had unhinged me. Why?

In my trouser pocket, a hard object was hurting my thigh. I took it out: it was the key to Bruno's house.

"We're going to Beco da Boiada," I said to the chauffeur in a choked, strange voice.

The place was quite some distance away. It was midnight when we got there. The rain had stopped, but thick, dark clouds . . . I got out of the car and told Adelaide to get out too. Bruno's house: old, tumbledown, surrounded by brushwood. Splashing through the mud, I made my way to the door. Adelaide followed me, whimpering. I inserted the key in the lock; the door creaked open. Bruno's distinctive smell—fustiness invaded my nostrils.

I groped for the light switch. There wasn't one. I struck a match and saw a table and on it, the stub of a candle. I lit it.

"I'm scared," moaned Adelaide.

"Shut up."

I looked around me. Books everywhere, piled on the shelves, on the floor, on the table. On the walls, reproductions of paintings. An old typewriter.

I went into the bedroom.

There it was—the coffin.

So, it was true. I had heard that Bruno had been sleeping in a casket lately. I never gave much credence to this piece of gossip. But there it was, before my very eyes, a plain coffin, with no frills, resting on a stack of bricks.

I let myself collapse into a chair.

Bruno slept in a coffin. I lived in fear of coffins, of cemeteries; but Bruno slept in a coffin. Any minor pain would send me running to the doctor. Bruno slept in a coffin.

Adelaide came in.

"A coffin!" She laughed. "Isn't that funny! A coffin!"

I gave her a slap across the face. She crumbled, and remained on her knees, crying.

I went near the coffin. With great fear. God, was I ever afraid! But as I inched forward, I managed to overcome my fear. What would I find in there? What if there were bones in there? Or hair, or fingernails?

Nothing. Nothing besides the bluish satin lining, lustrous in the flickering light of the candle.

"Let's go," begged Adelaide, and I wanted to go, too, but I couldn't: I had to get close to the coffin, I had to touch it.

I touched it. My vision became blurred. I was going to faint . . .

I didn't faint. I caught sight of the rip.

The rip in the lining of the coffin. I extended my tremulous fingers, I touched that rip, I began to explore that raw wound.

There was a sheet of paper in there. I pulled it out. I unfolded it in the light of the candle, I examined it in the light of the candle, and it was—in the light of the candle or in any other light—a Providence Bond!

I broke into laughter. And how I laughed! Laughing, I took Adelaide into my arms; laughing, I started to waltz with her; laughing, I pushed her into the coffin. Her feet wouldn't fit in. I kept laughing! She kept laughing! Then I jumped upon her and began kissing her furiously. The candle went out.

I've had but few moments of inspiration in my life. One was when I hatched this Providence Bonds scheme. Another, was that one, in Bruno's coffin.

Festive Dawn

AT SIX O'CLOCK the alarm clock went off. He got out of bed and went to the window. *Good weather, with cloudiness,* he thought; and upon seeing the news imprinted in large block letters on the low clouds, he compressed his lips: *Another Earthquake in China.* In smaller letters, the details, which he didn't want to read. I can't stand bad news first thing in the morning, he murmured. What? said his wife, shifting in bed. She didn't hear his reply; she was snoring again. She worked downtown as a typist, but she didn't start until nine o'-clock. Nothing, he said, looking at the picture in the sky: a man smiling. A huge man: his eyes would be bigger than the sun, if the sun were visible. Yes, bigger than the sun, even if it was a pallid sun, but less brilliant than the sun—even if it was a pallid sun. Probably the president of some country or other, he muttered. What?—his wife again. Nothing, woman, he said and closed the window. How in the world did they do it? Those news items printed on the clouds? And those huge pictures? The mouth of the president took up a whole cloud—a small cloud, of course, but still a cloud, a real cloud. Were they slides projected on the sky? I bet I'm the only one who sees such things, he thought; and he then concluded: It's because I'm the only one to wake up at six in the morning. His son never got up before eleven o'clock.

He went to the bathroom, determined not to let himself become annoyed again—at least not until he got rid of his morning flatus, which was already putting pressure on his entrails, trying to get out. He sat down on the toilet bowl, picked up a magazine that lay discarded on the floor—in this house everything is left lying about—and opened it at random. And there it was again, the picture of the man who a moment ago had been smiling at him from the clouds! Alarmed, he was about to rise to his feet; but he then heard a muffled rumbling inside the toilet bowl, a rumbling coming from the toilet bowl itself. He took a peak through the gap between his hairy thighs. Lightning was flashing there; and the water below was thrashing about like a choppy sea in miniature. Then a sudden downpour began to lash out from everywhere—but it wasn't the toilet flushing.

Repeated knocking on the door.

"Just a moment, love."

It was his wife.

"I'm leaving earlier for work today."

(A lover? An early morning lover?)

"Your coffee's ready. Did you hear?"

He made no reply.

"I'm taking the umbrella. It started to rain. A real downpour."

"I know," he said.

"Buy yourself another umbrella, will you?" (she had lost hers).

"All right," he groaned.

"What?"

"All right. No problem. Bye now."

A pause.

"You're not feeling well?" she asked.

"I'm fine," he said.

"Aren't you going to work today?" She was now getting worried.

"Sure. Of course I am. Later."

"Well," she said, hesitant. "Bye, then."

"Bye."

Upon hearing the front door slam shut, he got up, determined to take a pill for his constipation. He opened the door of the medicine cabinet only to find the bottle of pills empty. It should have been nearly full, but it was empty. He opened it. (What for?) A horrible stench assailed his nostrils.

"Gosh!" He recoiled in astonishment.

It was a physical presence, that stench—an invisible moth flitting about in the bathroom. And from the toilet bowl a thin vapor began to rise.

"I've swallowed a cloud. A cloud of rain."

He left the bathroom and went to the kitchen. The coffee was, as his wife had said, ready. The newspaper lay folded beside his cup. The main news item was about the earthquake in China; but there was no headline. The space usually taken up by the headline was blank. He quickly leafed through the newspaper. From in between the pages, small green pills—the laxative—began to roll out. He took three of them with a bit of water. He sighed.

"I think that things will get better now."

He helped himself to some coffee. He carefully examined the black liquid and sniffed at it; it was indeed coffee. He drank it in one gulp, with no sugar.

"I'm already feeling better."

He looked out of the window. It was no longer raining. A pallid sun appeared amid the clouds. He went to the bedroom to get dressed. But he didn't look back.

Because had he done so, he would have seen the face of the man with eyes as big as the sun emerge from the cup.

Skinny Enough to Become a Kite

I WAS ON THE VERGE OF—I don't even know what, I really don't, so fed up was I: fed up with the job, fed up with the boss.

It was then that I hit upon this idea of a kite. Oh boy, what a good idea! How in the world did it occur to me? I don't know. By looking at my arms, I guess. They were as thin as sticks, and so were my legs. *Beware of the September wind*, my old mother used to say, *or it will carry you away. Like a kite.* There, then: a kite!

I went to see the boss. A *kite?* He liked the idea. He laughed. It was the first time I had seen that man laugh. But it's only now that I know why he was laughing. It was because what I said evoked memories of himself as a boy, flying a kite. A long time ago. Long before he started bossing us around.

Seeing that he liked the idea, I lay down on the ground, belly up. He went and got a ball of strong twine. I spread my arms wide open, then stretched my legs out.

The first knot was on my left wrist. A double knot, very secure. *I still remember how to tie a knot*, he said, always smiling. I laughed, too. For once, we were getting along with each other. He wasn't calling me a loafer, or a thief. We were actually playing together. It felt good.

The second knot was on my left ankle; the third, on my right ankle—both of them single knots. The knot on my right wrist was double, like the one on my left wrist. The frame was now finished.

I've always used sturdy paper to make a kite; and that's what I told him, that for me, a kite had to be made of sturdy paper. But he winked at me: *I have another idea*, and I was afraid he wanted to use my skin—those loose folds of skin left on my arms and neck after I lost weight.

But no, it wasn't my skin, but the cloth from this tunic, this baggy tunic that I normally wear. I was so glad that he was no longer critical of my clothes, that he was, in fact, quite pleased with them.

He stretched out the cloth and started to sew it around the twine that ran from my wrists to my ankles. He worked diligently, always cheerful and whistling away. Really happy, he was.

He then proceeded to make the bridle leg: three pieces of string. One piece tied to my neck with a slipknot (he was careful not to tighten it too much); the other two tied to each one of my wrists. Neck, wrist, wrist: the three most suitable points. He sure knew how to make a kite. He tied one more knot to join the three loose ends of string, and the bridle leg was ready.

To this bridle leg he then attached the end of a large ball of twine. *That's a good two hundred meters of string I've got here*, he said, but I didn't believe him. Later I saw that it was really true.

He then lifted me to my feet, urging me not to move. I stood there, rigid, motionless, with the strong September wind swelling out my tunic. We were standing on the lawn in front of the metallurgical company. Beautiful, this lawn. Stretching for about one hundred meters.

He ran along the lawn, unrolling the twine. All of a sudden, I felt a strong jolt. I started to ascend! I was functioning as a kite! And before long, the kite was floating over woods and hills.

From way down below he kept waving at me. It was impossible for me to wave back, but I was hoping he could see the radiant smile on my face. It was the first time that I had seen him—that sad little man—looking so cheerful.

He tugged at the bridle leg twice, almost strangling me in the process. But even so, I responded with two jerks of my head. It was our code; at last, we understood each other.

He was giving me more rope. I was now flying high, with the strong wind tossing me about. But I bore up well. I was the framework.

Night began to fall. I knew that he had to go home. Which he did, after tying the end of the twine to the trunk of a tree. And there I remained all night long, floating in the black space, looking at the lights way down below, and at the stars above my head.

Beautiful, it was.

I no longer wanted to descend. Now that I knew about things, I no longer wanted to descend.

And I didn't: to this day I have been up here.

That dark little dot in the sky? That's me.

Profile of the Hen of the Golden Eggs
as She Lay Dying

IN ADDITION TO A DISTRESSING ANOMALY, the hen of the golden eggs was afflicted with a thwarted ambition and an unrequited passion.

The thwarted ambition: She had always wanted to be a singer. She came from a family that was in the habit of greeting the rising sun with vibrant hymns. However, even though the hen of the golden eggs had been born in an environment of euphonious creativity, she hadn't been endowed with a pleasant voice. Her raucous singing was so unpleasant, when not ridiculous, that it provoked the indignation of the other hens, who would peck her into silence.

But this hen wanted to be a singer. And she really exerted herself. Self-disciplined, she would practice indefatigably. There was no musical scale that she was not familiar with; there were no sharps that she hadn't attempted. The results, always precarious, didn't dampen her spirits. One day—she kept thinking to herself—a metamorphosis would take place; it was only a matter of perseverance, of effort. And she would go back to her exercises.

The distressing anomaly: She laid golden eggs. Joylessly; with displeasure, with pain even. She conceived hard, cold objects, which were then expelled amidst indescribable pains: a torture that she had to undergo day after day at dawn. Half an hour before, she could already feel that dreaded moment drawing near. The portent of what was to come manifested itself as an unpleasant sensation in her womb—a mixture of anguish and pain. Something—a ball—would grow inside her and expand inexorably, squeezing and crushing everything. Edgy, and not knowing what to do, she would then pace to and fro in an attempt to distract herself. And she would peck at the ground, and flap her wings, and sing a little (her voice being then more unpleasant than ever)—and nothing. Nothing but this everlasting anguish. She would jump into her nest, curl up, and try to sleep; maybe if she fell asleep . . . Nothing. Unable to fall asleep, unable to calm down. Quite the opposite: as the minutes went by, her anguish would grow more unbearable. In despair, she would shout for help, and turn to the other hens for comfort. Irritated, they would rebuff her. And the hen, with no bosom to retreat to, with no shoulder to lean on, would huddle up in a corner, all atremble, and in a near faint.

And then, in her tenebrous insides—a jolt. The thing would move. It would start on its descent, it would leave her body—tearing everything apart as it forced its way out. Hallucinated, the hen would kneel down: unbelievable that one single creature should have to endure so many tribulations! She was fainting! She was dying!

But the act of giving birth would run its course. Her suffering would reach a climax—the hen would see stars—and all of a sudden, it would be all over.

The egg would lie on the straw: a yellowish object covered with a thin layer of a bloodstained secretion. With a rancorous eye, the hen, exhausted, would observe the cold, hard fruit of her entrails.

A hairy hand would then find its way into the nest. Ramão, the owner of the chicken farm. Greedy, he could hardly wait for the hen to finish laying the egg. (As a matter of fact, he would often grab her while she was still in labor; he would squeeze her and cheer her on with rude words: Come on, lazybones, poop this egg out, you gun moll. Which only contributed to the suffering of the poor thing.)

With the egg finally in his possession, he would gaze at it, radiant, plant a kiss on it, and run to Amâncio's house, where this sharpie would be waiting for him, with the deck of cards all set up. Ramão would install himself on a chair and place the egg on the table:

"Today's the day, Amâncio! Today you'll be trounced, Amâncio!"

The other, a pro, would merely smile and deal the cards. The two of them would spend the whole day gambling.

By late afternoon, the egg would be in Amâncio's possession.

Ramão, his face congested, his hair disheveled, his countenance clouded, would get up and go home. He would have a few drinks and then throw himself upon his bed; he could hardly wait for the hours to pass, hardly wait for the hen to lay another egg. Amâncio would soon see who he was dealing with.

On the following day Ramão would again be the loser.

Amâncio had already won a fortune off Ramão. But he was still not satisfied; it wasn't gold, what he wanted from Ramão What he really coveted, and coveted most insanely, was Torpedo, the game-cock owned by the chicken farmer.

What a rooster! Not once had he suffered defeat in the cockpit. Amâncio owned many roosters, but none of them matched up to Torpedo. He was willing to bet everything he had on Torpedo—he had, in fact, already made a proposal in this regard, but Ramão wouldn't hear of it. Ramão was fond of this rooster; besides, he wanted to hold Torpedo as a trump card, should he one day lose his hen of the golden eggs, his chicken farm, his clothes, everything, to Amâncio. Not until then would he put a bet on his rooster. And he expected to win then, at least that once. But even if he lost, he wouldn't let Amâncio waltz off with his prize rooster. He would never give his partner this pleasure. If Amâncio ever dared lay his hands on Torpedo, Ramão would kill him right away.

Torpedo was beautiful and strong. And . . . he had a secret affection for the hen of the golden eggs. While Ramão and Amâncio were gambling away, Torpedo would caress and comfort her. He was a witness to the suffering of the poor creature; on several occasions he had almost attacked Ramão. It was the hen who would hold him back, for she would rather suffer in silence than become the pivot of a passional tragedy. And she would then give vent to her feelings by singing to the skies—her song a strange, dissonant cackling.

The unrequited passion: The hen of the golden eggs was in love with the chicken farmer Ramão. Love mingled with hatred, but yes, it was love—deep, abysmal love. With loathing—but with joy as well—she would deliver her golden egg to the bastard, because she would then have him beside her, albeit only for a few brief moments. She would have liked to have him lying beside her on the straw. If only she could nestle up against his hairy chest and peck at the matted hair for larvae and various tibits, ah, then she would finally find the inspiration for beautiful songs.

But Ramão only slept with women—with the two or three that he had. The hen was well aware of this fact, but she would delude herself: It's just a pastime, she kept repeating to herself, he doesn't love them. One day she would break into song and he would come to her. And it wouldn't be just for a golden egg . . .

As for Torpedo, the hen consented to his keeping her company— but that was all. He wasn't to expect anything more. They might be together on the straw, but that was all. Two birds befriending each other.

Ramão kept gambling and losing, gambling and losing. Amâncio's cupboards were already chock full of eggs; now that the price of the precious metal was being quoted at one hundred dollars an ounce, he couldn't find any buyers for all that gold. But even so, they continued with their card games—Ramão wanting to recoup his losses; Amâncio hoping to win the rooster Torpedo.

The night of December 31. On the streets of the small town, people in a cheerful mood walk in a hurry. They look forward to spending the New Year with their families, when they will eat roasted chicken stuffed with a *farofa* of manioc flour toasted in butter and mixed with olives and chopped eggs. Even the poor intend to have a celebration and eat chicken.

Ramão and Amâncio are oblivious to all the bustle outside. They are playing cards. Seated at a small table under a strong lamplight that makes their sweaty brows glisten, they hold their cards firmly in their hands. And they keep watching and examining each other closely, and they won't discard a queen or a jack before a great deal of pondering.

Ramão is edgy. He compresses his lips; at times he mutters unintelligible things. He drums on the table with his thick fingers.

Amâncio tries to feign unconcern; he hums away to himself, an enigmatic smile flickers on his face. And when he spreads his cards on the table—again the winner—he doesn't rush Ramão; with studied modesty, he waits for the other to admit defeat—which the chicken farmer finally does with barely contained resentment.

Amâncio then reaches out for the golden egg; he weighs it with his hands and examines it closely; pulling a handkerchief out of his pocket, he then proceeds to polish the egg; with the tip of a fingernail he removes a tiny speck of dirt. Sighing, he gets up to put the egg away in the cupboard. Upon which, he extends his hand to his partner:

"Well . . . so then, happy new year, Ramão. I hope that next year . . ."

"We'll go on with our card game," says Ramão, somber.

"How?" Amâncio laughs. "You've already lost today's egg."

"We'll go on with our card game," repeats Ramão.

The tone of voice makes Amâncio feel uneasy. But he is a gambler: he doesn't show fear.

"Come on, now: doesn't your hen only lay one egg per day, doesn't she?"

"That's right."

"So? How come you still want us to continue?"

"We're not stopping now, I've already told you so."

Amâncio carefully assesses the situation. He decides to take a risk:

"All right. Then go and get Torpedo."

"No."

Amâncio's patience is wearing thin.

"So, what's going to be the stake? Or are we playing just for fun? I don't play just for fun, you know that."

Ramão stands ups.

"Wait for me. I'm going to get another egg."

"Fine, but look," Amâncio warns the other, "I'll wait only until midnight. If your hen decides to wait until tomorrow to lay an egg, forget it."

"She's going to lay an egg now," says Ramão.

"Is she?" sneers Amâncio.

"You wait and see."

Ramão goes running to his chicken farm. He is upset, he is distraught! He rushes into the hen yard and turns all the lights on. Startled, the hens begin to cackle. Ramão comes to the nest of the hen of the golden eggs, who is reposing on the straw, with Torpedo beside her. Upon seeing Ramão, she neither moves nor emits a single sound—she just stares at him fixedly.

"So, you wretch, have you laid your egg yet?"

Grabbing her by the neck, he brutally wrenches her from her nest. There is no egg.

"Stupid you! Why didn't you lay an egg? It's already almost midnight. Are you waiting for the new year? YOU know nothing about time, do you?"

On the verge of suffocating, the hen flails about helplessly.

All of a sudden, a fluttering of wings: It's Torpedo, who makes a leap for Ramão's face and proceeds to strike at it fiercely with his beak. Taken by surprise, Ramão recoils, but he soon rallies. Pulling the rooster away from him, he throws him on the ground, then digs his boot into him, and continues to trample upon him until Torpedo is reduced to a bloody mass.

"There, you fucking bird," Ramão mutters, panting. "You've got your just desserts. I've turned you into chicken paste." He laughs:

"Amâncio's not going to like it at all."

He cleans his dirty and badly lacerated face, then lifts up the hen until she is on a level with his face:

"Now, you! See that you lay this egg of yours. And be quick about it."

He sets her down in the nest, then crosses his arms.

"I'm waiting."

He looks at his watch.

"I'll give you five minutes."

All of a sudden, the hen of the golden eggs begins to sing.

It is such a beautiful song that even Ramão is touched: he has gooseflesh, his eyes mist over.

"Aw, come on now, you floozy . . . "

The other hens sit motionless in their coops, their heads turned to them. Ramão waits in the expectation of some grandiose event.

"It's going to be something, this egg. Out of this world! Who knows, there might even be two of them."

Gingerly, he lifts up the hen. Nothing. He sets her down, waits a while longer, lifts her up again. Nothing. Just the straw, nothing but the straw. He becomes furious:

"Are you making fun of me, you shit-ass? But I'll show you! I'm getting this egg straight from the factory."

He hurls the hen upon the ground, pulls out the big knife that he carries at his waist, and at one stroke—with all the hens cackling in horror—slashes her womb open.

He then throws the big knife aside and proceeds to ransack her entrails impatiently. He plucks out her intestines, her liver, her gizzard:

"It should be here! In every other hen, that's where it is."

There are no golden eggs. What he finds is an ordinary ovary, with small, yellow ovules.

The chicken farmer rises to his feet. All of a sudden, he bursts into laughter.

The Tremulous Earth [1977]   205

"She was just like all the others, this hen. Just like all the others, Amâncio!"

He picks up the knife.

"You're down on your luck, Amâncio. Too bad!"

He walks away laughing.

"Too bad for you, Amâncio!"

On the bloodstained earth, the hen lies dying. Her beak still opens in infrequent spasms, but no sound comes out of it. And her eyes have become lusterless.

The hen dies. Her eviscerated carcass shakes with one final convulsion. From the cloaca emerges the rounded end of a great golden egg.

Capital Punishment

THE JAILER WAKES UP ROBERT, a certain Robert, at five o'clock in the morning. The jailer is brutal; he keeps shaking the prisoner—a young man with disheveled hair and congested eyes—who then rises to his feet.

"Are they here already?"

"And why shouldn't they?" asks the jailer in an unpleasant, screeching voice. "Why shouldn't they be here? It's five o'clock in the morning, isn't it?"

Robert lets himself collapse upon the bed. In a half faint? The jailer yanks him to his feet:

"Isn't it five o'clock now? Answer me. Isn't it five o'clock now? How come a smart-ass like you doesn't know? It's five o'clock, isn't it?"

"Yes," mumbles Robert. "It's five o'clock."

"So? It's five o'clock and they're here. They're on time," concludes the jailer, triumphant. "Here, put this on."

He hands a grey tunic to the prisoner, who has a hard time pulling it over his head. The jailer goes to his assistance.

"There now," he says. "All spruced up. My, aren't we cute."

He then peeps through the open door: nobody outside in the corridor. He then puts his mouth close to the prisoner's ear:

"Relax. Everything's been arranged. Do you hear me? Everything arranged. Everything fine."

He then gives Robert a shove:

"Get a move on, you clod!"

Winking at the prisoner, he continues to shout:

"Get going, you drag ass, you fraidy cat."

They leave the cell and proceed to walk down the long corridor, headed for the place where a small detachment of soldiers, standing at attention, awaits their arrival. The officer in charge talks to the prison chaplain, who then walks up to Robert.

"Are you the condemned man?" The priest looks at Robert in the eye. Does he give him a wink? He does.

Unsure, Robert stands still. The chaplain takes him by the arm.

"Come over here. Let's have a little talk."

"Sorry, Father," says Robert, "but I'm not a believer."

"It'll only take a moment. Come over here."

Pulling Robert aside, he makes him kneel down, and then he, too, kneels down.

The priest proceeds to intone something in Latin; all of a sudden, he murmurs:

"Have faith. Everything has been arranged."

The officer in charge approaches them.

"It's time, chaplain."

The two of them rise to their feet. The chaplain shakes Robert's hand and disappears down a side corridor.

The prisoner is positioned among the soldiers. *March!* shouts the officer. They start marching, Robert perfectly in step with the soldiers. And with his head held high. Not as high as the soldiers', but high enough.

"Psst!"

Psst? Who? Where has it come from, this psst?

"Psst!"

Again! But he has now located its source: the soldier beside him. Robert leans toward him.

"Everything's fine," murmurs the soldier, all the while looking straight ahead. "Know what I mean? Everything's fine." He gives his rifle a gentle tap. "Do you understand? Everything's fine."

The prisoners, as they peep out from the tiny windows of their cells, can detect a smile on Robert's lips . . . A smile. Lips.

Lips.

They reach the courtyard of the prison. The sky—it is sixteen minutes twenty seconds past five o'clock—begins to grow light. The sky—it is sixteen minutes twenty-one seconds past five o'clock—begins to grow light. The officer in charge consults his watch.

Two soldiers escort Robert to the middle of the courtyard, where they proceed to tie his hands to his back. One of the soldiers murmurs:

"Have faith," and the other:

"So far, everything's fine."

"Everything's fine," repeats the prisoner. Quite audibly. "Everything's fine," he says to the two soldiers, who bear a close resemblance to each other. They look like brothers. They are brothers.

A third soldier approaches with a strip of black cloth in his hand. "I don't want—" says Robert.

"It would be better," the soldier cuts him short.

While blindfolding Robert, the soldier whispers to him:

"Don't be afraid. Everything's all right. Do you hear me? Everything's all right."

The firing squad assembles. A journalist standing a short distance away writes down in his notebook:

The soldiers are standing at attention. The voice of the officer in charge makes the gelid morning air vibrate. Make ready! he commands, and the soldiers cock their rifles; but everything is all right, everything is fine. Take your aim! shouts the officer. Everything's fine, if only the prisoner knew . . . The face of the blindfolded man reveals a deep anguish. And yet—everything's fine. And now, fire! Fire, now!

A volley of rifle fire.

Robert, fallen on the ground. A thread of blood trickling out of his mouth forms a small puddle on the cement floor. The body still twitches convulsively. The officer approaches the dying man in order to have a close look. He draws his gun:

I rise to my feet, pick up the crutches, and start walking back and forth. I then hit upon an idea:

"Everything's fine," he says, and dealing the coup de grâce, we sign our names below.

Cordially.

The jailer.

The chaplain.

The soldier from the escort.

The prisoners.

The soldier with the ropes.

The other soldier with the ropes—his brother.

The journalist.

The officer.

A storyteller. A storyteller.

The Last One

"OKAY, WEASEL. Drop the weapon and turn around slowly."

Weasel turned around. It was Frog, with a .38 in his right hand.

"You're smart, Frog," said Weasel. "Real smart. But we're even smarter, aren't we, Cricket?"

"That's such an old trick, Weasel," said Frog.

"Okay, Frog. Drop that weapon, raise your arms, and turn around slowly."

Frog turned around. It was Cricket, with a 7.65 caliber pistol.

"You're smart, Cricket," said Frog. "But not any smarter than we are, isn't that right, Rat?"

"That's such an old trick, Frog," said Cricket.

"Okay, Cricket. Drop that pistol, raise your arms, and turn around this way, very slowly."

Cricket turned around. It was Rat, with a Springfield rifle.

"You're smart, Rat," said Cricket, smiling. "Real smart. But not smarter than we are. Right, Angel?"

"Wrong."

Astounded, they all turned to see a man holding a sword in his hand.

"And my name," he then said with a smile that froze the others with fear, "is not Angel."

The Riddle

AFTER THE BURIAL, upon returning home from the burial, he realizes, much to his annoyance, that his shoes are dirty from the mud of the cemetery. A red, sticky mud, it is.

He steps out into the patio, and with the help of a small shovel, he carefully cleans his shoes. He reenters the house only to see that his shoes are still muddy—this time it is the black mud of the patio.

"Shucks!" he mutters. "How aggravating!"

With a sigh, he returns to the patio and gets down to work. With the remainder of the gravel and the cement, he succeeds in paving the patio, which is small. He then goes inside the house.

The first thing he notices is that his shoes are still dirty. Now, it is from the cement. His shoes are still dirty! He takes them off. He goes to the kitchen, soaks them in a solvent, then burns them. He sighs, relieved.

But not for long. In the bathroom, while washing his hands in front of the mirror, he notices the fine ashes on his hair. With a blow of his fist, he destroys the mirror.

He calms down. He breaks into a smile. And it is still smiling that he drinks in one gulp the bottle of that thing that he put in his wife's coffee. Is it red mud? No, it's not red mud. Is it black mud? Is it cement dust? Is it ashes? Is it rat poison?

The Dream

MARTIM HAS THE FOLLOWING DREAM:

He sees himself entering a bedroom. He leans over a small bed, and in the semidarkness he looks at the child lying there.

The child is Martim himself, at the age of ten.

Contemplating the tranquil face with its rosy cheeks, he is suffused with a deep feeling of—

All of a sudden, the sleeping child breaks into laughter. Into rollicking, jeering laughter.

Martim is enraged. What is he laughing at, the little brat? What does he see in his dreams? If it's all that funny, why doesn't he open his eyes and tell him about it? He doesn't open his eyes, he doesn't tell anything; he is laughing again. Enraged, Martim lifts his hand to hit the child.

He doesn't hit the child. He stands there, gazing at the calm face. Because it has just occurred to him that—

He wakes up. His wife, looking at him with suspicion, is shaking him awake.

"Were you asleep, Martim?"

"Of course!" He—annoyed, drowsy.

"But you were laughing!" says the woman.

"Who? Me?" Martim finds it hard to believe.

"Yes, you, Martim. You."

Laughing at what, wonders Martim, the sorrowful Martim.

The Shadow

AS A MOVIE BUFF living in a small town in the interior, I always took great pleasure in helping the projectionist of the *Esplendor* Movie Theater—a gentleman of moderate means but of a certain refinement. From the cramped projection room, the two of us would watch the movies from a very original angle, and engage in interesting conversations.

The *Esplendor* Movie Theater was housed in an old, rundown building beset with problems: the large rats in the projection room was but one of them. Squealing, the rats would scurry back and forth and devour anything they could. But nobody ever noticed their presence. In the dark, couples went on kissing. Sounds of moaning continued to come from the washrooms. The rain persisted in pattering on the old tiles of the roof.

It was 1962. Or '63. A week came when we had but one movie to show—*The Adventures of the Shadow.* A second-rate production of the American movie industry. Directed by a Barry Dikes. Movie script by—? I no longer remember. The Shadow was, of course, a crude cinematographic trick, a dark blob of indistinct contours, vaguely reminiscent of the figure of a man wearing a hat. He always appeared on the left hand side of the screen. From there he would raise his voice against crime. And immorality. In the final episode, Pamela Archer would fall into his arms. In that shadowy region of the screen, she would dissolve herself in love. And that was the end.

Embarrassed, we would project the movie in silence. What could we do? There was no other film available. But that was not the end of our trouble.

One afternoon we arrived at the movie theater only to discover that the rats had been gnawing at the film. Upon projecting it on the screen, we saw that the Shadow no longer appeared: the left side of the film had been destroyed. What now appeared was just the patched-up fabric of the screen. Pamela Archer would open her arms, take two steps forward, and vanish into the emptiness. An absurdity.

In order to save the projectionist from being dismissed from his job, I decided that I would play the role of the Shadow. Positioned behind the screen, with a lamp illuminating me from behind, I was, there on the screen, nothing more than a silhouette with blurry contours. Just like the Shadow.

Night after night I would kiss Pamela Archer. I now saw her from a new angle. An enormous face, distorted and flawed. The blackhead, the wrinkle—they all had their territory there. As for depth, there was none, naturally. Her profile was nothing but a dark line no thicker than the fabric of the screen. What puzzled me was how that face could elicit so many amorous sighs from the audience night after night.

I worked really hard. Night after night I would raise my voice against crime. Against immorality.

I don't know . . . It was because of this movie, I suppose, that I became a lawyer. I moved to the capital city, where I've continued to raise my voice against crime and immorality. But Pamela Archer has never again fallen into my arms.

Stories of the Tremulous Earth

THE NEW MAID, they say, has but two flaws: she eats too much and—this is funny—she keeps complaining about the bugs in her bed; she doesn't complain about the bed, or the bedroom; she only complains about the bugs that keep her from sleeping.

But the new maid, they say, has desirable traits: she is clean, she is honest, and she works hard. All things considered, they are pleased.

They: Senhor Isidoro, Dona Débora, and their two sons— Alberto and Júlio. The consensus of opinion is that the new maid is very good, indeed. Gertrudes. A country woman of German descent; a giant of a woman. Quiet, hard-working. From work to bed, from bed to work. (There was no way they could imagine what was in store for them.)

One morning—two months after Gertrudes' arrival—the husband and the wife woke up with a feeling of asphyxiation. The windows were shut (it was winter), but even during the cold months, they always left their bedroom door open, in case the children called out in the night, and also to ensure that there was enough ventilation in their room. Dona Débora suffered from asthmatic bronchitis.

That morning, however, they noticed that the door was obstructed by a large mass of indistinct contours. Turning on the light, Dona Débora jumped out of bed and went to investigate.

The door was blocked by a foot. What she saw was the callous sole of a big foot. Alarmed, she called her husband: Isidoro! Isidoro! Come and see what we've got here at the door. It's a foot, Isidoro! I think it's Gertrudes' foot.

Groggy with sleep, the husband sat up in bed. I don't want this woman here in the bedroom, he muttered, searching for his eyeglasses. Send her right back to the kitchen.

"No, Isidoro." The wife was gasping for breath, already with a wheeze in her chest. "I don't think she'll be able to do that. She has grown huge, Isidoro."

He put on his glasses, got out of bed, and went to the door. He carefully examined the strange object. It's a huge foot, he said, the foot of a white person. Yep, it can only be Gertrudes'.

"And now what?" asked the woman, panic-stricken.

"First of all," the husband said, "we have to get out of here."

He peered through a gap between the foot and the door frame.

"I can't see a thing . . . Gertrudes! Move your foot away, will you?"

A muffled groan came from the distance. Senhor Isidoro listened attentively. I think that her head is in the kitchen, he said. Move closer, woman, and see if you can understand what she's saying.

Cupping her hand around her ear, the wife went near to the door.

"She's saying that she won't take her foot away. That she'll stay here. That she won't go back to her room because the bugs there bother her too much."

"That's outrageous!" shouted Senhor Isidoro, irritated. "Get your foot out of here, did you hear me? Get it out of here!"

A shout came from the adjoining bedroom.

"Mom!"

"It's Júlio," said Dona Débora, panic-stricken again. "It's my little son, my Júlio."

"Mom," Júlio went on, "there's a huge foot here at the door, mom. We can't get out."

"Don't be scared, sonny," said his father.

"I'm not scared," said Júlio. And in fact, he wasn't; he was only ten years old, but very alert and sharp-witted. The other boy, twelve years old, had a quiet temperament.

"It's Gertrudes' foot," said Senhor Isidoro. "But don't be scared, son, Dad will find a solution."

He then turned to his wife:

"One foot in our door, one foot in the children's door, the head in the kitchen. She's occupying the whole house. The legs and the thighs must be blocking the corridor."

"And now what?" asked the wife, growing increasingly more frightened.

Compressing his lips, the husband then looked steadily at his wife. "There's no other way," he said, "we'll have to amputate."

"A toe?" asked the wife, drawing back in alarm.

"At least."

She was horrified.

"But just like this, in cold blood? And the pain?"

"What else can we do? It's either she—or we."

"At least," she sighed, "let her know."

He stood close to the gap in the door:

"Gertrudes!" he shouted in the direction of the kitchen. "Gertrudes! We're going to take some minor precautions. We're going to make a small cut in your foot, can you hear me, so that we can pass through. Then we'll go out and get help, and everything will be all right. Did you hear me?"

There was a groan in reply.

"I wonder if she heard you," remarked Dona Débora.

Senhor Isidoro looked at his watch.

"I don't know. But I can't waste any more time. Let's get down to work."

He went up to the window, broke one of the panes and came back with a large shard of glass.

Have you got any alcohol here? Just a little, she said, and he, shit, now that we need it . . . He asked her to pour it over his hands. Then he climbed on the chair he had asked her to place by the door. He now stood level with the big toe. It's like the bark of a tree, he said, feeling the sole of the foot. There's a huge callous here, as big as the cover of a manhole, right where I was thinking of making an incision.

From the kitchen came a muffled giggle. "Poor thing, she must be ticklish," mumbled Dona Débora.

"There we go now!" shouted the husband.

Darting forward, he then plunged the glass blade into the base of the big toe. A howl shook the house. Blood gushed out and cascaded down the man. The foot began to flail about like a wounded monster.

"Stop it, Isidoro," Dona Débora, horrified, shouted.

"I can't stop now. Now that I've started I can't stop. I'll have to go on the very end."

The screams of Gertrudes turned into a continuous, ghastly ululation. In the adjoining bedroom, Júlio was weeping loudly.

"Stop this, Isidoro!"

"Shut up, woman!"

Cutting deeper into the flesh, Isidoro reached the bone. In order to disjoint the phalanx, he used the post of the table lamp as a crowbar. Finally, the big toe fell down like the severed branch of a tree. A gust of wind swept across the bedroom.

Senhor Isidoro then peered through the opening.

"What can you see?" asked the wife.

"It's just as I thought," he said. "It's a huge body, the whole living-room is filled up with it. The belly is like a mountain. The breasts, two mountains. The house is jam-packed with this woman."

"The poor thing," said his wife. "Don't talk like that, Isidoro."

He was now examining the wound of the amputation.

"It's still bleeding. I'll have to do something about this. Otherwise, it'll be impossible to climb up along this way, it's too slippery."

His eyes scanned the bedroom.

"Is that an electric iron?"

"Yes."

"Plug it in. Let it get really hot, then give it to me."

While waiting for the iron to get hot, Senhor Isidoro reassured the children:

"Relax. Daddy will be right there."

Suddenly he remembered the maid.

"Gertrudes!"

There was no reply. She must have fainted, he concluded. His wife handed him the iron—which was extremely hot—and he applied it to the bloody surface. A smell of roasting meat filled the room. Are you cooking something, Mom? Are you cooking for us? Júlio wanted to know. Poor child, she said, no, not yet, sonny, in a moment, wait for a little while longer, little Júlio, will you?

"It worked," shouted Senhor Isidoro. "I cauterized the wound. The bleeding stopped."

He climbed down.

"Come on, Débora. Climb here, and get out through that opening."

"But I won't be able to," she protested.

"Come on, get going."

But the woman was right. After several attempts, she still couldn't pass through the opening.

"You're a roly-poly of a woman," muttered Senhor Isidoro.

"It's not my fault."

Senhor Isidoro began to assess the situation.

"Okay, here's what we'll do: I'll go through the opening first and get the children—that's our priority now. Then I'll come and get you."

Dona Débora agreed. Senhor Isidoro kissed her, then he hoisted himself up the foot, and with some effort, he succeeded in crossing over the stump of the big toe. The first thing he saw were his tools scattered across the floor of the living room. He had been repairing a chair the night before; feeling sleepy, he had gone to bed without putting the tools away despite his wife's grumbles. Now, with those tools, he felt that he was well equipped to deal with the situation. Picking up the handsaw, he brandished it in the air and shouted:

"See, Débora? See how sometimes it pays to be disorganized?"

Scaling one of Gertrudes's thighs, Senhor Isidoro looked around him. As he had surmised, the body of the servant was virtually occupying the entire house. He began to walk over the mountainous belly, whose fat hung in folds down the woman's flanks. He felt the urge to lift her nightgown and have a peek at her private parts, but he resisted the temptation—it was not the time to be indulging in raunchiness.

The door of Júlio's bedroom was blocked by the other foot. The man climbed it with relative ease—he had become experienced in climbing; besides, there were the golden hairs he could hang on to as he ascended. He examined the groove between the first and the second toes: the filth of months had accumulated there. (Clean, she? Well, so much for that.) He wouldn't be able to get the children out through this passage. This foot, however, seemed smaller than the other, and it didn't completely seal up the door. He figured that if he clipped the nail of the big toe, he would be able to create an opening large enough for the children to get through. He used the handsaw to do this job, and he was successful. Before long, the children came out; no longer scared, Júlio was having great fun sliding down the servant's thighs.

But Senhor Isidoro was worried. There was no way out of the living room; all the openings were blocked. I'll have to dig a tunnel through this arm, he reasoned, so that we can reach the front door.

The children helped him in this work. They used a carpenter's chisel, a lathe, a plane—and of course, the electric iron for cauterization. Gertrudes didn't react to the blows inflicted on her, even though she was alive. Senhor Isidoro supposed that she had fainted (from hunger—it's not going to be easy to feed a body this size, he thought), but he wasn't worried. His only concern was to get out of there as soon as possible in order to seek help. All of a sudden, Júlio burst into tears:

"Poor Gertrudes! She's so kind, and we're hurting her. We brought the poor thing to Porto Alegre just to mistreat her."

Senhor Isidoro stopped what he was doing and took his son in his arms, which were covered with blood.

"No, sonny, that's not so. What we're doing is not just for our own good, but for Gertrudes' good too. We'll have to seek help, can't you see? Besides, we didn't make Gertrudes leave her home. It was she who wanted to come to the city so that she could better her lot in life, make some money, find a boyfriend . . . eat more. If it weren't for us, she would still be in the country, with no chance of getting ahead in life. Now, if she has turned into such a voracious eater, always gorging herself, she's only got herself to blame, right? What happened to her is a punishment. But I'm not mad at her, no, not all. We'll soon be out of here and then we'll get her a doctor."

When Júlio calmed down, they resumed their work, which was becoming increasingly harder to do. Senhor Isidoro had to build a supporting structure similar to the one used in mines. For this purpose, he employed wood taken from the furniture. The tunnel was so long that he also had to install wires for electricity. He digged on and on, and the boys would carry the rubble of flesh away.

It took them about twelve hours to finish the job. In the evening they reached the forearm, they bored a hole through the skin, and they jumped out onto the palm of the hand. When they spread the fingers apart, they found themselves at the front door. The exit!

Afterward they freed Dona Débora, and then they started to hug each other, and they laughed, and they kept recounting the story to each other zillions of times.

This is the story that they tell.

I have a different story to tell. I'm a servant, a farm girl from the interior, but I know how to read and write, and I know how to tell stories. The story that I'm going to tell is about four bugs that kept roaming over my body—stinging me, biting me, drawing blood from me. Four bugs that felt very much at home as they inhabited a friendly earth. But they'll find out, these four bugs, when the earth begins to tremble. They'll find out what kind of stories this tremulous earth has to tell them.

The Dwarf in the Television Set [1979]

The Prophets of Benjamin Bok

THE PROPHETS DIDN'T INCARNATE THEMSELVES in Benjamin Bok all at once. At first, it wasn't even a whole prophet that took control of him. Parts of a prophet, more likely. An eye, a finger. Paulina, Benjamin's wife, was later to recall the strange dilation of a pupil, the convulsive tremor of the thumb of his left hand. But Benjamin Bok, a small, thin man with a bald head and a hooked nose, a very ugly man—and to make matters worse, going through a mid-life crisis—and afflicted with a gastric ulcer—Benjamin Bok, poor Benjamin Bok, was regarded—in fact, had always been regarded, even during his childhood—as having a nervous disposition. His parents, in a constant state of alarm, had been overprotective toward him, partly because he was an only child, but mostly because he was so nervous, The boy didn't eat well, he slept restlessly, he had nightmares. His parents kept taking him from doctor to doctor. Leave the boy alone, the doctors would tell them, and he'll get better. But Benjamin's parents didn't leave him alone until he married. And even so, they never ceased to remind Paulina that Benjamin needed to be looked after.

Thus, knowing about her husband's nervous disposition, Paulina didn't attach much importance to what—as she later came to realize—could be interpreted as premonitory signs, and she remained unconcerned even when Benjamin Bok began to intersperse Hebrew words in conversation (which he would do in an odd, raucous voice, a voice that wasn't his). Paulina didn't question her husband about this matter, but had she done so, she would have found out that he *had never learned Hebrew*. Benjamin's parents, assimilated Jews, had never made an issue of it despite the fact that the boy had always enjoyed reading the Bible.

One day Benjamin flew into a tantrum. He kicked a small coffee table to pieces—right in front of his children, two girls aged eight and ten. Paulina became furious. But she still didn't realize what was happening to her husband.

Finally, it was Benjamin himself who became aware of his situation during a social gathering of co-workers in a *churrascaria.*

Benjamin was an accountant (in reality, something like a manager) in an investment company owned by Gregório, a childhood friend. Gregório, a burly, expansive man, liked to give parties; he wouldn't let the end of the year pass without taking all his employees to a *churrascaria* for a Brazilian-style barbecue.

While Gregório was gabbing away, Benjamin, seated beside him, had his eyes fixed on the remainders of the barbecued meat strewn across the table.

"Dry bones," he cried out suddenly.

Gregório stopped talking, and everybody turned to Benjamin. Dry bones, he repeated, like an automaton. What the hell, Benjamin? said Gregório. Why have you interrupted me like this? And what's the big idea, this dry bones crap?

Benjamin mumbled an apology, and the incident was soon forgotten. But it wasn't him who had said that, of this he was sure; the voice wasn't his. At home, already in bed, it occurred to him that *Dry bones, I heard the word of the Lord . . .* was one of Ezekiel's prophecies. The prophet had spoken through Benjamin's mouth, right there in the *churrascaria.*

Benjamin was a malcontent. He couldn't resign himself to being a mere employee, but he had no desire to become a boss. He was always disparaging the government, but he didn't think much of private enterprise either. He had the reputation of being an oddball, so nobody in the office was surprised at the oddity of his behavior in the *churrascaria.* But everybody commented on that dry bones incident. It didn't occur to anybody to connect those words with Ezekiel's prophecy.

Days later, Benjamin Bok went into Gregório's office. Without a word, he took a Magic Marker out of his pocket and proceeded to trace Hebrew letters on the newly painted wall. Flabbergasted, Gregório looked on.

"But what the hell are you doing?" he bellowed at last.

Benjamin then turned to Gregório and stared at him.

"You've been weighed in the balances and found wanting," he then said.

"Weighed in the balances? Found wanting?" Gregório was puzzled. He didn't know that he had just heard the prophet Daniel speaking, and that Benjamin, as he sat on the floor amidst the large vases that decorated the office, was in fact in the lions' den.

Gregório asked Paulina to come to his office for a private talk. Benjamin is bonkers, he said without beating around the bush, we'll have to commit him to a hospital, there's no other way. Breaking into tears, Paulina said that she recognized that her husband wasn't well, but a hospital would be the end of him. Besides, perhaps the whole thing was due to exhaustion. Benjamin works too hard, she said in a tone of voice in which Gregório detected a clear accusation. Subdued, and somewhat remorseful, he conceded that perhaps it wasn't a case for a mental institution.

"But," he was quick to add, "something has to be done. I can no longer put up with this situation, Paulina. The firm is buzzing with gossip. I become discredited, you must understand."

Paulina was again in tears: Ah, Gregório, if you knew what I've been going through, she sobbed. I can well imagine, he said, but so what, Paulina? Let's get down to the nitty-gritty: what's the problem? what's the solution? I haven't gotten all day. We already know what the problem is, so let's tackle the solution.

After considering various solutions, they opted for the one that seemed the most practical, at least for the time being. Gregório would give Benjamin time off for a vacation. Paulina was to take her husband to a seaside resort in the state of Santa Catarina.

At first Benjamin didn't want to hear about a vacation, much less about going to the beach. I get nervous having nothing to do, he said. Besides, I dislike beaches, I'm allergic to sand.

Gregório then intervened and threatened to make an issue of it— he would even fire Benjamin if it came to that. Reluctantly, Benjamin acquiesced. They left the children with Paulina's mother and went to the seashore.

The hotel where they stayed was nearly empty, for it was the off-season.

During the first few days Benjamin seemed to be getting better. He would rise early in the morning, do calisthenics, have breakfast, then read for a while—mostly the Bible, in which he was again very interested. At ten o'clock in the morning they would go down to the beach and stroll among the rare vacationists. In a rather talkative mood, Benjamin would reminisce about his childhood and recall funny incidents that had occurred during their engagement. The sea air can do wonders! Paulina whispered into the mouthpiece when she phoned Gregório to keep him posted.

On the days that followed, however, Benjamin was again in a state of perturbation. He had become very quiet; he slept restlessly. In his sleep he mumbled incomprehensible things. One night he leaped out of bed screaming: Be gone, you wretch! Leave me alone! Paulina had to shake him awake. He was beside himself.

Paulina didn't know what to do. She was afraid of an unpleasant scene at the hotel; she considered returning to Porto Alegre, but she didn't dare to take any steps without first consulting Gregório. She phoned him.

"I don't want Benjamin here, not in the condition he is in!"

shouted Gregório. "He is to stay there until he gets better. Don't bring this nut here, I already have plenty of other worries."

Paulina returned to the bedroom. In the semidarkness, with the shutters closed to keep the heat out, Benjamin was lying motionless in bed. Paulina went up to him.

"He wants me to return to Porto Alegre," groaned Benjamin. "He wants me to announce that the days of the firm are numbered. Because of Gregório's, and other people's, inequities."

"He, who?" asked Paulina.

"You know who." He pointed to the ceiling. "Him. He won't leave me alone."

"Perhaps we'd better go home," said Paulina, trying hard not to cry. Benjamin leaped to his feet:

"No!" he shouted. "I don't want to. I don't want to go back! I don't want to prophetize! I want to stay here, sunbathing!"

He gripped his wife's hand: "Why can't I be like everybody else, Paulina? Why can't I lead a normal life?"

Weeping, they hugged each other. Paulina then helped him back to bed, and then she, too, lay down. She fell asleep. When she woke up, it was already night. Benjamin was not in bed.

"Benjamin!"

She made a dash for the bathroom: He wasn't there either. Seized by a sudden foreboding, she opened the door to the terrace.

A figure was running down the moonlit beach. It was Benjamin. At times he would stop to gaze at the sea; a moment later, he was running again, at times in one direction, at times in another, as if not knowing where to go.

Paulina knew what he was searching for. The fish. The prophet Jonah was searching for the gigantic fish that would swallow him and take him to his destination.

Benjamin began to take off his clothes. Naked, he then proceeded to advance toward the sea.

Tearing down the stairs, Paulina ran to the beach, which was only a short distance away from the hotel.

"Benjamin! Don't, for God's sake, don't!"

He was standing still, with the water waist high. She entered the sea and tried to lead him away, but he kept resisting, and finally he gave her a shove; she fell, and a wave dragged her away from him. At that moment the hotel staff arrived on the scene. With great effort they managed to take Benjamin back to his room.

A doctor came and gave him an injection. Shortly afterward, he was asleep.

Next morning Benjamin couldn't remember a thing. But he seemed fine, although tired and depressed.

They spent a few more days at the seashore, with Benjamin getting increasingly better. Paulina was convinced that he was cured. Maybe it was the dip in the sea, she thought. Or maybe it was the injection.

They returned to Porto Alegre. I feel great now, Benjamin would say again and again. He could hardly know that the prophets were readying themselves for a new attack.

Gregório had a partner—Alberto, the son of old Samuel, the firm's founder, now deceased. Alberto, a shy, absent-minded man, had a degree in economics, but gardening was his passion. His dream was to develop a new variety of begonia, which he would name after himself. Before dying, old Samuel had asked Gregório, whom he had promoted from manager to partner, to look after his son. Which Gregório did for several years, but with growing impatience. Prodded by his wife, ambitious like him, Gregório started to devise a plan to rid himself of his partner.

Benjamin, who suspected that something was afoot, had his suspicions confirmed when he overheard, by chance, a conversation that Gregório had over the telephone. It was a long-distance call from São Paulo, where Gregório had a mysterious informant who would tip him off about such things as investment opportunities, new regulations still in draft form, imminent bankruptcies. Then a few days later, Benjamin saw Gregório in conversation with Alberto. He was trying to persuade his partner to trade his interest in the company for shares in business enterprises in São Paulo:

"Your profits will be much higher, Alberto. You won't have to work anymore, you'll be able to live on the returns of your investments. You'll be able to spend the rest of your life puttering around in your vegetable garden."

"Flower garden," corrected Alberto.

"You bet, in your flower garden. So? What do you think? Wouldn't it be great?"

Benjamin was outraged. Gregório knew very well that the sharp rise in value of those shares was only temporary: the market was jittery, unstable. Poor Alberto was being lured into a trap.

But it was really none of his business, Benjamin thought to himself. Besides, it was all one to him whether he had one boss, or two bosses; it really made no difference to him whether he had to work for Gregório or for Alberto.

He went back to his office and closed the door. Before reaching his desk, he stopped: He was feeling dizzy. It was starting all over again—that thing with the prophets. With his eyes closed, his teeth clenched, his face congested, he stood there motionless for a few minutes. He then opened his eyes and made for the door, but before he had time to open it, he had to stand still again. The same weird sensation was now returning, but with greater intensity.

Two prophets. Two prophets were trying to gain control over him at the same time. Two fierce prophets Elijah and Amos—were fighting and jostling each other in a scramble for what little space there was inside poor Benjamin Bok. They were scrimmaging inside his chest, inside his belly, trampling his entrails with their sandaled feet, their shouts resonating in his skull. At last, having apparently reached a settlement, they literally pushed Benjamin out. He went staggering down the carpeted corridor, and he opened the door of Gregório's office:

"You accursed man!" he shouted. "You want to seize your partner's share of the business just like King Ahab seized the vineyard of his subject Naboth!"

(It was Elijah speaking.)

"Woe to those who tread on the heads of the poor," he went on. "Woe to those who are unfair to the meek! Woe to those who falsify the balances by deceit! Woe to those who sleep in beds of ivory!"

(It was Amos speaking.)

Flabbergasted, Gregório watched him. Benjamin then started to sputter some garbled words. Inside him, they were fighting again, the two prophets. Finally, Elijah shouted:

"I'll say no more. I'm leaving now. I want my chariot of fire so that I can climb up to heaven!"

Gregório made a dash for the phone and dialed the number of a psychiatric clinic. An ambulance came. Benjamin didn't want to go, and he started fighting with the orderlies. Then all of a sudden he calmed down, and with docility, he let himself be led away. Had he convinced himself that the ambulance was the chariot of fire?

At the psychiatric clinic, Benjamin got to know the man who received the Holy Spirit.

"No, it's not a dove at all. It's more like a butterfly. It enters me through my right nostril and then it keeps flitting about inside my head. It's terrible."

He also got to know the woman in whom Buddha had once incarnated himself: "Just imagine my suffering—me, skinny like this, with that enormous roly-poly inside me."

And there was the mulatto upon whom saints were in the habit of descending; and there was the student who received Zeus. Everybody suffered. Everybody—except for a bearded, long-haired man, who seemed tranquil. He was not possessed—he *was* Jesus Christ. I do envy him, the man who received the Holy Spirit would say with a sigh. I'm afraid I've been allotted the very worst of the Holy Trinity. I don't know what God the Father is like, but he can't possibly be as jittery as this butterfly.

Benjamin, too, envied Jesus Christ—the limpidity of that gaze, the splendor of that face. If only I could be like him, he would say. He would do anything to be able to rid himself of the prophets. As a matter of fact, the worst part of the whole experience was the expectancy, for once the prophets took possession of him and started speaking through his mouth, he no longer suffered; he became nothing but an empty carcass—a kind of armor that the spirits utilized.

One day he told Jesus Christ that he envied him.

"If your intention is to take my place," said the mental patient, smiling all the time, "desist from entertaining any such notion. There is one and only Son of God—me."

"No, that's not what I meant, you misunderstood me," explained Benjamin. "All I want is to rid myself of these prophets."

"The first step," the other man went on, "is for you to become a Christian. I could even make an apostle out of you, there are openings for apostles. Sell everything you own, distribute the money among the poor, and follow me. Together, we'll then traverse the roads of the Earth, leading men to their salvation."

He took a scrap of paper and a pencil stub out of his pocket.

"Let's make an inventory. What do you own? A car? A house? Clothes?"

No, none of that had anything to do with what Benjamin had wanted to say. Nobody understood him, not even his psychiatrist, a young man named Isaiah. The coincidence of this name didn't escape the notice of Benjamin. Nor of the doctor, for that matter. Deep down, the doctor would say to Benjamin, what you fear is the prophet that I represent. What you're afraid of, Benjamin, is that I, the prophet Isaiah, will start fighting with your prophets.

Benjamin didn't believe in any of it, but he wasn't one to question the opinion of a doctor with postgraduate work in the United States. So, he would listen to the psychiatrist in silence; when it was time for occupational therapy, he would carve little wooden horses; and when it was time for recreation, he would compete in a ping-pong tournament. And he would take his medicine conscientiously. The worst of it was that the drugs gave him an allergy—a skin disease that quickly ulcerated. Here I am in the same condition as Job's, he thought, alarmed, but upon remembering that Job was not a prophet, he sighed, relieved.

Upon being discharged from the hospital, Benjamin found another job. For many years he led a tranquil life. That prophet thing seemed definitively over.

Then one day he disappeared.

Full of despair, Paulina notified the police. She then went to every single hospital in town—including the mental hospitals—and she ran ads in the newspapers, and put notices on the radio. She even went to the morgue. With revulsion and horror, she looked at the corpses that a sinister-looking attendant had taken out of the freezer. Luckily, Benjamin was not among them. But he was nowhere to be found.

Years later, the mailman delivered a yellow envelope to Paulina—mailed in Rio, but obviously originating from a foreign country. It contained nothing but a picture—a snapshot, badly out of focus, showing a smiling and somewhat fatter Benjamin Bok, in a safari outfit complete with a cork hat similar to the one the explorer Livingstone used to wear. He was sitting on a folding chair, in a barren plain. Beside him, lying on the ground, a huge lion. Standing somewhat farther away, a little black boy looked on curiously. And there was nothing else. No letter, not even a dedication on the back of the picture.

However, it didn't take long for Paulina to deduce the meaning of the message. At first she thought of Daniel in the lions' den, but Daniel had already had his turn. No, what was represented there was a version of Isaiah's prophecy: *the lion will lie with the sheep, and a child will lead them.*

Benjamin Bok had finally found his peace.

Ah, Mommy Dear

FOR THE FIRST TIME NOW I'm writing *and* telling you the truth. All my other letters, Mother, were written at the whim of illusions by this poor fool who happens to be your daughter. How sad it is! How could this have happened to me, that's what I have been asking myself, and that's what I'm now asking you and Dad. Lately I've been thinking a lot about both of you. I miss you so badly. How painful it is.

I see myself as a little girl, with a ribbon tied to my hair, and you and Dad are taking me to a matinee. Remember? It was a western movie. Everybody in the movie theater was rooting for the good guy, but I kept cheering the Indians on. (By the way, wasn't this already an early sign of something wrong? Shouldn't you and Dad have taken some precautions? I don't know. Besides, knowing won't do any good.)

I see myself in high school, and then in college. Now I wish I had never studied Social Sciences. I wish I had never studied anything. Knowledge brought me nothing but misfortune. If I hadn't gone to college, if I hadn't majored in Anthropology, I would never have met this husband of mine, this Peter. This bastard.

I can imagine the look on your faces as you read this. I can imagine you and Dad wondering, how can she say such a thing about her own husband? But I do say it, three times. Damn him. Damn him. Damn him. For now I know who he is. During my college days I didn't know the first thing about him. I, a student fascinated by Anthropology. He, a visiting professor—of Anthropology. It was bound to happen: He kept gazing at me, I kept gazing at him. We went out for dinner and with great pride he told me that he had Indian—Cheyenne—blood (and he as blond as they come, the devil!). I then told him about those western movies, and my passion for Indians. Assuming an expression of sorrow (he was so good at pretending, the bastard) he said that the American Indians were no longer what they once were, that it was only the Brazilian Indians that still preserved the purity of the primitive man.

The primitive man. I should have taken notice of those words, Mother. But I didn't: I was in love, all I wanted was to marry him, and you well remember my happiness when we became engaged. I, too, remember your pleasure at our engagement, and I don't blame you. A young American professor, intelligent, handsome, charming—how could you not have liked him, Mother. You and Dad were bursting with pride, you had to tell everybody about it, and you gave us a beautiful wedding party. It's all perfectly understandable. When Peter announced that we were going to live in the jungle, near a settlement of half-civilized Indians, you and Dad were disappointed, but you said at that time—and I understand your reasons for saying so—that a wife was supposed to follow her husband, as the Bible says. So, I packed the suitcases and went with him; and ever since, everything you know about me has been through letters, right? I always wrote that everything was fine; that Peter's research was progressing well; that I was happy looking after our house—modest but comfortable, the best house in the region. That's what I would say in my letters, and it's painful for me to confess now everything I told you was a lie, Mother. What I wrote to you had—has—nothing to do with reality, and that's why I never wanted you and Dad to come and visit us. By way of excuse, I would say that Peter had to concentrate on his work. A lie. I didn't want you and Dad to see the kind of life we were living here.

At first everything was fine. We settled in our house—an old wooden house that had been built on the edge of the jungle, not far from the Indian settlement. Peter always said that he felt at home here, that it was the kind of life he had always wanted for himself: authentic, rough, primitive, and in the midst of nature. I missed not having a few things—electricity, mostly, and the movies—but I tried to look cheerful. Every morning Peter left for the Indian settlement. I stayed home, cooking, and cleaning, and washing our clothes. But so far, so good.

Then a month after our arrival, Peter—who until then had always gone about in a suit and a tie started to wear some tattered old shorts and he no longer wore a shirt. This struck me as odd, but then it *was* hot. And he also insisted that I wear only a minimal amount of clothes. I thought it indecorous for a young woman alone in the jungle to be scantily dressed, but in order not to annoy him—and yet that's when I should have nipped this idea of his in the bud—I went along with him.

The following week he shows up wearing nothing but a *tanga*, you know, the G-string worn by the Brazilian Indians.

Yes, Mother. A *tanga* fashioned from the fur of some animal (a small ocelot, I think it was), tied to his waist with a liana. I'm returning to a primitive way of life, he announced with a smile that made my blood freeze. And from then on, it has been one thing after another.

He wrenched out all the floorboards in the house, saying that he wanted to feel the earth underneath his feet. He then started to sleep on the dirt floor. Before long, the house was full of wild growth;

I cooked (while I still could, as you'll soon see) amid the creepers and the bromeliads. And the whole place was just crawling with all kinds of creatures—ants, beetles, geckos; once I even killed a snake, Mother! I, who had always been scared to death of these creatures, had the guts to kill a snake that had started to climb up my leg while I was answering a call of nature (in the bushes, mind you, for we had no toilet anymore).

Next, he told me to stop cooking. We're going to feed ourselves, he announced, the way the primitive do: We'll eat only what we can kill ourselves.

That's how it went: He would come home with, say, a piglet. He would let go of the animal, which would then run all over the place, knocking down the few things that I managed to keep tidy. With Peter in hot pursuit. Holding a knife between his teeth, he would chase it, his eyes glittering. Suddenly, he would pounce on the animal. With a frightful scream, he would decapitate the pig and tear away bloody chunks of meat, which he then proceeded to eat—raw! And he made me eat it too. At first I wouldn't, with the excuse that I had an upset stomach. But it was impossible to resist hunger. And so it was raw piglet, and raw fish, and raw kid goat—and once we even ate a monkey, which he had killed in the jungle. We drank water from the river, and that's where we bathed too—or rather, I did, because he would rather go dirty. He looked ghastly: a profusion of matted hair and beard, and those eyes of his—they were like burning coals. He stopped going to the settlement of the Indians, who were afraid of him. He would climb up a tree, where he would remain, scratching himself until it was time to go hunting, or time to raid the granges in the vicinity. As a matter of fact, the grange owners were very kind; they didn't take action against him, they always offered to help me, and they mailed my letters to you.

Why haven't I told you any of this before? I don't know. Perhaps because I didn't want to alarm you. And also because—I admit—I

was hoping that Peter would change, that he would become a civi-
lized human being again.

Now, however, I no longer entertain any such hope. And I live in
fear.

It's that he started looking at me in this weird way, Mother. He
keeps looking at me, and he keeps laughing, and he keeps saying
that in the times of the cannibals, that's when they had it good.

Good Night, Love

NOT MANY PEOPLE KNOW where my store is located. Its name—
The Hamper—does not figure in any newspaper advertisement, not
even in a modest one. No jingle sings its praises over the radio. It is
not listed in the Yellow Pages.

Besides, it is not located on a street downtown. If you want to
shop at The Hamper, you'll have to walk along the narrow streets of
the Lower City. After a long walk, you'll come to a little old house
painted in dark blue, with a door and a window at the front, and a
sign showing the article that gave the store its name: a hamper.
After entering through the narrow front door, after walking on the
worn-out tiled floor, after scrutinizing the dimly lit interior, you will
finally see—amid the boxes of handkerchiefs and of bead necklaces,
amid the lingerie articles and the statuettes of shepherdesses, amid
the table lamps, the picture frames, and the clay pots—the shop-
keeper. A tall, middle-aged man, greying hair plastered on the skull,
close-shaven face, shirt buttoned at the throat, hands resting on the
counter—that's me. Dry-eyed, thin-lipped—that's me.

Contrary to what all appearances and derisive smiles might indicate, I say that I am happy here. I like this street, I like this store, I
like these objects that surround me. No sum of money could pay for
the pleasure I feel looking at them. If I had a choice, not one of
these articles would be for sale. But I have to eat. And so does my

wife. And so do my three children—the twins, and the baby of the family. If this weren't the case, ah, I would keep all the articles in the store for myself. Particularly the little wool animals.

They are made by a diminutive blind woman who lives in the Passo das Pedras district. Once a week I take a bus to her house. The blind woman (she is very old, she must be in her eighties) is already waiting with the articles I had ordered: half a dozen lion cubs, half a dozen teddy bears (three white, and three brown), half a dozen kittens. I don't care too much for the kittens, but I would never say so to the blind woman: in my dealings with her I use few but always courteous words. I receive the little animals, still warm, from her wrinkled hands, I pay her, and I take my leave. Upon returning to the store, I place the toy animals on a shelf somewhat out of sight, for the general assumption is that the store carries them, and then I go back to my usual pose—hands on the counter, eyes pinned on the front door. Waiting—albeit with a feeling of ambivalence—for the customers to come. Actually, there aren't many of them. Hardly anyone ever shops at The Hamper.

She, however, came. Ah, she couldn't help coming: always persistent, my ex-wife is. She came at about ten o'clock on a Monday morning. I remember the time very well because I'm in the habit of closing the store in the middle of the morning to go to the bathroom, which is in the back part of the house. So there I was, peeing, when I heard a strange noise, a rasping sound it was. Cursing, I buttoned up my fly and returned to the store proper to find her at the front door, scratching the pane with her car key.

Had she arrived later in the morning, she wouldn't have found me. I would be at the bar around the corner, having lunch: a cheese and salami sandwich, and a beer—a frugal meal as usual, but I like to linger over my meals. And after lunch, I'm in the habit of going for a walk in the neighborhood.

What if she had come at seven o'clock in the evening? She

wouldn't have found me, either. By that time I'm already home, watching television.

But it was ten in the morning when she came, and so she found me in the store.

There she was, watching me. With the usual expression in her eyes: a touch of sadness mingled with a great deal of impudence. Deep down, there had always been something impudent about her. Impudence and good looks—a combination that in the end made her walk out on me. And ever since, it's been cheese and salami sandwiches, beer. Television. Little wool animals.

I opened the door. She came in smiling. Very smartly dressed: her husband is rich. Good morning, she said, and I: Good morning. How are you? she asked. Fine, I replied, and how are you? She said that she was fine and then inquired after my family—I said that they were fine, but my mother hadn't been feeling well. (She and my mother were very fond of each other. Our divorce was a great disappointment to the old lady.) But it's nothing serious, I added, it's just some kind of rheumatism. Ah, well, she mumbled.

We stood in silence for a moment. In my mind, an image began to form: a round slice of salami. . . . But no, I should be looking at her. She was my wife once. For reasons of her own, she walked out on me. Now that she was paying me a visit, it was my duty to be pleasant. You look very elegant, I said, and she: Thank you, Jorge, it's nice of you to say so. She looked around: A nice setup you've got here. Then opening her purse, she took out a cigarette case:

"Do you smoke?"

"Thanks, but no," I said. "I have bronchitis and I'd rather not smoke. Sure, go ahead," I said.

She lit a cigarette, looked around her, and took an ashtray off the shelf.

"No, not that one!" I shouted. Then, lowering my voice, I explained that the ashtray was for sale. I then went into my office to look for an ashtray but I couldn't find one. I came back with a glass: "Use this as an ashtray, will you?"

She stood smoking, and she put the ash into the glass. We were not looking at each other, but once in a while we could cast surreptitious, sidelong glances at each other. All of a sudden, she said: "It was good with us, wasn't it, Jorge?"

We were both standing, I with my hands resting on the counter. She placed her left hand on my left hand.

For a moment I stood considering that hand. A hand treated with great care, the skin smooth even though she was no longer young—pushing forty, she was. The fingers were full of rings (three on the forefinger, two on the middle finger, and so on), which glittered in the semidarkness of The Hamper. And the fingernails were painted in some exotic sanguinous color.

I didn't withdraw my hand. Nor did I say anything. She kept looking at me, I kept looking at her, and that was all.

She sighed and started to walk about the store. Then pointing to a vase:

"How much does that thing cost?"

That thing, I felt like saying, is a vase. Not an exceptionally good vase, not a masterpiece, but still a good vase, bought from a potter that will be famous one day. Ninety, I said. Let me see it, she asked.

I took the vase from the shelf, and much to my displeasure, I saw that it was covered with a fine layer of dust—a disaster, my cleaning lady. Taking the vase, she examined it carefully, and with a pretense of know-how, tapped it with a fingernail. It's no great shakes, she said, returning the vase to its place. She sighed again. She then examined, but without touching, a porcelain elephant. And an enameled plate.

It was good with us, Jorge. True: inordinately good. Good on her uncle's farm; good on the backseat of my father's car; good on the beach; always good. Even during our marriage, it was good. But even so, one day she took off.

"I'd like to see that necklace over there."

I handed her the necklace, which she proceeded to examine, running her fingers on the beads. She asked me for a mirror. I went to my office, looked for a mirror, and found one. Already with the necklace on, she looked at herself in the mirror, moving her head from side to side. She sighed:

"No. I don't like it."

She then stared at me intensely. And all of a sudden, she began to sing in a weak, trembling voice:

"Good morning, love,

la-ri-la-li-la-la-la-la

good night, love . . . "

It had been our favorite song.

Embarrassed, I averted my eyes. What if somebody were to walk in? She stopped singing and grabbed me by the arm.

"Do you know what I'm talking about, Jorge?"

I did. But I said nothing.

"It's about love, Jorge! Love! Have you ever experienced love?"

She was practically shouting now. Oblivious to the fact that she was on the premises of a commercial establishment.

(Just a dinky little store, true. But I have plans. Dreams. A chain of stores is not utterly unthinkable. I'll have to learn about salesmanship. That's it: salesmanship. Perhaps it would help if I were to take some courses.)

I remained silent. She let go of my arm, and lit a cigarette.

"And this leather handbag, how much is it?"

"Four hundred."

"It's quite ugly."

Nothing suited her. I looked surreptitiously at the watch: almost time to close.

"Do you know that I've left Roberto?"

"So I've heard."

"Well, it's true."

Then pointing with the cigarette:

"And that handbag over there?"

"Five hundred."

"Outrageous."

She wanted to know the price of various other articles. Since she showed no intention of acquiring any of them—which in fact didn't displease me—I said that it was time to close for lunch. She looked at me (with anger and hurt), then stubbed out her cigarette in the glass, and left. Without a word. And slamming the door behind her.

On that day no other customer appeared.

It was not until late in the afternoon that I noticed that one of the wool teddy bears was missing: of the six, only five were left. At first I thought that the blind woman had cheated me: She had charged me for six and given me only five, that's what I thought. But she was much too honest to do such a thing.

And the cleaning woman? Honest, too. Therefore, it could have been only one person.

For a while I sat there, thinking. *It was good, Jorge.* It had, indeed, been good. "Good morning, love. . . . " True. But that's all dead and gone now. Besides, friendship is one thing, business another.

I picked up the phone and spoke to a friend I had in the police. I supplied him with her name and address, and with a brief description. Everything by the book.

I then locked up, went home, had dinner, watched television with my kids, and went to bed at eleven o'clock. As I turned off the light, I thought of her: *It was good, Jorge.* It was, indeed. Good night, love, I murmured before falling asleep.

The Apex of the Pyramid

IT WAS PERHAPS THE SMELL—a mixture of odors. Of earth, of damp sawdust, of sweat—the sweat of men or of exotic animals. It was perhaps the smell. Then perhaps not. The fact is that she was feeling sick there, quite sick. Oh God, she thought, I wish I were home; at this moment, there's nothing else I want as badly.

The man before her, Breno (Breno or Bruno), seemed unaware of her indisposition. He was smiling all the time; a shy smile—shy but mocking; the smile of someone with bad teeth. Those cavities are disgusting, she thought, and then it occurred to her: Is it his teeth that are making me sick? She became annoyed at herself: I shouldn't be posing questions to myself, but to him, after all I am a journalist. She corrected herself: an apprentice. A forty-year-old apprentice— still nothing but an apprentice. She hadn't completed her training in journalism yet.

She opened her handbag, from which she took a pen—a gold fountain pen it was (the eyes of the man glittered, or she imagined that they did)—and a note pad. Let's see, she said, your position is at the base. Yes, said Breno (or Bruno), at the base, that's right, I stand in the middle of the base. You know, they say I'm the strongest. Yes, I can see that, she said. I was the first to be recruited, added the man, proud. *He was the first to be recruited*—she wrote down and then asked: And when was that? Ah, replied the man, a long time ago, about ten years ago.

Ten years ago. What was she doing ten years ago? She was then living in that big mansion in the posh Higienópolis district, and the days fled one after the other. Mornings, her husband, briefcase in hand, would go up to her: I'm off to work now, Selma, have fun. He would then kiss her. She would kiss him back, knowing very well that she wouldn't have any fun—not on that day, nor on any other day for that matter. But her husband was in a hurry to leave, it.

wasn't the moment for complaints. She would take another sip of coffee, sigh, and pick up a magazine.

"It was Redhead who recruited me," the man went on.

She winced. Who, she said, trying to disguise her perturbation. Redhead, Breno (or Bruno) repeated; I don't know his real name, I don't think anybody does. Everybody around here calls him Redhead.

A very short man walked by—a man who looked like a dwarf: he *was* a dwarf. With difficulty, he was carrying a huge stool. He smiled at her and then disappeared from sight. She began to write down *Redhead recr*—but couldn't finish the rest of the sentence, for her pen ran out of ink. I should use a ballpoint pen like everyone else, she thought as she frantically shook the pen; but I'm not like everyone else, so I use a fountain pen and I keep forgetting to fill it with ink. She tried again: yes, it worked, and she finished the sentence— *recruited me*.

Full of animation, Breno (or Bruno), went on:

"Redhead, yep. We were kids then, me thirteen or so, he a bit older, sixteen, I guess. One day he came up to me and said: You know, Bruno . . . "

(Bruno! The name was Bruno. She mustn't forget. Just in case, on a corner of the page, she jotted down: Bruno.)

" . . . that house with the high wall around it? There's something going on there." What? I asked. But Redhead wouldn't say, that's how he was, mysterious. He just laughed and said, come, I'll show you. So I followed him. When we got to the wall, he asked me to crouch down, and then he climbed on my shoulders—and that's how the whole thing, ma'am, our whole enterprise, got started. Redhead was very nimble but I was somewhat clumsy, but he taught me what I had to do so that he wouldn't fall down. It took me a long time to get the hang of it, but I finally learned what I had to do. But, you see, ma'am, I was a bean pole even then, but Redhead was a peewee, he still is, so he still couldn't look over the wall. How much higher do you have to go, Redhead? I asked, a bit fidgety because his ankle boots were hurting my shoulders. At least a meter, he said. He then jumped down, terribly disappointed.

She was writing like mad. I don't want to look at this man, she was thinking, I don't want to look at these things around me. *Jumped down*, she wrote.

A scream. She heard a scream. No, not a scream, it was more like a squeal, an anguished squeal. Oh God, and again she was addressing a question to herself, how did I get myself in this pickle?

She was annoyed at herself: No, I'm not going to give up. I'm not going to let anything frighten me, I'm through with this phase in my life! She forced herself to stop taking notes, she forced herself to raise her head, she forced herself to smile and speak:

"It was then that the others joined in."

"That's right, ma'am," said Bruno (Bruno?). "Redhead then said to me, Bruno (Bruno!), we'll have to get more people, just you is not enough. "Redhead," I said, "I've got several brothers, I could talk to them." "Bruno" (Bruno!), Redhead said, "we'll need five guys altogether: three to form the base, two to stand on the base, and me . . . "

(—*on the apex*, she wrote in advance)

" . . . on top of all you guys. I was pleased as punch, ma'am" (he laughed, Bruno did), "because we happened to be five brothers: the twins, and the rest of us. The only problem was, I didn't know how they would like the idea. . . . But Redhead had no problem winning them over, he told them that everybody would take turns looking over the wall after he did so; after he took a look, he would go down to the base, then another guy would have a chance."

A scream—this time it was. A man's scream, followed by the shriek of an enraged animal. She winced again. The pen was now tracing invisible words on the paper. This time the ink had really run out.

Redhead had the gift of gab, the man was now saying with admiration in his voice. A crackerjack, Redhead was. . . . He talked my brothers into it. But it took us a week of training before we succeeded in forming a pyramid. Redhead blew his cool more than once, he would yell at us, saying we would never learn how to do it. But we did learn. And we were finally able to form a beautiful pyramid.

He wiped his eyes. Holy cow, he mumbled, hard to believe it's been ten years already.

Ten years ago, and it was summertime. Have fun, her husband would say, leaving for work. The maid would come, holding the boy by the hand: We're leaving now, Dona Selma, Serginho is already late for school. Bye, son, and have fun. Fun? the boy would say, peeved. How can I have fun in school? You're so stupid, Mother, you never learn anything!

He would leave, haughty like his father. With a sigh, she would pick up a magazine and head for the swimming pool.

One morning, Bruno (or Breno) was saying, we headed for that house. We hid ourselves in a vacant lot near the house because there was a big black car parked in front of the gate. When the car drove away, Redhead gave us a signal. We ran to the wall and formed a pyramid. Redhead climbed on our backs up to the top. He looked over the wall. Saying nothing, he jumped down and was gone.

A roar. But this must be a lion now! she thought, alarmed. What I've just heard must be a lion, perhaps on the loose. She bit the back of her hand and shook her head—she didn't give a damn whether the man noticed her perturbation. And what did Redhead see there? she asked.

Nothing, said the man. Redhead said there was nothing there.

Redhead lied—was what she should say or write down, but she wasn't going to do either. She was thinking of the red-headed teenager jumping from the top of the wall and landing on the edge of the swimming pool; she was thinking of her alarm, and of his derisive smile, and then of the idea, the fascinating idea that had occurred to her—*and why not?*; she was thinking of his trembling fingers opening her dressing gown . . .

Nowadays, the man was concluding, we all work here, in Redhead's circus. We still do our pyramid act. Except that Redhead no longer performs with us. Now that he owns all of this, he's on top of everything, said the man, with that smile full of rotten teeth.

On top. Redhead on top. She shrieked, she roared, she screamed, she moaned—nobody could hear her: the house was empty, the walls were high and thick. Ten years ago . . .

"Hi, Selma," said a voice behind her.

She turned around: a well-dressed man, an elegant man despite his short stature. It was him, yes, it was the

"Hi, Redhead."

apex of the pyramid.

A Porto Alegre Story

DON'T THINK THAT I'M COMPLAINING, I'm not. I'm just telling the truth, and telling the truth can't hurt anyone. And the truth is that I'm the one who is a native of Porto Alegre; you're the one who feels so proud of this city, but I'm the one who was born here. I was already living in Porto Alegre when you, the haughty son of a wealthy farmer from the southern regions near the Uruguayan border, arrived here. A long time ago, wasn't it? What is now the district of Petrópolis didn't even exist then, and Três Figueiras was nothing but scrubland. There were hardly any streetcars then. . . . Remember the streetcars? Ah, well. And I—I was the humble salesgirl in a notions store, remember? And you—you were the debonair student who would hang out in bohemian cafes until dawn, declaiming your poetry at the top of your voice. You were the rich young man who would come to the store where I worked, bringing me huge bouquets of roses.

WHAT A SCANDAL IT WAS, remember? Tongues wagged on Rua da Praia. All because you insisted on strolling arm in arm with me, all the way from Praça da Alfândega to the Conceição Church. I didn't even enjoy those walks, but you would saunter down the street full of defiance, your head held high—while the ladies and the gentlemen watched us, scandalized. Scandalized, were they? I'll show them, you'd say. You then did something even more outrageous: You rented a house for me in the Menino Deus district. And what a house it was! The old palatial residence of a baron, situated in the middle of a veritable park, with trees, and statues, and a pond full of little red fish. You installed me there because I was, you used to say, your queen; and in fact, I did lead the life of a queen there, with servants, and even a car at my disposal—one of the very first automobiles in Porto Alegre, an Edsel, remember? Your father footed the bill for everything. Your father, a wealthy farm owner, thought that his son was entitled to all the prerogatives of a male, regardless of what people said. Or of how much it cost. He always footed the bill.

And I? Well, I liked you. I truly did. It was because of you that I moved out of my parents' house in the Lower City to live like a courtesan in that mansion that you rented. But the truth is, I was fond of you.

YOUR RELATIVES—wealthy farmers like your father, but farmers turned city dwellers, who lived in the fashionable Moinhos de Vento district—stopped inviting you to their parties. Which only increased your irritation. But you got even with them by renting a house in Moinhos de Vento, in the very stronghold of the enemy. And there you installed us—me and all the servants (except for the cook, whom you fired because you considered my cooking superior to hers). You would drop by very often. You didn't want to live in the house with me because you wanted your freedom, but you did visit me frequently.

Moinhos de Vento . . . a beautiful neighborhood with fine houses. Your relatives were furious; they wouldn't even greet you. If they happened to run into you on the street, they would turn their faces.

All of them, except for your cousin Rosa Maria. She would look at you sideways and wink, naughty girl that she was. . . . You would smile. The two of you exchanged billets-doux. You think I didn't know? I knew. But the truth was, I liked you. And I liked the house in Moinhos de Vento. A paradise.

A paradise that didn't last long . . . You decided that I would have to move out. You liked that house, and you wanted it for yourself, and so I had to go. I moved into a house in Petrópolis. Together with the maid and the chauffeur, who was also a kind of guard. The gardener was dismissed, for the house, relatively modest, had no garden; besides, why have a garden? you rationalized. Gardening is such a demanding job. Although I liked gardens, I said nothing. Because I liked you.

YOU MARRIED YOUR COUSIN Rosa Maria and then you took on a managerial position with her father's business firm. From then on, your visits became increasingly rarer; the life of a businessman is burdened with work, you would say. I would agree, recalling my days at the notions store.

The city continued to develop, and at one point I no longer had a chauffeur because Petrópolis—you informed me enthusiastically—now boasted public transportation worthy of a modern city: there were plenty of streetcars, of buses.

Petrópolis was really a nice neighborhood, but as the years went by, some difficulties arose. Many of your friends—doctors, lawyers, businessmen—had moved into the area; besides, the ballet school that your daughters—two charming little girls—attended, was also located in Petrópolis. . . . So you decided that I would have to move away.

You sent me to Três Figueiras, an area that, although no longer scrubland, was but thinly populated. You installed me in a nice little house. A wooden house, but very nice. The rain leaked in but I wasn't going to bother you with such minor problems. It wouldn't be fair, when you hardly ever showed up. And the house wasn't ugly. I whiled away my time doing the domestic chores—I no longer had a servant. (Why have a servant in such a small house? you asked, and you were right. Truly, you were right.)

A FEW YEARS LATER—I can recall the time very well because by then I was already taking in sewing to make ends meet—the first elegant houses began to appear in Três Figueiras. Beautiful houses they were, with ornate masonry on the façades. . . . You then thought that I should move to Garden City. It's a bit far from here, you said, and you were right; but the place is a real garden, you said, the garden that you've been missing so much. It's true that the house had no running water or electricity; however, I didn't want to bother you about this matter. You were going through a phase of existential anguish. What good is money? you would ask me. We were both sixty years old then. What's the meaning of life?—your eyes brimming with tears. And I, almost toothless, only thought of a new set of teeth—but I never dared ask you for anything.

You then told me to move away from Garden City. The neighborhood was becoming quite well known, someone might see you there. You made me live in some sort of houseboat, which was moored in the Guaiba River—quite a deserted place it was. Interesting, that houseboat. More boat than house—the house was nothing but a simple wooden cabin covered with canvas.

Shaken by the winter storms, I would wait for you. There was a year when you came only once, on your birthday. You were feeling very depressed: Rosa Maria had died, your daughters didn't want to have anything to do with you, they were only interested in their European trips. At that time you were searching for the answers to life's big questions in Zen Buddhism. You said that we should plunge ourselves into nothingness. Watching the water seeping into the boat, I agreed with you.

ONE DAY I RECEIVED A NOTE FROM YOU—delivered by your chauffeur, or rather, our old chauffeur. . . . In a very quavering handwriting, you stated that life no longer held any meaning for you; that I should cut the boat's moorings and let the currents of the Guaiba River carry me at the whim of fate.

For the first time ever, I considered disobeying you. You see, the fact is, I like my hometown an awful lot; I like this Porto Alegre of mine, which I can only see from the distance and which I can hardly recognize. I remember that I shouted: No! I won't forsake my city! And then I decided that I would recall our story in a letter to you, and ask you to unsay what you ordered me to do.

I hope you'll get this letter. You see, it's that I'm writing already in the middle of the river—and it's the first time ever that I'll be sending a letter in a bottle tossed into the water. However, I do hope that you'll get it, and that it will find you in good health, together with your nearest and dearest, in this beautiful city of Porto Alegre.

The Noises in the Attic

IT IS ALREADY ELEVEN O'CLOCK in the evening, but they are unable to fall asleep. They are tired—both of them work very hard, he driving a taxi, she looking after the house—but they are unable to fall asleep. Lying side by side, they have their eyes fixed on the small spot of light that the street lamp below their window projects on the ceiling.

It is hot, they are perspiring, and yet all the windows are closed. They don't dare open them; there have been too many robberies in the neighborhood, too many murders. So they swelter, but better safe than sorry. True, the window in their bedroom doesn't close properly; it is boarded up for greater security, but there is a crack through which the light from the street sneaks in. But only this light, for they are awake, and while they are awake, nothing else will enter through the window.

ELEVEN FIFTEEN, ELEVEN-THIRTY—and they cannot sleep. They fidget, restless, and their sweaty bodies touch lightly. It is a familiar sensation—they have been married for a year, already—but at times it still feels strange to be together. Strangest of all, however, are the darkness and the noises that populate the darkness.

The whole house creaks. It is a small, crooked house, badly built. Since they couldn't afford the rent elsewhere, they had no choice but to move to this housing project, where they don't know any-one—and have no desire to do so. They don't want to get involved with the criminal types that infest the neighborhood.

Some of the noises in the house are already familiar to them: the creak of the kitchen door, the snap of the wardrobe, the drip of the tap. But there are always new and unsuspected noises; new insects, new pests keep arriving, despite all the poisons to destroy them.

It is past midnight. She dozed off, she had a brief nightmare, she woke up with a start; she has now calmed herself, and she lies star-ing at the ceiling. He hasn't had a wink of sleep yet. He, too, lies staring at the ceiling, at the same luminous spot.

It is then that the noises in the attic start.

Taken by surprise, she shudders with fear. It is the first time that she has heard noises coming from the attic, until now silent. This is something new. New and unpleasant. Something that does not bode well.

Reaching out a trembling hand, she touches her husband's arm; his muscles feel tense. So he, too, has heard the noises; he, too, is on the alert. Which doesn't reassure her at all; quite the opposite. (They are both frightened children: she, on the brink of tears; he, about to transform his fear into fury—but in fact, they don't know what to do; they just wait, their eyes riveted on the ceiling.)

It is not a continuous noise. It stops and starts anew. It could be the noise made by a body that is crawling. An animal? A big animal, then. Bigger than, say, a cat. A dog? But a dog in the attic of a house? No, it can't be a dog. Some animals live in attics; opossums, for in-stance. She, who is from the country, is familiar with opossums. But—and of this she is certain—it is not an opossum that is making this noise.

A man?

No. It is not a man, either. The boards are too thin to bear the weight of a man—especially of a burly man. Perhaps they could bear the weight of a skinny man. Or of a boy. Or of a dwarf.

The noise stops. Minutes trickle away. Maybe this time, she thinks hopefully, it won't start again. She wants to sleep. She is tired. She has to get up early in the morning, and so does her husband. It is a hard life, theirs. Don't they already have enough worries? They don't need this noise.

Out of the corner of her eyes, she watches her husband. She can barely see him in the semidarkness. But she knows that his eyes, like hers, are wide open. He is a nervous man, she is afraid of what he might do if he were suddenly to fly into a rage.

An idea occurs to her. She yawns noisily, in the hope that the sound of a relaxed, easy-going person will scare the intruder away and calm her husband (and herself as well). A prolonged yawn that she ends with gurgles of pleasure to translate her contentment in lying there beside him, in their own bed, in their own house. But her husband does not relax his muscles, and the silence that follows is ominous. A moment later, the noises in the attic start anew.

This time the noises are very loud. As if there were no concern about muffling them. The boards creak. The lamp hanging from the ceiling swings distinctly.

His hand comes out from under the bedsheet. It gropes about the night table for the .22-caliber gun, which he always carries with him in his taxi in the daytime; at night, he keeps it loaded and cocked, and always within reach.

The noise is now continuous. It is not difficult to locate its source: Right at the spot where the ray of light projects itself, the boards rise and fall rhythmically. He raises his arm—the nickel-plated gun glitters for a moment—she lets out a stifled scream; he fires.

The detonation shakes the house. The bedroom is filled with smoke and the acrid smell of gunpowder. They sit up in bed, the two of them, rigid, with their eyes, wide open, fixed on the ceiling. Outside, dogs begin to bark. (But no window will open, this they know for sure. A gunshot is a problem between gunman and victim. A problem for the police to handle.)

Gradually the barking stops. They remain seated, their eyes fixed on the ceiling, the bullet hole clearly visible in the center of the spot of light. The house is now dead silent. Not a single noise can be heard.

She begins to cry softly. Pulling her to him, he then kisses her hair, her eyes, her neck, her breasts. My darling, he murmurs, his trembling hands running over her firm thighs, feeling the slightly coarse down that covers them. No, don't, she murmurs, but he has already made her lie down, and he is already on top of her. No, don't, she murmurs with a moan, but she is already kissing him, and nibbling his ear.

(ON THE FOLLOWING DAYS they will smell the faint but pervasive odor of decomposing flesh. But they won't talk about it over dinner. He will tell her about his day at work, about the traffic jams, and she will complain about the time she wasted waiting to see a doctor at the clinic. But they will say nothing about the smell. They hope that it will vanish—and in fact, within a week or two, only the old, familiar smells will remain in the house—the smell of the food that she cooks, the smell of the plants that she grows in empty tin cans, the smell of the garbage that accumulates in the vacant lot beside their house.

As for the attic—he will never climb up there.)

Five o'clock in the morning. They yawn. One of these nights no human being will be able to take it, he says, and she laughs.

They decide that if they have a son, they will name him Alonso.

At the Figtree Retreat

I ALWAYS THOUGHT THAT IT WAS much too good. Especially the place. The place was . . . was wonderful. Just as the prospectus said: wonderful. Tranquil, full of trees, one of the very few places—according to the advertisement—where you could still hear birds sing. And in fact, during our first visit there, we did hear the birds. And we also ascertained that the houses were indeed solid and beautiful, just as the prospectus stated: solid and beautiful houses in modern style. We saw the lawns, the parks, the ponies, the small lake. We saw the airstrip. We saw the majestic figtree after which the condominium complex was named: the Figtree Retreat.

But what my wife liked most was the security. Throughout the fifty-minute drive back to the city, she enthused over the electrified fences, the outlook towers, the searchlights, the alarm system—and most of all, the security guards. Eight of them: strong, stalwart men—but also friendly and courteous. As a matter of fact, on our first and second visits, we were received by their leader—a gentleman so intelligent and cultured that it immediately occurred to me: *Ah, he probably holds a university degree.* And indeed: In the course of our conversation he mentioned—but just in passing—that he had graduated from law school. Which increased my wife's enthusiasm even more.

SHE HAD BEEN LIVING in fear recently. Our neighborhood had been plagued by a series of violent attacks; door bars and electronically controlled entrances no longer deterred criminals. A day wouldn't go by without the news of someone being robbed or mugged; and when a woman friend of ours was raped by two miscreants, my wife decided—we would have to move to another neighborhood. We would have to search for a safe place to live.

It was then that someone thrust the colorful prospectus under our door. Sometimes I think: had we been living in a building with tighter security, that circular would never have been delivered to our door, and then perhaps . . . But these are idle suppositions. Anyhow, my wife became enchanted with the Figtree Retreat. My children were crazy about the ponies. Besides, I had just received a promotion in my firm. There was a chain of events, and what had started with a prospectus thrust under our door became—just as the advertisement said—a new lifestyle.

WE WEREN'T THE FIRST PEOPLE to buy a residence in the Figtree Retreat. On the contrary: When we returned one week after our first visit, most of the thirty dwelling units had already been sold. The chief guard introduced me to some of the other buyers. I liked them: they were people like me—business managers, lawyers, doctors, two ranchers. All of them came attracted by the information in the prospectus. And almost all of them decided on this place because of the security.

In the course of that week I discovered that the prospectus had been sent out to only a limited number of people. In the business firm where I work, for instance, I was the only person that had received one. My wife attributed the fact to a careful selection of potential residents—which she regarded as yet another reason for being pleased. As for myself, I thought the whole thing was very good. Much too good.

WE MOVED IN. Life in the condo complex was really delightful. The birds were punctual: at seven o'clock in the morning they would start their harmonious concert. The ponies were gentle, the graveled paths were clean. The breeze would stir the trees in the park—one hundred and twelve trees, just as the prospectus had said. Besides, the alarm system was flawless. The guards—always polite, always smiling—would come to our home periodically to make sure that everything was all right. The chief guard was a particularly caring person: He organized parties and competitions, and he concerned himself with our well-being. He compiled a list of all the relatives and friends of the residents—in case of an emergency, he explained with a reassuring smile. Our first month there—just as the prospectus had promised—went like a dream. A real dream.

THEN ONE SUNDAY, quite early in the morning—I remember that the birds hadn't started singing yet—the alarm siren went off. Since it had never sounded before, we were somewhat—just somewhat, not very—startled. But we all knew what we were supposed to do in the circumstances, so in an orderly fashion, we headed for the recreation center by the lake. Most of us still in dressing gowns or pajamas.

The chief guard was already there, flanked by his men, all of them armed with rifles. He invited us to sit down and offered us coffee. Afterward, with profuse apologies for the inconvenience, he explained the reason for holding that meeting: The police had warned him about the presence of criminals in the woods surrounding the Retreat, and so he had decided to ask us not to leave the premises on that Sunday.

"After all," he said in a jocular tone, "it's a beautiful Sunday, and we've got ponies, tennis courts, everything, right here. . . . "

He was indeed a very nice man. Nobody got really upset about the situation.

BUT SOME PEOPLE DID GET UPSET on the following day when the alarm went off again at dawn. Once more we got together in the recreation center, some of us muttering that it was Monday, a workday. Always smiling, the chief guard renewed his apologies, then said that unfortunately we wouldn't be able to leave the complex; the criminals were still at large, hiding in the woods. Dangerous people, they were: among them, two escaped murderers. In reply to the question of an irate owner, a surgeon, the chief guard said that no, we couldn't drive out either, for the bandits might have blocked the narrow road leading to the Retreat.

"In this case, why don't you fellows escort us?" asked the surgeon.

"But then, there would be no one here to look after your families," replied the chief guard, always smiling.

WE WERE DETAINED in our condo complex on that day and on the following day as well. That was when the police surrounded the area: There were dozens of vehicles with armed men, some of them wearing gas masks. We could see them from our windows, and we had to admit that the chief guard was right.

We whiled away the time playing cards, going for a walk, or simply doing nothing. Some people were even enjoying the situation. But not me. It might seem presumptuous to say so now, but I didn't like what was going on at all.

Then on the fourth day an airplane landed on the airstrip. A small jet, it was. We all ran there.

A man alighted and handed a valise to the chief guard. The man looked at us—he struck me as being frightened—and he left through the main gate, practically at a run.

The chief guard signaled us to stay where we were. He then entered the airplane, leaving the door open, which enabled us to see him examining the contents of the valise. After closing it, he came to the door and signaled. The other guards then made a dash for the light aircraft, and they all climbed in. The door closed, the airplane took off, and was soon gone.

We never saw the chief guard and his men again. But I'm sure they must be enjoying all that ransom money they received for our release—a sum large enough for them to built ten other condominium complexes like ours which, incidentally, I always thought was much too good.

The Secret Tourists

THERE WAS A MARRIED COUPLE who were green with envy of their traveling friends—especially of those who took trips abroad. He, a minor clerk in a major company, and she, a schoolteacher, had never been able to save enough money to travel. When there was enough for the installments on the airplane tickets, there wasn't enough for the purchase of American dollars, and vice-versa. Thus. year after year, they ended up staying home. They would economize, they would spend less on clothes, they would always ride the bus, they would eat less—but they still couldn't afford to take a trip abroad. Occasionally they would spend a few days at the seaside, but that was all.

However, so great was their desire to tell their friends about the wonders of Europe that they concocted a plan. Every year, at the end of January, they phoned their friends to say good-bye: They were leaving for the Old World. And indeed, a few days later, postcards from various European cities—Rome, Venice, Florence—began to arrive in the mail; and a month later, the couple was back in town, inviting their friends to see the slides of their trip. And they had such interesting things to tell! They even divided the topics between them: His part was to comment on the hotels, the flights, the money exchange rates, as well as on the picturesque aspects of the trip; hers, to elaborate on the cultural side: the museums, the historical places, the plays that they had seen. Their ten-year-old son had no story of his own to tell, but he would confirm everything, and sigh when his parents said:

"We had such a good time in Florence!"

What their friends were unable to figure out was where the money came from to finance the trip; one of their more indiscreet friends even had the temerity to ask. Smiling mysteriously, the husband and the wife mentioned something about an inheritance and then changed the subject.

Eventually, the truth came to light.

As it turned out, this couple never went on a trip at all. They didn't even leave town. Throughout their one-month vacation, they would lock themselves up in their house. She would study travel brochures about, say, the city of Florence: its history, its museums, its monuments; he, in his small photo lab, would superimpose pictures of themselves on the pictures of Florence, and then make slides of this photomontage. He would also write the postcards, affix used postage stamps on them, then cancel them with a forged rubber stamp. As for the boy, he would memorize the stories told by his parents so that he would be able to confirm them if necessary.

They would only leave the house late at night: the boy, to get some exercise; she, to buy groceries in a distant supermarket; and he, to drop the postcards into the mail boxes of their friends.

THIS PLOY COULD HAVE GONE ON for years and years. It was she who ruined everything. In the course of time she got fed up with having a poor husband, who could only take her on make-believe trips. She fell in love with an airplane pilot, who promised to take her to many highly exotic places. She ended up asking her husband for a divorce.

UPON LEAVING THE LAWYER'S OFFICE, they kissed for the last time.

"The truth is," he said, "I really got a kick out of the whole thing."

"Me too," she said.

"We had such a good time in Florence," he sighed.

"True," she said, with tears in her eyes. And she promised herself never to go to Florence again.

Milton and His Competitor

MILTON HASN'T OPENED HIS STORE YET, but his competitor has already opened his; besides, he is already advertising his wares, he is already having a clearance sale with goods sold at a price below cost. Milton is still in bed with a woman, not his legitimate wife, a woman who is not even beautiful or nice; his competitor is already standing alert behind the counter. Together with his wife—the faithful companion of so many years, she, too, alert. Milton hasn't had breakfast yet (breakfast? a cigarette, a glass of wine, is this breakfast?); his competitor has already had orange juice, eggs, toast, cheese, and he has already finished drinking a mug of cafe au lait. A nutritious meal.

Milton is still naked; his competitor is already elegantly dressed. Milton has barely opened his eyes yet; his competitor has already read the morning papers, and is already up-to-date about the stock exchange quotations and the market trends. Milton hasn't said a word yet; his competitor has already been in touch with clients, with political bosses, with a friend in the revenue department, with his suppliers. Milton is still in the suburbs; his competitor, overcoming all the traffic problems, has already reached the center of the city and is already solidly installed in his own office building. Milton doesn't even know yet whether it is going to be a rainy day or a sunny day; his competitor already knows from reliable sources that the prices of leather goods are going up. Milton hasn't seen his children yet (not to mention his wife, from whom he is separated); his competitor has already raised his daughters, has already paid for their education—one girl graduated in law, the other in chemistry—has already married them off, and is already a grandfather.

Milton hasn't started to live yet.

His competitor is already feeling pains in his chest, he is already collapsing on the counter, he is already breathing stertorously, his eyes bulging—in short, he is already dying.

The Soothsayer

JUST AS BERNARDO HAS BEEN DOING for a very long time, at the end of this year he will again pay a visit to Miro, the soothsayer.

Not many people know about the existence of this soothsayer. He lives in an absolutely ordinary house in the district of Partenon. There is no name plate or any other clue indicating the occupation of the householder. The visitor, however, must ring the bell in a particular way: three long rings, three short, three long. The soothsayer Miro will then open the door cautiously and look at the visitor with distrust. If the visitor gives the password (a quote from Horace: *quid sit futurum cras fuge quaerere*—cease to inquire what the future has in store), he will be invited in. Through a narrow corridor, he will then be conducted to a room at the back of the house, where he will be asked to sit at a round table; he and the soothsayer will be sitting opposite each other.

The soothsayer is thin and very old. Nothing in his appearance indicates his occupation: he doesn't wear a turban, nor does he wear a tunic embroidered with stars, and his beard is not trimmed in the fanciful style favored by soothsayers. And there are no stuffed owls in the house, no maps of the heavens hanging on the walls, no crystal ball or tarot cards on the table.

There is, however, a book. That's what catches the visitor's attention: the huge book on the table. But even the book doesn't have the expected black binding. The cover, made of cloth, is a yellowish color.

Bernardo, then, in front of the old man. Tense, barely containing his nervousness. The soothsayer will ask him his name. At this moment, and just as in previous years, Bernardo will fly into a rage, and he will reply with insolence: You should know. Aren't you a soothsayer?

"Behave yourself," the old man will say sternly, "and answer my question."

After Bernardo reveals his name (the rest—age: forty-five; occupation: sales clerk; marital status: married, two children—is apparently of no interest), the soothsayer will open the book and carefully leaf through its handwritten pages:

"Bartolomeu . . . Batista . . . Bernardo. Yes, here it is. All right. Tell me about anything of importance that happened to you during this year."

Still reluctant, Bernardo will tell him. The soothsayer, his eyes half closed, will listen to him. Every so often he will consult the book, and nod approvingly. In fact, when Bernardo is finished, he will say that everything that happened to him is written down in the book.

A brief pause, during which they will stare at each other, with Bernardo barely able to sustain the gaze of the old man. I suppose that you've come here to find out about the future, the soothsayer will finally say.

"In this case, there's a fee. Two thousand cruzeiros, please."

"That much?" Bernardo will say, surprised. "Last year—"

"Last year," the old man will cut him short, "is over. This year it's a different price."

Bernardo will take the check book out of his pocket. Cold cash, please, the old man will say. Bernardo will take a sheaf of paper money out of his wallet; as in previous years, it will be the exact amount demanded by the soothsayer.

The old man will put the money into a pouch that hangs from his neck. Only then will he wear a wan smile:

"I'm ready now. Your future is here, in this book. Do you want me to read it to you?"

Bernardo will make no reply: With anguished, wide-open eyes, he will be staring at the old man, who will then repeat his question two or three times. Seeing that Bernardo remains silent, the soothsayer will then say:

"Good. I'll read it then."

"No!" Bernardo will jump out of his chair. "Don't! Please. I can't. I'm sorry, but I can't. You know I can't. I'll never be able to . . . Don't tell me anything. Keep the money, but don't tell me anything. Please."

In silence, the soothsayer will close the book. Bernardo will pick up his hat. Before leaving, he will turn to the old man:

"At least wish me," he will say, trying hard to smile, "a happy new year."

"I'm paid to make predictions," the old man will say without any emotion, "not to offer my best wishes."

A Vacancy

STRAPHANGERS die in a train accident (from a news item in the Jornal do Brasil).

POSITION AVAILABLE, says the sign at the door of the railroad station. I am unemployed. I go in.

The stationmaster, a diminutive old man, peers shortsightedly at me and says: I need a muscleman. I show him my biceps. And my acrobatic skills by executing a flawless somersault. A guy who doesn't talk too much. I stick my tongue out—or rather, what is left of it: the doctors had to cut off most of it because of the cancer. Good, mumbles the stationmaster approvingly. He hires me. I receive a denim jacket and a blue cap.

My job consists of pushing people into the commuter trains before the doors close. Too many people try to hitch themselves to the outside of the trains. They don't pay, and what's worse, they cause accidents. We have to do something to stop this practice. But without letting the newspapers get wind of what we're doing. Do you understand? I nod my head.

The trains arrive empty and leave crammed with people. I do my work with enthusiasm, shoving the passengers into the trains: those heading the pack go in easily, but there is no room for those at the rear; however, nothing is impossible for someone who, like me, wants to go ahead in life. A man gets stuck in the door: with a blow of my fist I send him flying indoors. A woman manages to wedge herself in, but her little boy remains outside. My son! My son! she shouts in despair. Hoisting the kid over the mass of heads, I throw him to her.

A fat woman comes. Putting one foot on the boarding step, she then flings herself forward only to be repelled by various elbows, but she keeps trying again and again, always unsuccessfully.

There's a problem here. No sweat, though, for a smart guy like me. Here's what I do: I grab the arm of a burly workingman who is already inside the train and I use it as a crowbar to shove the fat woman inside. The workingman howls, the fat woman screams—but at the last minute I succeed in pushing her inside. The train leaves.

I mop the sweat from my forehead and stand here wondering: Why don't they use the spaces above the mass of heads? Lots of passengers would fit in there. Lying down, of course. It's a suggestion that I'll be making to the stationmaster at an opportune moment. And maybe to the directorate of the company as well.

FOR SEVERAL DAYS NOW I've been aware of a young woman who has been watching me constantly. She never boards a train, she just stands here, looking at me. She looks at me and smiles. And she's quite pretty. . . .

It's past midnight. The last train has already left. We are alone in the station, the young woman and I. But I don't even pay attention to her. My arms are sore, my throat is dry. I need a drink. I make for the exit.

She follows me. I can hear her footsteps resounding on the cement. I stop. She draws near, and takes hold of my arm. I want to talk to you. I don't look at her, I just stand with my head lowered, I am an unassuming man. She persists: Don't you want to talk to me? Me, silent. Don't you like me? Ah, yes, I do; with a nod of my head I say yes, I like you an awful lot. Smiling, she goes on: I'm very interested in the work you do. You push people into the trains, don't you? I know, I've been watching you. Tell me: Who told you to do so?

A newspaper woman! The stationmaster knew what he was talking about. Don't you want to talk to me? She is beautiful. Her hand, worming its way under my shirt, begins to stroke my chest. We kiss. I look around and see a storeroom with the door open. I pull her toward the place and throw her upon a pile of old mattresses. Don't you want to talk, love? she moans as I tear off her dress. Her tongue rolls about inside my empty mouth. Extricating herself from me, she opens her purse and takes out a flashlight: Open your mouth. I do as she tells me. Ah, she says, that's why. An operation, was it? I nod my head. Good, she says, there's no need to speak. Just answer with your head. Who told you to push the passengers into the trains? Was it the locomotive engineer? I shake my head; the tears begin to run down my face. Was it the police? No. Was it the stationmaster? Yes. It was the stationmaster. She guessed it right. How smart she is! I laugh, happy. She picks up her clothes and leaves at a run.

The next day I'm back at my post, carrying out my task as usual: pounding an old woman in, hammering a cripple in with his own crutch.

Suddenly, somebody snatches my cap away. I turn around only to be punched in the face. Still groggy, I'm thrown into the train.

Into this train that runs on and on. Where are we going? I would like to ask the silent passengers. But I can't: I'm a mute. The train batters the rails with a clashing noise. And we keep going.

In a State of Coma

1902. ALL OF A SUDDEN—and with no previous illness, or fever, or head injury, or grief to trigger it—Jorge Henrique Kuntz, a thirteen-year-old boy living in the Floresta district of Porto Alegre, goes into a coma. At least this is the diagnosis reached by Dr. Schultz, the family doctor, perplexed by the strange case of this young boy who, without ever having been seriously ill before, one day lay down never to wake up again, notwithstanding all the screaming, all the pleading, all the cautious pricking with needles. He is in a coma, says the doctor, but the family refuses to believe him; the boy's rubicund face, the faint smile, the peaceful breathing—is this a coma? How can it be a coma, doctor? asks the boy's father, Ignácio José Kuntz, full of indignation. He works as a carpenter and a jack-of-all-trades. The mother, Augusta Joaquina Kunzt, neither asks nor says anything. She cries, hugging their other children: the twins, Suzana and Marlene, two years older than Jorge Henrique; and Ernesto Carlos, the baby of the family. Bewildered, the doctor picks up his valise and leaves.

1903. UNDER THE GUIDANCE of the kindly and patient Dr. Schultz, the parents become skilled in feeding their son; for this purpose they use a flexible rubber tube which, inserted through one of the nostrils, reaches the stomach. In this way they can feed the boy broth, gruel, juice—food he used to like when he was conscious. They learn how to move him on the bed, how to exercise his limbs, how to keep him clean. As a result, Jorge Henrique develops well. His muscles are strong, his skin is smooth and satiny. His fingernails and toenails grow and are clipped regularly; his hair also grows but it is never cut because of a vow that Augusta Joaquina has made to God.

Handsome, this boy who seems merely asleep. The faint smile never leaves his face.

1910. "YOU THINK ONLY OF HIM, you only care about him," Ernesto Carlos, now a strapping teenager with a pimply, pasty face and fierce blue eyes, bursts out one day during lunch. Livid with rage, Ignácio José rises from the table and orders his son out of the house. His mother and sisters start crying. Ernesto Carlos packs his things and leaves, banging the door behind him.

THE FAMILY IS IN THE HABIT of going together to Jorge Henrique's room to pay him a visit. He's a grown boy, murmurs Augusta Joaquina, and it is true: he already has a beard. While bathing him lovingly with a sponge, she can't help noticing the hair on his body, and the golden thicket that grows luxuriantly in his pubic area, already making inroads upon his belly. Augusta Joaquina blushes, but she continues with her task. She applies oil to the entire skin which, thanks to all this tender loving care, is smooth and flawless, without a single scab or blemish. Jorge Henrique can sleep his unbroken sleep in peace.

1914. WORLD WAR I BEGINS.

1915. JORGE HENRIQUE'S HAIR grows and grows. His mother tries to keep it clean and tidy. And beautiful: at times she will style his hair in braids, at times in ringlets, at times in a chignon. When fluffed out, the fine blond hair floats in the air before it flows down the sides of the bed all the way down to the floor—a scene that enraptures both parents and sisters. The beard, blond like the hair, doesn't elicit as much admiration.

1916. SUZANA, one of the twins, has a strange dream. She sees her brother in a palace, seated on a monumental throne, his blond mass of hair encircling his resplendent face like an aureole. Jorge Henrique smiles at her, and then speaks to her in an unknown language.

The dream, although of exceptionally short duration, is enough to make Suzana feel that she has been entrusted with a mission. Her task is to arouse her brother from his stupor, and to lead him to the position of honor and distinction that fate has in store for him. She discloses this fervent wish of hers to her parents. They vacillate, doubtful about the advisability of embarking upon a course of action for which there is no apparent logical basis, and which might even be harmful to the young man. However, their daughter's fervor finally persuades them; they give her permission to attempt to execute a seemingly absurd plan.

Suzana plunges into her task wholeheartedly.

There is a series of massage sessions, of shouts of encouragement, of prayers uttered by the bedside. Infusions of a great assortment of herbs are poured into the feeding tube.

After the flogging with wet towels come the applications of hot and cold compresses. The blood of a young chicken is poured over the chest and the genitals of the young man.

All to no avail. The sick young man remains as lethargic as before.

Suzana is driven to despair. As dawn breaks on the thirtieth day, she is found hanging from the avocado tree in the backyard.

1917. THE RUSSIAN REVOLUTION.

1918. THE END OF WORLD WAR I. The Spanish influenza spreads across the world. The disease spares the Kuntz family. But even so, Ignácio José and Augusta Joaquina go through days of anxiety; they are afraid that germs might infiltrate through a chink in the walls. They spray their son's room with carbolic acid, they watch over him constantly, and they take his temperature throughout the day.

The danger has passed. *Unfortunately, nothing happened to Jorge Henrique*, says Marlene, the flighty Marlene. Realizing her slip of the tongue, she apologizes with a smile; but her parents stare at her with suspicion.

1919. ON THE NIGHT OF DECEMBER 23, a hot, stifling night, Ignácio José wakes up startled. Seized by sudden foreboding, he jumps out of bed and runs to his son's bedroom. A dim night light illuminates the young man, serenely asleep under the bedcovers. Apparently everything is all right; but Ignácio José still feels uneasy. He sits down by the bedside and keeps vigil.

The young man's breathing becomes faster. Something is happening! Ignácio José rises to his feet, his eyes bulging. He approaches the bed and with trembling fingers, he pulls the bedcovers away.

His son's penis is beginning to rise. It is an enormous penis, emerging from the tuft of golden pubic hair; it stands erect, oscillating rhythmically. My God, murmurs the poor man, devastated, and he lets himself fall upon the chair.

The young man is tossing about in bed; with his forehead pearled with sweat and his mouth partly open, his face is a mask of anguish. Ignácio José cannot bear to see his son suffer. He goes back to his bedroom, gets dressed without making any noise, and then steals out of the house.

He heads for the Lower City, and soon comes to a lane frequented by hookers. Heavily painted women in slinky dresses, some in plumed hats, some with weird hairdos, pace their turf—shouting terms of abuse, laughing derisively, making obscene gestures. He finds them repulsive.

Suddenly he runs into a young woman leaning against a wall; with her downcast eyes and modest clothes, she seems more decorous than the others. Ignácio José still hesitates for a moment before accosting her. In a low voice, he then informs her of his reason for being there, and he makes her an offer. Surprised, and rather distrustful, the young woman looks at him; she asks him questions, she wants details. Ignácio José's honest face finally convinces her. Let's go, then, she says.

They hurry along the sleeping streets. They enter the house through the back door and go straight to Jorge Henrique's bedroom. Ignácio José opens the door, but he doesn't look at his son: Okay, young lady, he says in a low voice, go in.

She goes in and closes the door behind her.

Ignácio José, nervous, with beads of sweat running down his face, waits outside in the corridor. Minutes later, the door opens and the young woman comes out, tidying herself up. All set, she says. How did it go? asks the man, anxious. Fine, she says, and then she falls silent. How much? asks Ignácio José. She mentions a modest sum of money. He pays her and shows her to the door. She walks down the street, without turning around.

1920. DR. SCHULTZ THINKS that Jorge Henrique's condition is stable: it doesn't get better, but it doesn't get worse either. He is, however, alarmed by Ignácio José's appearance; he is not at all pleased with the purplish hue of the man's lips, with his shallow, labored breathing. The doctor warns him: You must take care of yourself, Ignácio José, who then says in reply: If you take care of my son, doctor, you're taking care of me. The doctor leaves, muttering: This is bound to come to a bad end; and with winter almost here . . .

But Ignácio José survives the winter. Spring arrives; then summer. One night he is sitting by his son's bedside, reading a newspaper, when there is a knock at the front door. Answer the door, will you? I'm busy, his wife shouts from the kitchen. With a sigh, he puts the newspaper down and goes to the front door.

It's a young woman. The shawl that covers her head partially conceals her face. She is carrying a baby.

"What do you want?" Ignácio José asks.

"Don't you recognize me?" she says in reply, and with an abrupt gesture, she pulls the shawl away.

Ignácio José recoils in surprise: It's the young prostitute that he had taken to his son. But his surprise soon changes to wrath. What do want from me? he blusters, closing the door behind him. I'm finished with you. I paid you, I owe you nothing.. . .

"Oh, yeah?" she says in a challenging tone. Then showing him the baby, "And what about this?"

Ignácio José looks at the child in astonishment: it's a blond, blue-eyed baby.

"It can't be," he mumbles.

"Yes, it can," she shouts, triumphant. "Yes, it can! Count up the months, old man."

"Don't shout," pleads the man. "My wife is in there . . ."

The young woman laughs.

"I know. And you're afraid, aren't you? Will she believe this story? Or will she think that the child is yours?"

Ignácio José is upset:

"Listen, we can't talk here. Let's go for a walk . . . "

"No. We're going to settle this matter right here. And right now."
She is firm and resolute in her demand: but he persists and even
pleads with her until she finally relents.

They start walking. Ignácio José leads her through dark, deserted
alleys. He doesn't speak. He doesn't know what to say. Or what to do.
Insane thoughts swirl around in his brain. A crime: he could pick up
a good-sized pebble from the gutter and . . .

As if guessing at his thought, she stops dead in her tracks:

"Listen, old man," she says, clutching the baby tightly in her
arms, a gleam of hatred in her eyes, "if you're thinking of doing me
in, forget it. I know how to defend myself."

Reaching down her cleavage, she takes out a razor, already unfolded, its blade glittering. The baby begins to bawl, the man steps
back. I'm sorry, young lady, he murmurs. I don't even know what I'm
doing. . . . This old head of mine . . .

Leaning against a tree, he bursts into tears, and he sobs convulsively. Astonished, she looks on. Putting the razor away, she goes up
to him and places her hand on his shoulder:

"I'm sorry, sir. I didn't mean to . . . "

"Ah, young lady," he says, his voice strangled by sobs. "Ah, young
lady, if you only knew what I've been through. . . . This son of mine
. . . Ever since he was thirteen years old . . . "

He wipes his eyes. "I, too, know," he says, looking at the baby
"what it's like to suffer because of a son."

Ignácio José takes a handkerchief out of his pocket, blows his
nose noisily, and smiles: And what's his name? he asks. Jorge Henrique Junior, she says. He is surprised: But how did you know . . . ?
You told me, she replies. Then laughing: Can I call you father-in-
law? Somewhat embarrassed, he nods his head. Well, then, father-
in-law, she says.

They remain silent for a moment. The baby starts to cry again and she soothes him with the pacifier. She then asks after Jorge Henrique: Is he any better?

"The same," sighs Ignácio José. "The same."

"Is he not aware of anything?"

"No."

"Gosh. What a terrible disease."

Another pause.

"I liked you son," she says. "I didn't mind his being a half-wit, I liked him." She falls silent again, and stands staring at her child. "I can't raise this baby on my own. Would you take me into your home, father-in-law?"

"I can't," he says in a muffled voice.

"I knew you wouldn't," she says, without feeling hurt. "But my son—will you take him in?"

Ignácio José extends his arms to receive the baby. He holds the child clumsily, and the baby starts to cry again. I'm out of practice, he mumbles. She shows him how to cradle the baby so that he won't cry. Then with a sigh:

"Well, father-in-law, I think I'd better go now."

On an impulse, he kisses her on the forehead. He offers her money. Refusing to accept it, she then walks away.

With the baby in his arms, Ignácio José returns home. His wife, annoyed, goes up to him:

"Where have you been? I've been calling you . . . "

On seeing what her husband is carrying, she interrupts herself, astounded.

"Look what I've found on our doorstep," he says, smiling.

1922. JORGE HENRIQUE'S CONDITION remains the same. One could even say that he is under a spell, exclaims Pastor Joseph.

As for the child, he grows and develops well; he is naughty and is always scampering all over the house, but he never goes into the bedroom of the comatose man, of whom he is afraid. The boy is very attached to Marlene, who doesn't get along with her parents. Throughout the celebrations of the 100th anniversary of the country's independence, she keeps making sarcastic remarks about family life.

Ignácio José doesn't have much time for the child; as for Augusta Joaquina, she ostensibly ignores the boy, leaving the task of raising him to her daughter. Come on, Bebê, Marlene says, let's go to your room, we're not wanted here. Ignácio José swallows his anger. There is nothing he can do.

1923. THE NEWS ABOUT the Revolution up north, about sons being dragged away from their homes, about battles and bloodshed, worry Ignácio José: Will the Revolution reach Porto Alegre? He worries so much that he can't sleep at night. He ends up with acute pulmonary edema. I've warned you, haven't I, says Dr. Schultz, who was quick to come to the house. He recommends hospitalization. And Ignácio José dies in the hospital after revealing the truth about the boy to his distressed wife.

Upon returning from the funeral, her eyes red and swollen, Augusta Joaquina goes straight to her son's bedroom. There he is, lying in bed, his countenance tranquil as usual—an ordinary sleep, it would seem, weren't it for the rubber tube inserted in his nostrils. *But why doesn't he die, this wretch?* shouts Augusta Joaquina (it's the bitterness accumulated for years now flowing out). *Why does he have to lie here, making us suffer?* (She feels like pouring caustic soda down the tube. She feels like decapitating that head, whose eyes won't open.)

Carrying a kitten in his arms, her grandson appears at the door. Look, Granny, he says laughing, look what I've found. Get out of here, you louse, she says in a hoarse voice. Startled, the boy runs to his room: Marlene! Granny yelled at me, Marlene.

Augusta Joaquina looks at her son again. The blond hair, spread across the pillow, shines in the sun, which is now entering through the window. Kneeling down by his bedside, she asks for his forgiveness and cries her eyes out.

1924. AFTER HER HUSBAND'S DEATH, Augusta Joaquina begins to sleep in Jorge Henrique's room. Her cot stands right next to her son's bed; at times, as she tosses about in her restless sleep, she sinks her face into her son's soft tresses. A soothing caress.

Marlene's attachment to the boy (whose nickname is Bebê), keeps growing. She showers him with hugs and kisses, but then all of a sudden, she pushes him away from her and runs to the bathroom, where she locks herself up. From there comes the sound of convulsive weeping. Bebê also cries, but not for long. Soon he begins to amuse himself by playing with his wooden blocks. Marlene always comes out of the bathroom looking different. Heavily made-up and dressed to kill, she sashays into the living room, laughing and pulling faces at Augusta Joaquina, who pretends not to see her. She opens the front door.

"Where are you going?" whines Bebê.

"It's none of your business, you runt."

She goes out. That's the way it is, night after night. And she never helps with the housework. Augusta Joaquina does all the washing and the cooking; she looks after Jorge Henrique and (reluctantly) after Bebê; besides, she takes in sewing in order to make ends meet. What she gets from her husband's pension is not enough.

Marlene returns home late at night. When her mother admonishes her for being late, she makes insolent retorts: I'll do as I well damn please, you can't boss me around, don't think that I'm like Suzana, so get off my back. I'm going to live my life my way. She reeks of rum and tobacco. Staggering to her room, she then slams the door shut.

Exhausted, her back aching, Augusta Joaquina lies down beside her son.

1925. MARLENE SPENDS WEEKS away from home.

One days she returns, accompanied by a stranger. A roguish type. A dude in a close-fitting jacket, a bowtie, two-tone shoes; a scoundrel with a neat hairline mustache and hair slicked down with brilliantine. A fellow with a very dark complexion.

"Who is this man? asks Augusta Joaquina, scandalized.

"My husband," replies Marlene. "We got married in the city of Rio Grande a week ago." And she hastens to add: "I'm forewarning you, Mother, he's going to live here."

"But you haven't consulted me," says Augusta Joaquina dryly and with a frown on her face.

"And I'm not going to. I'm forewarning you."

"I don't like him!" Bebê shouts.

"Shut up, you too!" bellows Marlene. Then turning to the man: "Let's go, Songbird, I want to show you our bedroom."

"If you'll excuse me, ma'am." The fop, who never stops smiling, has a soft voice. Carrying the suitcase, he follows Marlene.

Augusta Joaquina is most unhappy with the new way of life in her house.

Marlene and her husband spend the whole day at home—he, in pajamas, with his hair kept in place with a hairnet; she, in a dressing gown that partly exposes her ample breasts, with a cigarette dangling from the corner of her mouth. They laugh all the time. They play cards and drink beer. Bebê, in a sullen mood, hides in corners. Songbird doesn't want to have anything to do with the boy.

Then one day:

"My husband wants to take a look at Jorge Henrique," Marlene announces.

They are at the table, eating.

"Absolutely not," says Augusta Joaquina, without lifting her eyes from her plate.

"But why not?" Marlene persists. "He's his brother-in-law, for Christ's sake."

"I said no," Augusta Joaquina repeats.

Songbird heaves a sigh. Then folding his napkin carefully, he rises to his feet. And so does Augusta Joaquina. Songbird makes for Jorge Henrique's room. Augusta Joaquina runs ahead of him to block his path.

"Move back, you bastard."

But Marlene, advancing upon her mother, slaps her repeatedly, and shoves her away.

"That'll teach you, you witch!"

Marlene and her husband enter the bedroom, and close the door behind them. Augusta Joaquina lies on the floor, weeping softly.

"What happened, Granny?" asks Bebê, frightened. "What happened?"

The door opens, and Marlene and Songbird emerge.

"Talk to her," says the man, and he then goes to the veranda to smoke.

Standing before her mother with her arms akimbo and with a frown on her face, Marlene proceeds to disclose her husband's plan.

"Songbird thinks we could use Jorge Henrique to make a lot of money. He says it's a rare case, to have a man living like this, half-dead, half-alive, for such a long time. Songbird says there was a man who lived like this in his hometown, and he became a saint. People would come from far way just to look at him and pray in his house. And they were willing to pay a fortune to do so. We, too, could benefit from this case."

"No," says Augusta Joaquina, still lying on the floor.

Marlene decides to negotiate with her mother:

"Come on, Mother, there's nothing wrong with it. It won't harm Jorge Henrique in the least, he won't even know. And it will benefit us, we've been going through hard times . . . "

"No."

"But, Mother . . . "

"No."

Marlene's patience begins to wear thin:

"Stop being silly, Mother. You won't have any extra work to do, Songbird said he'll look after everything."

With a strangled scream, Augusta Joaquina pounces upon her daughter, her hands searching for Marlene's throat. Ah, you bitch! cries out Marlene, enraged. Without any difficulty, she extricates herself and then knocks her mother down. From the veranda, Songbird watches the scene, splitting his sides with laughter. Bebê starts to cry. Marlene is finally in control:

"Cool it, Mother!" she yells. "Stand still! From now on, I'm the one who's calling the shots around here, do you understand? Me— and Songbird."

"I'll order the posters, " says Songbird. "We'll be in business, starting next week. "

But that's not what happens. The police arrives and arrests Songbird, a well-known crook. As for Marlene, she disappears.

1929. THE CRASH OF THE STOCK MARKET in New York; the depression. It's God's punishment, murmurs Augusta Joaquina while bathing her son. A just punishment, she says as she combs his beard (some of the hairs are more than a meter long). From the door, Baby, impassive, looks on.

1936. BEBÊ, NOW A FINE, strapping youth. Dark-skinned, blue-eyed. The girls in the Floresta district sigh for him, notwithstanding their parents' admonitions: He's bad news, he's tainted with illegitimacy.

Bebê enlists in the army. When he comes home, looking elegant in his uniform, his grandmother can't help feeling admiration for him: against all odds, she thinks, the boy has succeeded in mastering his fate, in doing something worthwhile with his life. She feels like revealing the secret of his birth to him, but she refrains herself: It's not the right moment yet.

Bebê now treats her with indifference. He has never swallowed the humiliations he has suffered. It is his turn to show contempt, and he is now in a position to do so: in the barracks, people look up to him; the captain's daughter winks at him.

1938. DR. SCHULTZ DIES. Among his papers, they find a notebook containing a detailed description of Jorge Henrique's case. The many probing questions registered there are evidence of the anxiety experienced by the old doctor: up to the very end, he tried unsuccessfully to come up with a diagnosis.

1939. WORLD WAR II BREAKS OUT. People of German descent are under suspicion. Worried, Augusta Joaquina tosses about in her cot: Will her house be attacked? Frightened, she gets up and turns on the light. Jorge Henrique continues to be submerged in his calm sleep. She examines his serene face, still boyish despite the wrinkles; she strokes his long hair, which is already turning gray.

1943. ON THE EVE OF LEAVING for Italy with the Brazilian Expeditionary Force to fight against the Nazis, Bebê, accompanied by his wife, visits his grandmother. Augusta Joaquina has prepared a nice lunch: roulade, braised cabbage, apple strudel. Bebê, however, does not eat. He is in a gloomy—and belligerent—mood: It's all because of the Germans, he says gruffly. Shut up, Bebê, whispers his wife (a tall, beautiful woman). Augusta Joaquina hangs her head and hides her tears; now is the time to tell Bebê, she thinks. But she doesn't have the courage. With a handshake, the soldier takes leave of his grandmother. He merely casts an abstracted glance at Jorge Henrique.

1944. AUGUSTA JOAQUINA turns seventy-five years old. Her neighbors want to celebrate the occasion with a party for her, but she declines, saying that she sees no reason for a celebration. She would rather stay alone, with her son. The fact of the matter is, she sees death approaching.

She sees death approaching, and there is nothing that she can do. But she isn't worried: for months now, she has seen a figure with indistinct contours, a figure enveloped in an aura of soft splendor, standing by Jorge Henrique's bedside. It is to this being, to this guardian angel, that she will entrust her son when she finally departs.

One day at dawn she wakes up choking and breathing sterterously; it is, she realizes, her old heart finally giving out. Lifting herself up on the cot, she turns to her son, her eyes wide open:

"Son!"

She is unable to get up.

With trembling hands, she takes hold of his hair, and presses it against her face. Son, she murmurs, I'm going to heaven, I'll be praying for you. . . . She dies.

HADN'T IT BEEN FOR THIS—her death—she would have seen Jorge Henrique open his eyes, smile, stretch his limbs, and say in a baby's faint voice: Gee, guys, that was quite a nap I had.

The Dwarf in the Television Set

IT IS TERRIBLE TO BE A DWARF and have to live inside a television set—even if it happens to be a gigantic color TV; however, there is at least one advantage: When the TV is turned off, it is then possible to watch some very interesting scenes from behind the screen. And what's more, it's possible to do so without anybody noticing—after all, who is going to pay any attention to a television set when it is turned off? If people paid attention, they would be able to see—deep down where the small luminous point disappears at the moment when the TV is turned off—my attentive eyes. In the daytime I watch, that's what I do. At night . . . Well.

It was Gastão who brought this TV set to the apartment. It is a huge apartment—an extravagance, for a man who lives alone (seemingly alone)—and in each room there is a TV set. Gastão can afford to have as many as he wants, for he is now the owner of the department store. The death of his father forced him to withdraw from the course in dramatic arts that he was taking (incidentally, that's where I first met him) in order to run his father's business.

It is a very big department store.

Gastão describes it like this: In the basement, bicycles, motorcycles, tents, fishing and hunting gear. The entire first floor is the territory of the television sets; there are about eighty on display, arranged in rows—a battalion of TV sets, both color and black-and-white, in all shapes and sizes, all of them tuned in to the same channel. One smiling face—eighty smiling faces—one weapon being fired—eighty weapons being fired. When the security guard turns off the main switch, eighty images flee; eighty screens turn dark. And in not a single one of them—and Gastão is constantly repeating this to me—in not a single one are there any peering eyes. In not a single one—he says, with a note of censure in his voice. In not a single one! he repeats, with great annoyance.

Gastão finds it very stressful to run the store. When he returns to the apartment after work, all he wants is to take a bath, put on his silk dressing gown, and sit sipping whiskey. All of this I watch from here, from amid the wires and the transistors—and I, too, am dying for a whiskey, but I manage to control myself. I can't leave my hiding place until all the servants are gone. So here I remain, cramped for space. There's no room to swing a cat in here, far less a dwarf.

(Funny that I should think of this remark now. It was my first line in a play in which Gastão and I were acting together. He would appear on stage, walking in that peculiar way of his, and he would open a suitcase that was in a corner—and at that point I'd come in, saying: Shit, there's no room to swing a cat in here, far less a dwarf! Gastão would then break into a smile and take me in his arms. Night after night.)

Nowadays, night after night, and day after day, I have to remain here, hidden inside this boob tube. Thank God, at least he brings me food—a few sandwiches prepared in a slapdash way, and cold milk. Cold milk! He has a grudge against me, I know.

The servants have already appeared at the door to ask if the boss needs anything else, and he has already replied in the negative, and they've already said their good-nights and are now gone—but he still hasn't taken me out of here. I could come out on my own, if I wanted to. But I don't want to. He knows that he is supposed to come and get me. But no, he chooses to play dumb. This has been going on since he became a businessman. With arrogance, he is now holding the glass of whiskey against the light to examine it. Handsome, this devil . . . A carefully trimmed beard, manicured fingernails—he is handsome, I admit, with a constricted heart. Handsome—but he won't come and get me out of here.

The doorbell rings.

Of course—he lingered over his drink for such a long time that the door bell was bound to ring. Deep down, that's what he was waiting for. With a sigh—but what a fakey bugger he is—he rises to his feet and answers the door.

I can hear some muffled exclamations, and a moment later he is back in the room, accompanied by a couple I have never seen before. But they are obviously common people. The man is young and dressed in a manner that he must consider stylish: checkered jacket, purple pants, platform shoes (and he isn't a dwarf!), red tie. The woman is dressed in a more simple way. And she is pretty, a salesgirl type, but nice.

Gastão invites them to sit down. Ill at ease, they sit on the edge of their armchairs. Conversation is difficult and spasmodic. From what they say, I gather that they are Gastão's employees. Newlyweds, who first met at their place of work. They exchanged passionate glances amid the bicycles and the motorcycles (they are both from the basement) and finally got married. And now they are here to pay a visit to the boss.

(What a riot! If I weren't imprisoned here, I would laugh uproariously. To pay a visit to the boss! What a riot!)

They talk about their honeymoon, which they spent in a resort town. Without too many details, they describe the roast chicken dinner they had at the house of an uncle.

A prolonged silence.

The young woman gets up. Blushing, and twisting a handkerchief in her hands, she asks where the bathroom is. Gastão, courteous, gets up to show her the way.

He returns to the sofa, where he sits curled up like a cat. Like a cunning cat. His employee—up to now sitting motionless and tongue-tied—starts talking. Senhor Gastão, he says, I've got a problem. I'm telling you about it, Senhor Gastão, because you've been like a father to me, you've given me a TV set as a wedding gift. Senhor Gastão . . .

The problem, he tells Gastão, is that his wife is frigid. When he is through with his story, he buries his head in his hands.

Gastão, sympathetic, asks him to come and sit on the sofa beside him.

"Here, right beside me. Let's talk," he says in a low, slightly hoarse voice, a gleam of sympathy in his eyes—what an artist he is! He learned a lot in that dramatic arts course. He was the top student. . . . But wait a moment—what he is saying now?

He is saying that frigidity is quite common, that many women have this problem. That often young women are not prepared for sex.

"But it's nothing to worry about," he adds, taking the young man's hand. "You're a handsome man . . . "

But what a sleazeball he is, this Gastão! How dare he, and right under my nose! And the young woman, what's taking her so long? Then it dawns on me: She is lingering in the bathroom on purpose, so that her husband will have plenty of time to ask his boss for advice on their problem. A prearranged thing. Such idiots they are!

I'll have to do something right now, and here's what I do: I stir myself inside the television set, and I produce crackling and snapping noises.

"What was that?" The young jumps to his feet.

"Don't be alarmed," says Gastão. "It's just the TV set, there's something wrong with it."

He then looks at the screen—at me—and I see hatred in his eyes. "You'll pay for this, you dwarf," his eyes threaten me. Beautiful, his eyes.

"I'm sending it back to the warehouse tomorrow. Come, sit here."

But the employee doesn't sit down. He has become quite nervous, and he is unable to look at his boss in the face.

"I've never thought that you, Senhor Gastão . . . "

The young woman returns. The young man takes her by the arm

and says that they should be going now, they will have to get up early. They take their leave, and are gone.

Gastão remains seated on the sofa, snorting with rage. All of a sudden, he throws his glass away, rises to his feet, and comes near the television set. He looks at the screen—but not at me.

"This TV has had its day. It has outlived its usefulness. I don't think it works anymore."

"Don't, Gastão!"

He presses the button. A thousand jolts send me into a screaming fit. Sparks fly, and they dazzle and burn me. Gastão is delighted. He has never seen such a good program on television before.

The Memoirs of a Researcher

IT WAS NOT SO MUCH LIFE AS LETHARGY—but anyway, it was bearable and even pleasant. It ended abruptly, however, when I was twenty-eight years old, at the moment when a small container of gas exploded right in front of me, in the electronics laboratory where I worked as an assistant. I was rushed to the hospital, and the doctors didn't hold out much hope that I would make it. I did make it, though, but the accident left me disfigured. I lost all the fingers on my left hand, and three on my right hand (only the thumb and the little finger remained). Besides, my face was seriously burned. I wasn't handsome to start with, but the end product, even after two plastic operations, wasn't a pleasant sight. Oh God, not at all pleasant.

But even so, during the first few months following the accident, I saw no reason to feel depressed. I retired from work, and I drew a good disability pension. My old aunt, with whom I was living, was full of solicitude for my welfare. She would make my favorite meat turnovers, cut them into bite-size pieces, and put them into my mouth—all the while shedding heartbroken tears, for reasons that, frankly, I couldn't understand. You should cry for my father, I would say, for my mother, for my older brother—they're the ones who are dead, and yet you cry for me. Why? I escaped alive from an explosion that would have killed any other person, and I don't have to work anymore, and you pamper me—I have no cause for complaint.

But I was soon to find out that I did. Upon visiting a certain dressmaker.

This lady, a prim and proper but passionate widow, had always received me on Saturdays, when her children were away. So, when I felt strong enough, I phoned her to explain my prolonged absence, and we set a date.

Not surprisingly, she was shocked when she saw me. You'll get used to it, I said, and I suggested that we go to bed. She loved me, so she agreed. I soon ran into difficulties: the stump (that's how I called what remained of my left hand) and the pincers (my name for the two remaining fingers on my right hand) didn't give me the necessary support. The stump, in particular, had a certain tendency to slide across the sweaty body of the poor woman. She lay there, staring goggle-eyed; the more frightened she became, the more she sweated, and the more the stump kept sliding.

I'm ingenious at finding solutions. I've learned a lot by working together with technicians and scientists, and so it didn't take me long to solve this particular problem: with a pair of scissors, I made two incisions on the mattress. And there I anchored stump and pincers. In this way, I could make love to her, and I was in great form.

"I was dying for this," I confessed afterward. "Six months without scoring!"

She made no reply. She was crying. "I'm sorry, Armando," she said, "I like you, I love you, but I can't bear to see you like this. I ask you, love, not to come anymore."

"And who's going to satisfy my needs from now on?" I asked, affronted.

She started to cry again. I got up and left.

However, that was not when I became depressed. It wasn't until later; exactly one week later.

I was lying in bed, thinking of the dressmaker. With feelings of hatred, but also of sexual arousal; in fact, the feelings were more of arousal than of hatred.

I tried to masturbate. Impossible. The pincers (the stump was out of the question) were a completely inadequate tool for this purpose. The two fingers, separated by a mass of scarred tissue, were too far apart. Besides, the thumb, although strong, lacked sensitivity. A gross finger. As for the pinky, it had neither strength nor sensitivity. An inept finger. I finally gave up.

It was then that I sank into a real depression: I would just lie motionless, staring at the ceiling; I wouldn't eat, I wouldn't talk to my aunt. I believe that at that point in time I didn't want to live anymore. I think all I did was to ask myself continuously: Why didn't the explosion finish me off? Why?

On the third day my belly was swollen and my mouth was parched dry. Alarmed, my aunt sent for the doctor. He came, he sat down on the edge of the bed, he watched me for a while, he asked me questions—to which I gave monosyllabic replies—and then he made the correct diagnosis: depression. He put on a rubber glove, lubricated it with Vaseline, and asked me to lie on my side. Introducing his fingers into my rectum, he then proceeded to extract lumps of feces—hardened, petrified, almost fossilized turds they were. I didn't protest. I only envied the quantity of fingers that he had, that was all.

When he was finished, he removed the glove, and after throwing it out of the window, he sat down to talk to me. You should go out for a walk, he advised me, and do things that interest you. What are you interested in?

What was I interested in . . . ? I turned the matter over in my mind for a while but I couldn't come up with a satisfactory answer. After the dressmaker, nothing seemed interesting anymore. The doctor tried to be helpful: Fishing, perhaps? I laughed: Fishing, doctor? How can I fish, with this stump? How am I going to hold the fishing rod? (I spared him the description of a similar but far more anguishing recent experience). He, again: What about sports? Soccer, perhaps? No, I wasn't interested in soccer. In volleyball, yes, but volleyball . . .

All right, he mumbled. I felt that he had given up: After scrawling a prescription, he got up and left.

There was, however, some merit in the doctor's visit. I felt that my situation was a challenge to my inventiveness—an inventiveness that used to elicit the admiration of the technicians at the laboratory where I had worked. I mulled over my case, and on that very night I thought of an activity that could be both useful and pleasant, an activity that would enable me to kill two—if not three or four—birds with one stone.

Some time before the accident, I had read a licentious poem in the washroom in the laboratory, and I had written it down in my notebook as a unique example of a type of literature that was still little known. I now hit upon an idea: I would go to all the washrooms in the city and copy out whatever happened to be written on their walls and doors. Thus, I would get plenty of exercise; thus, I would overcome my constipation (and in case of need, there would always be a toilet close at hand); thus, I would demonstrate interest in something; thus, I would be able to collect some curious bits of information, which might even be of cultural interest and later I could put this information together in a book, which might even become a best-seller.

A bright idea! In the middle of the night I rushed to the phone to call the doctor.

Even though abruptly awakened in the middle of the night, the doctor, still groggy with sleep, gave me his full support. He suggested that I describe my experiences in a journal; he volunteered to put in a good word for me with an editor—a friend of his, and he even wanted to take me to a TV talk show (which I refused to do, mostly because I didn't want to shock the viewers). He was a good doctor; somewhat old, but very humane.

I followed his advice. So, here it is: Everything written above has been included in the journal as an introduction. At this point the journal proper begins, with dates and everything. By the way, I had quite a job writing in this journal; it wasn't easy to hold the pen with my pincers. Which, I hope, will increase the value of this work all the more.

APRIL 19. I start my research in the downtown area. In the Public Market, an excellent washroom; quite filthy, but rich in sayings: poems, proverbs, denunciations. And lots of drawings (impossible for me to reproduce them, however; perhaps with a camera, but handling a camera is an impossible dream for me). In a bar near Praça da Alfândega, another excellent find: fewer sayings, but also fewer foul odors, which enables me to conduct a more thorough examination and make a more careful selection. I begin to realize that the extremely hackneyed and salacious ditties cannot be included in the anthology, for they would lower the standard of the publication. I must select only the kind of writing that truly represents the finished product of the habitués of washrooms; that truly represents the essence of the act of scribbling; that truly represents the interrelation between the author and his peculiar milieu. Thus, *shit isn't paint, a finger isn't a paintbrush,* will not be included in the anthology. But reflections on the human condition, yes.

APRIL 25. Not everybody understands my work. There are people who keep pounding on the door, saying I'm taking too long. There are peeping toms who watch me from above or under the door. There are those who look at me with suspicion, and those who threaten to call the police.

Today I was brusquely interrupted by the janitor of a washroom in Praça da Harmonia. With the help of a hook, he lifted the door latch and then stormed in. But what the hell, I protested, can't a guy even answer the call of nature in peace anymore? You've been in here for almost half an hour, he shouted. Other people also have the right to use the john.

Then he stared at me in amazement: What the hell are you doing here? You haven't even pulled your pants down! Underneath the scars in my face I felt myself blushing. That's because I was already leaving, I mumbled. Look! and I pointed to a turd floating on the water of the toilet bowl—see, I'm finished!

He flew into a rage:

"You liar! That's not yours! It was already there before you came in. You liar!"

"That's no way to treat a cripple," I shouted as a last resort but he was already pushing me out.

APRIL 30. There's another problem looming with my aunt, of all people.

She has been hatching out a plan. She read in a magazine that artificial hands—electronic devices analogous to human hands—are available in the United States. She showed me the magazine picture: You've worked in electronics, you could easily make one of these for yourself. I showed her the stump and the pincers: And how would I manage to work with these, auntie?

She said nothing else for the rest of the evening. In the morning, however, she woke me up and suggested that we should buy those electronic hands. They are only available in the United States, I reminded her, yawning. In this case we'll have to send for them, she persisted, anxiously. She had every reason to feel anxious, for she had promised my dying mother that she would look after me. And ever since, she has lavished all her spinsterish affection on me.

I sat up in bed and patiently explained to her that the hands were far too expensive and inaccesible to poor people like us, what with the restrictions on imports, among other things.

She seemed convinced by my argument, but in fact, she wasn't. On the following day she showed me a letter. It was addressed to a radio program, and it asked the host and his listeners to help us acquire those electronic hands.

I took offense. She had gone too far. I said I would never accept charity from anyone. I'd rather lose the two fingers I've left, I shouted. She left my room in tears. On the following day she announced that she was going back to her hometown in the interior. She asked me to understand: She was sick and tired of feeding me pieces of meat turnover. Go, auntie, go, and God be with you, I said, already dismissing her from my mind, for I was engrossed in putting my notes in order. She left.

MAY 5. The departure of my aunt caused me some problems. I tried to do the house cleaning on my own, but it is impossible to handle a fishing rod with stump and pincers, just as impossible it is to handle a broom or a vacuum cleaner. Not to mention the floor-waxing machine, which would escape from my hands (?) and start dancing all over the house. Not to mention the dishes, which would slip from my fingers (?) and smash to pieces on the floor. Not to mention the slippery tomatoes; not to mention the perfidious string beans, the treacherous eggs.

I finally gave up. I don't clean the house anymore. I now live on bread rolls, cheese, apples—things that you buy and eat as they are.

MAY 10. A feeling of dissatisfaction is beginning to take hold of me.

Today, from a washroom in a government office located on the tenth floor of a downtown building, I was watching another washroom—this one in a luxurious office in the building opposite, a building owned by an insurance company. A man was sitting on the toilet bowl. A bald, middle-aged man, and as far as I could tell, very well-dressed. Through the narrow window of the washroom, he would look at the city lying at his feet for a moment. Then he would look straight ahead, then upward, then sigh and strain himself. He obviously suffered from constipation, for he sat there for a good fifteen minutes—even though it was a very busy time at the office. Suddenly he noticed me. With a grimace of disgust, he closed the window.

I became envious of him. I can't deny that I felt envious. This man, I thought, doesn't need an aunt to put food into his mouth. Thirteen liveried waiters would do this for him, if he wanted. This man doesn't have to do any house cleaning himself. This man doesn't need any neurotic dressmaker. He lies down on his back and three or four foxy ladies go down on him and he gets his rocks off without him having to lift a finger, or a pincer.

I left the washroom without even copying out the graffiti—I just plain forgot. For the first time. Not that I missed anything of great significance—there was nothing there, only the usual malicious remarks about the department head—but even so, the incident scared me, because I could already feel the specter of depression closing in on me once more.

MAY 16. Occasionally, as I go through the washrooms of the buildings, I run into a young woman who does the cleaning. A farm worker type—a strong woman, not entirely ugly. I like her freckles, I like the shrewd expression in her eyes, I like the fact that she is always smiling, even when she is washing the toilet seats.

We usually chat for a while. Her name is Marta; she is from the same town in the interior where my aunt lives. This, of course, has given me some ideas.

MAY 19. I went with her to her tiny room in the boarding house where she lives. There was no need to make any preparations: The rips already present in her mattress were perfectly suitable for the stump and pincers.

She is fiery. And she doesn't sweat. She smells funny—a mixture of shit and detergent, but it's not her own smell. And for a country girl, she is quite skillful. Her hands are somewhat rough. . . . But it shouldn't really matter. She's not going to handle any electronic instruments. But even so, I don't know; I'm still undecided.

MAY 31. To my delight, I've discovered that she knows more about graffiti than I do. Not just the vulgar ones; the witty ones too. She didn't copy them down; she stored them in her memory, which is prodigious, and she is willing to recite them to me so that I can write them down.

I've now made up my mind.

JUNE 10. I brought her to my place, to live with me. If things work out well, I promised her, we'll get married—after I finish my book about the inscriptions in the washrooms.

First thing she did was to clean the house, which had become a real garbage dump. She then prepared a hot meal (something I hadn't savored in ages). She put the food into my mouth—first the soup, then the risotto, then the pudding. Afterward we went to bed. She enfolded me in such a way that I didn't have to make use of the stump and pincers.

"Doesn't my face turn you off? " I asked her.

"No," she said. The scars, she told me, reminded her of the wrinkles on the face of her old father, already dead. Which moved me to tears.

JUNE 11. It was bound to happen. She was in the kitchen getting lunch ready (a carrot soufflé), and I was sitting in front of the television, when all of a sudden there was a tremendous explosion. *The gas container!* I thought, and ran to the kitchen. But even before I went to her aid, even before I took her to the hospital, even before the doctor announced the result of the operation, I already knew how many fingers were left: two on her right hand, none on her left.

IN JULY, when she is discharged from the hospital, we'll start visiting all the washrooms in the city. And as I ponder further upon this matter: I've always needed a female partner, who would have access to the women's washrooms.

The Loves of a Ventriloquist

A FAT WOMAN LOOKS AT ME AND SMILES; a thin man looks at me and smiles; a father points me out to his son, then they both look at me and smile. People know me. I'm the famous Albano, the ventriloquist. I'm well known throughout this state. I've been everywhere, performing solo (no, not solo: with Peewee) in theaters and movie houses in the interior, in cabarets and in *churrascarias*; it was me who would make the sirloin steak say good night to the sausage, it was me who would make the bottle of beer sing happy birthday to you. And of course, I would make my dummy, Peewee, talk. How is it going, Peewee, fine? Terrible, Albano. What's wrong, Peewee? Lack of women, Albano! The audience would go wild with delight. We were happy—Peewee and I. We didn't have a woman—just one would have been enough for the two of us—but even so we were happy. In the dingy rooms of the cheap, run-down hotels in the interior we would talk far into the night. Just the two of us. No woman. Timid as I was, I could never summon up enough courage to ask some floozy to go to bed with me. To talk to a woman? Only through Peewee's mouth.

"Look at that gorgeous brunette over there, on the second row! Isn't she gorgeous, Albano? Come over here, brunette!"

The brunette would climb onto the stage and kiss the dummy. Occasionally, I would indulge in an escapade and visit a brothel, which would give me some relief. Upon returning to my bedroom, I would be assailed by remorse: Lying helpless on the bed, Peewee would look at me, hurt. But afterward he would take his revenge on me: Whenever I fell ill, he never came to my aid. Me: burning with fever; he: sprawled out in a chair, his mouth agape, an insolent expression in his eyes: it was a sneer, pure and simple. One of these days I'll die because of this son-of-a-bitch, I would think to myself. When Ramão invited me to work in his circus, I accepted the offer. I would be losing my freedom, I would no longer be able to do as I pleased—but at least I wouldn't have to live in a hotel room and feel lonely. I now shared a trailer with the fierce Anteu, the weightlifter. He hated me, this Anteu. He hated me for no reason at all (or perhaps he hated me because he had to share the trailer with me, I don't know). The way he looked at me would send shivers down my spine. During my performance everything was fine—Peewee would talk to the audience, to the camel; the camel would talk back to Peewee, the audience would double up with laughter—but as soon as I returned to the trailer, my joy would fade at the sight of the sinister weightlifter eyeing me darkly. And worse still: even greater disturbances were in store for me.

I fell in love.

I fell in love with the gorgeous Malvina, the animal trainer. Like me, she was shy; and like me, she, too, was transformed in the course of her performance. She would enter the animal cage, fix her eyes on the wild beasts, and soothe them with a firm voice and a crack of the whip. As a matter of fact, it was the whip that made it possible for me to let her know about my feelings.

I had been watching her for a long time, and I think that she, too, had been watching me; but every time that we ran into each other, we both blushed and lowered our heads. One day, however, I mustered courage and:

"Ah, how delicate are the hands that wield me," sighed the whip.

She was so startled that she dropped the whip.

I then stepped out of my hiding place—I had been hiding behind a stool in the deserted riding arena, watching her rehearse for that evening's show. She turned red, and so did I, but:

"Your eyes have tamed my heart," said the Bengal tiger.

She looked at the wild beast—which was phlegmatically licking its paws—then looked at me, broke into laughter, and hurried away.

That was all. My mouth, my own mouth, never spoke to her of love. Not once.

It was Anteu who won her love. Won isn't really the right way of putting it—what he did was to overpower her and drag her to his trailer one Monday afternoon. He came in, carrying her in his arms (the poor thing in a half faint) and he kicked me out: Get out, you idiot, he shouted, slamming the door in my face. Through a window that had been left ajar, I did what I could: dumbbells, boots, ashtrays—they all voiced their protest. All of them threatened to call the police. All them, except Peewee. The son-of-a-bitch was the only one that remained silent.

All my protests were in vain, and so were the protests of the bearded woman, of the dwarfs, of Ramão. Anteu wasn't one to pay heed to anybody. He threw my belongings out of the trailer. I had to find another place to live. Malvina then moved in with him.

She suffered a lot, the poor thing. Her face was always covered in bruises, which her makeup could barely conceal. She spoke to no one, and she spent all day crying. But in the evening, when she entered the animal cage, she became her old self again—she was Malvina, the beautiful animal trainer. Only then was it possible for me to talk to her—through the animals. Malvina, you can't go on like this! You must rebel, the lion would say. She would make no reply, but her eyes would glitter and her fingers would tighten their grip on the whip. Put an end to it today! the tiger would plead. Today, Malvina! Go back to your place, animal, she would shout. And I, hidden behind the stool, would feel the tears welling in my eyes.

When my turn came, I would enter the ring running, and after greeting the audience, I would sit down, with Peewee on my lap.

"You clown!" he would shout. "You can't make it with women, can you, clown? You're such a wimp!"

Everybody would laugh. Which would make my blood boil. I then decided to take action.

One night I made up my mind: I downed a whole glass of cognac and ran to the weightlifter's trailer.

"Anteu! That's enough, Anteu!"

I threw myself against the door as if I weighed one hundred kilograms instead of a paltry fifty-two; and as if under the weight of one hundred kilograms, the door yielded, and there he was, on top of Malvina, crushing her with his monstrous body.

"That's enough, Anteu!" I shouted, and then to Malvina: "Scram, Malvina! Now!"

Anteu, naked, got up—how huge he was! and he advanced upon me, growling: "You're now going to pay for this, you rat!"

Malvina managed to escape through a window, and I readied myself for the showdown with Anteu. Over here, you coward! Here! shouted the dumbbells, but Anteu was familiar with my tricks, and he didn't turn around. He seized me, lifted me in the air, then threw me away—as if I had weighed three, not fifty-two, kilograms. Almost at the same time, he raised his hands to his head, and letting out a scream, he collapsed to the floor.

I never saw him again. I know that he was committed to a nursing home for the destitute after the stroke left him paralyzed. I never heard from Malvina, either. And Peewee, well, I burned him; it was with great pleasure that I watched his sneering face being consumed by the flames.

As for myself—I've been bumming around. I've been unemployed since I lost my voice. That's right: that night, after Anteu threw me into the air, I wasn't able to speak anymore. I became a mute, a dummy. I spent all my money on doctors; they were unable to find out what was wrong with me. There's nothing wrong with your vocal cords, or with your tonsils, they would say. They finally gave up trying to cure me. One of the doctors suggested that I should always have paper and pencil on me. That's what I do now: I write. I'm pretty good at writing, what else can a voiceless ventriloquist do?

I wander about the streets, and I go into bars and stores. People recognize me and point me out. And when in a men's clothing store a mannequin says—

Good afternoon, gentlemen, what I lack is women—everybody laughs. They think it's a prank of mine. They don't know—and this frightens me—that it is the mannequin himself that is speaking, saying things off the top of his head. The mannequin, the statue of Saint George, the vase, the radio—the world is full of crazy, crazy voices.

The Peal of Bells at Christmas

PURSUED BY THREE POLICEMEN, a man runs along the streets of a small town.

He is exhausted, and desperate; it is just before dawn now and his pursuers have been hard on his trail since nightfall. They don't give up the chase. The man is panting. He trips over something, falls down, picks himself up, and starts running again, in a hobbling way.

On the verge of surrendering himself, he sees a church. He runs to it. A window happens to be open and he slips through it. In the darkness, he comes upon the handrail of a staircase; he climbs up the narrow stairs, without knowing for sure what he will find at the top. Suddenly, he feels the wind on his face. He is in the belfry. There is a huge bell there, a bell that is out of all proportion to the size of the church and the tower. It is famous, this bell (but the man does not know this), for its size.

Warily, the man peers down. He sees luminous spots—the flashlights of the policemen—shifting from place to place. The policemen are confused: they have lost his trail. . . . The man smiles. He is safe. Just then he feels dizzy and he staggers; on the verge of falling, he hangs on to the rope of the bell. The enormous clapper detaches itself and comes crashing down to the narrow platform where the man is standing—and from there, it rolls down through an opening in the wall of the church. And it disappears. It must have fallen into the attic.

For a few minutes the man remains motionless, panting, his eyes closed. He recovers from his fright. He was pursued, but he saved himself; he almost fell down, and again he saved himself. He opens his eyes and smiles. He is safe.

Safe, but with a problem.

He must put the clapper back inside the bell. Otherwise, when the sexton comes to ring the bell to call the faithful to Mass, he will notice that something is amiss. And then he will climb up the stairs to the tower, for sure.

Slowly and with the utmost care, the man begins to haul on the rope. The very heavy clapper keeps coming closer. The man can hear the dull sound that it produces as it trails across the boards of the attic.

Suddenly, there is resistance. The clapper is stuck, maybe caught in a rafter. The man tugs at the rope adroitly but sharply. Nothing. The clapper is stuck. Good and stuck. It won't budge. Take it easy, easy does it, the man keeps saying to himself.

He takes stock of the situation. Should he enter the attic and free the clapper? Impossible. The opening—probably a ventilation hole—is not wide enough for a burly man like the fugitive to pass through. Thrusting his arm down the opening, he can feel the rope, but not the clapper. The attic is way below. Apparently, there is nothing else the man can do except to tug at the rope, so, that's what he does, feeling increasingly more exasperated, until finally a hard tug suddenly overcomes the resistance and the man falls on his bottom on the platform. With the rope in his hand. It has detached itself from the clapper.

The man stares in disbelief at the frayed end of the rope. And then he starts to berate himself: What an idiot I am, now I've really bungled it. I was already safe and sound, and I had to bungle the whole thing.

All of a sudden, a fit of laughter: But after all, he has nothing to do with the clapper. Or with the bell, or with the tower for that matter. He is worried for nothing. He is going to scram, that's what he is going to do now. As soon as he rises to his feet, he hears the barking of dogs and he sees the beams of flashlights: the policeman have returned. And what's worse, the day is now dawning. Soon the sexton will be here, too.

Panic-stricken, the man cringes. I'm lost, he mumbles. Completely lost.

The Dwarf in the Television Set [1979]   303

Lost? No. He won't give up so easily. They haven't found him yet, and they won't find him. Unless the sexton, unable to strike the bell, decides to climb up the stairs to the tower.

He examines the bell. It is really colossal: a good two meters in diameter, at least as much in height. The rim, turned inward, forms a sort of lip wide enough for him to rest a foot there. The man enters the bell and climbs on the lip as if it were a running-board. Balancing himself with difficulty, he gropes about, trying to find the place from which the clapper was suspended. As he expected, he finds a metal hook. Now, all he has to do is to find an object that can replace the clapper, and then attach it to the hook.

But—what object? The man looks around him. What is he looking for? A spare clapper? There isn't one. There is nothing, there in the tower. The man climbs down the bell. He empties his pockets: a jackknife, a notebook, a few coins. Nothing that could be used as a clapper. He takes off his right boot and weighs it by hand: much too light. Maybe a brick . . . ? Using the jackknife, he furiously starts digging into the wall of the church.

Half an hour later, he gives up. He has barely made a dent in the hard roughcast. And even if he succeeded in taking a brick out, he realizes, he wouldn't be able to suspend it from the hook. And even if he were able to do so, it wouldn't work, for the brick would crumble at the first clangs of the bell.

And yet, he has to find a solution. It is growing light, and now it is impossible for him to escape. One of the policeman is mounting guard at the front of the church: They suspect that the fugitive is somewhere in there. And they are waiting for the arrival of the sexton so that they can search the church. The son-of-a-bitches, mutters the man, they don't even respect God's house.

The sexton is on his way.

He slowly walks up the street where the church is located. The policeman meets him halfway. They stand talking for a while before the main entrance. The sexton gropes for the key in his pocket; the man doesn't know what to do—he opens the door—the man still doesn't not know what to do—he walks in with the policeman—and now the man knows what to do: with the rope held firmly between his teeth, he climbs inside the bell and stands on the lip inside. He is taking the place of the clapper.

The sexton doesn't start pulling on the rope right away. He is undoubtedly waiting for the policeman to finish his search of the church. Motionless inside the bell, and holding on to the hook, the man waits tensely—and what's worse, with his bladder about to burst: oh God, don't let me piss in my pants.

Finally, there is a vigorous thug at the rope; it is the sexton. Imitating the movement of the clapper, the man begins to move his head to and fro. Suddenly now!—he throws his head against the bronze.

It is an excruciating pain, an explosion inside his head—but he has produced a beautiful clang: clear, resounding, indistinguishable from the sound that the bronze clapper would produce. But the man has no time to rejoice at the outcome, or even to rest for a moment. The sexton continues to pull on the rope, and the man again strikes the bell with his head, then again, and again, and again. Twelve strokes of the bell in all.

DIZZY, HIS HEAD BURSTING WITH PAIN, the man climbs down the bell and he stretches himself out on the small platform of the tower. He lies there, unable to move, the strokes of the bell still resonating in his skull.

Finally he opens his eyes, and he takes a peep at the street down below. The faithful are beginning to arrive to hear Mass. As for the policeman, he is gone. The man sighs. He then becomes aware of the wetness on his leg: he has just pissed in his pants.

HE NEVER LEAVES THE PLACE AGAIN. He has made the tower into his permanent home. He lives on pigeons, mice, and bats; he drinks rainwater.

And he strikes the bell. In the course of time, he gets used to striking the bell. His skull, although deformed from the blows, has acquired the rigidity of metal. The man doesn't envy the lost clapper, a mere article of bronze. And, one could say, he is even happy.

There is only one period of time during the year when the man really suffers: on Christmas Eve. The sexton, habitually indolent, is then suddenly seized by a burst of energy and he starts pulling on the rope like a madman. The man has to strike the bell desperately. In the midst of his agony, he even has visions: He is lying in a manger, like the Infant Jesus, and he laughs and claps his hands. Except that the three men kneeling before him are not the Three Wise Men. They are the policemen who once pursued him as far as the church.

The Phantom Ship

HERE, ON BOARD THE PHANTOM SHIP, the days and the nights are identical, for we always sail amid a thick fog.

In silence, we—officers and crew—go about our work. The officers in their velvet tailcoats and tricorn hats; we, in the simple garb of sailors. Our job consists in lowering or hoisting the sails, according to the type of wind that suddenly blows from unforeseen directions. During our leisure time, we read or play chess. If anything, fever or pain, ails us, we are required to see the doctor on board. Strange dreams also warrant a visit to the doctor—my reason for seeing him. He receives me in a cabin that serves him as a consulting room—a cramped cubicle stuffed with books, surgical instruments, and flasks containing malodorous liquids. Suspended from the low ceiling, a skeleton oscillates with the movements of the vessel.

He asks me to sit down. For some time (which may well be a long time—time doesn't count on a phantom ship), the two of us, the old doctor and I, sit staring at each other. The old, white-bearded doctor in his tricorn hat, velvet tailcoat, and gold-rimmed eyeglasses. What's the matter, my lad? he finally asks.

"I had this strange dream."

"Tell me about it."

I hesitate; however, I have no choice but to tell him:

"I dreamed about a penis. A penis. A penis and a vagina."

He furrows his brow.

"That's what it was, a penis and a vagina?"

"Yes."

"Interesting . . . Penis and vagina. Interesting."

A pause. He looks at me keenly.

"Tell me," he says, leaning forward, "in this dream of yours, did the penis enter the vagina?"

"Ah, yes, it did. It entered, yes, sir. It went in and out, in and out."

Another pause.

"Is that all?" the doctor asks.

"That's all. Yes, sir, that's all."

"Ah!" He smiles. "So that's all, is it? Nothing to worry about, son. It's quite a common dream among the sailors on board our ship. It's not difficult to decipher it: the penis symbolizes the ancestral ship, the ship after which all the phantom ships were built."

"Interesting. And the vagina?" I ask.

He smiles again. "The vagina, you naughty boy. . . . The vagina. Yes. Tell me: in your dream, did you by any chance see the pubes?"

"Yes."

"The pubic hair?"

"Yes."

"Was the hair blond? Very fair hair on a soft, rosy skin?"

"Yes! Blond hair. Soft skin. Yes!"

I contain myself: I can't weep now. Not now.

"But then everything is all right," he says. "Don't you see? The vagina symbolizes the mist through which we sail. Deep down, what you want is to return to the ancestral ship. . . . But don't let this upset you. It's not unusual, you know, among sailors. Not unusual at all."

He stands up. I stand up.

"Out you go now! Back to your work."

He winks at me:

"I'll authorize an additional glass of wine for you at dinner. In this way you'll sleep well and won't have any more dreams. Go now."

At the door I turn around.

"Doctor," but I'm almost shouting, "is it true that islands exist? Is it true that the islands are full of fruit trees? Doctor, is it true that women exist?"

He stares at me fixedly.

"No, son. It's all legend. You know very well it's all legend. Islands? No, of course not. The same goes for fruit trees. And for women. It's nothing but a dream, a fantasy. Forget about it. And now go back to your work, there's a wind already picking up."

I open the door. He holds me by the arm.

"And above all," he says (but the tone of voice is now harsh), "don't write anything. Don't put a message inside a bottle, do you hear me? It's for your own good."

I mumble a thank you and leave. The door closes behind me. Trembling, I lean against it, with my eyes shut. How did he guess? How does he know that I already have, hidden under the pillow, a pencil stub, a scrap of paper—and a bottle?

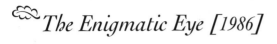 *The Enigmatic Eye [1986]*

The Enigmatic Eye

A MAN GOES TO A MUSEUM.

He is a wealthy man; in fact, one of the wealthiest men in the country. He is not an art enthusiast, neither does he have a special liking for museums; as a matter of fact, he is not in the habit of frequenting public places. And yet, there he is, piqued by the same curiosity that has drawn thousands of people every day to this small, and in all respects, uninteresting museum. He is there to see the small painting that a custodian found in the basement, buried under a pile of loose-joined frames—a painting which, after being examined by both national and foreign experts, was pronounced to be nothing less than an original by Rafael Sanzio. How it ended up in this museum is a mystery. Anyway, there it is, the masterpiece, exposed to the admiring eyes of the public. It is a portrait of an old man of aristocratic bearing. What impresses visitors the most is his gaze, which is truly enigmatic.

The portrait fascinates the man as nothing else in the world—whether it be magnificent landscapes, or luxurious buildings, or precious jewelry—has ever fascinated him. In the half light of the air-conditioned room (the preservation of this piece of art requires special conditions), he spends countless hours; the guard has to warn him that the museum is about to close and that he must leave now. He leaves; but on the following day there he is again, motionless, magnetized. Finally, he makes a decision: The painting must be his. In order to reach this objective, he is willing to spare no expense and to run all kinds of risks.

There is one person he can turn to for this purpose—Jorge: In addition to being an aide, he is also a devoted friend and a jack-of-all-trades. The man sends for Jorge and entrusts him with his wish. Leave it to me, says Jorge. And indeed, three days later, Jorge hands a cardboard box over to the man. With trembling hands he opens the box, and inside is the portrait of the old man with the enigmatic gaze. That the painting is authentic there is no doubt, for the newspapers report in banner headlines that the masterpiece at the museum has been stolen.

It's important that the painting be well hidden; the man hangs it in the attic in his mansion, and he is the only one to have a key to that room. There he spends hours looking at the painting, lit by spotlights that he himself has installed. It is with tenderness that he gazes at the face of the old man; he even strokes the wrinkled surface of the canvas with his fingers, moist with perspiration. Merely looking is not enough, he has to touch the painting, too, in order to experience the real feeling of ownership.

The servants wonder about what their master (a childless widower, he lives alone) is up to. But nobody dares ask him a question, and thus, without being disturbed, he can remain in the attic for increasingly longer periods of time. He goes downstairs only for his meals, when he then amuses himself by reading the news in the papers: There are still no clues to the whereabouts of the painting, the chief of police believes it has been taken to New York. New York! The man laughs so hard that he chokes. The servants exchange glances. The man knows that they think him crazy, but he couldn't care less. Now that he has his painting, nothing else matters to him. All he wants is to sit before the old man with the enigmatic gaze. With his brow creased and his lips compressed, the man studies the face in front of him just like an explorer studies the map of the unknown region he is to traverse. The man knows this face thoroughly; at least he thinks he does; however, as soon as he closes his eyes, the face disappears from his memory—completely erased. Which is frustrating, for the face is not as completely his as he imagined it to be; he does not possess it in its entirety. *Once more,* he murmurs, and drawing the chair up closer to the painting, he starts the undertaking anew, trying to memorize the outline of the eyebrows, of the labial commissure, of the wrinkles.

But then—due to the heat of the lights or to moisture, or some other unknown reason—the painting begins to fade, to vanish. At first the man thinks it is his imagination, an illusion caused by his prolonged effort to engrave in his mind the small details of the portrait. But no, the face is indeed vanishing; day after day the lines keep fading. Inexorably, the painting is vanishing and there is nothing the man can do about it. He cannot consult the experts, he cannot call in the restorers; helpless, he stands rooted before the painting until all that remains of the old man is—for some mysterious reason—his right eye, which glitters, enigmatic. But even this eye vanishes, and one day the man finds himself standing before a blank, empty canvas. And on that day he falls down on his knees; and on that day he weeps as he has not wept since his childhood, and he even calls out to his mother, dead for many years.

The man falls ill. Doctors, several of them, are sent for; they examine him thoroughly, take blood for numerous tests, x-ray him from top to bottom, but they find nothing wrong. His condition deteriorates, the doctors give him up, his death is even announced on television; but, as suddenly as he fell ill, he recovers. The first thing he does after getting rid of the servants, who urge him to stay in bed, is to go upstairs to the attic. Cheered by the hope that everything might have been just delirium, he climbs the steps two at a time. He unlocks the door, turns on the light—and there it is, the blank canvas, before which he sits down, devastated.

Suddenly an idea crosses his mind: what if Jorge were to return the canvas to the museum? It is possible that once there, under the specific circumstances of that environment to which the painting, after all, belongs, the figure will reappear. But why in the world would the museum's curator want to replace a Rafael painting with a blank canvas? And suppose the face were to reappear, what would he do then? Would he have the painting stolen again?

No. No, this is not the right solution. Opening the door—there is no longer any reason to keep it closed—the man calls a servant and dispatches him to a store to buy painting supplies. Later, the man mixes paints, then clumsily wielding the paintbrush, he gives himself over to his work. What he has in mind is just an eye, an enigmatic eye. To begin with. Later, he will see.

Inside My Dirty Head — The Holocaust

INSIDE MY DIRTY HEAD, the Holocaust is like this:

I'm an eleven-year-old boy. Small, skinny. And dirty. Oh boy, am I ever dirty! A stained T-shirt, filthy pants, grimy feet, hands, and face: dirty, dirty. But this external dirt is nothing compared to the filth I have inside my head. I harbor nothing but evil thoughts. I'm mischievous, I use foul language. A dirty tongue, a dirty head. A filthy mind. A sewer inhabited by toads and poisonous scorpions.

My father is appalled. A good man, my father is. He harbors nothing but pure thoughts. He speaks nothing but kind words. Deeply religious; the most religious man in our neighborhood. The neighbors wonder how such a kind, pious man could have such a wicked son with such a bad character. I'm a disgrace to the family, a disgrace to the neighborhood, a disgrace to the world. Me and my dirty head.

My father lost some of his brothers and sisters in the Holocaust. When he talks about this, his eyes well up with tears. It's now 1949; the memories of the World War II are still much too fresh. Refugees from Europe arrive in the city; they come in search of relatives and friends that might help them. My father does what he can to help these unfortunate people. He exhorts me to follow his example, although he knows that little can be expected from someone with such a dirty head. He doesn't know yet what is in store for him. Mischa hasn't materialized yet.

One day Mischa materializes. A diminutive, slightly built man with a stoop; on his arm, quite visible, a tattooed number—the number assigned to him in a concentration camp. He arouses pity, poor fellow. His clothes are in tatters. He sleeps in doorways.

Learning about this distressing situation, my father is filled with indignation: Something must be done about it, one can't leave a Jew in this situation, especially when he is a survivor of the Nazi massacre. He calls the neighbors to a meeting. I want you to attend it, he says to me (undoubtedly hoping that I'll be imbued with the spirit of compassion. I? The kid with the dirty head? Poor Dad).

The neighbors offer to help. Each one will contribute a monthly sum; with this money Mischa will be able to get accommodation in a rooming house, buy clothes, and even go to a movie once in a while.

They announce their decision to the diminutive man who, with tears in his eyes, gushes his thanks. Months go by. Mischa is now one of us. People take turns inviting him to their homes. And they invite him because of the stories he tells them in his broken Portuguese. Nobody can tell stories like Mischa. Nobody can describe like him the horrors of the concentration camp, the filth, the promiscuity, the diseases, the agony of the dying, the brutality of the guards. Listening to him brings tears to everybody's eyes.. . .

Well, not to everybody's. Not to mine. I don't cry. Because of my dirty head, of course. Instead of crying, instead of flinging myself upon the floor, instead of clamoring to heaven as I listen to the horrors he narrates, I keep asking myself questions. Questions like: Why doesn't Mischa speak Yiddish like my parents and everybody else? Why does he stand motionless and silent in the synagogue while everybody else is praying?

The Enigmatic Eye [1986] 315

Such questions, however, I keep to myself. I wouldn't dare ask anybody such questions; neither do I voice any of the things that my dirty head keeps imagining. My dirty head never rests; day and night, always buzzing, always scheming. . . .

I start imagining this: One day another refugee, Avigdor, materializes in the neighborhood. He, too, comes from a concentration camp; unlike Mischa, however, he doesn't tell stories. And I keep imagining that this Avigdor is introduced to Mischa; and I keep imagining that they detest each other at first sight, even though at one time they were fellow sufferers. I imagine them one night seated at the table in our house; we're having a party, there are lots of people. Then suddenly—a scene that my dirty head has no difficulty devising—suggest that the two men have an arm-wrestling match.

(Why arm wrestling? Why should two puny little men, who in the past almost starved to death, put their strength against each other? Why? Why, indeed? Ask my dirty head why.)

So, there they are, the two men, arm against arm; tattooed arm against tattooed arm; nobody has noticed anything. But I have—thanks, of course, to my dirty head.

The numbers are the same.

"Look," I shout, "the numbers are the same!"

At first, everybody stares at me, bewildered; then they realize what I'm talking about and see for themselves: Both men have the same number.

Mischa has turned livid. Avigdor rises to his feet. He, too, is pale; but his rage soon makes his face and neck break out in red blotches. With unsuspected strength he grabs Mischa by the arm; he drags him to a bedroom, forces him go to in, then closes the door behind them. Only my dirty head knows what is going on there, for it is my head that has created Avigdor, it is my head that has given Avigdor this extraordinary strength, it is my head that has caused him to open and shut the door; and it is in my head that this door exists.

Avigdor is interrogating Mischa, and finding out that Mischa has never been a prisoner anywhere, that he is not even a Jew; he is merely a crafty Ukrainian who had himself tattooed and who made up the whole story in order to exploit Jews.

So, once the ruse is exposed, even my dirty head has no difficulty in making Avigdor—and my parents and the neighbors—expel Mischa in a fit of fury. And so Mischa is left destitute, and he has to sleep on a park bench.

My dirty head, however, won't leave him alone, and so I continue to imagine things. With the money Mischa gets from panhandling, he buys a lottery ticket. The number—trust this dirty head of mine to come up with something like this—is, of course, the one tattooed on his arm. And he wins in the lottery! Then he moves to Rio de Janeiro and he buys a beautiful condo and he is happy! Happy. He doesn't know what my dirty head has in store for him.

There's one thing that bothers him though: the number tattooed on his arm. He decides to have it removed. He goes to a famous plastic surgeon (these are refinements devised by my dirty head) and undergoes surgery. But then he goes into shock and dies a slow, agonizing death. . . .

ONE DAY MISCHA TELLS MY FATHER about the soap bars. He says he saw piles and piles of soap bars in the death camp. Do you know what the soap was made of? he asks. Human fat. Fat taken from Jews.

At night I dream about him. I'm lying naked in something resembling a bathtub, which is filled with putrid water; Mischa rubs that soap on me; he keeps rubbing it ruthlessly while shouting that he must wash the filth off my tongue and off my head, that he must wash the filth off the world.

I wake up sobbing, I wake up in the midst of great suffering. And it is this suffering that I, for lack of a better word, call the Holocaust.

Five Anarchists

THE SECRET SERVICE of King Igor XV has captured five anarchists.

"I'm going to teach those bastards a lesson," the monarch declares to the press.

The five are locked in the same prison cell: Louis Halm, thirty-two, the ringleader; Ruiz Agostin, thirty-eight, father of six children; Georges Pompeu, twenty-three, the only son of a widow; Miro Levin, twenty-four, the intellectual of the group, the author of *Anarchy and Independence*; Amedeo Bozzini, twenty-two, the youngest and least experienced.

Ruiz Agostin, on the first day:

"Friends, let's not worry. There's no evidence against us. Soon the king will have to set us free. Cheer up!"

The jailer comes in with the day's ration: five rolls and five mugs of water.

"Is that all?" Amedeo Bozzini protests.

"It's a diet devised by the prison's physician," the jailer replies. "A roll and a mug of water a day will guarantee a person's survival. Enjoy your meal."

The first day goes by, the second goes by, the tenth goes by. The jailer was right: Their hunger is satisfied and they are not undernourished.

To maintain themselves in high spirits, they hold debates:

"The present predicament propritiates . . . "

"Wrong, wrong."

"But the facts of reality . . . "

"Wrong!"

"It's undeniable that . . . "

"You idiot!"

Unfortunately, they begin to lose their tempers.

On the twenty-eighth day the guard comes in with four rolls and four mugs of water.

"There's one roll missing," shouts Georges Pompeu.

"And a mug of water!" chimes in Amedeo Bozzini.

"I'm following orders," replies the jailer, and he closes the heavy iron door.

"Friends," says Louis Halm, "we'll survive this trying ordeal. Our solidarity and our faith will help us succeed."

Each one gets four-fifths of a roll, and four-fifths of a mug of water.

On the following day, it is the same thing; and on the following, and on the following.

At the end of the week their bones begin to show through their skin. Louis Halm calls a meeting.

"Friends," he says in a strained voice, "as we can see, this is killing all of us. It would be better if we sacrificed one of us. Those who remain will wait for freedom, which will be here before long."

"I'd like to volunteer," says Ruiz Agostin.

"No. You've got six kids."

"Me, then," says George Pompeu. "Why not me?"

"Your old mother needs you."

"And who needs me?" asks Miro Levin.

"The people, for you do brainwork for them." A pause, after which Louis Halm goes on. "Everybody is indispensable, but somebody will have to die."

With the help of his companions, Amedeo Bozzini hangs himself from the bars of the jail.

On the following morning the jailer comes in with four rolls and four mugs of water; before leaving, he remarks: "The newspapers are saying that Amedeo has killed himself out of guilt."

"A lie!" shouts Louis Halm.

The jailer shrugs his shoulders, and leaves whistling.

On the fortieth day the ration is once again reduced: three rolls, three mugs of water. The prisoners protest. "I'm following orders," says the jailer.

"Another one of us will have to be sacrificed," says Louis Halm when the jailer is gone.

Ruiz Agostin volunteers again, and so does Georges Pompeu; but this time the chosen one is Miro Levin. "Well, I was really beginning to get tired of being an intellectual," he says before hanging himself

"The newspapers have reported that Miro Levin was a drug addict," says the jailer on the following morning.

"A lie!" shouts Louis Halm in a weak voice. The jailer leaves.

On the following morning: two rolls, two mugs of water.

"Tell my mother I died for a just cause," Georges Pompeu requests before hanging himself.

On the following morning the jailer remarks: "According to the newspapers, Georges Pompeu's mother will be spitting on her son's grave daily."

Louis Halm and Ruiz Agostin, now reduced to spectral figures, don't even protest.

On the fiftieth day the jailer comes in with one roll and one mug of water.

"Farewell, my friend," says Ruiz Agostin. "I hope you'll soon leave this place to provide leadership to our people. Look after my children!"

Louis Halm helps him hang himself. After ascertaining himself that Ruiz is indeed dead, he goes to the door.

"Hi, there! Jailer!"

The jailer appears.

"That was the last one," says Louis Halm with difficulty. "Go and tell the king that I've carried out my task according to our agreement. And now let me out."

But the jailer stands motionless, blocking the door with his corpulent body.

"Haven't you heard?" says Louis Halm gruffly. "Let me out! And go inform the king. Hurry."

"I've already done so," says the jailer.

"And?"

"He has sent you this."

The jailer produces a tray: one half of a roll. And a mug of water, half filled.

Among the Wise Men

THEY WENT IN SEARCH of the boy and found him among the wise men, who were dazzled by this whiz kid.

One wise man: "What's an abyss?"

"A natural cavity which opens itself in the ground in a roughly vertical way, and whose bottom is practically unexplorable. Next!"

Another wise man: "And a pyramid? How should we perceive a pyramid?"

"It's a solid figure, limited by a flat polygon ABCD and by the triangles, VAB, VBC, and others, having as a vertex a point V not situated on the plane of the polygon, and as opposite sides all the sides of the polygon. Another wise man, please."

Another wise man: "And what about Xerxes the First?"

"An Achaemenid king of Persia. He squelched uprisings in Egypt and Chaldea. In the year A.D. 480 he began an expedition into Greece. He fought in the Thermopylae and finally reached Athens. He was defeated in several battles. Another one. Hurry!"

Another wise man hurried forward: "The opening lines of the Odyssey, please."

"Sing to me, O Muse, of the industrious man who, after he sacked the sacred city of Troy, wandered about countless lands, visiting cities and learning the minds of so many men."

And he added peevishly: "A second-rate question. Is there anyone who can come up with a better question?"

An old man drew near. Respectful but challenging, he asked: "And what do you have to say about Aristotelian philosophy?"

The boy smiled approvingly yet condescendingly. "In Platonism, the problem of Oneness is decisive. Aristotle breaks away from this unity, and for this reason he is to be applauded. He has also stated, in his *History of the Animals*, that women have fewer teeth than men. Such a statement is regarded as an aberration. However, I see amazing transcendence in it."

The elders stirred, uneasy; then one of them raised his finger. "What do you have to say about fish?"

"Provided they are carefully chosen, fish can turn into yummy dishes. But only a fish that has bright, clear eyes, red gills, a well-shaped belly, firm flesh, a pleasant albeit peculiar smell, well-attached scales, and perfect fins. Take this fish. Then scrape the scales off carefully so as not to damage the skin. Gut the fish by slitting the belly open; it's not advisable to pull the guts out through the gills. Then fry it, piece by piece, in some good olive oil. Serve it with round slices of lemon."

Pushing his way to the front of the group, an old man then looked straight at the boy. "What's the meaning of life?"

At that moment the boy's parents took him away. It was lunchtime. Fish was the main course.

The Conspiracy

WHENEVER A TEACHER WAS ABSENT, Dona Marta was called in as a substitute. She taught singing, a subject regarded as being of secondary importance; besides, her classes were dreadful—but, on the other hand, she was always on call. Mornings, afternoons, evenings. She practically lived in the school. When we arrived in the morning she was already sitting in the staff room, always with that smile of hers, a smile somewhat resigned, somewhat silly; and even after the last of the night-class students had left, she would stay on. Waiting for one of her brothers to pick her up, but since nobody had ever seen this brother, rumor had it that she slept in the attic of the school building. That she had her meals on the premises was certain. At noon she would head for a bench in the school yard, take a sandwich from her bag, and sit munching on it, melancholy.

One day our Portuguese teacher didn't come. Dona Marta was brought in. Entering the classroom in her unsteady gait, she greeted us, then apologized for the absence of her colleague. We wouldn't be singing, she announced, for her voice was hoarse (something difficult to verify, as her voice sounded normally hoarse. Which even gave rise to jibes: Rusty Gullet, we had nicknamed her. Which she ignored, or pretended to ignore).

"We're going to do something different," she said. Then, trying to assume an air of mystery, of complicity: "We'll pretend this is your usual Portuguese class, okay? I'd like you to write a composition. On a topic of your own choice. Then I'll pick five students at random; they'll read their compositions aloud and the best one will win a prize."

She paused, then added: "Here it is."

She took a chocolate bar from her purse. A small, ordinary chocolate bar. And that bar she held up in the air for at least a minute, smiling, happy.

Ours was a school attended by the children of wealthy people. Chocolates, bonbons, candies—we could have them every day, at any time. A chocolate bar? Some of us snickered in derision. But at that moment the school principal appeared at the door and cast a stern look at us. Right away we set to work.

The Enigmatic Eye [1986] 323

I was sure I wouldn't be called upon to read my composition aloud. I was never called upon to do anything, which suited me fine. This fact, as well as the many mystery books I had been reading at that time, might explain the title of my composition: "The Conspiracy Against the Blind." In it I described a distant country which was ruled by a caste of blind men: a blind king, blind ministers, blind generals—all of them ruthlessly oppressing the people, who couldn't rebel or even conspire: The extremely sharp sense of hearing of the blind detected the slightest muttering of discontent. But even so, determined leaders of the people succeeded in hatching a conspiracy based exclusively on the written word. Books as well as magazines and newspapers denouncing the blind were published. All antiblind thoughts were voiced in writing only. Finally, the oligarchy was overthrown and a new king mounted the throne. His first acts were to destroy all the printing presses, close down the newspapers, and declare literacy illegal.

I finished my composition and sat quietly, waiting. The others were also finishing theirs. "Ready, everybody?" she asked. Everybody said they were. Except me. I kept quiet. But (as ill luck would have it), it was at me that she pointed her hesitant finger.

"You . . . what's your name?"

"Oscar," I replied (a lie; my name is Francisco Pedro; I could hear some stifled snickering but I stood firm).

"That's a beautiful name," she said, smiling. "Will you read your composition to us, Oscar?"

There was no way out. I glanced at the sheet of paper, then, after hesitating for a moment, I announced: "I wrote about a walk in the country."

She smiled approvingly. Then I gave an account of a walk in the country. I described the landscape: the trees, the brook, the cattle grazing under a deep blue sky. I concluded by saying that a walk in the country taught us to love nature.

"Very nice," she said when I finished. And she added with emotion: "I'd like to keep your composition."

"It's not worth keeping," I said. "But I'd like to," she persisted. "It's not worth keeping," I repeated. She laughed. "Come on now, Oscar, don't be so modest, let me have your composition."

"This composition belongs to me," I said, "and I can do with it whatever I want. This was supposed to be a singing class, not a Portuguese language class. You have no right to demand anything from me, ma'am."

"I'm asking you for the last time," she said, and her voice was trembling. "I'd like to have your composition. Please."

Taking the sheet of paper, I tore it up amid a sepulchral silence.

She said nothing but all of us could see the tears streaming down her face. Which surprised me: I didn't know then that the blind can cry.

The Prodigal Uncle

A WEALTHY ENTREPRENEUR SITS in his mansion watching television with his family when a servant comes in to announce that there is a young man at the door wanting to speak to him.

"He says he's your nephew."

The man gets up and goes to the door, where he finds a plainly dressed youth in his late teens, with an anxious expression on his bearded face. How are you, Uncle, he says; the man hesitates. Who are you? he asks. I'm your nephew Milton, says the youth.

"Milton? You, that little kid?"

"That's me all right, Uncle. Time goes by."

The man opens his arms.

"Here, let's have a hug, Milton!"

The man embraces him for a long time. Then he shows the youth into the room where the family is gathered, and introduces him:

Here's the son of my brother João; I hadn't seen him since he was a little boy. Everybody gets up to greet the newcomer; Aline, the eldest daughter (eighteen years old), smiles shyly. After the greetings, the man asks the youth to sit down by his side on the big sofa and asks him if he has had dinner yet; when the youth replies that he isn't hungry, the man insists that he have something, a whiskey, a beverage; the youth accepts some fruit juice, and while the servant is seeing to it, the man, his eyes bright, turns to the youth.

"Well, now tell me about your parents. I haven't seen them in years."

Whereupon sadness casts a shadow over the youth's face: with his voice cracking, he says that his father is dead and that his mother is in a mental hospital. I didn't know, said the man, dejected. Saying that he was quite fond of his brother, he then reminisces about their childhood days on a small farm full of fruit trees. The conversation drags on; then, noticing that the youth appears to be tired, the man asks him where he is staying; nowhere, is the reply; he has just arrived in town and hasn't found accommodation yet. The man insists that the youth stay at his house. The youth, apparently somewhat reluctant, accepts the invitation. The servant is called to show him to the guest room.

Days go by and the youth stays on. In fact, much to the delight of the family; the entrepreneur's wife enjoys talking to him; the eight-year-old son has found a playmate in him; and Aline, well, Aline is clearly in love. Her parents have noticed, and at the table they exchange glances, smiling.

The entrepreneur offers the youth a job in his company. He accepts. From then on they leave the house together every morning; the young man now dresses in a befitting manner. As a business manager he proves himself to be dynamic, enterprising, intelligent; the entrepreneur's aides are delighted with him. It is predicted that after his engagement to Aline, he will officially take up his duties as executive director.

One night he asks his prospective father-in-law if he can have a word with him. There is a personal matter he would like to discuss. They go to the library; as soon as the entrepreneur closes the door behind them, the young man, on an impulse, kneels down and kisses the entrepreneur's hands. But what's going on, says the man, at once surprised and moved, but the young man, in tears, is too distressed to reply. Finally he calms down, and then he says that he is grateful, very grateful, but not for the reasons the entreprenuer imagines; he is grateful for other, entirely different reasons. The young man then proceeds to tell the entrepreneur that after dropping out of school, he spent a long time loafing around the country, sleeping in shacks and abandoned houses, until he fell in with a group of lawbreakers. Together, they devised a plan to kidnap the entrepreneur and de- mand a large ransom. Entrusted with this mission, the young man was at first firmly determined to carry it out. Not just for the money; well, for the money, too; but mostly because he believed he would be meting out justice. He carefully studied all the details of the operation. . . .

But the warmth with which he was welcomed, the atmosphere of genuine family love that he found in the house, and also the dy- namism, the intelligence, the kindness of the entrepreneur—all of this (contrasting so sharply with the erroneous ideas about business- men that the youth used to have) caused a change of heart. Re- nouncing violence, he now wants to forget the past and turn over a new leaf. I realize, he says, that I was living before in a world of fa- natical fantasies, in a world of dangerous illusions; thank goodness, I withdrew in time, before I turned into a criminal. All I want now is to build a home full of love and comfort for my wife and children. I owe my good intentions to you, sir. I'll never forget the lesson in life that I've learned here, a lesson for which I'll be grateful to you forever.

The entrepreneur listens in silence. But you're really my nephew, aren't you? he finally asks. The young man hesitates; he hesitates for a long time before saying that he made up the whole story. He used to know the entrepreneur's real nephew; from that youth, later killed in an accident, he obtained all the information he needed to pose as the entrepreneur's nephew.

Then the entrepreneur rises to his feet, says he has some matter to attend to, and asks the young man to wait in the library. He leaves. Ten minutes later he returns, accompanied by two of his security guards. Arrest this man, he says dryly. The young man looks at him with disbelief, horror even; slowly, however, a smile begins to open his face. Thank you, Uncle, he says at last. After kissing the man's hands once more, he leaves, escorted by the guards.

Root Canal Treatment

STILL DIZZY FROM THE DRONE of the dentist's drill, and with part of her face frozen, she left the dentist's office and walked toward the elevator. Wanting above anything else at that moment to get home and lie down, she pressed the button.

A man stood there, waiting for the elevator. Partly because she wasn't feeling well, and partly because the corridor—notwithstanding the fancy building—was poorly lit, it wasn't until several seconds later that she noticed his presence. The man was still young and—a detail that didn't escape her—relatively well dressed. Had he been raggedly dressed and, on top of that, evil looking, she wouldn't of course have stayed there for another moment and would have hastily sought refuge in the dentist's office. But no, nothing in the man's appearance roused distrust. So, she looked at her watch—six o'clock in the evening—and pressed the elevator button again.

Suddenly the man let out a moan, staggered, and leaned against the wall. Startled, she looked at him. Startled and annoyed. That's all she needed, to have to help a stranger when she herself could barely stand on her own two legs. She wanted to ignore him; she wished she could. But no, it wasn't in her to ignore other people. For which she often censured herself: I'm always taking care of others, I'm neglectful of myself, a patsy, that's what I am. She looked around; her last hope was for someone to appear and take charge of the case (if it was indeed a case; everything seemed to indicate that it was; the man seemed really ill). But no, nobody appeared. Only the two of them in the long corridor. God's will be done, she thought. She addressed the man.

"Aren't you feeling well?"

He looked at her. He wasn't ugly; he wasn't good-looking, either. A man with an ordinary face—like her own, as a matter of fact (I have an ordinary face, she was in the habit of whispering as she looked at herself in the mirror at night; an ordinary face, an ordinary life).

"What?" The voice was weak, a child's voice, almost.

"I asked if you weren't feeling well."

"If I'm not feeling well . . . ?" He looked at her as if he hadn't understood. "If I'm not feeling well . . . ? I don't know. I think I'm not feeling well. Yes, I'm sick. I have cancer."

"Gosh," she murmured. She didn't know what to say. To her own indisposition was now added the discomfiture created by this situation; a horrible situation. And to make matters worse, the elevator wouldn't come.

Fortunately, the man seemed to be rallying. Taking a deep breath, he pulled a handkerchief out of his pocket and mopped his forehead.

"Cancer," he said. "The doctor said there's no doubt about it. He's quite frank. One of those that will hold nothing back from you, you know. You have cancer, my friend, you're not going to live much longer, you'd better set your affairs in order."

Poor man, she thought. Poor, poor man. Suddenly she was struck by remorse—what was her root canal compared to this man's cancer?—and at the same time by relief: root canal was preferable to cancer. Anything would be preferable to cancer. Not that she was safe from cancer, of course; all it takes for a person to fall ill is to be alive, but it wasn't her turn yet; no, it wasn't. At that moment it fell to her lot to suffer from a tooth infection; at that moment she was safe; in that corridor, with the two of them, Death had drawn lots and the lot fell upon the man. Not my turn yet. Relieved, she felt generous, ready to offer help.

"Is there anything I can do?"

The man raised his head, and looked at her again, as if only at that moment he had become aware of the presence of another person, of a woman.

"You . . . "

He hesitated. Of course. Confronted with his own death, how could a man not hesitate? This confrontation gave him the right to say whatever he wanted—which he wouldn't do under other circumstances (perhaps because of his upright character). This confrontation gave him the right to ask, to demand, anything from any person, from any woman. For the time being, he still hesitated, but despair would break down barriers and overcome scruples, and he would end up by making her a proposition which, he imagined, was on his mind, as it was on the mind of every other man, good or bad, healthy or dying. He would end up by inviting her to go to a motel with him. And she wouldn't be able to recoil, offended, from a proposition that was, after all, merely normal; a proposition that any man, even if stricken by cancer, or for this very reason, could make to any woman, no matter how straitlaced she was, for the very reason that he was near the end, near the stopping point of a countdown now measured in months, perhaps days, hours. And what would she say, then, to get out of this situation? But, my friend, I don't even know you, we haven't been introduced—would she say that? Would that do as an excuse? This banal line, this stock phrase with which she warded off brash males (who, in fact, were growing scarcer as her youth retreated)? But he wasn't a brash male, nor was he an opportunist. Or, if he was an opportunist, he had every right to be one. I'm a virgin—would she say that? Could she use as an argument the very thing she now regarded as a stigma, a sign of her inability to live? No. There was nothing she could say. The man would invite her to go to a motel and she would have to accompany him, the two of them marching, on their respective paths, toward the gallows.

Just then the elevator came.

Mumbling a vague good-bye, she rushed headlong into the elevator, settled herself amid the other people, then stood still and shaky. It wasn't until the doors closed that she realized that the man hadn't followed her. The elevator slowly went down: 12, 11, 10. . . . The man had remained up there. In the gloomy corridor.

At the front door she stopped and peered outside. A street in the downtown area of a big city, a busy street—people, cars, motorbikes. On the facade of the store across the street, the lights of a neon sign went on and out. CORA FASHIONS, CORA FASHIONS. My God, she thought, what have I done? I've run away from a sick man, a man in need of help; it was fear that has made me run away—but fear of what, when he didn't harm me?

No, she couldn't accept this. Her self-dignity wouldn't let her. She had behaved like a coward, like a frightened rat; she had behaved like a fool. But there was still time to right her fault. All she had to do was to return to the fourteenth floor, speak to the man, justify herself (she could say something like I thought you were going to take the elevator, too; any explanation would do), ask again if she could be of any help, and then, yes, say a friendly good-bye. She went back to the elevator; when the doors opened, she hesitated again; then the doors began to close—but at the very last moment she managed to leap in. That was a bit of luck! she thought. Was it, really? (That doubt, again. Again and forever: doubt, indecision, fear.) Should I go back? Won't I get involved in a mess? She was annoyed at herself: A mess? What mess? A mess, why? There won't be any mess. She would simply speak to the man, justify herself with a carefully prepared excuse, then politely say to him: Would the senhor (senhor? Why not você or tu, the informal way of addressing a person? No. No familiarities even taking into account the man's predicament; even taking into account her possible earlier rudeness to him. Você? No. Nor tu. Later, perhaps—but when would this later be? Would there be any time left for "later"? Did she want it? Questions, questions.) please finish what you were saying before?

The elevator stopped. The doors opened. She stepped out, looked to this side, to that side. Nobody. The corridor was deserted.

It occurred to her that the man might have returned to his doctor's office: Maybe he was really feeling ill, maybe he was feeling even worse now. Anyhow, she thought, if he had decided to see his doctor again, then this matter is no longer in my hands. However, she had to admit to herself that she was disappointed; frustrated; distressed even; on the verge of tears. It would be nice if everything could be solved once and for all.

The door to the doctor's office was open; this fact struck her as a sign, an encouraging sign, so, she decided to make another attempt. She would go in; if she found the man in the waiting room, she would ask him if everything was all right; then, regardless of the answer, or the connotations or veiled propositions of the answer, she would consider the case closed, say good-bye, and leave.

But she didn't see the man in the waiting room. The doctor and the receptionist were there, both getting ready to leave. Can I help you? asked the receptionist politely. No, she replied, embarrassed, I must have entered the wrong room, sorry. She hurried out.

She was feeling sick now, so sick that she had to lean against the wall: dizzy, nauseated, sick, sick. What in the world made me come back? she kept asking herself. Why didn't I go straight home?

The elevator came. It wasn't the one she had taken before. Then it occurred to her: While I was going up, he was going down; such things do happen. Things that are funny in the movies.

With a faint, absurd hope, she stepped out of the elevator. Maybe the man was still somewhere in that area: standing at the main entrance, for instance; he could well be watching the neon sign and be pondering on the significance of the lights going on and off; or he could be watching the street, the passersby, the cars.

No, the man wasn't there. As she reached the main entrance, she looked to this side, then looked to that side. She didn't see him among the people walking by. Or in the cars parked on the street. Or anywhere.

She hailed a taxi. She got in and gave the driver her destination. Normally, she would have taken the bus; although she earned a relatively good salary, she tried to save. At the moment, however, she felt she was in no condition to stand on a bus line.

They drove in silence. After a remark or two about the weather—it's been very hot, it's going to rain—the taxi driver fell silent. They arrived at the neighborhood where she lived; three blocks before her street, she asked the taxi driver to stop and she got out of the car. She wanted to walk for a while. But walking didn't dispel the anxiety she had been feeling. Perhaps she should have walked a longer distance. Perhaps: too late now.

At home, her mother was waiting for her; worried, of course. Her mother worried about everything. I was delayed at the dentist's, she said. She couldn't tell her mother about the incident with the man; she wished she could; she wished she could talk to her mother more

The Enigmatic Eye [1986] 333

openly; her mother was the only person she had, now that her sisters were living far away, one in Rio, the other in Recife. But her mother got upset easily; sometimes she would lose sleep over a movie she had watched on television, and would have to take sleeping pills. So, she merely made a remark about something or other—it's hot, isn't it?—then went to the kitchen to get dinner ready. This was something her mother couldn't do because of her arthritis. There was hardly anything her mother could still do. So, she had to do the cooking, run the household, and look after everything. But she didn't complain. She did all the work and didn't complain.

The effect of the anesthetic was wearing off, and she was feeling better; but she couldn't stop thinking about the man. She was annoyed at herself. The matter is closed, I should have spoken to him but didn't, now there's nothing that can be done, and if there's no solution to a problem, the problem is thus solved.

She didn't eat much. Her mother noticed. You didn't eat much, she said. It's the tooth, she explained. Does it hurt? asked the mother, alarmed—everything was cause for alarm: the flu, a headache. No, Mother, it doesn't hurt, but the dentist told me not to chew on this side. She waited until her mother finished eating, then she cleared the table and did the dishes. Later they sat down to watch some television. At ten o'clock she bade her mother good night and went to bed.

Naturally, she found herself unable to sleep. The image of the man haunted her; in particular, his beseeching eyes. Tossing about in bed, she cursed herself, she could have prevented all of this, she could have made the dental appointment for some other day, but no, she had insisted on this day because business at the office happened to be slow; and now she was paying for her insistence, for her compulsion to do the right thing. Everything right: everything wrong. As usual.

It was hot; she was drenched in sweat. I need a shower, she murmured. Sometimes she would get up in the middle of the night to take a shower. An adventure, in a way. Innocuous, but still an adventure. She jumped out of bed, and after ascertaining herself that her mother was asleep, she went to the bathroom She stood a long time under the tepid shower, which normally had a wholesome effect on her, as if the water, cleansing her mind, carried her torments down the drain. Now, however, it was impossible for her to relax; because of the man, of course. She seemed to see him there, in the bathroom, looking at her desperately. She closed her eyes tightly; and suddenly she wished she were ill. She wished she had cancer. Not something annihilating, terminal cancer; a modest tumor, which would be able to soak up her anxiety like a sponge soaks up water. She would like to have the opportunity to be cut up; to suffer pain; to have a big, conspicuous scar. She began to palpate her belly, her neck, her breasts (which no other hand, except the hand of her female gynecologist, had ever touched)—nothing. Just the usual flesh, fat, tendons. The same ones with which she had been endowed at birth, and which she had nourished with sandwiches and fruit juices; and a skin that was now beginning to turn flaccid. Grabbing the towel, she dried herself vigorously, then put on her nightgown and went back to bed. She fell into a doze, woke up, then dozed off again, dreaming about entangled, anguishing things. With relief she saw the day dawn.

She got up early, washed, got dressed, had a cup of black coffee. Flipping through the newspaper, she lingered over the announcements of deaths. Mario Mendes, could that be him? Francisco (Chico) Westdorfer? Dr. Armando Fonseca? How could she know? She couldn't even recall the man's face, she discovered, feeling uneasy. That's how flighty she was. Grabbing her purse, she went out. The bus took a long time to come, and she was late for work. Berenice, the other secretary, was already in the office. Beautiful, charming, and elegant as usual, Berenice wanted to know if everything had been all right at the dentist's. Yes, she replied, everything went well. She couldn't tell the other woman about the man in the corridor. She wouldn't understand. A free, emancipated woman, Berenice lived alone; she had several boyfriends and took turns going to bed with each one of them; and she never missed the chance to rebuke her fellow worker: You keep blaming yourself for things that aren't your fault.

She sat down at the typewriter—and couldn't help thinking again: Even this shows how different our situations are. In this export company where they both worked, Berenice, a bilingual secretary, was responsible for typing the letters in English, and for this reason she had a better quality typewriter, an electronic Olivetti. She, however, had an ordinary typewriter on which she typed the letters in Portuguese. But she refused to ask for a better one, despite Berenice's insistence that she do so: I really like this typewriter, it was on a similar one that I learned how to type.

The man. What was he doing now, the poor man? Was he at his home? At work, trying to keep his mind off death, now near (how near?)? Already in the hospital? Already?

At lunch in a luncheonette, she couldn't eat a thing. What's the matter? asked Berenice. It's my tooth, she lied, it hurts a little. Why don't you go back to that lady dentist of yours, said Berenice, she'll have to do something about it. Go, I'll look after the office.

That's how Berenice was—bossy, determined. Which rather annoyed her, for she thought that Berenice meddled too much in her life. But now an idea struck her: Yes, she would go back—not to the dentist's office, but to the doctor's office. She would pour out her heart to the doctor; she would talk about the man she had met in the corridor, speak to him of her remorse, ask him to help her find the man. Undoubtedly, the doctor would show sympathy for her; doctors are trained to be sympathetic to people.

Upon returning to the office, she consulted the telephone directory and found the doctor's phone number. Before dialing, she hesitated: Should I or shouldn't I? She dialed the number. The receptionist answered. Yes, the doctor was in, but only for a short time; he had come to the office just to pick up some papers for the income tax people. Please, she whispered, ask him if he can see me. The receptionist said she would speak to the doctor. Minutes went by, long minutes they were, before finally the receptionist came back on the phone. The doctor said he'll see you but you'll have to come right away.

Quickly grabbing her purse and her coat, she said to Berenice, I'm leaving now, I'm going to the dentist.

AND SUDDENLY SHE IS HIT by an urge, a great urge, to hurry away: she runs out of the building, hails a taxi, gets into the car, tells the taxi driver to head for downtown. The cabbie—young, handsome, and garrulous—talks nonstop about politics, about soccer, about the heat. But what am I doing, she wonders, what in the world am I doing? She's on her way to the doctor, she'll tell him an entangled, crazy story, what will the doctor think of her? And yet the taxi is already in the downtown area; she's getting closer and closer to the final catastrophe.

They arrive. She pays, gets some change back, but doesn't alight from the taxi. What is she hoping for? Is she hoping that the taxi driver will guess at her dilemma? That he will offer to help her? That he will declare himself in love, I love you, ma'am, let's go to a motel right away? I can't stop here, says the man, already impatient at the delay, would you mind getting out quickly, ma'am? She gets out, the taxi speeds away, the tires screeching on the asphalt.

For a moment she stands still. She sighs, then heads for the entrance of the building, goes in, and walks down the long corridor. The elevator is there, its doors open. She steps in, presses a button, the doors close, and there she is, slowly ascending in a closed compartment, immersed in the brightness of the fluorescent lights. She gets out of the elevator, takes a few hesitant steps, stops. In front of her is the door to the doctor's office. Some time ago she devised a plan, which consisted in her going in there and telling this man, this doctor, about something that had happened to her. But she can't carry out this plan. She just can't. The absurdity paralyzes her.

Suddenly her tooth starts to hurt.

With growing elation she realizes this fact: Her tooth hurts. A pain that grows by the minute, an excruciating pain; a pain that, triumphant, imposes itself; a pain that immobilizes her, that galvanizes her. With simple but genuine joy she receives the good news—the pain; it is the answer to all her anxieties; better yet, it makes answers unnecessary. In the canal of her tooth another creature is in a period of gestation—herself, in the process of being reborn. Her old carcass will burst open, and here in this corridor, resurrection will take place. Slivers of light dance before her eyes; she turns around, and like an automaton, she advances toward the dentist's office. She doesn't have an appointment for today, but what does she care? Whoever is in pain has rights. She opens the door and walks in. With her head held high.

The Interpreter

WHEN I ARRIVE, they are already seated at the table—the father, the mother, the son. But they haven't started dinner yet; they're waiting for me. I'm late. I've walked all the way here.

On my arrival, their heads rise briskly. The father's gray. The mother's, gray, too, despite the hair tint. The youth's, shaved (it is, I know, a form of protest). The eyeglasses—all three wear them— glitter in the strong electric lights, hiding their eyes and whatever they might be expressing—anger, or fear, or sorrow, or even hope.

They—the father and the mother—rise and walk up to me. We exchange greetings and remarks about the weather. This winter has been awful, says the mother, it makes people feel under the weather. I agree; her eyes are congested; it could be from crying, but it could also be from a cold. One shouldn't dramatize. I say good evening to the youth, who mutters something in reply and remains seated, motionless. I put my hand on his shoulder: It's a friendly gesture. A buzzer sounds in the pantry, which adjoins the dining room. The button is under the table; while the mother was sitting down again, she pressed it with her foot, thus summoning the maid. The family enjoys all the comforts of life; the father, a prosperous sales representative, can afford to provide his family with all the amenities, if not luxuries, of life. The maid that appears at the door wears a cap and a starched apron; and the soup tureen that she brings in is made of porcelain. But when the father eats the first spoonful, the slurping noise betrays his humble origins which, incidentally, he doesn't repudiate: I started from nothing, he often says with pride. The son, however, makes a grimace of disgust. His father's table manners annoy him. He can't stand the boorishness of the bourgeois.

Good soup, I remark with joviality. I'm forty-two years old, and I live alone (I'm considered a weird, albeit charming, bachelor), but even so I maintain my sense of humor and I know how to look straight at life with one eye ironic, the other tender; with one eye mirthful, the other serene. I'm a judicious man; this couple—my cousin and his wife—know this. That's why they keep inviting me over for dinner. They know I won't let silence descend upon this table. To let silence envelop them like dense, dark magma? Unthinkable. I'm a geology professor (currently unemployed; this dinner, by the way, is very timely, it's the first decent meal I've had in many months); but I know that such things upset people. Before I'm through with the soup, I have time to comment on three different things:

—a movie depicting the facetious side of life, recently shown in
the movie theaters of the capital city;

—the playoffs in the soccer championship;

—a modular stereo system consisting of a receiver, a record
player, and a tape deck (which I'm hoping they'll give me as a
birthday gift).

To my first comment the youth reacts by merely raising his head,
without displaying any further interest; to the second ditto; to the
third he reacts by smiling, for I'm now telling them about my outrageous experience with a stereo system—I wanted to tune in to
an FM station, but instead I somehow triggered the tone arm of
the turntable, which then kept joggling back and forth like a crazy
turkey. Like a crazy turkey! I repeat, hitting the table with my fist
and roaring with laughter. The youth smiles.

The salad is brought in and for one full minute—but not exceed-
ing one—we munch in silence on the leaves of lettuce and on the
round slices of cucumber. The dressing is superb—at once mild and
peppery—and I say, The dressing is superb, Cousin. Grateful, she
smiles.

Next comes the main course: roast beef garnished with peas, car-
rots, and french fries, everything topped with a remoulade sauce. Before I start helping myself, the father leans toward me: *Ask him*, he
murmurs, *how things are*. The moment has come!

Laying down my knife and fork, I pick up my napkin. After wiping my mouth carefully, I turn to the youth.

"So, young man, how are things?"

He doesn't look at me. He's cutting the meat, and, still cutting it,
he replies, "Everything's fine, everything's the same."

The mother lifts her napkin to her eyes. It's not the most suitable
kind of fabric—the napkin is stiff with starch—with which to wipe
tears, but she doesn't have a handkerchief handy; it seems that tears
have taken her by surprise in the course of this dinner. But it's a

fleeting emotion; before long, she heaves a sigh and mumbles something. Unintelligible words addressed to everybody, or to nobody, or to me, or to God, or to her son, or even to the maid, although she isn't in the room at the moment.

Once again the father leans toward me. *Ask him,* he says in a tense, quite audible voice, *if he has changed his mind.*

I'd say he hasn't, it doesn't seem to me that the youth has changed his mind; but it doesn't behoove me to have an opinion. My cousin wants me to ask the question, so I ask.

"Well, my lad, have you changed your mind?"

Although he doesn't reply, it's obvious that his mind is made up. He's leaving. Soon. Tomorrow. Or tonight. Maybe after dinner. Maybe he won't even finish dinner.

The father is terrified. He doesn't know what happened, or what's happening, or what will happen. He knows nothing, he doesn't even know how to talk. Shaking, he leans toward me once more: *Ask him what he wants,* he whispers, *in order to change his mind.*

I take a sip of wine, then put the glass down. I won't make my cousin's words mine; I find them unsuitable. The proposition may even be sound, but the way it has been presented is totally wrong. I have a better way.

"Isn't it possible, perhaps," I say in a casual tone, "that on second thought you might change your mind?"

I wait for several seconds before adding: "Isn't there anything that could perhaps make you change your mind?"

"Shit!" he cries out, throwing his napkin aside and rising to his feet. "Shit! Can't people even eat in peace?"

Then the worst happens: The father and the mother get up and start to scream and to cry, and the mother, like a madwoman, starts to pull at her hair. For a few seconds the son looks at them full of hatred, of despair, of bitterness. Then he walks out.

Devastated, the two of them let themselves collapse on their chairs. With a mingle of despair and accusation, the father looks at me: Why don't you do something? But there's nothing I can do now. However, I want to show them that life goes on; with this intention, I cut a piece of meat, stuff it into my mouth, and chew vigorously. "Scrumptious, this roast beef!," I say with my mouth full.

Even though there's something missing, hmm? There's something missing. There's a certain emptiness inside me, an emptiness that can't be filled with meat or peas or wine—it will take this one specific thing to fill it, such a plain and delicious thing whose name escapes me at the moment. My mouth opens but no sound comes out; I raise my hand, make a gesture, point to it—but I can't remember the name of this thing, which is so good, of this thing whose image is so clear to me: a slightly crisp crust, with a soft, fragrant, warm core. The name suddenly pops into my mind and, joyful, I cry out as they, stunned, stare at me, as if I were speaking in that language of the yellow race:

"Bread!"

Atlas

I

It fell to the giant Atlas's lot to support the world upon his back, a task that had been assigned to him by—whom? He no longer remembered. By whom, and why, and when, he no longer remembered. Neither did he know when he would be relieved of this duty, or when he would be replaced. All he knew was that he had to support the world and there he remained, motionless, on his knees, stooping under the weight of the globe. Without complaining, without seeking help from anyone. As a matter of fact, nobody would ever offer him help. Younger and stronger, the other giants didn't commiserate with him on his fate at all; what's more, they would even reproach Atlas for his alleged arrogance: Did he then see himself as being very important? Did he think of his job as being exceptional?

"The Earth! It's not even one of the biggest planets!"

They were wrong. Atlas was unpretentious. And he didn't even look upon what he did as labor. Labor? Certainly not. Now, if he were carrying the Earth from one universe to the next, if he were shifting it, say, one meter, even one millimeter, then yes, one could consider this labor. But no, Atlas was always motionless, frozen still, and for this reason he kept reproaching himself day in, day out, year in, year out: I'm a bum, I'm a bum. He envied those who roamed across the skies, taming comets or rekindling the flame of the stars— tasks that demanded great skill, if not virtuosity. But he did nothing, and there was no call for any skills. A rock could replace him. A giant tortoise. Four elephants.

And yet his was a hard, arduous responsibility. The mountain ranges bruised his shoulders; the tropical rain forests irritated his neck, giving him a rash; and once a peninsula had penetrated the auricle of his ear, causing a serious infection. Just think how much worse it would be if you had to carry the sun, his wife would say, try-ing to comfort him. Atlas had to admit that she was right. At least the Earth was cool, except for the occasional eruption of a volcano, when he would receive second- or third-degree burns.

2

Atlas rarely slept. Sometimes he managed to have a nap. And in those moments he would dream about the inhabitants of his planet: tiny creatures whom he had never seen, but he imagined that, smil-ing, they waved at him from their tiny houses or from their tiny ships. On waking up, he would try to forget those dreams. There was no way he could substantiate them; this impossibility depressed him, and it accounted for the sadness on his face and the vacant gaze of his eyes, lost in the infinity.

3

The wife of the giant Atlas was a bitter woman. She envied her friends, whose husbands had interesting jobs and earned decent wages. My husband, she would write in her diary, has a weird occupation for which he doesn't get paid. She would turn to knitting for comfort.

As for his children, they were pranksters. Seeing Atlas stooping under the weight of the world, they would tickle him in the armpits. And they would laugh, they would split their sides with laughter. Atlas would have loved to join in the laughter, too. However, were he to do so, he would run the risk of dropping the world, a catastrophe of unpredictable consequences. For Atlas, being tickled was a really unbearable torture. All his muscles would contract in his effort to remain motionless; beads of sweat would gather on his forehead; tears would stream down his face. But even so, he would wear a fixed wooden smile, a smile that was almost a grimace—until the children, bored by their own pranks, would go away.

4

On a certain Saturday, Charles Atlas took his children to the zoo. While they were running through the graveled alleys, he stood admiring a lion. The feline was dozing. Or perhaps, treacherously, it was just pretending to be asleep, because all of a sudden it opened its eyes. For a few seconds they—the man and the beast—stared at each other; the puny man and the magnificent beast. Then the lion stretched its limbs. My God, thought Charles Atlas, its muscles run under its skin like bunnies running under a carpet! And the lion isn't even doing calisthenics or lifting weights, it's merely exercising its willpower. An animal's willpower, infinitely weaker than the will of a rational human being like me!

He felt he was on the verge of making a major discovery—a method using self-control by which it would be possible for him to develop powerful muscular masses in his arms, in his legs, in his abdomen, even in his scalp. He would become as strong as—a lion! A tiger? Much stronger than a lion or a tiger! He wouldn't have to put up with his boss's insults anymore. And, by teaching his method to others, he would become rich. He would be able to bedeck his wife with jewels and to afford expensive toys for his children.

Shouts of distress aroused him from his thoughts. He turned around, his children were nowhere in sight. A small crowd had gathered in front of the tigers' cage. Running to it, he elbowed his way through the crowd—and he couldn't contain a scream of horror. His younger daughter had managed to squeeze herself through the bars of the cage and there she stood now, among the beasts. Charles Atlas took a step forward and fell to the ground, unconscious.

When he came to, the little girl stood in front of him, looking at him curiously. She had come out of the cage with the same boldness that had prompted her in. Weeping, Charles Atlas threw himself at her.

He bought his children popcorn and ice cream; he loaded them with popcorn and ice cream. Then he took them to the amusement park, and he spent all his money, down to the last cent—what did it matter?—on the children. At nightfall they returned home, Charles Atlas carrying the tyke on his shoulders. He wasn't loaded down with her weight; she wasn't a burden at all.

His wife, worried about their delay, greeted them. You'll have to be up early tomorrow, she reminded him. True: On the following day Atlas would have to resume his usual task of carrying the world on his back.

But he didn't go to bed. He sat down on a chair in the living room, and there he remained, smoking in the dark. He was envisioning a new method for developing muscles. A method that would make him strong, rich, famous. One day, he was thinking, I'll hold the world in the palm of my hand.

A Brief History of Capitalism

MY FATHER WAS A COMMUNIST and a car mechanic. A good Communist, according to his comrades, but a lousy mechanic according to consensus. As a matter of fact, so great was his inability to handle cars that people wondered why he had chosen such an occupation. He used to say it had been a conscious choice on his part; he believed in manual work as a form of personal development, and he had confidence in machines and in their capability to liberate man and launch him into the future, in the direction of a freer, more desirable life. Roughly, that's what he meant.

I used to help my father in his car repair shop. Since I was an only son, he wanted me to follow in his footsteps. There wasn't, however, much that I could do; at that time I was eleven years old, and almost as clumsy as he was at using tools. Anyhow, for the most part, there was no call for us to use them since there wasn't much work coming our way. We would sit talking and thus while away the time. My father was a great storyteller; enthralled, I would listen to his accounts of the uprising of the Spartacists, and of the rebellion led by the fugitive slave Zambi. In those moments his eyes would glitter. I would listen, deeply affected by his stories; often, my eyes would fill with tears.

Once in awhile a customer appeared. Usually a Party sympathizer (my father's comrades didn't own cars), who came to Father more out of a desire to help than out of need. These customers played it safe, though: It was always some minor repair, like fixing the license plate securely, or changing the blades of the windshield wipers. But even such simple tasks turned out to be extraordinarily difficult for Father to perform; sometimes it would take him a whole day to change a distributor point. And the car would drive away with the engine misfiring (needless to say, its owner would never set foot in our repair shop again). If it weren't for the financial problems (my mother had to support us by taking in sewing), I wouldn't have minded the lack of work too much. I really enjoyed those rap sessions with my father. In the morning I would go to school; but as soon as I came home, I would run to the repair shop, which was near our house. And there I would find Father reading. Upon my arrival, he would set his book aside, light his pipe, and start telling me his stories. And there we would stay until Mother came to call us for dinner.

One day when I arrived at our repair shop, there was a car there, a huge, sparkling, luxury car. None of the Party sympathizers, not even the wealthiest among them, owned a car like that. Father told me that the monster car had stalled right in front of the shop. The owner then left it there, under his care, saying he would be back late in the afternoon. And what's wrong with it? I asked, somewhat alarmed, sensing a foul-up in the offing.

"I wish I knew." Father sighed. "Frankly, I don't know what's wrong with it. I already took a look but couldn't find the defect. It must be something minor, probably the carburetor is clogged up, but . . . I don't know, I just don't know what it is."

Dejected, he sat down, took a handkerchief out of his pocket, and wiped his forehead. Come on, I said, annoyed at his passivity, it's no use your sitting there.

He got up and the two of us took a look at the enormous engine, so clean, it glittered. Isn't it a beauty? remarked my father with the pleasure of an owner who took pride in his car.

Yes, it was a beauty—except that he couldn't open the carburetor. I had to give him a hand; three hours later, when the man returned, we were still at it.

He was a pudgy, well-dressed man. He got out of a taxi, his face already displaying annoyance. I expected him to be disgruntled, but never for a moment did I imagine what was to happen next.

At first the man said nothing. Seeing that we weren't finished yet, he sat down on a stool and watched us. A moment later he stood up; he examined the stool on which he had sat.

"Dirty. This stool is dirty. Can't you people even offer your customers a decent chair to sit on?"

We made no reply. Neither did we raise our heads. The man looked around him.

"A real dump, this place. A sty. How can you people work amid such filth?"

We, silent.

"But that's the way everything is," the man went on. "In this country that's the way it is. Nobody wants to do any work, nobody wants to get his act together. All people ever think of is booze, women, the Carnaval, soccer. But to get down to work? Never."

Where's the wrench? asked Father in a low, restrained voice. Over there, by your side, I said. Thanks, he said, and resumed fiddling with the carburetor.

"You people want nothing to do with a regular, steady job." The man sounded increasingly more irritated. "You people will never get out of this filth. Now, take me, for instance. I started at the bottom. But nowadays I'm a rich man. Very rich. And do you know why? Because I was clean, well organized, hardworking. This car here, do you think it's the only one I own? Do you?"

Tighten the screw, said Father, tighten it really tight.

"I'm talking to you!" yelled the man, fuming. "I'm asking you a question! Do you think this is the only car I own? That's what you think, isn't it? Well, let me tell you something, I own two other cars. Two other cars! They are in my garage. I don't use them. Because I don't want to. If I wanted, I could abandon this car here in the middle of the street and get another one. Well, I wouldn't get it myself; I would have someone get it for me. Because I have a chauffeur, see? That's right. I drive because I enjoy driving, but I have a chauffeur. I don't have to drive, I don't need this car. If I wanted to, I could junk this fucking car, you hear me?"

Hand me the pipe wrench, will you? said Father. The small one.

The man was now standing quite close to us. I didn't look at him, but I could feel his breath on my arm.

"Do you doubt my word? Do you doubt that I can smash up this car? Do you?"

I looked at the man. He was upset. When his eyes met mine, he seemed to come to his senses; only for a moment, though; he opened his eyes wide.

"Do you doubt it? That I can smash up this fucking car? Give me a hammer. Quick! Give me a hammer!"

He searched for a hammer but couldn't find one (it would have been a miracle had he found one; even we could never find the tools in our shop). Without knowing what he was doing, he gave the car door a kick; soon followed by another, then another.

"That's what I've been telling you," he kept screaming. "That I'll smash up this fucking car! That's what I've been telling you."

Ready, said Father. I looked at him; he was pale, beads of sweat were running down his face. Ready? I asked, not getting it. Ready, he said. You can now start the engine.

The man, panting, was looking at us. Opening the car door, I sat at the steering wheel and turned on the ignition. Incredible: The engine started. I revved it up. The shop was filled with the roar of the engine.

My father stood mopping his face with his dirty handkerchief. The man, silent, kept looking at us. How much do I owe you? finally he asked. Nothing, said my father. What do you mean, nothing? Suspicious, the man frowned. Nothing, said my father, it costs you nothing, it's on the house. Then the man, opening his wallet, pulled out a bill.

"Here, for a shot of rum."

"I don't drink." said my father without touching the money

The man replaced the bill in his wallet, which he then put into his pocket. Without a word he got into his car, and, revving the engine, drove away.

For a moment Father stood motionless, in silence. Then he turned to me.

"This," he said in a hoarse voice, a voice that wasn't his, "is capitalism."

No, it wasn't. That wasn't capitalism. I wished it were capitalism—but it was not. Unfortunately not. It was something else. Something I didn't even dare to think about.

A Public Act

RECENTLY, IN BRUSSELS, a public act was staged as a protest against the arms race and the armed conflicts that keep erupting in various points of the globe. The event took place in an auditorium, which wasn't very big, but it was filled to capacity. Speaker after speaker took to the podium, and particularly vehement was the last speaker, a highly respected physics professor who described at length the horrors of an atomic war. While the old professor was speaking, a man in the second row stood up, walked up to the podium, then, in front of the stunned audience, he drew a gun and fired five shots at the professor, who fell down.

The incident created panic and confusion, with everybody wanting to leave; but suddenly the man shouted: "Wait! Wait a moment!"

The audience turned to the podium: There he was, and at his side, smiling, stood the professor. The man then explained that the whole thing had been just an act—blank cartridges had been used in order to give the audience a dramatic, therefore didactic, demonstration of the savage and treacherous tactics of the warmongers. While he was speaking, a man in the third row got up; he walked up to the podium, drew a gun, and shot both the speaker and the professor.

Again, panic and confusion; again, the audience scrambling for the exits; and again:

"Wait! Wait a moment!"

The audience turned to the podium, and there stood the two men who had fired the shots, as well as the professor—all three of them smiling; the second gunman then explained once more that the incident had been just an act to give the public a dramatic, and therefore didactic, demonstration of the savage and treacherous methods of the warmongers. While he was speaking, a man in the sixth row stood up; he walked up to the podium, drew a gun, then shot the speaker, the fellow who had previously staged the act, and the professor. This time the panic and confusion weren't as great; people walked toward the exits but in no great hurry; and when the man shouted for them to wait, they returned calmly to their seats. The third gunman then explained that the whole thing had been just an act, etc. And at that point a man in the fifth row stood up.

There was a succession of such acts, with the shooting followed by an explanation. Except that now the people heading for the exits were in fact leaving; it was getting late and the whole thing had become an utter bore. Finally, there was only one person in the auditorium, although by then there was quite a crowd on the stage itself— the professor and all the fake gunmen. The last of these gunmen was explaining that the whole thing had been nothing but an act, etc., when the lone member of the audience rose from his seat in the twentieth row; he walked up to the podium, and, taking a machine gun from under his raincoat, he opened fire on the current speaker and everyone else around him. When he was finished, he left.

There was no one else in the auditorium; therefore, nobody went up to the stage to find out whether or not the men were dying. As it turned out, they did die—which happened in minutes or years.

The Enigmatic Eye [1986]   351

Burning Angels

IT HAPPENS AT ANY TIME of the day or night, even in the course of a meal, or during a party. Suddenly, Munhoz becomes pale and distressed. The film, I've completely forgotten about it, he mumbles, and runs to the small room that he uses as a photographer's studio. Everybody knows, however, that he's not going there to develop films: it is an open secret.

As soon as he enters the studio, he lights a candle. In the dimly lit environment, his face, which has absolutely ordinary features, acquires a phantasmagoric expression: a prelude to what is about to happen.

Motionless, his mouth partly open, Munhoz waits. If after four or five minutes nothing of what is supposed to happen happens, he makes a sound with his lips, the kind of sound that others would make to attract doves. Then, at that moment, from the cracks in the wall and from amid the piles of cardboard boxes that fill the shelves, comes something like a crackling sound, soon followed by a faint rustling and buzzing—and what has Munhoz got now?

Angels begin to flutter around the candle. Diminutive, they are: not more than two centimeters tall. It would be really difficult to fit them into the same category of the celestial creatures who, to the right and to the left of God, intone hosannas. It is well known, however, that when it comes to angels, there's room for a great diversity in appearance; besides, their tiny white cotton robes and the lyres they carry affixed to their backs are unmistakable. Angels, yes. Miniature angels, but angels nevertheless.

The light attracts them in the same way that beautiful women attract certain men. They describe circles, which grow increasingly smaller, around the flame of the candle. From a corner Munhoz watches them surreptitiously. With apprehension: He foresees what is going to happen.

The angels draw closer and closer to the flame; they are now just millimeters away. Then suddenly the robe of one of the angels catches fire, and, floundering, he falls to the floor, a horrible sight to behold. But it's a short-lived agony: A small noise, something like a muffled shriek, is heard, and presto, it's all over with that angel. The same happens to another angel, and soon to another, and thus, in a short while, eight or nine angels are exterminated by fire.

Munhoz does nothing to prevent the carnage. On the contrary, he derives pleasure from what he sees. He smiles, rubs his hands, and doesn't leave until the last little angel has been reduced to ashes. By then there is a lack of oxygen in the small room: The flame flickers, already on the point of becoming extinguished, and Munhoz himself feels asphyxiated.

He leaves his room to face the reproachful eyes of the members of his family. Munhoz is aware of what they say about him: That he is wicked, that he takes the trouble of dressing beetles like angels, only to immolate them in the fire.

Munhoz doesn't accept such accusations. The winged beings go to their death because they want to; he doesn't prevail upon them to do so. Besides, these creatures aren't the charming insects known as beetles. They are indeed angels.

Free Topics

BECAUSE OF THE TIME LIMIT, I'll be brief. The purpose of my presentation is to relate the results of a survey conducted in one of our suburbs, Vila Armênia, to find out about consumer practices among the lower classes. Since time is short, I'll abstain from dealing with the question of methodology and go straight to the conclusions.

The first slide, please. There you see, ladies and gentlemen, the universe that we've researched: a thousand and one hundred people, 62 percent of whom are female. . . . And you can see the other details for yourselves, I'm not going to examine them because I'm pressed for time. . . . The second slide, please. There you can see the distribution by age group. . . . Most of the population consists of children and young adults. . . . The next one, please, quick, because we haven't got much time left, the chairman of the board is already signaling to me. . . . Here's a chart showing family income. . . . The income of some of these people is less than the minimum wage. . . . Next. This slide shows consumer practices. . . . It refers to the to-bacco question. . . . As you can see, about one-third of the cross-section smokes. You can well imagine which brands of cigarette are favored. Next. This one here refers to the mass media. Notice that the majority prefers radio, followed by television. . . . Next. There you have their eating habits. . . . It's a complex chart, so I won't be able to go into it. . . . How much time have I got left Mr. Chairman. . . ? Two minutes. Well, let's press on. Next! This slide isn't very important, let's go to the next one. . . . This one refers to en-tertainment. . . . In this suburb in particular, the townspeople have a big barn dance that's very popular. My own wife did research on it. Next. Well, this slide is only to show you the team that conducted the research on this barn dance of theirs. The one standing over there with a smile, that's me, of course. That's my wife by my side. The young man with the mustache is Chico, one of the local resi-dents who helped us a lot in the course of our work. . . . Next. That's a shot of the barn dance: there's my wife dancing with Chico. . . . Next. There's my wife arriving at a motel together with Chico. The motel, it was later discovered, was my wife's own choice. This Chico had never until then set foot in a motel. Next. I took this picture through the window, see . . . the two of them lying there. . . . Ob-serve the lascivious expression on her face, the glitter in her eyes. . . . Observe that salacious smile. . . . She's spreading for him. . . . And he's drooling over her. . . . Just look at him, see if he's not. . . . Look carefully, because time is running out. Time's up, isn't that right, Mr. Chairman? It is. That's it, then; time's up. That's for sure. Lights on, please. Please, lights on.

The Password

AN OLD CORPORAL IS RETURNING to his army camp late at night. His figure is barely discernible in the faint moonlight that bathes the stretch of prairie land; it's not surprising, therefore, that the sentry, weapon in hand, should order him to halt and not make another move. The corporal stops, annoyed (he can barely stand on his feet, and is eager to lie down), but he is not alarmed. The soldier draws near.

"The password."

Password? What's going on? Password? He tries to remember. His mind—befogged with drink, for he had been imbibing all evening— isn't of much help, but he somehow manages to remember: Yes, there's something. Some new rule: Nobody can enter the camp without giving the password. As a matter of fact, he himself relayed this rule to the rank and file. But the thing is, the password now escapes him. It's a word . . . or a phrase. . . . It's no good, he can't remember it. The soldier persists: The password, give me the password. Be patient, will you? mutters the corporal, I'm trying to remember. He hazards some humor.

"I'm old, son. Old people forget things, especially things like passwords."

Impassive, the soldier looks fixedly at him. Obviously, he doesn't care for humor—or for explanations. He wants the password. The soldier's stubbornness irritates the corporal. Damn it, don't you recognize me? he asks. I do, replies the soldier, I recognize you perfectly well, but I want the password; without the password nobody enters the camp. But I can't recall it, says the corporal, let me in, will you? I'm sleepy, who's going to know I didn't give you the password? The soldier makes no reply. Motionless, weapon in hand, he waits.

The corporal tries to remember. Is it a word, or is it a phrase? In his effort to remember, he closes his eyes, his face screwed up in a painful grimace. Phrase or word? It must be a word. But there are so many words, so very many. Even a humble, almost illiterate man like him must know millions of words. From the dusty corners in the dark cellar of his memory, the words are now watching him. Then he starts searching for one, groping about in the dark with difficulty, trying to fit the sounds of every word that occurs to him into the ill-defined mold he has in his head. Naturally, he starts with the most imposing words. Is it pátria, fatherland? No, it can't be pátria, pátria is a word of the feminine gender, and he thinks (but perhaps this is just a macho hangup) that no word of the feminine gender would be used as a password. Is it duty? Is it heroism? Or is it a combination of two words, like duty discharged? It occurs to him that he may have jotted down the password on a scrap of paper, which he then put into his pocket. He often does this: He writes things down in order not to forget them. Sometimes he forgets where he wrote them down. But in the case of the password, it's possible that he has it on him. Thrusting his hands into his pockets, he empties them out: money, identification papers, medical prescriptions, a letter from his daughter, a pack of cigarettes. Each piece is examined, for the password might have been jotted down on the pack of cigarettes, for instance, or on the back of a receipt. And indeed, there is something written on the back of a receipt; something he can't read in the semidarkness. Have you got a lantern? he asks the soldier. The youth says he hasn't. You're on duty as sentry and you haven't got a lantern? The corporal finds it peculiar. I haven't got one, repeats the soldier. The corporal searches for traces of irritation or mockery in the soldier's tone of voice; there aren't any. The tone is neutral; there's no reason for the corporal to suspect harassment. The corporal squats down, lays the receipt on the ground, strikes a match, and tries to read what's on it. A complicated operation, for he can barely coordinate his gestures; besides, the wind keeps extinguishing the flame. But there is something written down, and finally he manages to read: horse.

Horse. Could this be the password? It's impossible for him to remember. If this is the password, wouldn't he be overcome by sudden jubilation, by that kind of joy that strikes scientists upon making a new discovery, or gamblers upon hitting the jackpot? Perhaps. Perhaps his age and all he has been through in life have cast a damper over such raptures of joy. *Horse,* even if it doesn't kindle enthusiasm, could well be the password. Could it, really? Is it possible that the lieutenant—the man responsible for passwords—could have chosen such a word? A word not entirely ridiculous, of course, but somewhat silly. Why horse? There are no horses in the camp. There are farms in the area—but would this fact be sufficient reason for the lieutenant to have chosen the word *horse* as a password?

On the other hand, if it is not the password, why in the world did he write it down? He usually jots down things that he is supposed to buy to take home, things that his wife wants him to get; but was there a moment when he considered buying a horse? (And where would he find the money to buy one?) Was there a moment when his wife asked him for a horse? Could the word stand for something else, say, a tip on the illegal animal numbers game? No, he has never gambled on the animal numbers games. He wouldn't even know how to go about it. He's not a gambler at all. He's an honest corporal who sometimes drinks too much—but then, who doesn't? Is there anyone who doesn't get stewed to the gills every once in a while, especially if he happens to have a daughter in poor health, and a mentally retarded son? Horse. A mystery, this horse.

He looks at the soldier who, impassive, continues to look fixedly at him. The corporal could test out the word. He could say horse in the casual tone of someone speaking to himself. If this is the password, then everything will be fine; the sentry will let him enter the camp; if it is not, it could be interpreted as a drunkard's muttering. Before saying the word, however, the corporal decides to see what else is on the list; the next word is orange, yes, he promised to take some oranges home, his wife wanted to use them in a dessert. Such a good, talented woman.. . . . Therefore, orange is not the password; or is it? Could it be that besides alluding to one of the ingredients in the dessert, it is also the password? Rather unlikely.

The third and fourth words are absolutely illegible. He strikes one match after the other, trying to read his own scrawl, but he can't; his handwriting has always been atrocious. During his few years of schooling, his teachers kept warning him: You'll have to improve your handwriting, or one day you'll get into hot water. And that's precisely where he finds himself now—in hot water. Because quite possibly, the password is there, lost in this illegible scrawl of his.

The light of the match goes out. It's his last one, too. With difficulty the corporal stands up, looks at the soldier—and he is overcome by a sudden fit of anger. No, he doesn't remember the password. And so what? He's not obliged to remember every single thing he is told, there's enough nonsense in his head already. He has forgotten it, that's it. He feels like sending the soldier packing; but he can't, he's not in a position to do something like that. Instead, he tries reasoning, and argues that in fact, he knows the password, that he has it stored somewhere inside him, that it's only a matter of pulling it out of the bottom of the well of memory. All he needs is time. And perhaps a hint. Yes: A hint would help.

I'm not giving you any hint, says the soldier in the same neutral tone as before; every man has to remember the password unaided. Oh, yeah? says the corporal with indignation. Every man for himself, is that so? Unaided, repeats the soldier.

"And what if you were on the battlefield? What if you lay wounded on the battlefield? Would it still be every man for himself? Or would you at that moment ask for help?"

The soldier makes no reply. Those are his tactics, concludes the corporal—not to make a reply, not to get involved. The password. That's all he cares about. The password? He'll get the password. The corporal will utter every single word he remembers. Every one of them. Beginning with the most important ones in the life of a warrior.

"Cannon! Is cannon the password? Hmm? Is it cannon? Is it rifle? Is it bayonet? Is it mortar? Is it ammunition? Is it howitzer? Is it shrapnel? Is it tank? Is it flask? Is it haversack? Is it binoculars?"

The soldier, impassive. But the corporal continues, after the words related to the army camp, others from the civilian life come to his mind—house, wardrobe, bed, patriot, bathroom, store; then, words at random—moon, star, sea, brook; next, names of plants, of animals (including horse); finally, swear words: finally, one single swear word:

"Shit, shit, shit, shit," he repeats in a monotone. "Shit, shit."

Panting, the corporal falls silent. He stands glowering at the soldier; he's angry, really angry.

But he controls himself. *Take it easy, you old corporal, take it easy, you idiot. Don't lose your head. Think it over, put on your thinking cap.* Yep, it will take cleverness. It will take some bargaining, I'll have to win this guy over, after all, he's merely carrying out his duty. And what's more (and at this thought the corporal even becomes soft-hearted), there was a time when he, too, was a young recruit who took pride in being on guard at the gates of the barracks.

No, he has no reason to quarrel with the soldier; they are brothers in arms—the corporal the older brother, the soldier, his kid brother. It falls on the older brother to be tolerant and understanding, to give in when there's an impasse.

"Well? What do you say?"

"I say that I want the password," replies the soldier in a firm voice.

"Yeah, sure, the password. But before I—"

"The password!"

The soldier cocks his rifle. The corporal takes a deep breath. The moment has come, at last. It would have to come one day, and now it has come. It is something that the corporal has always feared: How am I going to behave? Because, even though he is a military man, he has always been a peaceable person, he has never quarreled with anybody. And what is more, he has never been in a narrow-escape situation, he has never been seriously ill, he has never undergone surgery. And now the moment has come. Suddenly, without fore-warning. Triggered by something stupid: first the drinking spree, then this password thing. He would have expected something more solemn, more spectacular. Sometimes he would think of a war, and in his imagination he would see himself collapse, wounded, on the battlefield. But we're in Brazil: we're peace-loving, not warmonger-ing people. Sometimes we have to make threats, take security mea-sures, but deep down everybody knows they aren't for real. Every-body? No. This little soldier here doesn't know. And there's no time to teach him now, it's too late. There's no time to say, look here, buddy, forget it, nothing of this is to be taken seriously.

Nevertheless, the whole thing is the staging of an act. An act in which the corporal has to play his role. Reluctantly, for he's tired and sleepy, but there's no other way. The youth must be taught a les-son. So, with a sigh, the corporal smiles—but there's nothing ironic in his smile, he's sure there isn't; nothing challenging, either—and he steps forward. The soldier, motionless, looks at him. Six foot-steps, ten footsteps, twenty footsteps, and now the corporal's back is already turned to the soldier—and at this moment, so unbearable is his anxiety, and so violent the contraction of the muscles in his neck, in his back, even in his scalp, that he—but this takes but a fraction of a second—stops short. The moment he stops, though, a dead calm invades him; it's as if he were floating on a huge lake of tepid waters. And as in a dream, he resumes walking. He's not going to shoot me in the back, the corporal is thinking with diffident joy. He won't do such a thing, nobody would.

But then he stops again: And he turns around; he opens his arms and there's a blast, and he falls to the ground, the smile frozen on his face at the precise moment when he was about to utter—and why was it that he just couldn't recall it before?—the password, the real password, so obvious it was, this password which he had on the tip of his tongue, and which was, yes precisely that: a *dead shot.*

The Emissary

ON SATURDAYS I WOULD VISIT HIM in the hospital. Every time I saw him, I thought he looked worse. But to him I would say You're looking good, Pedro. To which he would reply with an impatient—and yet grateful, undoubtedly grateful—gesture.

I would sit down and give him the usual small bag of apples (he would thank me; he wouldn't eat them, though; could this perhaps explain why he was getting worse?). Then he would chat for a while—about the weather, about the news in the papers—but I was well aware that he wasn't interested in any of it. I always sensed that he was eager to go straight to the point. But even so, we—he or I, or both of us—would prolong the small talk. Anyhow, it fell on me to give the cue.

"I saw Teresa yesterday." The tone of voice was, of course, nonchalant.

He: "Did you?" trying, of course, to show little interest. I would wait for a while before continuing with a carefully thought-out statement.

"She struck me as being rather down and out."

"What makes you think so?" he would say, barely containing his anxiety. "She was shabbily dressed," I would reply—and from then on the conversation would proceed in a crescendo. I: She struck me as being rather ill. He: Poor thing—a remark made with some plea-sure. I: She's been evicted from her apartment. He: Poor thing—a remark made with a small smile—poor thing! I: She's been hitting the bottle. He: Ah! I: She now walks with a gimp. He: The poor bitch! I: Her women friends have been shunning her. He: You don't say! I: It's true, Pedro. She's really gone to seed. He: Oh God.

He would throw his hands up and let himself collapse on the pil-low, where he would lie panting, eyes closed, nostrils quivering. In a state of bliss, obviously. In seventh heaven.

I would wait in silence. Soon he would open one eye: Tell me more, he would ask.

I would look at my watch: I can't Pedro, I must be going now.

He would beg: For the love of God. But I would remain adamant in my refusal to tell him more. I had a feeling that it was his curios-ity that kept him alive. And I wanted him alive.

Because Teresa always got a kick out of it whenever I said: I went to see Pedro in the hospital.

Tell me all about it, she would then say with a small smile, do tell me what you've seen.

I always told her. Which gave Teresa great pleasure. And I was not one to deny Teresa a pleasure.

The Candidate

WE ARE A GROUP OF ABOUT THIRTY ENTREPRENEURS working in all lines of business. We do not, however, constitute an association; what brings us together are our common interests—not always brought up at our dinner parties, as well as the bonds of friendship among some of us—the latter always extolled on the occasion of drinking a toast. Menezes is our leader. Neither the oldest nor the richest among us, he is, however, a man of vision, and for this reason his opinions are always respected. Therefore, when he said that we needed a representative in the City Council, we agreed right away. Since the elections would be held five months from then, we would have to set things in motion without delay. Menezes himself volunteered to search for a candidate. His incredible efficiency was again in evidence: At the following dinner party he was already announcing that he had found the ideal person for our purposes.

"Young, charming, elegant, articulate, smart as a tack. He rose from nothing. Do you really know what nothing is?" He gave us a challenging look." "Many of you claim that you rose from nothing, but that's not so. Your nothing and his nothing are not the same. All of you had something, some education, a relative with clout, some money you inherited, even if it was a mere pittance. Whereas he— you can't even imagine the kind of life he had. The father, a drunk. The mother, in poor health. They lived in a shack. Often, there was nothing to eat. Very early in life he was forced to earn a living. He attended school in the evenings. He soon distinguished himself in student politics and in soccer, both of which, he told me, gave him his remarkable sense of timing. He graduated in law. He married the daughter of a merchant, a wealthy man who unfortunately lost everything in a series of unsuccessful business ventures. But this fact is of no consequence to him because, he told me, he wants to make it on his own. For this reason he is willing to have a go at anything. What do you say, gentlemen? Is he eligible?"

We had to agree: He was eligible. Then, excusing himself, Menezes left the hall and soon returned accompanied by a man still young and—just as he had told us—charming and elegant. That he was articulate and clever became apparent as soon as he started to speak. Everybody was thrilled; but I, and I don't know exactly why, hesitated. It was a slight hesitation, but hesitation nonetheless. Caused perhaps, by a certain expression that I saw, or thought that I saw at one moment on the closely shaved face of our candidate. At one moment, on that face, I detected, or thought that I detected (perhaps because of a certain innate distrust in my nature, a trait that I have never succeeded in shaking off, notwithstanding the great harm it has already caused me), an expression of a certain melancholy; at one moment his look became vacant, the corners of his mouth drooped, and all of a sudden he looked much older than his twenty-seven years. But this melancholy, whether real or imagined, vanished immediately, and soon he was laughing and greeting one and all with handshakes and hugs.

Menezes was right. The election campaign turned out to be expensive, but the young man got an impressive number of votes. Quite pleased, we decided to have a dinner party in his honor. On the night of the dinner we were all gathered at the club, still jubilant over our victory—but he was late. Eight o'clock, eight-thirty, nine, nine-thirty—and still no sign of him. Some of us were already annoyed: The fellow is already getting up on his high horse was a comment I heard in various groups. We were thinking of starting dinner without him (this would teach him a lesson, too), when an employee of the club came to say that there was a phone call for Menezes. Menezes went to the phone and returned soon, looking pale. He drew me aside.

"It was his wife. She asked us to hurry there. He's in his study, with a gun on his head, threatening to kill himself."

We—Menezes and I—went there in a taxi. The woman was waiting at the door. Tearful, she told us that her husband sometimes had these bouts of depression, but they were rare, and nobody knew about them because he never mentioned the matter; this time, however, things had gone too far, and frightened, she had decided to call on us for help. She showed us into his study. And indeed, there was our alderman with the gun barrel against his head. What struck me right away was the expression of deep melancholy on his face: the vacant look, the drooping corners of his mouth.

Placing himself in front of the young man, Menezes fixed his eyes on him.

"How much?" Menezes asked in a firm voice.

Our alderman looked at Menezes as if he hadn't understood. "Come on," Menezes insisted, "we've got no time to waste; tell me straight out, how much do you want not to kill yourself?"

Slowly, a smile began to open the young man's face.

"A lot," he said.

"We'll talk about it later," Menezes said. Then, taking the gun from the young man's hand, he put it into his pocket. "Let's go now, we're already late for dinner."

We got into the taxi; I sat on the front seat next to the cabbie. Menezes and the alderman, together on the backseat, were engaged in a lively conversation. I was now convinced that this alderman-ship was going to cost us a lot of money; but I was also convinced that it was money well invested.

General Delivery

ONE DAY I GOT OUT OF BED, washed my face, combed my hair, got dressed, drank coffee, and went to the house of the widow Paulina, a neighbor of ours.

The widow Paulina was an elderly lady, very friendly. For this reason, and also because she was an invalid (she moved about in a wheelchair), I was always rendering her a small service, such as mowing the lawn in her garden, walking her dog, Pinoquio, and mailing her letters at the post office.

There were always heaps of letters. The widow Paulina sub-scribed to a publication that listed pen pals all over the world. Thus, she would write to countries as distant as Sri Lanka, Japan, Tunisia. Letters and more letters; a good part of her modest income was spent on postage. With almost negative results; only occasionally did she receive a reply. But this fact didn't discourage her; on the contrary, she stepped up her letter-writing. By writing letters, according to her, she remained faithful to the memory of her husband, a humanitarian doctor who, to his dying day, had dreamed of a united world. To his widow he had bequeathed a message of love. And little else: a few old books, an ancient car, which she sold, and a modest nest egg. He hadn't owned much because his patients, who were poor, couldn't afford to pay him—a fact that the widow always recalled with emotion. My father had been one of his patients. So, there was also a component of gratitude in my lending assistance to the old lady.

Well, I dropped in on the widow Paulina. She was waiting for me in the garden, smiling as usual. She asked how I was doing in school, and gave me a slice of the cake that she had baked herself. Then she handed me a letter. Just one? I found it strange. Yes, just one, she replied, giving me a level look. Taking the letter and the money, I said good-bye and left.

As usual, I headed for the park. I threw away the piece of cake—it tasted awful—sat down on a bench, and, as I always did, I opened the letter. By and large, I got a kick out of reading her letters.

On that day, however, I was in for a surprise.

The letter was written to me. The envelope itself was addressed to somebody in the United States, but the letter, the letter itself, started with a Dear Chico. Chico, that's me. It's my nickname. And the widow wrote on: *I would never expect this kind of thing from you, Chico. You, of whom I've been so fond.*

The fact is that she had found me out. She knew that I didn't mail her letters, that I pocketed the money for the stamps. The new post office master, who happened to be a relative of hers, told her that I never set foot in the post office. And the widow concluded by saying: To think that I trusted you. To think that I handed you the money taken from my dwindling savings when instead I could have invested it. I could have exchanged it into dollars, Chico.

Crumbling the letter, I threw it away. Dollars! I would keep this in mind until it was time for me to make my first investments.

In the Submarine Restaurant

JERÔNIMO RINGS ME UP. I have some great news, he says, the excitement in his voice sounding strange in a man who is normally reserved. Great news, he repeats, adding that he can't tell me about it over the phone. He suggests that we meet for lunch: the two of us, and also Hélio and Sadi. Where? I ask rather uneasy. At the Submarine Restaurant, he replies. I argue that it's way out; besides, it's not the best time of the year to go to the Submarine Restaurant; not in this cold, rainy weather. That's precisely why we're going there, says Jerônimo, I don't want anybody to see us. As a matter of fact, I've already phoned and reserved the entire restaurant just for us.

I ended up accepting the invitation. What else? Jerônimo is well known for his tenacity, for his iron will. He lets nothing stand in his way, that's what everybody says about him.

I drive to the place where the Submarine Restaurant is located. On the highway, I'm overtaken by Hélio, who looks at me with an inquiring expression. It seems that he, too, doesn't know what is going on.

Upon arriving at the beach, I leave my car in the parking lot. The cars of the others are already parked there. As usual, I'm the last one to arrive.

I walk along the ancient wharf, at the end of which the restaurant was built. Entering the lobby, I greet the circumspect manager, then climb down the winding staircase. The restaurant proper is below sea level. Through its windows, or rather scuttles, diners can watch the marine fauna of the area.

Jerônimo and the others are seated at a table in a corner. Greeting them, I take a seat. They are engaged in small talk. But it's obvious that Jerônimo is radiant.

A loudspeaker placed right above our heads squeaks, then emits a shrill sound. "Hello!" says a man's voice. "Hello, hello. Testing, testing. One, two, three. One, two, three. Testing, testing."

A pause, then the voice goes on.

"Gentlemen, welcome to the Submarine Restaurant, the only one of its kind in Brazil. The management would like you to make yourselves at home. While you savor our delectable dishes, we'll give you some information about the marine creatures surrounding us. We'll return in a few moments. Thank you for now."

Hélio, who had never been to the place, is amazed. Wonderfully well appointed, isn't it? he says. What an ingenious idea.

"Attention," it's the loudspeaker again. "Gentlemen, your attention, please. There's an octopus approaching us from the south. The octopus, gentlemen, is not a fish, it's a mollusk. I repeat: a mollusk. And here comes our hero!"

It is, in fact, a small octopus. Slowly, it passes across our scuttle and disappears. Fantastic, cries out the enthusiastic Hélio. This place here is fantastic, Jerônimo! Jerônimo says nothing; he merely smiles.

The loudspeaker again:

"Attention! What we see now is a dogfish. It's a close relative of the shark, the killer of the seas."

Swiftly, the dogfish swims away.

The waiter comes with a huge platter. I took the liberty of ordering this for all of us, Jerônimo explains. You're going to like it. It's snook. Super. Really super.

I don't like fish, says Sadi, I'd rather have shrimp. His voice is tinged with huffiness; but Jerônimo is already asking the waiter to get his shrimp. Certainly, sir, says the waiter, who then goes away.

Jerônimo raises his glass: To us, he says. We drink and afterward silence falls upon us, a silence that strikes me (but then, I m rather paranoid) as oppressive. I lean toward him.

"Well, let's hear what you have to say to us."

Jerônimo takes another sip of wine. Good, this wine, he remarks. He wipes his lips with the napkin, looks at us—always smiling—and announces: "The man's finished. He'll be kicked out next week. And I'll get the post, it's in the bag! Can I count on you?"

But you're a genius, Hélio cries out. A real genius, I agree. Only Sadi says nothing. He's looking through the scuttle: There's a school of fish out there. The loudspeaker doesn't tell us their name, but I'll bet they are robalo, also known as snook. They stare at Sadi with their inexpressive eyes.

Peace and War

BEING LATE FOR THE WAR, I had to take a taxi. Much to my annoyance: with the recent increase in the taxi fares, this expense, unforeseen and ill timed, was a hole in my budget. However, I did make it, and was able to clock in just in the nick of time, thus averting further hassles. There was a long line of people waiting to get to the time clock: I wasn't the only latecomer. Walter, my partner in the trench, was there, too, muttering: Like me, he had been forced to take a taxi. We were neighbors and we had joined the war roughly at the same time. Every second Thursday of each month we would take a bus at an intersection of our street in order to take part in the war activities.

I'm sick and tired of the whole shebang, said Walter. Me, too, I replied. Sighing, we clocked in and headed for the quartermaster's depot, where the locker room was temporarily (but this had been so for over fifteen years) located. Aren't you late today? asked the youth in charge of the locker room. We made no reply. He handed us the keys to our lockers. Quickly, we change out of our clothes and into our old fatigues; then, grabbing the rifles and the ammunition (twenty cartridges), we headed for the line of battle.

The setting for the armed conflict was a stretch of prairieland on the outskirts of the city. The battlefield was surrounded by a barbed-wire fence with signs saying WAR, KEEP OUT. An unnecessary warn-ing: hardly anybody went there, to that site of bucolic granges and small farms.

We, the soldiers, occupied a trench roughly two kilometers long. The enemy, whom we had never seen, were about a kilometer away from us, and they, too, were entrenched. The terrain between the two trenches was littered with debris: wrecked tanks and other de-stroyed armored vehicles lay jumbled together with skeletons of horses—reminders of a time when the fighting had been fierce. But now the conflict had reached a stable phase—of upkeep, in the words of our commander. Battles were no longer fought. But even so, our orders were not to leave the trench. Which posed a problem to me: My youngest son wanted me to get him an empty shell fired from a howitzer, but there was no way I could get one. My kid kept pes-tering me about it, but there was nothing I could do.

We—Walter and I—climbed down to the trench. The place wasn't totally lacking in amenities. It was furnished with tables, chairs, a small stove, kitchen utensils, not to mention a sound system and a portable television set. I suggested that Walter and I play a game of cards. Later, he said. With a wrinkled forehead and an air of dissatis-faction, he was examining his rifle: This fucking thing doesn't work anymore, he stated. But after all, I said, it is more than fifteen years old, it has seen better days. Then I offered him my own weapon: I had no intention of ever firing a shot. Just then we heard a detona-tion and a bullet came hissing over our heads. That was a near miss, I said. The idiots, muttered Walter, one of these days they'll end up hurting someone. Grabbing my weapon, he rose to his feet and fired two shots in the air. That's a warning to you, he shouted, and sat down again. A manservant appeared holding a cordless telephone: Your wife, Senhor Walter. What the devil, Walter cried out, not even here will this woman leave me in peace. He took the phone.

"Hello! Yes, that's me. I'm fine. Of course I'm fine. No, nothing has happened to me, I've already told you, I'm fine. I know you get nervous, but there's no reason why you should. Everything's okay, I'm well sheltered, it isn't raining. Did you hear me? Everything's okay. There's no need to apologize. I understand. A kiss."

What an utter bore, this woman, he said, handing the phone back to the manservant. I said nothing. I, too, had a problem with my wife, but of a different nature. She didn't believe that we were at war. Her suspicion was that I was spending the day in a motel with someone else. I would like to explain to her the nature of this war, but in fact, I myself didn't know. Nobody knew. It was a very confusing thing; so much so that a committee had been set put to study the situation of the conflict. The chairman of this committee would sometimes visit us, and then he would complain about the car he had been given to go on these inspection trips: a jalopy, according to him. It was, in fact, a very old car. To practice economy, his superiors wouldn't change it for a newer model.

The morning went by serenely; somebody from our side fired a shot, somebody from the other side fired back, and that was all. At noon we were served lunch. A green salad, roast beef, rice prepared in the Greek style; for dessert, an insipid pudding. This is really going downhill, Walter grumbled. The waiter asked him if he thought this place was a restaurant or what. Walter made no reply.

We lay down for a nap and slept peacefully. When we woke up, night was falling. I think I'll go home now, I said to Walter. He couldn't leave with me: He was on duty that night. I went to the locker room and changed. How was the war? the smartalecky youth asked me. Good, I replied, really good. I dropped by the administration office, got my paycheck from a sour-looking employee, and signed all three copies of the receipt. And I arrived at the bus stop just in the nick of time.

At home, my wife, dressed in a leotard, was waiting for me. I'm ready, she said dryly. I went to the bedroom to get my sweatshirt. We went to the fitness gym and mounted the exercise bicycles. Where exactly were we? I asked. You never seem to know, she answered in a reproachful tone. Picking up the map she studied it for a moment, then said: "Bisceglie, on the Adriatic coast."

We started pedaling vigorously; when we stopped two hours later, we were approaching Molfeta, still on the Adriatic coast. We figure it will take us a year to complete the circuit of Italy. Then, we'll wait and see. I dislike making long-term plans because of the war, of course, but mostly because the unknown element of the future is for me a source of constant excitement.

The Blank

AT THE AGE OF TEN HE DECIDES to keep a diary—and from then on there won't be a day when he doesn't record something—an event, a thought, a daydream. The years go by, the notebooks pile up. At the age of fifty, the man, driven by some obscure motive, decides to review, not his life, but his diaries. It is something he never did before. So, he reads on, at times with a smile; at times with tears in his eyes; at times enraptured; at times bored. Suddenly, he realizes that there is no entry at all for one particular day; it is the only day when he wrote nothing, as he verifies by leafing through the rest of this notebook and of all the others that followed it. Why, he wonders. Why is this particular day missing? At first the most obvious reason occurs to him—a leaf torn from the notebook. But no: The same page on which the entry for that particular day should have been also contains the entries for both the preceding and the following days. Brief notes as a matter of fact, like all the others. He is, therefore, facing an inexplicable fact: an unrecorded day. Why? Because of a trip? No. Even when he went on a trip, he always took the diary with him. An illness? Again, no. Even when ill (and he was never seriously ill), he never failed to record something. What was initially intriguing has now become a torment: The man doesn't want merely to find out, he has to. The mystery tortures him, he has lost his appetite, he can't concentrate on his work. His wife and friends ask him what is wrong: They've never seen him like this. But there's no one he can tell anything because he feels that nobody would understand him.

He is determined to clear up this mystery. It won't be easy. At the time when that particular entry should have been made, he was living alone. Newly graduated from college he was still jobless. And it wasn't until months later that he found a girlfriend. So, there were no connecting elements, nobody he could ask. To whom should he turn for help? After mulling over the matter, he goes to a fortune-teller who, rather surprised, says there's nothing he can do. He specializes in predicting the future, not in disclosing the past. He suggests that the man go to a hypnotist. The man tries hypnosis, but without success; whenever he is about to fall into a trance, he is frightened, and is again on his guard. Noticing the man's great anxiety, the hypnotist advises him to see a psychologist. The man goes to a psychologist, who listens to him attentively for forty minutes; at the end of the session, the psychologist shakes his head and looks at the man sympathetically. Yes, he says, the memory of that day must be in your subconscious, buried somewhere deep down, but I don't see how I can retrieve it. He gives the man some hope, though: It's possible that it will surface unexpectedly, like the corpse of a drowned man.

"Maybe during a dream. Pay attention to your dreams."

The man begins to sleep with pencil and notebook at hand.

Should a dream bring him the recollection he has been yearning to remember, he wants to write it down immediately, before he forgets it again. Then one night, he does in fact remember; he remembers everything; with a trembling hand he writes down in the notebook what he has remembered, then, exhausted but pleased, he falls asleep. In the morning he discovers that the pages in the notebook are blank. The act of writing something down was also a dream.

Now the man is convinced that something serious must have happened. He goes to the morgue of a major morning newspaper and asks the person in charge for a copy of the newspaper published on that fateful day. The attendant brings him the requested newspaper and the man leafs through it impatiently. Then, in the crime section, he finds what he has been searching for. A loner was murdered, and the police had no clues.

The man doesn't feel well. He goes to the men's room and washes his face. Then he raises his head, and in the mirror he sees the smiling face of his victim.

Many Many Meters Above Good and Evil

AT THE END OF THE STREET there was an empty lot, and at the back of this lot stood the house in ruins where Lúcia and I used to play. Everybody said that the house was haunted, that ghosts were often seen there. But Lúcia and I weren't afraid. We feared nothing. We were both ten years old then, an age when children are usually afraid of ghosts; we, however, were afraid of nothing—until one afternoon, as we were about to enter the house, we heard muffled moanings coming from inside. A moment later I was already far away from the house, with my hair standing on end and my heart pounding fiercely. Lúcia didn't run away. Come back here, she shouted, this is no ghost, it's a person.

Warily, I approached the house. The two of us went in. We

waited until our eyes got adjusted to the darkness. Look, over there, whispered Lúcia.

I looked and saw an old man—the oldest and most shriveled old man I had ever seen. He was lying behind a heap of bricks, all huddled up inside his tattered clothes.

Lúcia squatted down by his side and remained looking at him. I would rather have fled, but she seemed fascinated by that old ragamuffin who looked ill—and who stank something fierce. "Are you feeling ill?" she asked, a question that struck me as obviously unnecessary; the old man was ill, desperately ill. He didn't even make a reply; he moaned and moaned. Lúcia put her hand on his forehead. "Does he have a temperature?" I asked. "I don't think so'" she said, "it feels ice cold, poor little fellow."

(Poor little fellow. That's how she would refer to the old man from then on: poor little fellow. The poor little fellow is hungry. The poor little fellow is cold. We never found out his name.)

Lúcia rose to her feet, her mind made up: We're going to bring him food. Food, clothes, and a blanket.

I wasn't in complete agreement with her. Yes, I thought that the old man was possibly starving and freezing; it was winter, and winters in Rio Grande do Sul can be severe; however, to take steps to supply the old man with the basic necessities and look after him was a whole new ball game. We had better notify someone, a neighbor, the police.

"Lúcia, maybe we should . . . "

But she wasn't even listening. Already acting on her decision, she ran to her house and was back in a jiffy with bread, a chicken leg, apples; then she began to press food on the old man. A well-intentioned but useless try. Whimpering, the creature kept shaking his head. Lúcia stood staring at him, her forehead creased. I know, she finally said. He can't eat because he's got no teeth.

Again, she ran home and returned with her baby sister's feeding bottle, which she had filled with milk. She inserted the nipple into the old man's mouth and he began to suck it ravenously. The problem is solved, she said, pleased.

Was the problem solved? I didn't think so. How were we going to look after the old man, there, in that house in ruins? And without anybody knowing? (For Lúcia had sworn me to secrecy: Don't tell anyone, not even your brothers.)

She entrusted me with the task of arranging for clothes and blankets. In the attic of my house there was a chest containing the belongings of my dead grandfather, and that's where I got hold of those items. And I even took a mattress to the old man in the dead of night. Great, Lúcia said. We have to take good care of the poor little fellow.

The old man improved somewhat. The milk agreed with him, and sometimes he accepted a grated apple, a small banana mashed up with sugar and cinnamon, some broth, some mashed potatoes. But he never rose from his mattress; he was always lying down, apathetic. And he never talked; we didn't know who he was, where he came from.

Looking after him was no picnic. He was unable to feed himself; he befouled the mattress. We had to change him twice a day; we washed his clothes at home, in secret, of course, then took them to another empty lot, a good distance away, to dry. A real hassle. Frankly, I was fed up with the whole thing. I couldn't wait to get out of this situation.

The old man noticed my ill will. Whenever I walked up to him, he started to cry; sometimes he tried to claw at me, or to bite me. Lúcia thought it funny: He doesn't like you, she would say.

He liked her. It was obvious. As soon as we entered the room, he would reach his fleshless, puny arms to her. Lúcia would cuddle him, kiss him, talk to him as if he were a baby; sometimes she would lay his head on her lap, and the old man would purr contentedly. Which would upset and annoy me. A dirty old man, that's what I thought he was. Or he wouldn't be rubbing himself against the girl like that. And that's what I said to Lúcia: He's a dirty old man. She took offense, and wouldn't talk to me. Later we made up, but only after I apologized not only to her but to the old ragamuffin as well.

One day we found him dead; apparently, he had suffered a heart attack, or something like that. Lúcia was inconsolable: Why now, when he was getting better? she kept saying in tears. I did my best to comfort her, then I saw to it that the old man was buried. Right there, in the empty lot. That night I got a spade from my house, then I dug a hole, into which I placed the body, wrapped in a blanket that used to belong to my grandfather. After covering him with earth, I put some stones and branches on top, and presto, the deed was done.

Many years later, a huge apartment building was erected on that empty lot. After we got married, Lúcia and I went to live there. We have two children, a boy and a girl. We're very unhappy. Sometimes Lúcia says that our unhappiness stems from the fact that we live atop the old man's bones. I don't think so. After all, the building stands twelve stories high, and we live in the penthouse. Many many meters above good and evil.

Prognoses

THE MILLIONAIRE TEOBALDO has his own physician. The function of the physician is, first, to give Teobaldo a monthly checkup; second, to frighten him. To frighten him to death. Almost to death. The tests, the physician says gloomily after one such checkup, have revealed cancer. "Oh no," says, Teobaldo, turning pale (a genuine, not a put-on pallor). "And is it serious doctor?"

"Deadly'" says the doctor, dryly.

"How much time do I have left? Two, three years?"

"Less than that."

"Five, six months?"

"Afraid not."

"Weeks, then?"

"Should you be so lucky."

"Will there be pain?"

"Excruciating. Nothing will allay it."

Teobaldo bursts into tears. He weeps convulsively until suddenly:

"It was a lie!" the doctor cries out.

Teobaldo raises his head, his eye still brimming with tears, but he's already smiling.

"A lie, Doctor? Was it all a lie?"

"A lie, yes. A lie."

"It wasn't cancer?"

"No."

"Not even a benign tumor?"

"No. You're in the pink of health." The physician extends his hands. "Come on, let's shake on it."

Teobaldo clasps the doctor's hand, and then, he leaves, light-hearted. About two weeks later he is back, and the doctor says: "Your blood pressure is way up, your kidneys are not functioning well. I foresee a stroke in the near future."

"Is it serious, Doctor?"

"Terribly serious. Serious enough to send you to the intensive care unit."

"And my chances?"

"Slim. But even if you were to survive the stroke, paralysis will be inevitable, you'll never be able to speak again.. . . Reduced to a vegetable. A bedridden vegetable."

"But—"

No buts: Ruthless, the doctor continues to describe the picture: Spoon-fed like a baby. The cleansing of the private parts performed reluctantly by an orderly, a brute of an orderly, who very likely says humiliating words to his charges, and even hits them. Fits of crying for no reason. A burden to the family. Why is he taking so long to die will be the question most often asked by friends and colleagues at the club by fellow party members. The newspapers will have the obituary in readiness.

The millionaire weeps until:

"It was a lie!" says the doctor, smiling.

Then Teobaldo smiles happily. But a month later the doctor again: "I'm concerned. The tests have revealed a serious blood disease. . . . "

And so it goes. Teobaldo suffers and suffers. There was a time when the suffering gave place to instantaneous euphoria, to an exceedingly heightened faith in reality, to an iron disposition to suffer the reverses of life, to an ever-increasing belief in the values of society. Lately, however, this hasn't been the case. Underlying the cathartic relief is a residue of disconsolation, of distrust, of bitterness. With bleary eyes Teobaldo studies the doctor's facial expression as he discourses on the degradation brought about by Alzheimer's disease: There's too much enthusiasm on the doctor's face. One of these days, the millionaire is thinking, it will be true. One of these days, I'll be lying on a hospital bed, weak, sick, worn down to a shadow. One of these days I'll have to change to a new doctor.

Real Estate Transactions

A REAL ESTATE AGENT must sell a condo. It's a superb apartment: a four-hundred-square-meter penthouse in an eighteen-story building, with four bedrooms, a living room with wide floorboards, a terrace with a swimming pool, and a sun deck. But he can't find a buyer: the asking price is too high.

Then the real estate agent finds a potential buyer: a man, young and rolling in money. This man is in a state of confusion. He is going through a major crisis. He has walked out on his wife. He wants to find out the meaning of all this. This what? asks the real estate agent. This, replies the man, all this—life, the world, everything. He has already searched for an answer in books, he has already had several long conversations with a priest, he has consulted a psychiatrist: in vain. In his despair he has considered taking his own life by jumping out the window of his twentieth-floor office. Not just to die; dying would be a side effect of this fall—a by-product in which he is not particularly interested; what he would like is to find the meaning of life in the vertiginous trajectory leading to the asphalt.

The real estate agent is intrigued by what he has heard. Do you believe, sir, he asks, that you would then find the answer you've been searching for? Of course, says the man. But, persists the real estate agent, at what moment would you find it? At what distance from the ground? Ah, I wish I knew, replies the man. At one millimeter from the asphalt, perhaps? the real estate agent persists. The man smiles. Perhaps, except that it would be a bit too late, I'd rather have more time left—it would be nice if I could enjoy the answer for at least a few meters. This, reasons the real estate agent, would depend greatly on the speed of the fall; if the fall were to occur slowly, say, at the speed of a falling feather, you'd be able to find the answer sooner, let's say, at ten meters from the ground. After thinking for a while, the man agrees. The real estate agent then goes on: But suppose the fall were to be very, very slow, wouldn't it be possible for you to find the answer soon after jumping? I'd think so, says the man who, beginning to grasp what the real estate agent is getting at, is now all keyed up.

"And suppose that the fall were to be extremely slow, that the fall were to amount to practically motionlessness"—the real estate agent, triumphant, is now standing on his feet "wouldn't it be possible for you to find the meaning of life at the exact moment that separates the intention to jump off from the act of jumping off?"

"Yes!" cries out the man, tears streaming down his face. "Yes, yes!"

Panting, the real estate agent sits down again.

"Then," he says slowly, "I have the solution for you."

Opening his briefcase, he takes out a photograph of the building and the blueprints.

"From the terrace of this penthouse here, you'll be able to find the meaning of life, should you wish to do so, sir."

The man writes out a check for a deposit: The deal is closed.

Days later the real estate agent is about to pay a visit to his client, now living in his new penthouse. He gets out of the car—and astonished, he stops short. In front of the building a crowd looking up: Way up, a man is standing on the edge of the terrace, ready to jump off. "Jump, jump!" many are shouting. "No, don't jump, don't!" shouts the real estate agent, overcome by anguish. Perhaps because the mob outshouts him, the man ends up by jumping off.

The real estate agent opens his briefcase: There it is, the receipt for the down payment that he was taking to his client. With a sigh he tears up the document. Then he gets into his car and speeds away, following a virtually horizontal trajectory.

Life and Death of a Terrorist

FERNANDO WOKE UP STARTLED with the alarm clock ringing. He pressed the button down, sat up in bed, sighed. Sighing once more, he got out of bed and drew the curtains open. A beautiful day, he found out, and heaved yet another sigh: Beautiful days didn't agree with him. He'd rather have gray skies, which were more compatible with the emotional climate he needed to carry out his daily assignment. An assignment whose steps he reviewed as he shaved: (1) Pick up the small parcel lying on the kitchen table; (2) go to any neighborhood in the city, pick a store, a restaurant, or supermarket; (3) surreptitiously insert the parcel into a niche somewhere, or drop it into a garbage can; (4) affecting insouciance, leave the premises and go into a coffee shop across the street from the chosen commercial establishment; at the moment of the blast, run to the door and with the same expression of incredulous horror as all the other bystanders watch the Dantesque scene of the bloodied bodies amid the smoldering rubble; (5) find a telephone, then dial a certain number; to the usual curt hello, say nothing but perfect. Mission accomplished. Chalk up another win.

He was sick and tired of the whole business. But there was no way he could get out of it. If only he had chosen some other occupation. If only he were, say, a bank teller in a quiet neighborhood bank: a peaceful, pleasant job. But no, he had opted for danger, for excitement. So, now he had to bear the consequences of his choice; and one of the toughest to bear was the transformation of what should have been a thrilling adventure into a tedious routine.

He got dressed, drank coffee, picked up the parcel. Before leaving, he cast one last look at the small apartment where he had been living alone since he separated from his wife. With a sigh he left. He got into his car in front of the building and started the engine. Before driving away, he hesitated: Where, today? The branch of a bank, it occurred to him, and he smiled at the thought. He headed for a distant neighborhood, then drove slowly along its tranquil streets until he arrived at a small bank. He parked and got out of the car.

HE WENT IN, greeted his fellow workers, and posted himself at the wicket. The security guard unlocked the front entrance and the first customers walked in. A lady came up to him, smiling. How are you, Dona Amélia? he asked. Fine, Senhor Fernando, you're always so nice. He took her check and handed her some money. And when she put it in her purse, he said: "Perfect."

Surprised, she looked at him.

"Perfect, what, Senhor Fernando?"

"Nothing'" he said, smiling. "Everything. This day. Life. Every-thing, Dona Amélia. Everything's perfect."

"You have the soul of a poet," said Dona Amélia, touched. "You're like my late husband. He, too, all of a sudden would say beautiful things."

She said good-bye and left. Fernando attended to a few more clients, then chatted with the manager, and thus the morning went by. At lunchtime he took the parcel he had left under the counter and unwrapped it. A cheese and ham sandwich, at which he stared with a mixture of displeasure and satisfaction. I'm going to tear this thing to pieces in nothing flat, he muttered and indeed, in six bites he devoured the whole sandwich. Perfect, he said, when he finished.

Resurrection

ONE OF THEM WAS TWELVE YEARS OLD; the other, thirteen. They were sitting on the beach—deserted at that hour, five o'clock in the afternoon. All of a sudden:

"Look, there's a man over there'" said the first boy.

"Where?" The second boy, who was tracing lines on the sand with his finger, raised his head and looked, but without great interest.

"Over there. In front of the surf."

"I don't see anything."

"There, see. Over there. Can't you see his little head? Now it's gone. Look! Now it's there again."

"I don't see any head."

"Look carefully. Keep looking. It appears, then disappears. Look, there it is again."

"But how come I don't see anything?"

"Well, it's because . . . Look, it has appeared again."

"I don't see anything."

"Look, there it is" persisted the first boy. "Follow the direction of my arm."

The other boy was already annoyed.

"I don't see anything. I don't think there's a man out there."

The first boy sighed.

"But there is. There's a man there. Now I can see his arm. He's waving his arm."

"I'll bet he's waving good-bye to you."

"Now he's gone again."

The other boy rose to his feet.

"Oh, shucks. I'll have to see this man. Even if it means going home and getting my binoculars."

The first boy was gazing at the sea steadily.

"Now he's gone. Gone, for sure. I don't see anything. No head, no arm, nothing."

"Just now, when I was getting the binoculars'" says the other boy, skeptical. "Too much of a coincidence, isn't it? Quite a coincidence."

The first boy wasn't listening.

"He's gone, yes. Completely gone. Not a sign of him."

"Sure. As soon as I mentioned the binoculars—"

The first boy, who was younger, made no reply. In silence he sat gazing at the sea.

The second boy sat down again. He, too, was looking at the sea. In silence. Suddenly:

"Look over there'" he said, pointing to the horizon. "Look, there's a man out there."

Genesis

THE THREE OF THEM—father, mother, and daughter—were in a restaurant. The mother got up to go to the washroom. The girl, four years old, sat looking at her father, who was chewing on his food in silence, a distant look in his eyes. Suddenly, she asked: "Daddy, how was I born?"

Perhaps because he was absentminded, he made no reply. She asked again: "Daddy, how was I born?"

He looked at her but made no reply. He helped himself to some more rice. She persisted.

"Daddy, how was I born?"

Putting down his fork and knife, he sat thinking for a few moments. "You'd better eat and stop asking so many questions'" he said.

"I don't want to eat. I want to know how I was born."

"Well." He took a sip of beer. "Do you really want to know?"

"Yes."

"It was like this: First Daddy met Mummy, he liked her, and they got married. There was a beautiful wedding party."

"Was I there?"

"No. You weren't born yet. And that's what I was about to tell you: Daddy and Mummy got married. Then they wanted a little daughter. After a while Daddy began to feel a strange thing on his back. Mummy took a look and said: You have a little mole there."

"A what?"

"A little mole. A little lump. A very tiny lump. Daddy ignored it; but the tiny lump started to grow, so he went to the doctor."

"My doctor?"

"No. Another doctor. He said it was nothing, and told me to rub on it some of the ointment that he prescribed."

"Like the one Mummy rubs on me?"

"Yes. Except that in Daddy's case, it didn't work: The lump kept growing until it became the size of a ball."

"As big as my ball?"

"Bigger. By then Daddy was quite scared. He went back to the doctor, who ordered an X ray."

"What's that?"

"It's a kind of picture that shows what's inside people. But let me finish the story, will you? As I was saying, they took the X ray and the doctor said: Hmm, there's a tiny creature in there, it's small but it's going to get bigger."

"And did it get bigger?"

"It did. The swelling got so big that Daddy could hardly walk. He had to lie on his side. And he grew thinner and thinner. The bigger the swelling grew, the smaller Daddy grew. It looked as if Daddy was going to disappear."

"And did you disappear?"

"No. Don't you see I'm right here? I didn't disappear. One night that huge swelling burst open, and a little girl sprung out. It was you. That's how you were born."

"Ah," murmured the girl. The mother was back from the washroom. "What have the two of you been chatting about?" she asked, smiling.

"I was telling our daughter here," he replied, "that we found her inside a head of lettuce. Isn't that right, daughter?"

"Yes," she said. Lowering her head over her plate, she began to eat.

Van Gogh's Ear [1989]

The Plagues

THE WATERS ARE TURNED TO BLOOD

Our life was regulated by a seemingly eternal and immutable cycle. Periodically, the waters of the great river would rise, inundating the fields almost as far as our house; afterward they would recede, leaving a coat of fertile slime upon the soil. It was then the planting season. We would plow the land, sow the wheat, and months later, the golden spikes would be swaying in the sun.

And then came the harvest season, and the harvest festival, and again the floods. Year after year.

We were happy. Occasionally we had problems: an illness in the family, or a quarrel, but by and large, we were happy, if happy is the right adjective to qualify a life without major worries or fears. Of course, we were poor; there were many things that we did not have. But what we lacked did not seem important to us.

There were six of us in the small house: my parents, my two brothers, my sister, and I. All of us devoted ourselves to our agricultural tasks. Later I was to learn the craft of writing; it was my father's wish; I think that he wanted me to tell this story, so here it is.

One afternoon we happened to be strolling, as was our wont, along the riverbank when my sister noticed something strange. Look at the color of the water, she said. I looked and at first I saw nothing unusual. The water was muddy, for our river was not one of those mountain brooks with crystalline waters that run friskily amid the stones; it was a mighty watercourse that came from far away, flowing sluggishly, and dragging with it the soil of the banks (but what did we care? It was not our soil); a huge animal, quiet but powerful, this river, which had over the centuries gained the right to its wide bed. It was by no means a beautiful river; but then we did not want it to beautify the landscape—we wanted it to integrate itself into the cycle of our lives, of our work, and in this respect, it fit the bill. There was no need for us to contemplate it in ecstasy. Our secret gratitude was enough.

But there was indeed something strange. The color of the waters tended toward red rather than toward the usual ocher. Red? It had no part in our lives. There was nothing red around us; no red flowers, for instance. As a matter of fact, flowers were something we never planted. We could not allow ourselves such indulgences. On the other hand, it is true that sometimes at sunset, the sky was painted in various colors, scarlet being one of them. But by that time we were already back home. We went to bed early.

My sister (one day she might be acknowledged as an exponent of the new scientific spirit), halted. Surprised, the rest of us halted too. Then leaving us behind, leaving behind the familiar group, her own family, the flesh of her flesh, the blood of her blood (attention, here: the blood of her blood)—she moved forward, as vivacious as ever, and entered the river. She stooped down to pick up something, which she then examined attentively before bringing it to us.

"What is it?" asked Father, and I noticed the furrow in his brow; a furrow that rarely appeared but when it did, it was an ominous sign, as were certain black birds that sometimes would flutter over the region, invariably heralding the death of one of our rare neighbors.

"Don't you people know what it is?" replied my sister, with that superior smile of hers that so irritated Mother: This girl thinks she knows everything, but she still hasn't found a way of freeing us from poverty. "It's a clot. A blood clot."

Strange: a blood clot floating on the waters of our river. Father, who always felt that he was under an obligation to provide an explanation (logical, if at all possible) for everything, suggested that it might be the blood of an animal that had perhaps been immolated in the river. There are superstitious people, he assured us, who resort to such practices to control nature, hoping to harmonize the flux and reflux of the river with the planting season. Sheer nonsense, explicable in terms of the eternal warped notions of human beings.

Yes—but what about the coloring of the water? About this, he did not say anything, and neither did we ask.

We returned home. My sister and I were walking side by side, in silence. Then all of a sudden: Father is wrong, she said, and I was seized with fear. A daughter talking like this about her father? A girl who, strictly speaking, should stay home to help her mother, and who only came to the fields as a special privilege accorded to her by the head of the family? But unaware of my perturbation, she went on: With one of those gadgets capable of magnifying the size of things enormously, she said, we would see corpuscles of various sizes. Some are reddish, and they can color a liquid; others are whitish.

"In other words," she concluded, staring at me fixedly, "the river has been turned to blood."

Blood! Yes, it was blood and I had known it all along. Except that, unlike her, I had not had the nerve to utter the word, far less say it with such confidence and easiness. Blood!

Father either had not heard or he pretended that he had not. But on the following days, even he had to admit that there was in fact a transformation. The river that flowed before us was a river of blood. And there was no possible explanation for this fact. Not even from the veins of all the animals in the world, slaughtered simultaneously, could such a torrent gush out. We were confronting an extraordinary and terrifying phenomenon. Mother wept day and night, convinced that the end was near.

My older brother, a practical-minded lad (and perhaps for this reason, Father's favorite), thought that we could take advantage of the situation by selling the blood to foreign armies, for as everybody knows, hemorrhage was a common cause of death among badly wounded soldiers. However, this was not going to be possible: Even in the waters of the river, and at the slightest manipulation or turbulation, the blood immediately cohered in clots. Of a colossal size. Every so often, we saw monkeys perched on them.

Father did not let himself become discouraged. He lost no time in trying to find a solution to the problem. Before long, he discovered that he could get clear water by digging wells along the bank of the river; it seemed that the sand of the bank filtered out the blood (all of the blood? Even those elementary particles that my sister had been talking about? I didn't dare to ask her. Neither did she say anything about this matter. The particles in question were added to the list of embarrassing matters, never verbalized, that exist in every family, to a greater or lesser extent. Unuttered words haunt homes like specters, especially on stifling nights when people, their eyes wide open, unable to sleep, look fixedly at the same point in the ceiling. At the very place where, in the attic, a skeleton remains unburied).

We built a cistern. Day and night, without stopping, we would pour ewers of water into it. And thus we had enough water to drink, to cook, to irrigate the crops until one day the waters of the river began to clear up. The blood clots disappeared. Apparently, things were getting back to normal. We've won, Father shouted as Mother wept for joy.

THE FROGS

As it turned out, Father's exultation was premature. One day, a frog appeared in our kitchen. Frogs were not a rare sight in the region, and that one was an absolutely ordinary frog, of a size and appearance normal in such batrachians. It was surprising, though, that it had ventured this far; however, the fact merited only a good-humored remark on the part of Father. On that same day we came upon several other frogs in the cultivated fields; and down by the river there were dozens of them croaking endlessly. This was now rather intriguing but, as Father stated, still within the normal limits, considering that wide variations are not unusual in natural phenomena.

Still, it was an awful lot of frogs. . . . And on the following days their number increased even more. The situation was becoming unpleasant. It was impossible to walk without trampling on frogs; at mealtimes, we had to remove them from the table so that we could eat; and at night, we found them in our cots.

But even so, we did not lose our sense of humor. My younger brother even adopted one of the batrachians as a pet. For several days, he took the little frog with him everywhere he went; he would feed it flies and rock it to sleep. One night the frog ran away; it was impossible to tell it apart from the thousands, millions of other frogs that were now leaping here, there, and everywhere. Father would laugh at the boy's distress, but Mother was not amused: removing so many frogs from the house was getting to be quite a chore.

My older brother was already thinking of turning the situation to our advantage. There are people that eat frogs, he assured us. The meat has delicate flavor, it's like chicken.

"Of course, we can use only the thighs, but if we wash them quickly in cold water; if we steep them in a marinade of wine with nutmeg and pepper; if we soak them in milk; if we coat them with flour; if we fry them in butter; and finally, if we arrange them on a platter, we'll have, I'm sure, a delicious dish. Actually, it's just a matter of promoting the recipes skillfully and of marketing the product properly in order to overcome a natural, but inexplicable, repugnance on the part of the public."

It seemed like a good plan, but it was impossible to carry it out. The entire region was having an invasion of frogs; people did not want to hear about the batrachians, much less eat them. Finally, Father became irritated. This is all the government's doings, he said; the politicians don't care a hoot about us, they only think of the farmers when it's time for them to collect taxes from us.

As if in reply to Father's complaints, on the following day a representative from the government showed up. We knew him: He used to be a neighbor of ours, a man nicknamed the Gimp because of a defect in one of his legs. Being unable to work, this man devoted himself to witchcraft. True, without much success, but since he had influential connections, he had obtained a high-ranking post in the central administration of the government. And now he had been sent down our way to find out about the situation.

We followed him as he plodded painfully alongside the river, at times tripping over the batrachians heaped on the sand. So many frogs, he kept exclaiming, amazed, so many frogs!

"Well?" asked Father, impatient, at the end of the inspection. "Can anything be done about it?"

"Certainly." He smiled. "Just as they appeared, they can disappear."

"And what made them appear?" Father persisted.

"Don't you then know?" he asked, surprised. "It's a curse. Put on us by the workers who are erecting the monuments. They are outraged; and they say that their god is punishing us. Us, the powerful! Such gall they have!"

Father was perplexed. He never invoked the deities, for he thought that doing so would be unfair. He believed that human beings had to survive by means of their own strength, without the help of mysterious entities. Besides: we, powerful? We who always toiled arduously, we who never exploited anybody? Perplexed and outraged, Father stood there. The wizard promised that the frogs would be eradicated within a short period of time, a promise that pacified Father somewhat, but left my kid brother disconsolate. Bursting into tears, he asked the man to spare his pet frog, wherever it was. The man promised to take his request into consideration. He did not.

MOSQUITOES, FLIES

The frogs disappeared, but a few days after they were gone, clouds of mosquitoes invaded the region, attacking us fiercely. We could not work, we could not sleep; the mosquitoes gave us no respite. My sister put forth the hypothesis of an environmental disequilibrium (the frogs, she said, had devoured the mosquitoes; after the killing of the batrachians, the insects began to proliferate), and my older brother was thinking of marketing an insect repellent made from cow dung—but Father was sick and tired of explanations and daring projects. He kept killing the mosquitoes with his big hands:

"I'll show this god! I'll show him!"

It was all in vain. When the mosquitoes finally disappeared, the flies came—huge gadflies that buzzed incessantly around us. They did not sting us, but they tormented us just as much as the mosquitoes had.

"Why don't they let them go?" Mother would ask, anguished. She was referring to those people that were building the monuments. We, the children, thought that letting them go would be a logical arrangement, but Father was becoming increasingly more indignant. No, he did not want them to go; he did not even know them, but he wanted them to stay; now he wanted them to stay.

"To see how far this god of theirs will go. Just to see how far he'll go. Blood, frogs, mosquitoes, flies, I want to see how far he'll go," he would say while furiously milking the cows (we had two), which kept tossing their tails in a vain attempt to protect themselves from the pertinacious gadflies.

PESTILENCE

One morning one of the cows was found dead. This time Mother lost her patience. She started to scream at her husband, accusing him of having mistreated the animal, thus causing its death. Father said nothing. He was staring fixedly at his own arm, where he saw the first in a series of

TUMORS

Could there be a link between the man's gaze and the tumor? Could the intense emotion of that fixed stare, in which hatred and defiance, bitterness, and even irony were blended together (in variable proportions depending on the particular moment) have induced a pathological process in the integument of this man, a process that initially manifested itself as a painful bump, which soon turned into a fetid ulcer? My sister did not have an answer to this question; neither she nor anyone else. As for Father, he remained silent. Even when the lesions spread all over his body, even when they began to appear in his wife and children, he still said nothing. Clamping his jaws shut, he would set to work with a vengeance, plowing and sowing and pulling out the weeds with fury. In spite of everything, the wheat was going to thrive; in spite of everything, there was going to be a bumper crop. Or so we hoped until we were struck by

HAIL

It happened unexpectedly: one afternoon, heavy clouds obscured the sun, the wind began to blow—and all of a sudden, we were pelted with pebbles of ice, some as big as a clenched fist. Part of the wheat field was destroyed. Father, immobile, his expression somber, seemed bewildered by this disaster. For how much longer, my sister heard him say, for how much longer? And, we had to admit, even an expert in weather forecast would be unable to provide a satisfactory answer to this question. Moreover, the next plague had nothing to do with meteorology. Soon we would be confronting the

GRASSHOPPERS!

The days go by, and one afternoon we are all sitting in front of our house, when a neighbor comes running to us. Gasping for breath, he breaks the news to us: The grasshoppers are coming. An immense cloud, driven by the strong wind that is blowing from the south. Yet another plague!

Father rises to his feet. On his face, an expression of determination:

"That's enough! That's now enough!"

We're going to put up a fight, he decides. With every power we have, we're going to fight the designs of this god whom we don't know, whom we don't worship, and who has been using us for his own obscure purposes. Who is this god, after all? Father cries out, and his voice echoes in the distance. With no reply.

He devises a plan of action. About gods, he knows nothing; but he does know all there is to know about grasshoppers. Voracious insects that can finish off what is left of the wheat field in no time flat. We've got to prevent them from alighting. How? By making noise, says Father. An awful lot of noise, without any letup. The noise will frighten the grasshoppers away. The noise will save us from this evil.

At dawn on the following day we position ourselves on the edge of the cultivated field. In single file, immobile, facing south: Mother, the firstborn, myself, my sister, the baby of the family. Each of us holding a bowl (five altogether: all we've got) and a stone. We stand there, immobile; only the wind ruffles our hair. How do I know this? Well, it's true that the wind is ruffling their hair: my siblings', my mother's, my father's; but I can't see the wind ruffling mine, no, this I can't. I do feel something on my scalp, though: it could be the wind ruffling my hair; but it could be an error of judgment, for my hair is cut short, much shorter than theirs (I like to wear it closely cropped) and it is stiff: of course, it is badly in need of a wash. It could be an error of judgment caused by my desire to have the wind ruffle my hair the way it is ruffling theirs. Or it could be my anxiety. . . . In short, I have been seized by doubt, and I believe (inasmuch as it is possible for a skeptic to believe) that this doubt will never relinquish its hold on me. God has succeeded in carrying out his designs.

Father, his forehead creased, reviews his small army. He counts on us; or he imagines that he can count on us, that we are with him. Are we? Speaking for my myself: I am. But am I really? Entirely? Completely? But what about these indefinable feelings? And what about these harrowing doubts? God now dwells in me. Inside me he will grow, and he will prosper, and he will triumph. I am lost. We are lost.

We look southward. Southward and upward. Father is now standing by my side. I can only look at him sideways; I can't look him in the eye, but I can guess the multiple components present in his gaze: Hatred. Bitterness. Disbelief. Mockery. Helplessness.

"Why?" is a question, among many others, held within this gaze. A mute, agonized question.

All of a sudden, a dry rustling. My hair, I can feel it (or I think I can), stands on end. Anxious, I scan the horizon; there, a dark cloud begins to emerge: Thin and small at first, it soon grows bigger and denser. It's the grasshoppers. Carried by the warm wind.

It takes them but a few minutes to get where we stand. A nightmare, those billions of insects buzzing around us.

"Noise!" Father shouts out, but his voice is muffled by the frightful drone of the grasshoppers. "Noise!"

So noise is what we make, banging away on our bowls as if possessed. But it is in vain: the cloud of grasshoppers has already alighted, and the ground is covered with a moving mass.

"The wheat field!" shouts Father. We run there, and with our hands and feet we try to remove the creatures. Before long, however, we give up; the entire field of wheat, or what was left of it after the hail, has already been devoured—spikes, leaves, stems, everything. The baby of the family, amused, laughs and claps his hands; in his innocence, he thinks that it is all a game. Pipe down, bellows my older brother, and bug off. Let him have some fun, shouts Mother amid the infernal noise of the grasshoppers. He's a child, he's innocent. And at least one of us is not suffering. My brother, full of distrust (such is the consequence of this calamity: a son, and the eldest one too, begins to distrust his own mother), makes no reply. He continues to bang on his bowl, already badly battered.

My sister picks up one of the insects, and proceeds to examine it, oblivious to what is happening around her.

"Yes," she murmurs, "they're grasshoppers alright. But . . . "

"But what?" I yell, impatient. "What new discovery have you made? Is it of any significance?"

My sister shakes her head.

"I don't know. They do look odd to me, these creatures."

Father draws closer. Ashen-faced, he looks at us. He shivers as if he had a fever, his teeth chatter. He asks my sister something; she doesn't understand. He repeats his question: He wants to know if grasshoppers are edible. Alarmed, my sister and I exchange glances—could it be that this latest tragedy has made him lose his mind? But she is not one to lose her sangfroid in a situation like this: Yes, she replies warily, there are people in the South who eat grasshoppers.

Father then scoops up a handful of grasshoppers, and begins to devour them. He exhorts us to do the same: Eat, eat while they still have our wheat inside them. We avert our eyes from this scene. Father starts vomiting: Let's take him home, says my older brother in an imperative tone of voice. The voice of someone taking control: A father that quails before grasshoppers, a father that vomits (albeit after ingesting the insects) is not worthy of trust. He cannot head a family. Following our brother, we march toward our house. The baby of the family is quiet, strangely quiet. He is, as later I will deduce, the bearer of one of those secret premonitions that sometimes befall young children, enabling them to foresee, several days in advance, the

THE DEATH OF THE FIRSTBORN

During the days when Father, delirious from a high fever, was confined to bed, my older brother took charge of the family. He would milk the only cow we had left, and distribute the milk among us while expounding on his plans: He intended to bury the dead grasshoppers, and in this way fertilize the soil; later he was going to install a watermill to grind the wheat and then export the flour thus produced to far-off regions. And he was counting on us to help him carry out this intensive program of work.

In the meantime, Father recovered from his illness. He resumed his place at the head of the table (even though there was no food to eat); and again he was ordering us around in his booming, authoritative voice. Which my older brother could not accept. He simply could not reconcile himself to the situation. Stubbornly, he refused to obey; one day, in the presence of the whole family, Father cursed him. Affronted, my brother demanded a retraction. And since Father would not comply with his demand, he left the room, slamming the door behind him. On the following day a messenger arrived with the news: All the firstborn were doomed. The Angel of Death would soon be passing through in order to smite them with his sword. All of us happened to be at the table at the time; the reaction of my older brother was astonishing. Atremble, he rose to his feet, his eyes bulging:

"Why me? Why me, when I've always helped around the house, when I've always looked after my brothers and sister? Why should I die? Is it fair? Tell me: is it fair?"

The baby of the family was laughing, thinking it was all in fun (and in fact, my older brother was always very playful with him). Father remained quiet and motionless; as for my sister and me, we averted our eyes. My older brother then ran into Mother's arms, and bursting into tears, he cried convulsively for . . . how long? I don't know. I didn't pay much attention to the passage of time then, to the days that kept flowing slowly and heavily like the logs that drifted down the river. But he must have cried for a long time. Suddenly he raised his head and stared at us in a challenging way. I'm not going to surrender, he said. I'm not going to die without putting up a fight. Then he opened the door and left the house. He was eighteen years old.

He did not return home that day; nor did he return on the following day. Had he run away? Had he been struck by the Angel of Death, like a leaping deer felled by a spear? Our fears did not materialize: He returned at nightfall, exhausted but seething with excitement. He had, he announced, something of great importance to impart: He had discovered a way of evading sure death.

"Yes, the Angel of Death will smite every firstborn child. But he will pass over the houses whose doorways are marked with the blood of an animal killed as a sacrifice."

We stood looking at him. The baby of the family, very astounded. My sister and I, rather astounded. Father and Mother—well, I don't know; if they were astounded, they did not manifest their astonishment. But regardless of the degree of individual astonishment, we all stood there motionless, our eyes fixed on him. He:

"But can't you understand?" he shouted. "I'm safe. Practically safe!"

Practically: It was what he said. Later on I even checked with my sister, who confirmed: yes, he did say *practically safe*. And ever since that moment I have been wondering if it could have been the word *practically*—which at the time struck me as rather unusual, even strange and suspicious, a word tinged with malignity (the subsequent

Van Gogh's Ear [1989] 401

events were to confirm this unfavorable impression; only recently, after I became more familiar with words and certain facts of life, have I been able to accept, although with some nervousness, the adverb. *Practically*! I shudder)—I have been wondering, as I was saying, if it could have been this word, so odd, to say the least, if not sinister, as I have said earlier—if it could have been this word, this *practically* that precipitated everything: because, all of a sudden, he ran up to my father, grabbed him by the shoulders, and started to shake him (he was strong, this lad, except that his strength was of no help to him):

"I'm safe, Father! All you have to do is to sacrifice an animal. Kill the cow. Collect the blood in a pail, then pour the blood over our door. Use plenty of blood, all of it, so that the Angel of Death will have no doubt about it; so that he will pass over our house; so that he will go away; so that he will spare me!"

They stood gazing at each other at that moment. What kind of a gaze it was (the son's, the father's), I had no way of knowing. They were standing in profile to me. I could see their noses, their compressed lips; but I could not see their eyes. If I were endowed with an unusual imagination, I could have made their gaze visible (in the form, say, of luminous rays varying in color and intensity), but even so, how to interpret the expression in their eyes? And what is more—in the perfect superposition of the luminous radiations, how to tell apart the look of the father from the look of the son? How to fit the expression in their eyes into the complex classification of feelings and emotions devised by human beings, especially when at the time I was far from being familiar with such classification? Even if I had been face to face with my father and my brother, I don't think I would have been able to describe the expression in their eyes adequately. Actually, I don't even know if they were in fact looking at each other. They were standing face to face; but one of them, the older man or the younger man, could have been watching the south, could have been watching the north, could have been watching the spot from where the Angel of Death would supposedly come. But who would be capable of identifying the components of such a look? Or to put it in a different way: How does a person wait for death (in general)? How does a person wait for death, when it is his own death? How does a person wait for death, when it is the death of his firstborn? A father looking at a son who is about to die, a son looking at a father who will die later—who is capable of describing such a gaze? Such are the dilemmas that appear in times of plagues.

The firstborn loosened his grip, and his arms fell to his sides, helpless. You are not going to kill the cow, he mumbled. Yes, it was more than a supposition, it was an assertion, but what the hell did he mean? That we were unwilling to save his life? That we should not kill the cow, now our only source of nourishment? That he loved the cow, whose milk he had drunk ever since he was a child? In short, what was he talking about?

We never knew. Without a sigh, he collapsed heavily to the floor. Father still tried to catch him in his fall, but he simply could not hold him: He was too frail. Nobody had ever obtained proper nourishment from grasshoppers.

We buried our brother on the following morning. As we learned later, he was not the only firstborn that was buried that day. But—it was the last of the plagues to afflict us. Since then, no god has bothered us; at least not significantly; now and then there has been a crop failure, or a minor disaster, but nothing serious. Nothing serious. One could say the following (and it is not one of the most pompous statements that a person can use to end a narrative): Life follows its course in a seemingly eternal cycle.

Don't Think About It, Jorge

"I'M GROWING OLD, ZILDA. Old and frail. I feel I won't last much longer."

"Don't think about it, Jorge. Think about the good things in life."

"These stomach pains. It must be cancer. The doctor says it isn't, but I think he's deceiving me. It must be cancer, Zilda."

"Don't think about it, Jorge. Think about the happy moments we've spent together."

"I know it's cancer, Zilda. I've seen lots of people die of this disease. It's a terrible death, Zilda. You waste away little by little."

"Don't think about it, Jorge. Think about your job. Think about your colleagues, and about your boss, who's so fond of you."

"First, you start losing weight. I'm already losing weight. I've lost five kilograms this year. As a matter of fact, this year has gone by so fast. Amazing, isn't it, how the years go by so fast. How the days, the hours, go by so fast. When you notice, it's already night. When you notice, the month is over. When you notice, life has come to an end."

"Don't think about it, Jorge. Think about your bowling buddies; they're a cheerful, fun-loving bunch."

"It won't be long before I have to be hospitalized. And once in the hospital, Zilda, people cash in their chips pretty fast. I think it's because they feel so helpless. Helplessness is terrible."

"Don't think about it, Jorge. Think about your children. Think about Rosa Helena, about Ze. Think about Marquinhos, Jorge."

"I'm afraid of dying, Zilda. I'm ashamed of feeling this way, after all, I've had a long life, but the truth is, I'm afraid of dying. I don't believe there's life beyond the grave. I think everything ends in the tomb. The flesh detaches itself from the bones, the hair falls off, the skull becomes exposed. This is death, Zilda. This is what death is like."

"Don't think about it, Jorge. Think about your vegetable garden.

Think about your chickens, Jorge. Think about a hen incubating her eggs, Jorge."

"A hen with cancer, Zilda?"

"Why not, Jorge, why not."

Van Gogh's Ear

WE WERE, AS USUAL, on the brink of ruin. My father, the owner of a small grocery store, owed a substantial amount of money to one of his suppliers. And there was no way he could pay.

But if Father was short of money, he certainly wasn't lacking in imagination. He was an intelligent, cultivated man with a cheerful disposition. He hadn't finished school; fate had confined him to a modest grocery store where, amid baloneys and sausages, he bravely repulsed the attacks of existence. His customers liked him because, among other reasons, he granted them credit and never exacted payment. With his suppliers, however, it was a different story. Those aggressive gentlemen wanted their money. The man to whom Father happened to owe money at that point in time was known as being a particularly ruthless creditor.

Any other person would have been driven to despair under the circumstances. Any other person would have considered running away, or even committing suicide. Not Father, though. Always the optimist, he was convinced that he would find a way of dealing with his creditor. This man must have a weakness, he would say, and that's how we're going to get him. By making some inquiries here and there, Father dug up something promising. This creditor, who to all appearances was a boorish and insensitive man, had a secret passion for Van Gogh. His house was full of reproductions of the work of the great painter. And he had seen the movie about the tragic life of the artist, with Kirk Douglas in the starring role, at least half a dozen times.

Father borrowed a biography of Van Gogh from the library and spent a whole weekend immersed in the book. Then, late on Sunday afternoon, the door of his bedroom opened and he emerged, triumphant:

"I've found it!"

Taking me aside—at the age of twelve I was his confidant and accomplice—he then whispered, his eyes glittering:

"Van Gogh's ear. His ear will save us."

What are the two of you whispering about over there? asked Mother, who didn't have much tolerance for what she called the shenanigans of her husband. Nothing, nothing, replied Father, and then to me, lowering his voice, I'll explain later.

Which he did. As the story went, Van Gogh had cut his ear off in a fit of madness and then sent it to his beloved. This fact led Father to devise a scheme: He would go to his creditor and tell him that his great-grandfather, the lover of the woman with whom Van Gogh had fallen in love, had bequeathed him the mummified ear of the painter. Father was willing to let his creditor have this relic in exchange for the cancellation of his debt and the granting of additional credit. "What do you think?"

Mother was right: He lived in another world, in a fantasy world. However, the main problem wasn't the absurdity of his idea; after all, since we were in such dire straits, anything was worth a try. Rather, it was something else that was open to question.

"But what about the ear?"

"The ear?" He looked at me astounded, as if the matter had never crossed his mind. Yes, I said, Van Gogh's ear, where in the world are you going to get it? Ah, he said, no problem, we can easily get one from the morgue. A friend of mine works there, and he'll do anything for me.

On the following day he left home early in the morning. He returned at noon, radiant, with a parcel which he then proceeded to unwrap carefully. It was a small jar filled with formaldehyde. Inside, there was something dark, of an indefinite shape. Van Gogh's ear, he announced, triumphant.

And who would say that it wasn't? Anyhow, just in case, he stuck a label on the bottle: *Van Gogh—His ear.*

In the afternoon the two of us headed for the creditor's house. Father went in, and I waited outside. Five minutes later he came out, disconcerted and indeed quite furious. The man had not only rejected the proposal but he had also snatched the jar from Father and hurled it through the window.

"Of all the gall!"

On this point I had to agree with Father, although I had sort of expected such a denouement. We started to walk along the tranquil street, with Father muttering all the time: Of all the gall! Of all the gall! Suddenly he stopped dead in his tracks, and stared fixedly at me:

"Was it the right one, or the left one?"

"What?" I asked, without getting it.

"The ear that Van Gogh cut off. Was it the right one or the left one?"

"How should I know?" I said, already irritated by the whole thing. "You're the one who read the book. You're the one who should know."

"But I don't," he said, dispirited. "I confess that I don't know."

We stood in silence for a while. I was then assailed with a nagging doubt, a doubt that I didn't dare to articulate because I knew that the answer could well be the end of my childhood. However:

"And the one in the jar?" I asked. "Was it the right one, or the left one?"

He stared at me, dumbfounded.

"You know what? I haven't the faintest," he murmured in a weak, hoarse voice.

Then we continued to walk, headed for home. If you examine an ear carefully—any ear, whether Van Gogh's or not—you'll see that it is designed much like a labyrinth. In that labyrinth I got lost. And I was never to find my way out again.

The Fragment

FOR MANY YEARS NANDO had been playing the role of a dwarf with success; after all, since he was no more than one meter twenty centimeters in height, that's exactly what he was—a dwarf. A happy one, too; his job as actor gave him money, recognition, and pleasant companions. As happy as a dwarf can be, Nando was. But then he was asked to play a different role. Actually, it was still the role of a dwarf, except that he was a giant that had been transformed into a dwarf. As a matter of fact, the giant never appeared in any of the scenes; his existence was merely implied.

Nando accepted the part. As usual, his performance was a success. Particularly moving was the final scene in which the dying character kept pleading with the witch for the magic word that would transform him again into a giant. But the witch remained adamant in her refusal, and in the end the giant died.

After acting in this movie, Nando was never the same again. To have lived the part of a giant, albeit only a potential giant, unsettled him. He asked various clairvoyants, astrologers, and mediums for the magic word; nobody knew what he was talking about. Frustrated, he took to drinking, which led him to his ruin.

Years later he died. In accordance with his wishes, he was buried in a three-meter long coffin. Sacks of shredded paper were used to hold the corpse in place; among those scraps of paper, there was one with a mysterious word written in Gothic characters. Perhaps it was the magic word, perhaps not; perhaps it was the fragment of a word sectioned into two parts by the scissors of some unknown person.

Perhaps the magic word was just this—a fragment. As a matter of fact, shortly before his death (perhaps out of pique, perhaps not; but, as the endocrinologist attending him said afterward, in a dying man, this doesn't really matter), Nando said that from certain aspects, a giant was nothing more than a fragment of a dwarf.

The Decision Tree

A MAN—he could be a systems analyst—is suddenly afflicted with amnesia. Deprived of his memories, but not of his intelligence, and still in control of certain techniques that seem to have become part and parcel of his way of being, he decides to evoke the past by going back over the decision tree which, as he supposes, has directed his life. Thus, if I happen to live in this house, it's because I made this decision after choosing from various options; if I married this woman . . . . The method turns out to be a success, and from decision to decision he retrogresses down to the distant years of his childhood . . . . The man who suffers from amnesia manages to remember far more than anyone else. But then he reaches the culminating moment just before his birth. There are two options, naturally: to be born, or not to be born; he knows, of course, that he must have chosen the first option; however, with consternation and even fear, he realizes that he doesn't know why. Why did he leave a situation of perfect amnesia to enter a life that consists of nothing but memories? And then it dawns on him that the reason for his amnesia is amnesia itself; that to forget is an option, the reason for which is definitively forgotten. An extreme fatigue engulfs the man, and he no longer remembers anything. All that is left to him is sleep, and so he sleeps, and he dreams about a tree, which is not the tree of his decisions, but an actual tree, a common tree, a humble specimen of what once upon a time was known as the Vegetable Kingdom.

Jigsaw Puzzles

FOR MY MASTER'S THESIS, I had access to the unpublished work of Armando Cossio. And once again I had the opportunity to marvel at his style—sober, clear, and so deeply resonant. However, a surprise was in store for me; when I thought I was finished with my survey of Cossio's fiction, his widow presented me with an envelope:

"His last short story," she said, gazing intently into my eyes.

(It disturbed me, the way she was looking at me. Cossio had died at the age of sixty-two, but she was not even forty yet. Still a young woman, beautiful and fiery. And the two of us alone in that house . . . No, it hadn't been easy.)

I took the envelope and opened it. Inside were carefully cut bits of paper, each one containing a typed word.

"One of his jokes," she said, smiling. "It's a short story that he wrote just before his death; he dedicated it to me. He cut up the short story, word by word, and then he challenged me to reconstruct it. He wanted to know how much I loved him, that's what he said. But I didn't even open the envelope."

Then after a pause:

"Would you like to give it a try?"

I would have to. It was my work that was at stake. Perhaps more than that.

I plunged into this task right away. On a large table I spread all the bits of paper, just like children will do with the pieces of a jigsaw puzzle. A preliminary examination revealed that there was no set pattern to follow; therefore, I started by placing the capitalized words at the beginning of sentences, the verbs in the middle, the adjectives next to the nouns, and so on. I would then put the sentences thus assembled on a corner of the table, under a sheet of glass to hold them in place. On the night when I put the last word (which happened to be *finally*) in place, the widow slept with me. We spent hours of intense passion. In the morning, she got out of bed and went straight to the table to read the short story. "Is this what the story is supposed to be?" I asked from the bed.

She shrugged her shoulders.

"I don't know. He didn't let me read it before he started cutting it up."

She then lifted the sheet of glass, and with one single puff of air, she sent the bits of paper flying in all directions.

Smiling, she returned to bed: We made love again. But this time in a different position: She on top, I underneath.

The March of the Sun in the Temperate Regions

THE SUN OF THE TEMPERATE REGIONS shines upon the lands of Santa Catarina, a state in southern Brazil, with a brilliance that is naturally less splendorous than it is in the tropics.

It is Sunday. The year is 1957.

On the top of a hill, two sisters—Marta, sixteen, and Marlene, nineteen—are seated on the grass, chatting and doing needlework. It's Sunday, yes, and it's been three years since President Getulio Vargas killed himself. Down below, they can see the small town, and the river glittering in the sun. In the sky, black birds of an unknown kind or species flit about (later, in retrospect, this fact will strike Marlene as ominous), at times flying from east to west, at times from north to south, at times from south to west.

The sun is at its zenith, and the shadow—Marta's—that it projects on the ground is, although deformed by the unevenness of the terrain, the shadow of a beautiful young woman. Marlene, too, is beautiful, both in shadow and in reality, but not as beautiful as her sister. Less beautiful.

"I'm pregnant," announces Marta, without interrupting her needlework.

"For heavens' sake!" exclaims Marlene, turning pale. "For heavens' sake, Marta, Father will kill you."

She knows what she is saying: Their father is a strict man. Strictness characterizes the inhabitants of their small hometown, all of whom descend from upright German immigrants who settled in the area, but the baker Wolfgang is particularly strict. A widower, he has raised his daughters according to rigid moral principles. And he had endlessly warned them against incurring pregnancy out of wedlock.

"Who's the father?" asks Marlene, distressed. Marta shrugs her shoulders. She thinks it's a traveling salesman with whom she had been only twice, a *carioca* who returned to Rio after complaining about the cold weather in the South.

Marlene is now devastated. A young woman of model behavior, married to a textile engineer with a serious demeanor, she doesn't know what to say to her sister. Marta, however, already has a plan: She will give birth to the child (she doesn't even consider having an abortion, for she wants the baby) and, if her sister agrees, she will leave the baby with her. She will then go in search of a husband, any husband.

What can Marlene say in reply? Marta is her only sister, her only and dear sister, the kid sister with whom she used to play when they were children, and toward whom she has always felt protective. In tears, Marlene hugs her: I'll do anything for you, Marta darling, I love you. She cries so much that Marta has to comfort her: Take it easy, sis, everything will be alright. Of the two, Marta is, and has always been, the bravest; she used to confront the street urchins, whereas her sister would seek refuge under their mother's skirts. You're tough, says Marlene, wiping her tears. I know, Marta says with a sigh.

That very night Marta announces to her father that she found an excellent job in the town of Lajes, and that she has to leave right away. The father, although somewhat suspicious, consents. He is strict but fair; he realizes that children must eventually follow their own path, even though the price is a painful separation. He trusts his daughter; besides, he loves her. If that's what you want, he says, you can go with my blessing.

On the following day Marta sets out on her journey. In Lajes, she stays with a friend. Then one night six months later, she knocks on the door of Marlene's house. She is with the baby, a beautiful girl. With profuse thanks, she entrusts her daughter to Marlene's care. And she leaves a message for her father: All she wants is his forgiveness.

She then travels north, to São Paulo; there, in the streets thronging with zillions of people she will certainly find a man. She finds accommodation at a boardinghouse—and for three days she is unable to leave her room: She cries nonstop. She cries for her daughter. She cries for her father. She cries for her sister. She cries for herself. She cries and cries: All the tears that she managed to hold back for months on end now gush forth.

On the morning of the third day she suddenly stops crying. Enough is enough, she says with determination. Now let's get down to business.

She needs a husband—but first she needs a job, for she is short of money; besides, a job will give her the opportunity to meet various men (among them, perhaps, her future husband). She dolls herself up, and makes for the door, but as she is about to get out, she stops, intimidated by the crowds of people hustling and bustling on the broad avenue. The sun of Santa Catarina, the sun that shines upon the placid valleys and the soft hills of Santa Catarina, has never seen so many people! Her unease quickly turns into panic, but she reacts. What the hell! That's what she wanted, wasn't it? People, men galore, so that she could choose a father for her daughter? Well, here are the men of São Paulo, the audacious *paulistas*, the leaders of the country. As she looks at the faces passing by, her interest gradually turns into childish enthusiasm. Look, there goes a Japanese! Straight from Japan! His father committed harakiri, his mother became a geisha, but he picked up the pieces and came to São Paulo. Look, there goes a *nordestino*—a migrant from the depressed areas of northeastern Brazil! The drought killed his crops, two of his children starved to death, the breasts of his wife shriveled up, but he, too, picked up the pieces and came to São Paulo. Look, there goes a black man! His grandfather was a slave, his parents are illiterate, but he is getting ahead for he believes in São Paulo! Look, there goes a German! He can barely speak Portuguese, but he, too, is getting ahead because he is a mechanic and this place here is São Paulo, an industrial megalopolis. Look, there goes a . . . a . . . but what is he? A Javanese? Look, there goes an Indian! At least he looks like an Indian! Look, a fat man! Look, a cross-eyed man, as cross-eyed as they come!

Ah, São Paulo. Ah, Brazil. Everything is fine in Brazil, that's what she hears people say; this country has everything, cars, radios, bicycles, you name it. The president of the country is a likable, cheerful man. In this city only people who don't want to get ahead fail, Marta's landlady assures her, before adding:

"But watch out, or you'll drift into prostitution."

She won't. Her destiny has been charted under the benevolent sun of Santa Catarina: a path leading northward and upward. She crosses the street, buys a newspaper, and begins to scan the classified ads, looking for work. There are many jobs advertised in the paper, and she is in luck: She is hired as a waitress in an elegant bar. There she meets the first man in what was to be a long succession of men.

He is old. A rich old man. An industrialist, a former congressman, the vice-president of a soccer club. A pleasant little man, affable and fatherly. She likes him and it is not just for his generous tips; she likes him especially for his endearing gentleness, for his kindness toward her.

Soon they start dating; on one occasion he takes her to a restaurant; on another, to a nightclub. Marta thinks that despite his age, he would make an ideal husband—a father for her daughter. Thus, it is with spontaneity that she accepts his invitation to visit him at his house in Jardim Europa, a high-class district. While going through the gates of the imposing mansion, while walking along the graveled paths escorted by a silent security guard, while passing by two threatening dogs, while wiping her feet on the doormat, while crossing the threshold of the massive door, while entering the spacious foyer with the marble floor—not once does she falter in her belief that she is prepared for anything. Should he greet her with a glitter in his eyes, she is prepared. Should he take her by the waist and propel her to his bedroom, she is prepared. Should he take a showy negligee out of a wardrobe, she is prepared. Prepared for anything. Prepared to lie down on the wide, canopied bed; to spread her legs open; to receive this gnome of a man. What sustains her is the thought that her daughter will soon have a father, an old and ugly father, a lecherous father, but a father nonetheless. She is prepared.

She is prepared for anything, but she never expected what is to follow.

We're going to play a game, announces the old man, smiling. What game? she asks, rather suspicious. Nothing to be afraid of, he reassures her, it's a game that my late wife and I made up: it's called mommy and sonny. Mommy and sonny? She is not too keen on the idea of playing this game, but he persists: I want to, he now says categorically, and she thinks she had better acquiesce; her future marriage is at stake; besides, it can't be anything too terrible, this mommy and sonny thing. Anyway, what difference does it make, she's in fact a mommy, isn't she, she thinks with bitterness.

Come over here and sit down, says the old man, pointing to a comfortable rocking chair. Sit down, and wait a moment. I'll be right back.

He leaves the room. A few minutes later he is back. Upon seeing him, Marta, astounded, opens her eyes wide: the old man has stripped his clothes and is now wearing nothing but a diaper. A diaper made to order, for sure, but exactly like a baby's diaper. And what's more: a pacifier hangs on a thin gold chain around his neck; and in his hand, a baby bottle filled with milk.

"So?" he says, triumphant. "Don't you think I'm a cute baby, hm?"

Flabbergasted, Marta is at a loss for words.

"Can I sit on your lap?" he asks in a tiny voice that sounds, in fact, rather babyish.

"What?" She thinks she must be hearing things, but he repeats what he has just said, this time with a certain impatience.

"May I sit on your lap? Baby wants to snuggle up to mommy."

Ah, yes, so that's what it was: mommy and sonny, that's what it was. Of course you may, senhor, she hastens to say. Don't call me senhor, he says. I'm a baby, your baby. And without further delay, the little man, so tiny and wizened, nestles himself in the lap of the robust Marta. Hug me, he demands, and she hugs him. Nice, comfy lap you've got, he says.

"Do you have children of your own?"

She hesitates. Is this the right moment to—?

"A girl."

"It's obvious: you have a knack for mothering. Your girl, does she live with you?"

"No, she's in Santa Catarina, with my sister."

She stifles a sob. Don't be sad, says the old man, sympathetic, sometimes children are better off away from their mothers. Then, animated:

"Stop thinking about it, I'm your child now. Rock me to sleep, will you?"

She starts rocking him vigorously. Slow down, he warns her, be careful, or I'll fall. It happened before, some stupid broad let me fall and I almost broke an arm.

Marta rocks him more gently. That's it, says the old man approvingly. Now give me the pacifier.

She tries to put the pacifier into his mouth. But he keeps his lips tightly closed, and then he starts moving his head from side to side, whimpering like a baby. She looks at him, perplexed.

"What are you staring at?" he asks, irritated. "Don't you then understand? What kind of mother are you?" Then controlling himself: "All right. If I don't want the pacifier, and if I'm whimpering, it's because I'm hungry, can't you see?"

Marta picks up the baby bottle from the night table and then tries to insert the nipple into the mouth of the old man, who protests:

"No! Not like that. First you have to taste the milk to find out if it's warm enough, if it needs more sugar, things like that. Hey, wait a minute! Don't put the nipple in your mouth, you nitwit! Do you want to contaminate me with your germs? Taste the milk by putting a few drops on your arm. On your arm, you idiot! Right. Now taste it. Is it good?"

"Yes," murmurs Marta, her face bathed in tears. The old man then starts to suck at the bottle. Little by little, the expression of displeasure disappears from his face; he is now tranquil.

"That was good," he says upon finishing the bottle. "Very good. Now you must sing me to sleep."

Marta begins to rock him: *Sleep, baby, the cuca will soon be here . . .* , she sings. No, not this one, the old man protests feebly. It frightens him, this song about the *cuca*, a horrendous creature from Brazilian mythology. She then starts humming an old lullaby that her mother used to sing at bedtime. It works: With his eyes closed, the old man smiles; before long, he is asleep.

After putting him to bed, Marta takes off the negligee. She gets dressed. She climbs down the stairway, walks past the butler, who maintains an impassive manner, past the dogs, past the security guard, and leaves the property. She won't be back.

For some reason, she is dismissed from the job at the bar. She tries to find employment, but this time she is not as lucky as before, and she can't find a good job. She has no experience in office work. No typing skills. No knowledge of English. She is a girl from Santa Catarina in search of a father for her daughter; but nobody is interested in her story. Finally she lands a job as a salesgirl in a store.

It is arduous and fatiguing work. The pay is low. What she earns is barely enough to make ends meet; besides, since she insists on defraying part of the expenses that her sister incurs in raising the baby, she has to deprive herself of even the barest essentials. There are days when she eats only one meal; she begins to lose weight quickly, and she is always exhausted. Rita, a girl who works with her, suggests that she return to Santa Catarina. No way, says Marta. Not until I have a father for my daughter.

Upon leaving the store one evening, she falls unconscious in the middle of the street. She is taken to a doctor's office in the vicinity; there, after a shot of glucose, she comes to. The first thing that she sees on opening her eyes is the pleasant, kind face of the young doctor, Ricardo. And it is love at first sight for both of them.

Every day Marta goes to Ricardo's office, where she can hardly wait for his last patient to leave. Then they make love—on the old couch, on the floor, on the examination table. But despite the passion, the love-making leaves much to be desired. He is a nervous, insecure man. He feels guilty and uneasy about using his place of work for clandestine trysts; his anxiety is such that it rubs off on Marta. Sex between them is far from being satisfactory. She finds it painful, and she never reaches an orgasm. As for him, his problem with premature ejaculation worsens.

He is married, which further complicates the situation. He doesn't love his wife. On the contrary. He describes her as being a cruel, authoritarian woman who takes pleasure in tormenting him, either by calling him a failure (you're nothing but a two-bit doctor in a low-class neighborhood), or by making fun of his physical defect—Ricardo walks with a slight limp. She doesn't want to have children, and she dares him to walk out on her. However, despite the constant humiliations, he tries hard to prevent the breakup of their marriage. Partly because he fears, naturally, a scandal, which might damage his reputation as a physician, but mostly because he is in fact hopelessly attracted to his wife, who is not only a woman of great beauty but also a real demon in bed. She knows how to make him get his rocks off, ah, does she ever. At anytime, anywhere (often while bathing, she pulls him into the bathtub with her), and in any position. She dominates him; by pulling the strings of sex, she can manipulate him as if he were a marionette. Day and night he lusts for her, and whenever his thoughts turn to her, he can't help masturbating. If only I could rid myself of this woman, we could then marry, Marta darling; because it's you that I love, no one else but you.

Marta tries to be supportive: I love you too, Ricardo, and I'll wait as long as necessary.

Inwardly, however, she is filled with anguish at the thought of her daughter growing up away from her. It won't be long now, Marlene—she writes, and it is what she hopes: soon to be able to return to her daughter in the company of a husband, even if he happens to be divorced.

One night there is a knock on the door of her room. She opens the door to find Ricardo standing there, suitcase in hand. He looks upset, really upset: bug-eyed, his hair disheveled, his necktie undone:

"I did it!" he shouts. "I managed to rid myself of her, Marta. Thank God, I did it!"

Weeping, he falls into her arms. For a long time they just stand there, locked in an embrace. Later they go and see the owner of the boardinghouse—Ricardo wants to ask her permission to spend what he considers his wedding night in Marta's room. The landlady, showing understanding, accedes to his request, especially because she already knows about Marta's affair with him and wants to help her out.

The two of them are too excited to fall asleep. They spend the night making plans—they will travel to Santa Catarina, they will choose a small town to settle down: He will practice medicine there, she will look after the house, and little Clara will grow up happy (together with her little brothers and sisters—for they intend to have lots of children). The sun of Santa Catarina will see them happy, always hugging each other. In the morning they have coffee with the landlady, who makes a brief speech, wishing them every happiness in the new life they are about to start, and then Marta and Ricardo leave for work. She goes straight to the store where she works, and he to his office; they will get together again in the evening, in her boardinghouse. At work, Marta keeps glancing at the clock, yearning for the moment when once again she will be embracing her Ricardo, her man.

But he doesn't show up. Neither that night, nor the next night. Worried, she doesn't know what to make of it all. The telephone in Ricardo's office rings unanswered; she doesn't want to phone him at home. Finally, it is Ricardo who rings her up. Sobbing, he tells her that he has returned to his wife.

"She's a devil, Marta."

Ricardo goes on to say that his wife came for him while he was in his office getting things ready for their journey, and that she seduced him then and there, and as he was moaning from pleasure, she made him promise that he would move back with her.

"Forgive me, Marta! Forgive me!"

Without a word, Marta hangs up on him. She returns to the counter and mechanically resumes measuring a length of fabric for a shopper. It is not until the evening that she gives full vent to her feelings: in the arms of her landlady, she weeps and screams: Why, oh God! Why do these things happen to me? Don't take it so hard, says her landlady, your sorrow will pass.

It passes. It is not easy, but it passes. Three weeks later, Marta feels better: she manages to write to her sister and tell her about the incident, saying that she has learned a lesson.

However, the letter goes unmailed: on that very day, there is again a knock on her door. It's Ricardo, this time without a suitcase, without anything, looking radiant:

"At long last, Marta! I finally did it! I'm rid of her."

His exultation is so genuine that it is impossible for Marta to distrust him: Weeping, they throw themselves into each other's arms. Later they invite the landlady to join them for dinner at a restaurant to celebrate the occasion. The old woman looks surprised, but she accepts the invitation, wishing them—again—much happiness.

Three days of ecstasy follow. Marta has forgotten everything that went on before; they are now starting from scratch, and everything will turn out alright.

But then Ricardo does his disappearing act again.

This time he doesn't even phone; he has simply vanished.

"I knew it," remarks the landlady, not without a certain amount of censure. "I knew he would do this again. He's a coward, Marta. Like all of them, as a matter of fact. Typical of the Brazilian male, you just can't trust any of them. Peruvian men aren't as bad, believe me."

Marta doesn't want to think about him anymore, she doesn't want to think about anything. She moves about like an automaton, from the boardinghouse to the store, and from the store to the boardinghouse. She thinks only about her daughter, about this daughter growing up away from her mother; she feels like going back to her hometown; one day she even goes to the bus station; but at the last moment, realizing what she is about to do, she hastily walks away from the line of people at the ticket counter. She will only return home with a husband.

Ricardo comes to her place once again. But he isn't alone; his wife is waiting for him on the street.

"Go and tell her," he entreats Marta, "that we love each other. Go and tell her, Marta. See if you can persuade her to leave me alone, Marta. Do it, because I can't!"

Marta looks at him without saying a word. Suddenly she starts shaking; she looks so unhinged that Ricardo, startled, steps back.

"Get out! Get the hell out of here! Take your wife and get out! Get out before I kill you."

Frightened, he tears down the stairs. Bursting into tears, Marta flings herself upon the bed; and there she remains for one day and one night, crying nonstop. Nurses finally come to take her to a mental hospital.

A month later she is discharged from the hospital. Unemployed, and not knowing what to do next, she wanders about the city, amid the hurrying crowds of people. As she walks along the Viaduto do Chá, a small boy hands her a leaflet: *Madame Olga. Clairvoyant. Family problems? A missing child? The whereabouts of a spouse? Come and see me.* A sudden hope: Perhaps this Madame Olga could help her find a husband. Perhaps.

Marta calls on the clairvoyant. Madame Olga greets her and listens attentively to her story. Afterward, she invites Marta to sit down at the table. Taking hold of Marta's hands, the clairvoyant then asks her to close her eyes and concentrate on herself. Tense minutes trickle away. In a wavering voice, Madame Olga, who has fallen into a trance, says that she can see a man; his features are not clearly discernible; however, she knows that he lives in a comfortable house because she is watching him through one of the windows of this house. Marta insists on more details. How does the man look like? Is he tall or short, thin or fat? Does he wear glasses, does he have a mustache? And the house? What can Madame Olga tell her about the house? Is it a two-story house, a palatial residence, or what? But the clairvoyant doesn't answer any of her questions; she says that the vision is beginning to dissolve; the two women finally open their eyes and there they are, face to face. I was discharged from the mental hospital a week ago, says Marta in a low, subdued voice. It was horrible. I can imagine what it was like, says the other woman with a sigh. Then, after some hesitation, she goes back to her vision:

"No, I don't know where the house was, or in which city. But I'd say it was somewhere in the north rather than in the south. Try your luck in . . . Belo Horizonte. That's it: Belo Horizonte, give it a try."

Marta's landlady pays for the bus ticket, and she travels north to Belo Horizonte, the capital of the state of Minas Gerais. She finds a job in a garment factory; she manages to scrape a living. Periodically she receives a letter from her sister, sometimes with a picture enclosed: Clara in her crib, Clara taking her first steps. The first birthday, the second, the fifth, the sixth. . . . Every letter brings on a crisis: Marta cries and rages. But she remains steadfast in her resolution: She will only return to Santa Catarina with a father for her daughter. On Saturdays she dolls herself up and goes out: to nightclubs, to dances, to parties organized by her Workers' Union. She has boyfriends—ugly and handsome, old and young. But proposals of marriage? None. It's your own fault, her fellow workers keep telling her amid the deafening noise of the machines. Because of her anxiousness, she puts too much pressure on the men. We *mineiros*, we folks from Minas Gerais, are very distrustful, one of her lovers says to her in a hotel room before he puts on his pants and disappears forever.

At one time she actually becomes engaged to a bank manager, an earnest, methodical man still in his prime: Every time they go out on a date, he records the fact in his appointment book. They go to movies, to restaurants; over dinner they discuss the details of their wedding plans.

One day she summons up enough courage to mention her daughter. He turns pale:

"But you've never told me anything about this."

"I know, but it's because . . . "

"And here I was, thinking all along that you were a virgin. I've always shown the greatest respect for you. I've never made an indecorous proposal to you. And now you tell me that you even have a daughter."

On the following day he announces that he is breaking off their engagement. And he presents her with a bill containing three columns, with the headings: *Date, particulars, expenses incurred.* All their dinners and outings are itemized there.

"I've converted the expenses from cruzados into dollars," he explains. "Due to the galloping inflation, we have to think of costs in terms of a strong currency. I think we should share the expenses. If our relationship had worked out, I wouldn't be making this suggestion. However, since our paths now diverge, through your own fault, it's only fair that I should get some indemnification."

"But . . . I—I don't have this kind of money," Marta, bewildered and dejected, falters out.

He hesitates.

"Well, I'll tell you what I can do: I can give you a discount of, let's say, about twenty-five percent. After all, it was only at my insistence that you went to some of those places; and if my memory serves me right, you didn't eat much when we dined out. And you never drank wine. But I can't forgo the money. That's completely out of the question."

Then, on a sudden impulse, he discloses, in strict confidence, that he has been investing. And investing heavily. He has been buying bonds, shares of stocks. It's the right time for this sort of thing. It's a bull market; he has it from reliable sources that the prices of shares will skyrocket. Anyone willing to take risks will strike it rich.

Fortunes will be made overnight. You're probably right, says Marta, but I've got no money. He makes her sign some promissory notes. Frightened, she runs away to the northeastern city of Salvador, the capital of the state of Bahia.

There she meets a young *paulista*—a native of São Paulo—named Jorge. He is a university student who is spending some time in Bahia in search of solutions for his anxieties. For the first time in her life, she experiences the heat of passion: on one occasion they spend two days in bed, making love nonstop. They don't even eat: they merely drink coconut milk.

She is unable to find a job. And he, although he has a rich father, has severed relations with his family. When her money is gone, they leave Salvador and go to a commune near the city of Porto Seguro. There the days flow placidly; she is head over heels in love; and he . . . he is too. He, too.

She tells him about her daughter. He shows interest, inquires after the girl, wants to see pictures of her. But when Marta suggests that they get married and move to Santa Catarina, he turns down her suggestion: He is trying to find his own way, and it will lead to politics, not marriage. Besides, he takes a dim view of the whole thing: family, bourgeois possessiveness: People should give of themselves to everybody. And as if to stress his point, on that very night he returns to their shack with a girl newly arrived at the commune:

"She'll be sleeping with us."

Jorge lies down between the two women. He takes turns making love to them. Marta wakes up early in the morning. She kisses the student, who is asleep, and leaves.

From Porto Seguro to Brasilia. From Brasilia to Campo Grande. From Campo Grande to Belém. From Belém to Manaus. Armando, a geologist; Rui, a truck driver; Aristeu, a priest from a secret sect. César, an alderman. Peixoto, a street vendor who sells fruits and vegetables. Negrinho, a construction foreman. Ignácio, a farmhand.

In the city of Goiania, she meets José Reis, an old Portuguese actor who presents himself at circuses, old movie theaters, anyplace, always enacting the same play, *The Drama of Tiradentes*. It is a tribute, he says, to Tiradentes—the Toothpuller—who died a martyr in the cause of freedom. He was the leader of the patriotic movement of 1789 that tried to liberate Brazil from the Portuguese regime. It was, José Reis declares, Brazil's greatest movement ever of national liberation.

A good man, José Reis is. A good but bitterly dissatisfied man. He left Portugal to escape from the Salazar dictatorship, and arrived here with high hopes of seeing Socialism become successfully implanted in Brazil—a new country in the tropics, with none of the depravities of Europe. In 1961 he actually believed that his dream would come true.

"It was soon after the resignation of President Jânio Quadros, when the military attempted to stage a coup. I was then in the city of Porto Alegre, where I participated in the movement to defend the legality of the constitution. That was really something, those crowds of workers demonstrating on the streets. Unfortunately, it all ended much too soon: the politicians came up with a solution—compromise. It really shattered my illusions. Deep down they're all the same: the Brazilians, the Portuguese. All of them congenital, dyed-in-the-wool reactionaries.

He would argue with people on the street, he would insult the shoe shiners: Why do you humiliate yourselves like this? Why are you on your knees? To earn a pittance, is that it? Money changers in the temple, he would mutter upon seeing the street vendors. Nothing but money changers in the temple. They should be driven out with lashes of a whip. Even the capitalists have no use for the likes of them. If only they could be used as a target in the class struggle—but no, they fall somewhere between the bourgeoisie and the proletariat, between heaven and earth.

He would go to the airport and approach a cleaning lady who happened to be sweeping the floors:

"Have you ever traveled by airplane?"

"No," the woman would reply, astonished.

"And you never will. Never. Take a look at these people around you: They travel. To São Paulo, to Rio. To Paris, to Vienna. Do you know where Vienna is?"

"No."

"You don't know where Vienna is. You know nothing. Do you know how to read?"

"No."

"So I thought. While you're here sweeping floors and cleaning toilets, those people are above the clouds, sipping whiskey. Don't you find this outrageous?"

"Well . . . I'm poor . . . you know, sir."

"I know. Poor and stupid. Poor, stupid, and resigned. You'll go on cleaning toilets, what else? You'll go on crawling for the rest of your life. Have you ever heard of Tiradentes?"

"I've heard of him, yes."

"You've heard. And that's about it, right? You've heard of him." Then suddenly angry: "Get lost!"

An embittered man. A good but embittered man. Too embittered, he was. Marta lives with him for three weeks: She is deeply touched when she watches him perform in his play, but she can't stand his constant griping. Besides, José Reis doesn't want to be a father to anybody.

"Me? A father? Why should I? I don't believe in having a family. Or in anything for that matter. Each man for himself. . . . "

She leaves him and heads west. In search of a father, a father for her daughter.

Being sterile, Marlene raises Marta's girl as if she were the daughter that she cannot have. It is Marlene whom Clara calls mother. Of

Marta, Marlene never speaks; on the contrary, in her prayers she implores God (while at the same time asking for forgiveness for her ghastly selfishness) to keep her sister away forever. Marta never returns home.

But don't their paths—the mother's and the daughter's—ever cross? Yes, it happens one day. At a bus station in Buenos Aires. Clara is there together with her boyfriend and a group of friends. She is now eighteen years old, and this is the first time that she has been away from home.

Marta, too, has just arrived; she is with an Argentinian businessman whom she met in Cuiabá, a city in west-central Brazil—a man who is willing to discuss marriage after they give their relationship a tryout in his distant hometown.

For a few seconds they—Clara and Marta—look at each other. They look intently upon each other's faces, like explorers studying the map of an unknown region. Except that there is not enough time for them to absorb through this gaze (however intense it is) their respective facial features and to store in their memories the recollection of a well-shaped mouth, of an eyebrow, of an incipient wrinkle. And yet it is possible that something—a disquieting particle, the germ of a passion—will remain, something that will perhaps have to lie dormant for a long time. But behold! Marta, propelled by the Argentinian, is already boarding the bus. She is going south, headed for icy Patagonia, where the snow will stir up in her yearnings for the pale sun of the temperate regions.

The Diary of a Lentil Eater

AS ONE CAN EASILY IMAGINE, lentils were never the same to Esau after he lost his birthright. Esau, who had never been particularly fond of lentils and who would say to certain hosts, no, no, not the lentils, I'd rather have the suckling goat, was now obliged to reflect seriously upon a dish that had until then played only a relatively modest role in his emotional makeup. In this undertaking, he went through several phases. The first one, naturally, was of rage: I've lost my birthright! Something very precious to me. And for a plate of lentils! His grief was aggravated by the gibes of friends and relatives: Never has a plate of lentils been so expensive, they would say, breaking into derisive laughter. And still laughing, they would suggest that Esau open an establishment specializing in lentil dishes (and a wag even came up with a name: *The Lentil of Gold*).

Such ready wisecracking hurt Esau more than anything else. A hairy boor of a man, he used to embarrass other people with his off-color jokes; but now that the tables were turned on him, and he was on the receiving end of his peers' cruel taunts, he realized how painful the role of victim could be. If anything, the lentils have taught me this lesson, he would sigh.

He suspected that he was at the start of a new road in his life. It is possible that at the time he was haunted by dreams of giant lentils; however, no such dreams are recorded in his diary, a lengthy manuscript found hidden in a clay ewer that was recently discovered in a cavern not far from the place where he is supposed to have lived. The diary begins with the day when he lost his birthright; and the first word, spelled in a way that is incomprehensible even to renowned experts, is presumably a swear word, even though the swear words of those days are not recorded anywhere.

It is of course possible that the vibrations resulting from the voices of those people that clamored to the skies are still diffusing in space; however, the process of capturing, decoding, and placing such voices in a historical context is something still beyond the technical possibilities available to even the most sophisticated exegetes.

One can only surmise that Esau, like all human beings, also felt the immemorial impulse to emit certain sounds that conventionally express displeasure, especially after the pleasant (or perhaps not so pleasant; the diary makes no mention of this matter) sensation of gastric fullness gave way to a feeling of disquiet, a feeling which in many individuals manifests itself as questionings (who am I, what am I doing here on earth, why does the bamboo grow so impetuously?).

The first phase, therefore, can be considered as being one of rebellion. Which up to a point, is understandable. Esau was a young man. He didn't have much tolerance for certain rigid precepts of communal life. Although he wouldn't say so, he felt that Cain had been right in killing Abel, and that in this world there was no place for the weak. He didn't think it fair that some people should have everything, or almost everything, and others nothing, or almost nothing. That some should laugh, shamelessly, while others wept, copiously or not, silently or not. That some should crow while others had to hold their tongues. Moreover, on several occasions he had hinted to his father that he intended to shave on a daily basis (fully aware that elderly people didn't like to see a clean-shaven face). The look of pain on the face of the man to whom, in accordance with the moral codes of the time, he was supposed to show respect, did not arouse in him the slightest remorse. On the contrary: His smile evinced a barely contained feeling of pleasure.

And now on top of this, lentils. Lentils! Is it fair, he kept asking himself as he paced to and fro in the room to which those that had lost their primogeniture had to betake themselves, is it then fair for someone to be stripped of his prerogatives just because out of hunger (and what could be more human than hunger?), he lets himself be tricked out of his birthright with a plate of lentils?

Lentils, plain food: nothing fancy, nothing that would lead anyone into thinking that Esau had yielded to a gastronomic temptation (especially because he was reputed to be a man of simple tastes). In a nutshell, here is what happened: A man is on his way home; being exhausted and famished, he is not in full possession of his mental faculties, and thus he falls into a treacherous trap, whose lure is a plate of harmless lentils.

He could go a step further in his reasoning and suspect the lentils themselves. Not that they might have contained strange substances: No, he wouldn't carry his suspicions that far. But—were they really nothing but ordinary lentils? Perhaps not. Perhaps they resulted from some elaborate process of genetic selection aimed at obtaining a vegetable capable of—by means of its appearance, or aroma, or both—beguiling a firstborn out of his birthright. He remembered now that the aroma of the lentils had aroused in him a strange sensation, which he had attributed to hunger—to pure and simple hunger.

There was nothing that could be done now. A victim of his own gluttony—and once again he bemoaned the fact—he had polished off the plate of lentils. Therefore, he lacked any proof to substantiate his accusations. Besides, his aged father, although wise, suffered from various sensorial privations, of which blindness was the most serious; thus, behind the guileless appearance of the lentils, his father would be unable to detect any evidence of a perfidious enticement contrived by the woman whom he had, in an evil hour, married, and whom he trusted—for he loved her very much. So, what else could Esau do? React, fight back, that's what. Turn defeat into victory. Which wouldn't be easy, especially because he would have to start waging battle in a state of bitterness and humiliation. But perhaps he could start from the very trap into which he had fallen. *The Lentil of Gold*, why not. *Have a taste of the lentils that seduced Esau.* He could make a lot of money out of the treachery perpetrated on him. Or he could, as another option, hoist the flag of idealism. He could warn people against the immoderate eating of lentils; he could champion the abolition of primogeniture; in short, he could fight for a world in which everybody is equal, for a world in which eating lentils does not result in danger. A dream? Delirium attributable to the residual effect of a certain intrinsic or extraneous—substance in the lentils? Perhaps. However, what else can a firstborn stripped of his rights do, except dream, or even rave?

Esau's diary, long and uneven, leaves much to be desired regarding the importance of his cogitations (one might even say ruminations; not to mention the spelling errors and the intricate syntax, which make reading the diary a real chore). So, once all this lucubration is expurgated, what else is left? Nothing but the basic fact that Esau lost his primogeniture by eating a plate of lentils. For this reason, the scholars that had been perusing this document abandoned any and every attempt to extract from it a piece of work that would be remarkable from an academic or any other point of view. They then turned their attention to other, more promising fields. Three of those scholars, for instance, set up in business as exporters of legumes. They now follow the quotations from the Chicago Stock Exchange attentively. However, the matter of interest is not the lentil, about which Esau had so many complaints, well founded or not. It is the soybean, whom many call "the seed of gold."

Misereor

AS HE ENTERED THE HOSPITAL, Fernando realized that Suzana had been there for one year. Already one year. One year of pain, one year of anguish, one year of suffering: one year.

This realization struck him suddenly: for a moment he even thought that he wouldn't have the strength to proceed, that he would beat a retreat. But he fought off these feelings. He clenched his teeth, and with firm determination, he forged onward. He walked past the information desk; the receptionist barely glanced at him; most of the hospital staff were already used to his presence there. He climbed a flight of stairs and turned right. He walked down the long corridor, glancing at the numbers on his right and on his left: 1010, 1011, 1012. He already knew them by heart, and he also knew some of the occupants of those rooms, the old-timers: the man with the kidney disease, the girl in a coma for two years. Sometimes he would run into their relatives in the corridor, and then they would exchange those half-anguished, half-conniving glances that unite people going through the same grievous plight.

Suzana's room was the last one, at the end of the corridor. Its door was next to a large window from which the hospital garden could be seen: pine trees, beds of flowers, graveled paths along which children were always running. Fernando knocked on the door.

(He always knocked. It was a tacit agreement between them: He would knock and wait for a while, giving her time to recompose herself, in case she had to.)

Come in, said a weak, almost inaudible voice, and he opened the door. Right away he was assailed by the smell—a vague, nauseating smell of sickness, of disinfectant, to which he hadn't been able to get used. But he managed to smile at Suzana, who lay in bed, propped up by several pillows. Her appearance, he verified with an anguished heart, kept deteriorating day by day: Her cheeks were becoming increasingly more hollow, her lips increasingly more shrunken. Only her eyes still retained some of her former self, but the glitter in them—and the comparison presented itself to him implacably—was of the kind seen in the eyes of a trapped animal.

After bending over her to kiss her on the face, he pulled up a chair and sat down.

"You're looking very well today."

She smiled feebly. He knew that she knew that he was lying; but she kept smiling, and so did he. It was part of a tacit game of compassion that had replaced so many of the other games that they used to play throughout their married life in order to live together in an atmosphere of respect, of affection—and why not? of love (for who said that love exempts anyone from playing games?).

"Has the doctor come around yet?"

"Yes. He was here early in the morning."

"And—?"

"He said I should continue to take this new drug for another twenty days."

Yes, that's the way it was. Time was now divided into limited units. Another twenty days with this particular drug. A week from then, another X ray. If the blood count shows no improvement by the end of the month . . . That was the doctor's game: To demarcate the dark road with boundary stakes, thereby maintaining the illusion that they would get somewhere and reach a happy ending. Willingly, the patients subjected themselves to this game, and felt grateful to the doctor. After all, he was human, the doctor was. Besides, he was an old family friend. He, too, had to be protected from pain.

"Everything okay at home?" She was now playing her part, throwing a difficult question at him, just as someone would throw a lifesaver to a drowning man. *Everything okay at home?* She always helped him out, by giving him the cue to start talking about the children, about the maid. And implying that he could talk without feeling guilty, and without censuring himself for being alive and in good health. So he started talking about things at home: about the risotto that the maid had cooked for dinner the night before, about the report card that their eldest child had brought from school, about the faces that their youngest daughter had been making at their next-door neighbor, about his intention of having their apartment fumigated in the next few days. He talked on and on, without a pause, partly out of gratitude, partly out of fear—fear that any interruption (even to catch his breath) might turn into an impassable ditch, into an abyss into which they would both plunge headlong. She listened to him in silence, a wan smile on her face; at times she would nod her head, and this very unobtrusive encouragement gave him the strength to proceed. At one moment, however, he lost heart; the constriction in his throat had become unbearable, and his voice came out strangled; as panic was about to overtake him, there was a knock on the door, and a nurse's aid came in to give the patient an injection. While she was busy preparing the hypodermic, Fernando, in a state of exhaustion, managed to pull himself together.

"Will you give me a hand, sir?" said the nurse's aid. "We're going to lay Dona Suzana on her stomach."

With a determined gesture (but much too abrupt, he thought, much too abrupt), the woman pulled off the blanket, exposing a ravaged body: arms and legs thin as reeds, a hollow belly. It was almost impossible for him to bear the sight, which didn't seem to affect the nurse's aid very much:

"Stand here next to me, will you? When I say *now* we turn her over."

She was a young, beautiful woman; a disturbing presence there, which only served to increase Fernando's anguish. Eager to put an end to the situation, he drew nearer the bed and positioned himself next to the young woman. And then her arm brushed against his. At the touch of that warm, solid flesh, he quivered—and at that moment he caught Suzana looking at him. There was no accusation in that look, no grief or anything. She had just looked at him. The next moment she was lying on her stomach.

The nurse's aid administered the injection, helped Suzana lie on her back again, put the pillows in place, and left. Fernando sat down again. For a moment the two of them remained silent, she still gasping for breath. Suddenly she spoke, without looking at him:

"It's hard, isn't it, Fernando? I know it's hard."

He couldn't believe his ears. He couldn't believe that before this day was over they would have to put themselves through this ordeal, to yet another ordeal. What is hard? he asked in a voice that came out almost as a whisper.

"You know. Being without a woman. It's hard, isn't it?"

He made no reply. Oh God, he was thinking, let this be over soon, oh God. But she went on, in a voice that although neutral, was as faint as it was implacable:

"Is there someone else, Fernando? You can tell me. We've reached a point in which there's no need for us to keep secrets from each other. After all, it's been one year today."

Shit, he thought, shit. But then he reacted. And displaying an energy that surprised even himself, he lifted his head and said:

"No, Suzana, there's no one else. You know there isn't."

She said nothing. She lay in silence, her eyes fixed on the ceiling. But now he wanted to hear more, he wanted to get to the bottom of this matter; and as if reading his mind, she then asked in the same feeble, flat voice:

"How do you manage then?"

"You know. I masturbate."

"I know. I know you do. But thinking of whom, Fernando?"

"Of you. Of who else but you, Suzana?"

"Of me?" There was now bitter mockery in her voice: Her tolerance had reached its limit. "Of me, Fernando? Of me as I am now, or of me as I used to be?"

He was now feeling devastated. An absurdity, this whole thing. An absurdity that would clamor for God's attention if God existed, if it were possible for God to exist. He did what he could do: He took her hand—and said nothing. She closed her eyes. The tears were now streaming down her face.

In silence, they remained motionless until the shadows of the evening started to grow denser in the room. Seeing that Suzana had fallen asleep, he got up and without making noise, he left the room.

He took a taxi home. The children were out; they had gone to Suzana's sister for dinner. After telling the maid that he didn't want to be disturbed, he went to his bedroom and locked the door behind him.

He stripped off all his clothes and lay down, naked.

He then closed his eyes, and without effort, he yielded himself to a fantasy in which he had been indulging ever since Suzana was admitted to the hospital. He imagined himself lying in bed, in a luxurious motel room. Suddenly the door opened and a gorgeous woman dressed as an odalisk slowly drew nearer. Enraptured, he waited for her, his mouth parched by desire.

She then threw herself upon him. But before he closed his eyes, before the devastating passion obliterated everything around him, he still caught sight of someone peering at him through the window of the motel room.

Suzana, naturally.

The Calligraphers' Union

THE CALLIGRAPHERS' UNION is in permanent session. This decision was not reached abruptly, nor was it made in response to a crisis situation. On the contrary, this course of action became necessary because of the aggravation of the calligraphers' already poor working conditions, which led them to convene a series of meetings—initially once a month, then once a week, finally every day—until eventually the assembled members (numbering thirty at the present time) decided that they would be in permanent session as a form of constant mobilization. Besides, they have no other alternative. Would they rather stay cooped up in their dinky little houses located in distant neighborhoods, mulling over their lives, ruminating on sorrows, waiting for death? Never. At least here in the headquarters of their union—and until the time when a judge makes his final decision on the eviction order pending against them—they find shelter and companionship (no minor matter to these elderly gentlemen whose circle of relations keeps narrowing) and they feel that they are fighting together for a major cause. The preservation of the art of calligraphy, says Alcebiades, one the founders of the union, is a pre-requisite for the survival of our culture. Sipping their watery tea, the other calligraphers concur, but quite a few of them can't help recalling the days when it was customary for their association to offer its members sumptuous dinners during which the wine poured freely.

Time drags as they sit in permanent session. Once the discussions of various issues (ranging from demands for the elimination pure and simple of the typewriter to the need to appeal to the government and charitable organizations for help) are over, the chairman loses no time in steering the conversation toward other topics, for he knows that there is nothing more terrible and threatening than absolute silence—the kind of silence unbroken by the rasp of writing pens on paper. Therefore, discussions of a technical nature as well as accounts of personal experiences are also placed on the agenda.

Different styles of calligraphy are analysed and compared; the remarkable modifications that appeared with the advent of the steel nib are discussed. Reminiscences abound. I still remember, says Honório, the very first sentence that I wrote as a calligrapher: *And this above everything else—be faithful to thyself.* It's from Shakespeare. Does anyone nowadays know who Shakespeare was? Does anyone know the work of the immortal Bard of Avon? Hm? And I ask you, my dear fellows: Do you believe that today's youth care a hoot about such matters?

Nobody replies; there is no need to. Honório merely wants to unburden his heart, and his fellow calligraphers listen to him in silence. Those who believe that calligraphy and Shakespeare are two separate issues and that the audience should not be overawed by British writers, keep such objections to themselves. This is not the occasion for dissent, not even for a spat over trivia. Unity—as the Constitution of the Calligraphers' Union states—should be everybody's objective. It is for this reason that Almeida does not voice his criticisms of Valentim's work. He would never say in public what he recorded on page seven of his journal: "Valentim's M resembles a camel in the desert." The members respect one another; even though they might belong to different schools of thought, they recognize the fact that pluralism is a condition for the survival of calligraphy.

I've always preferred the R, says Evilásio, or even the W—perhaps because they enable me to trace fanciful scrolls, which suits my baroque temperament to a T. But then I discovered the i, yes, that's right, the lower case i, and what a revelation it was. The modest simplicity of this letter! And with the point suspended in space! This point, believe me, fascinated me. I think that in it I've found the true meaning of calligraphy. Whereas some people—my own son, for example—tend to exaggerate the size of what they call the "dot of the i," and even go as far as to draw a small circle to represent it, I, on the other hand, during a moment of deep introspection, came to the conclusion that I should in fact endeavor to achieve the opposite, that is—reduce the point over the i to its minimum dimensions. In fact, as everybody knows, the point is completely dimensionless. The number of points is infinite. Invisible, omnipresent. Could the point be God, or could God be the point? To accept such an idea, however, I would have to be annihilated by it; that is, I would only be able to apprehend the point at the exact moment of my total extinction. I wasn't, and I'm still not, prepared for this, and for this reason I continue to put a point over the i, but I do so by barely touching the paper with the tip of my pen. A very contained gesture, certainly, but a gesture nonetheless. And to those of you who believe that calligraphy is born of gestures, let me say this: It is my conviction that authentic calligraphy is characterized by total inaction; potentiality rather than factuality distinguishes it.

"God," concludes Evilásio, "is the grand calligrapher."

I've heard, Marcondes whispers to whoever is next to him, that they now have electronic devices capable of capturing sounds and transforming them into writing. I don't believe that they've reached this point yet, retorts the bitter, skeptical Amâncio. But Rebelo says: I don't find this surprising. The typewriter started a course of action that would inevitably lead to disaster. And the tabulator is merely speeding up the end of calligraphy. Calligrapher Rosálio disagrees with him. He is not against progress; he even has an interesting project in mind that involves tracing letters in smoke up in the sky, with him flying the airplane (but first he will have to take flying lessons, but that's all right, he says, for he is quite willing to put up with anything in order to make his dream come true). To those who see this as treachery to the art of calligraphy, he retorts: The hand that now gently handles the pen is the same hand that will firmly hold the control stick of the airplane. Actually, Rosálio's only problem is the fact that altitudes give him vertigo, from which he has suffered since childhood, and for which there is no known cure, according to the various specialists that he has consulted.

For quite some time now, Inácio has been corresponding with a young woman whose name he once saw in "Love's Mail," a popular column in a major newspaper. One letter from him, and bingo! she professed that she had fallen in love with his handwriting: "The way you cross the T clearly shows a vigorous mind; the gentle curves of your S indicates an affectionate heart." Inácio weeps every time he reads these missives from her, but he has decided that he will never meet the young lady in person. His love will subsist only on handwritten pages.

Feijó has just come in. The last one to arrive, as usual; and as usual, with that superior smile of his. He has every reason to be smiling. Of all the union members, he is the only one to have an assured job. Once every four years he is responsible for writing the name of the Governor elect on a special certificate. With great care, Feijó prepares himself for this task: he starts exercising and he goes on a special diet. The job pays well and Feijó is treated with deference; however, he has noticed over the years that the names of the governors keep getting shorter and shorter; he suspects that this fact is not just a matter of chance, but rather the product of a conspiracy in which radical elements are involved.

What if we were to revitalize our profession? bursts out Alonso (who often brags about having an entrepeneurial mind); we could, for instance, run ads in the newspapers, like: *Your beloved won't resist a letter penned in a beautiful handwriting.* Alonso has also plans for setting up courses geared to people from every walk of life. He then starts talking about calligraphy for politicians, calligraphy for executives, calligraphy for proletarians. Mercedes, the only female member of the union, makes a serious accusation against graphologists: They were the ones, she states, that discredited our profession by disseminating the idea that a person's handwriting can reveal his character. We must introduce into the schools' curriculum the concept that calligraphy unites people, she says.

The Calligraphers' Union is housed in an old mansion located in the oldest part of the city. It is a legacy left to them by Abelardo, a calligrapher of international renown (at one time he had even prepared documents for the Belgian monarchy). Those were the days! The calligraphers had just then established a famous Brotherhood. The Union was not formed until much later, at a time when job opportunities began to get scarce. The meetings they used to have, Damião reminisces, were real celebrations. Dressed in formal attire, the calligraphers, accompanied by their wives and children, would arrive at the headquarters, ablaze with lights. The meetings started punctually at 8 P.M. The minutes of the previous meeting— in longhand, naturally; being asked to record the minutes was a much coveted honor—were circulated among the members, not so much for comments as for admiration (or scorn). Afterward the orchestra played the Calligraphers' Hymn (*With a thousand serifs and a thousand scrolls / I'll trace the name of my Brazil / While in the bluest of the skies* . . . etc., etc.). Glasses filled with imported champagne were then raised in a toast; dinner was served—trout or salmon or lobster, finished with dessert—a torte with the words "Long Live Calligraphy" written in whipped cream. And then there was dancing, which was always lively. Nobody ever left before five in the morning. Ah, the good old days, sighs calligrapher Moura. Days that will never return, adds calligrapher Felipe (even though they have fallen out with each other, they are united in sorrow).

"Fanti!" shouts calligrapher Reginaldo. "Fanti de Ferrara!"

The other calligraphers exchange glances. They know that he is referring to Fanti de Ferrara, who in 1514 introduced the geometric method into gothic calligraphy. They know that Reginaldo owns an extremely valuable copy of the *Theorica et practica perspicassimi Sigromundi de Fantis: De modo scribendi fabricandique omnes litterarum species*, published in Venice. But since Reginaldo won't lend this book to anybody, they deliberately ignore the provocation. Calligrapher Guilherme then changes the subject: Calligraphy, he states, is the art of beautiful handwriting. Inspired, he goes on: It is freedom united to discipline. It is the past speaking to our hearts. This is all very nice, mutter a few calligraphers, but what about the labor laws?

We have nothing in common with this new group the key punch operators. If we have an affinity with anyone, states calligrapher Ludovico, it is with those monks who in the silence of their monasteries used to copy texts in gothic handwriting and intersperse them with exquisite illuminations. Which was also—calligrapher Arthur cuts in abruptly—a protection against fraud: The more intricate the handwriting, the more difficult it would be to falsify a papal bull. This unexpected interruption silences calligrapher Ludovico. He dislikes being reminded of the practical aspects of the art of calligraphy. It is a known fact that Pope Eugene IV had ordered that a special type of handwriting—the cursive script—be reserved for documents that had to be written quickly—*brevi manu*—from which the word *brief*, meaning a summary, is derived. Briefs! Briefs in an art characterized by unhastiness! Equally deplorable is the fact that Pacioli—a priest who was a friend of, incredible! none other than Leonardo da Vinci—made a close study of the geometry of the letters. As if it were possible to compare feelings to squares and hexagons!

Calligraphers Raimundo and Koch are engaged in a lively controversy. Raimundo charges that Colbert, the finance minister of Louis XIV, was responsible for the demise of the gothic when he recommended that all government employees adopt the type of writing known as *financière:* It was already the bourgeois tastelessness taking over, he bellows. Koch, in a subdued voice (in which, however, hidden vibrations of resentment can be detected), reasons that the gothic contained in itself the germ of its own destruction. Because of its angularity: Life, states Koch, favors soft curves. It's not by striking the paper with a pen that we will be able to imitate the flux of existence. Two or three calligraphers applaud timidly. Raimundo remains silent. Deep down, however, he believes in returning to the gothic style as a way of projecting himself into the dizzy heights there where the stars twinkle. Calligrapher Ronildo agrees with Raimundo: as far as he is concerned, the era of the Sun King had a disastrous effect on calligraphy, notwithstanding the efforts of Danoiselet and Rousselot to counteract the damage. Nowadays people say that it is more important to have character than to write legibly, but—and at this point Ronildo's voice quivers with unrestrained indignation—isn't this a *reductio ad absurdum?*

What is elegance? asks calligrapher Dimone. And he himself supplies the answer: It's the opportunity for embellishment.

I think of the trajectory of my life as if it were the tracing of a letter, says calligrapher Epaminondas—of the lower-case *l*, to be precise. I climbed up; when I reached the top, I turned around and began to climb down; I then reached the lowest point, and ever since I've been waiting for the final turn upward, however slight it might be.

"At times I wonder," he sighs, "if I shouldn't call myself Luís. Luís with a lower-case *l*.

Nobody replies to his remarks. Besides, it is getting late. One by one, the calligraphers get up and leave, headed for their dinky little houses. They will be back on the following day. There is no life outside the permanent session. There is no life outside calligraphy.

French Current Events

IN THE MIDDLE OF THE NIGHT, he is brusquely awakened. It is his father who, terrified, roughly shakes him awake:

"Tiago's been arrested, Leo! You've got to run away!"

Bewildered, he sits up in bed and begins to explain to his father: It's Tiago who is a political activist, not he, all he ever did was to take part in a few student demonstrations, innocuous things, really. His father, however, won't listen; he has already made a phone call to a friend of his, he has already gotten in touch with a lawyer, he has already made up his mind: His son will have to flee the country. And without further delay. Leo doesn't argue. He packs his things in a hurry. At dawn, he boards the *Colossus*, about to sail for France. In Paris he finds accommodation in a run-down hotel in the Quartier Latin. He hopes that he will be able to return home soon, as soon as all fears and apprehensions dissipate. But in fact, he won't return soon. Six years will pass; his father will die, and soon afterward, his mother; with no parents and no friends left, he will no longer have any reason to go home.

He is yet another Brazilian expatriate. Unlike the other expatriates, however, he doesn't want to have anything to do with Brazil. Or with anything else for that matter. He manages to make ends meet thanks to a modest job working as a janitor. At night, in his room in a boardinghouse, he watches TV. Whenever he has enough money, he goes to a concert. He has always had a passion for music. Sometimes he gets drunk, sometimes he picks up a woman—a salesgirl, a divorcee. They don't last long, these affairs. Then, it's back to the usual routine.

One rainy night he is standing in front of the Pleyel Concert Hall. Frustrated: The tickets for that night's performance are sold out, or at least the seats he can afford are all gone. He is about to walk away when a well-dressed young man approaches him. He has a ticket for sale: Due to an unforeseen circumstance, he won't be able to attend the concert. One hundred and twenty francs. Leo shakes his head sadly: He doesn't have that much money. The well-dressed young man persists: You can have it for one hundred francs. No? For ninety then. No? Seventy? Suddenly irritated, the young man does something surprising: He stuffs the ticket into Leo's pocket—it's yours, for free—and disappears amid the crowd.

Perplexed and suspicious (can the rich be trusted?), Leo enters the concert hall, finds his seat—which is in fact excellent—and sits down. Just in time: The orchestra begins to strike up the opening bars of the *Jupiter Symphony*.

Mozart is Leo's favorite composer, and the performance of the Philharmonic is breathtaking—but he finds it impossible to concentrate on the music. Because of the young woman beside him: She keeps looking at him, but she doesn't do so surreptitiously, with sidelong glances. No, she stares at him persistently. What does she want from him, this beautiful and elegant young woman? He can't imagine what, and he becomes more and more disconcerted, to the point of thinking that he will get up and leave. But no, it's a matter of honor: He will remain seated. He is not indebted to anyone, he owes no one any explanation. He won't leave. The hell with the rich.

During the intermission the young woman addresses him: Do you mind if I ask you something? She speaks in French, but to his surprise, he realizes that she is Brazilian; her accent is unmistakably *carioca*, a Rio de Janeiro accent. You can speak in Portuguese, he says, smiling. Ah, you're Brazilian, too! It's her turn to be surprised. He says that yes, he is Brazilian, but he has been living in Paris for many years. She then tells him that she has just arrived in the city, that she came to study for a doctorate at the university, but she missed the registration deadline; anyhow, she decided she would stay in Paris for a while. Daddy vouches for me, she says with a grimace.

They laugh. She then repeats her initial question. She would like to know how Leo happened to get this particular seat. He tells her. I see, she murmurs. She is upset, obviously upset, but she says nothing else. At the end of the concert, however, she speaks to him again:

"I should tell you . . . " She hesitates for a moment, and then goes on: "This ticket entitled its holder to have dinner. At my place."

He accepts the invitation. How could it be otherwise when he is already passionately—whatever the meaning of "passionately" is—in love with her. Passionately in love. And it is with passion that they yield themselves to each other in the beautiful apartment where she lives alone.

He spends the night there; on the following day he doesn't go to work. Instead, he takes her for a walk. It is a beautiful day, the first beautiful day after a week of rain. Occasionally he plays the tour guide and shows her around the Eiffel Tower, Notre Dame Cathedral—places that she didn't have the patience to visit before, places that now, she admits, she is delighted to see.

As night descends, Leo becomes increasingly restless (later, in retrospect, she will recall that strange restlessness of his at sunset). He tells her he has to go, he has an appointment. She makes him promise that he will phone her. I will, for sure, he says.

Before he leaves, he asks her for money. What for? she wants to know, surprised, and even somewhat offended. It's none of your business, he says dryly. Taking the money, he stuffs it into his pocket, and without another word, he walks away.

On that same night he returns to the Pleyel Hall to attend another concert. Whether by coincidence or not, he occupies the same seat. Whether by coincidence or not, it is again the Philharmonic playing. Except that it is Beethoven this time. Halfway through the symphony known as *The Pastoral*, Leo stands up, and removes from his tote bag what later will be identified as a Molotov cocktail; after igniting the wick, he hurls the bomb onto the stage. However, aside from the fact that the musicians are thrown into a panic, there are no other consequences, for the crude artifact fails to explode.

Leo is arrested and deported. Handcuffed, he arrives in Rio. He is interrogated by the police, who ask him if he is a terrorist. Leo makes no reply. In doubt, the clerk records the answer as being in the affirmative.

A Job for the Angel of Death

EVERY YEAR, ON HIS BIRTHDAY, the boss treats us to lunch. A huge marquee is set up in the courtyard of the factory, and all of us—more than six hundred workers, together with supervisors and department heads, sit down at the long tables to relish the magnificent spread: potato salad, chicken, rice, beans, pasta. A menu chosen by the boss himself, who is, as he himself insists on pointing out, a person of simple tastes. And with his feet on the ground.

The food is good, and the meal is eaten in an atmosphere of cheerful camaraderie: a few beers and we are already pelting each other with potato salad. The boss and the company directors smile at our antics. Everybody is having fun.

Then at a particular moment, a bell rings. Silence falls: The boss is about to address us.

He starts by saying that he is very happy to be with his employees, whom he considers as his own children, particularly because he is an old man, much older than what people think. Then he adds:

"I know that many of you consider me a cantankerous old man

because I am very demanding, but I am just as hard on myself as I am on you. Many of you think that I should have retired a long time ago."

"That I should have died even, to make room for a new boss, a younger man, less strict."

He pauses and then goes on:

"Let me disillusion right away those of you who entertain such thoughts. I have good reasons to believe that I'll be around for a long time."

He then proceeds to tell us the story about the Angel of Death:

The boss had just established his own company. At that time, he manufactured only small boilers. He had five workers to help him, but the bulk of the work was done by himself. One night he was working late. A boiler had to be ready for delivery on the following day, but the workmen had already gone home, leaving the work half-finished. So he decided he would finish the job himself. And there he was in his shop, all sweaty from soldering metal plates together, when all of a sudden he saw before him a strange-looking person: tall, thin, with hollowed cheeks and a sinister aspect. He asked the individual who he was. I'm the Angel of Death, he replied, I've come for you. The boss was then a young man in the pink of health, and the idea of dying had never even crossed his mind. But he knew that things like a heart attack, a stroke, could happen to anyone. Therefore, resigned, he told the Angel of Death that he would go with him. But he would like to have his permission to finish the boiler first, for he didn't want to leave his customer in the lurch. After some hesitation, the Angel of Death allowed him to finish the work. However, he said that he would wait only until daybreak. As soon as the first rays of sun entered through the fanlight, the boss would have to go with him. Under these circumstances, the boss lost no time in going back to his work. The Angel of Death stood watching. At a given moment, he drew closer; curious, he asked the boss what he was doing. The boss gave him an explanation without, however, interrupting his work. The Angel of Death then asked if he could be of any help. At first the boss considered the offer of help with suspicion; he thought that the Angel of Death was in a hurry to take him away; however, at that moment he would accept help even from the devil himself, and so, handing the Angel of Death a monkey wrench, he told him to tighten some bolts. And together, they worked. When they realized it, it was already day, and the workmen were beginning to arrive. The Angel of Death was panic-stricken. And now, what am I going to do? He was whimpering. I've failed in my mission, I can't return to the place where I came from.

Taking pity on the Angel of Death, the boss offered him a job, with the warning that he would be paying him only the minimum wage, for he was after all just an apprentice. The offer was accepted.

"And thus," says the boss winding up, "I've gained a loyal and helpful partner. I'm sure that as long as he is satisfied—and he is indeed satisfied—I'll remain here and I'll run this company my own way. And that's it, my friends."

The air resonates with a burst of enthusiastic applause. It is true that a few, the malcontents, keep casting surreptitious glances around them; they are trying to identify which one of their fellow workers could be this Angel of Death who had failed to carry out his task. Most people, however, are intent on savoring the dessert. Guava paste with cheese. Delicious and nourishing.

The Right Time

THE AIRPLANE HAD BEEN IN THE AIR for about thirty minutes when my husband suddenly realized: No, he didn't really want to walk out on me.

Everything—the rash decision, the hasty departure (he hadn't even packed a suitcase!), and then boarding the airplane—everything amounted to nothing more than precipitation. To a terrible mistake. In fact, he didn't want to live with the other woman; he really wanted to stay with his wife and children.

Fifteen years of married life, a family—this wasn't something that he could discard as if it were a banana peel,

(A banana peel: at the thought, there in the airplane, he couldn't help smiling. Because he now recalled a funny incident: On our very first date he had slipped on a banana peel right at the door of my parents' house. Both of us had laughed, although I was somewhat annoyed, I hoped it wasn't an omen, a bad omen. He must have read my mind: I'll never slip again, never, he assured me.)

A veritable oath, which came to mind as the airplane proceeded along its route across black clouds, which were at times illuminated by threatening bolts of lightning.

A veritable oath. Which he had been on the verge of breaking: In a moment of folly he had decided to abandon his family, his friends, in short, everything, for a woman that had just arrived in town—an actress; true, she was a beautiful, intelligent, educated woman, but a stranger nonetheless. Typical of an adolescent. But lucidity was back: The flight was long enough to allow him to come to his senses. Thank goodness we live in a country of vast distances, he thought, in a country of long flights. Shucks, all this money spent on the airfare—and only then did he notice: it was a round-trip ticket. Meaning what? Well, that he had in fact thought of going back, that he had never meant to cut himself loose from everything. Unconsciously he had taken a providential precaution against this possibility. All that he had to do after getting off the plane was to go to the ticket counter of the airline company and book a seat on the first returning flight. The young woman behind the counter would find it odd, for sure—but so what? Let her think it odd. It wouldn't upset him. He might even reveal to her the fact that he was returning home. You know, I've made a mistake, I've walked out on my family, but during the flight here I recognized that what I was doing was a mistake and now I'm eager to go back to my family as soon as possible. Smiling sympathetically, the young woman would then ask if he had any luggage; and after he replied in the negative, she would then verbalize what he himself must have known before setting off on this trip: Ah, I see, so you probably weren't all that serious about embarking on this adventure, sir. And the two of them would laugh.

"Dinner, sir?"

It was the flight attendant, with a tray. My husband declined: No, he didn't want anything; he was hoping he would be home in time for dinner with us, his family. It would be a reconciliation dinner, even though we wouldn't know this because he would tell us nothing about what had happened; he would disclose nothing to us. Why spoil the enjoyment of having dinner with us? Dinner was our best moment together. Always. What a foolish thing I was about to do, he murmured. The man beside him, surprised, looked at him suspiciously. My husband smiled at him. He considered telling the man: You know, I almost walked out on my family—but then decided against it. He looked at his watch: 7:45 P.M. No, I'm wrong: the time was 7:42 P.M. Five minutes later the plane crashed into a mountain. And everything that my husband had been thinking about has remained a secret; a secret between the two of us, a secret that I carefully keep.

As I carefully keep his watch, stopped forever: 7:45 P.M.

The Public Enemy

THE ACTIVITIES OF ARÃO, the public enemy, start at seven o'clock in the morning of any day, winter or summer. It is not easy for an almost sixty-year-old man afflicted with chronic rheumatism to get up so early, but Arão never wavers: He has a mission to accomplish, and so he gets dressed and goes out, headed for the bus stop. The bus comes. He gets on the bus, makes a quick assessment of the situation, and finally takes a seat, usually next to a fat and ugly old woman. As soon as the bus pulls out, Arão leans toward the woman:

"You're very ugly, lady," he whispers.

At first the woman doesn't understand: What? You're very ugly, lady, Arão repeats, you're the ugliest woman on this bus, in this city. The woman thinks that he must be joking, but Arão continues with his torrent of insults: You're a witch, lady, you're a hag, you're a miscarriage of nature, you should be devoured by voracious alligators. Curiously enough, there is no hatred in his voice; the whole thing sounds like some kind of a sour litany, it is as if Arão were going through some ritual; this fact, however, doesn't pacify the woman, who suddenly gets up screaming—you dirty, disgusting bastard—and then she slaps him on the face several times. With blood trickling from his split lip, Arão is thrown out of the bus by the indignant driver. He falls down and rolls on the dusty sidewalk—one of the vicissitudes in the life of a public enemy—but he soon picks himself up and gets into a taxi that happens to be parked nearby. The cabbie, a fat mulatto, makes small talk: What a beautiful day, isn't it, we haven't had a day like this for quite some time. Ignoring the cabbie's remarks, Arão asks to be taken downtown. As soon as the taxi pulls away, he leans forward:

"You stink."

Like the woman on the bus, the driver's first reaction is surprise: He thinks he must be hearing things. But no; Arão is now saying loud and clear that the man stinks, that he stinks really bad, that he stinks more than a mountain of shit; that he is polluting the car, the whole street, the city itself, with his stench. Angered, the cabbie (a peaceable man under other circumstances) brings the car to a halt, then opens the door and orders Arão out of his taxi. Since Arão refuses to get out, the cabbie grabs him by the coat, drags him out of the car, and then drives away without even thinking of collecting the money owed to him. Arão recomposes himself and starts walking. From a doorway, a beggar, who happens to be a cripple, asks him for money.

"For the love of God."

Arão ignores him and continues to walk. All of a sudden, however, he stops; he turns around, walks up to the beggar, and for a while stands staring at the man.

"Drop dead," he finally says.

Like the taxi driver and the woman on the bus, the beggar is taken aback; he goggles at Arão in surprise. To leave no room for doubt, Arão repeats:

"Drop dead."

And before the beggar has time to get his wits together, Arão bursts into a ferocious tirade: The world is already overcrowded with the poor—with the poor and the crippled, and beggars should really die. Then all of a sudden, the crippled man rises to his feet, and balancing himself precariously on his one leg, he delivers such a violent blow of his crutch that Arão staggers and falls down. People, filled with indignation, rush to his aid: It's unheard-of, a beggar assaulting an elderly gentleman, heaven knows why. Angry voices shout *lynch him*. A policeman wants to arrest the beggar, but Arão won't let him. He says that he is fine, that the whole thing was nothing but a misunderstanding. Then he hobbles away, headed for home.

He arrives home, takes off his hat, hangs it on the hatrack. He examines himself in the mirror: a split lip, an abrasion on his chin. Has he had enough for one day? Perhaps. But . . . what about that man selling lottery tickets that he saw a while ago? "You bring bad luck." Yes. Why not. "You bring bad luck." He smiles, grabs his hat, and goes out again.

The Message

THE KING USED TO ORDER that the heads of the messengers that brought him bad news be cut off. In this way, a process of natural selection was established: The incompetents were gradually eliminated until there was only one messenger left in the country. He was, as one can easily imagine, a man that had mastered the art of imparting bad news surprisingly well. Your son died, he would announce to a mother, upon which the woman would start chanting jubilant hymns: Hallelujah, Lord! Your house burned down, he would inform a widower, upon which the man would break into frenetic applause. To the King, this messenger would relay the news of successive military defeats, epidemics of the plague, natural catastrophes, the devastation of entire crops, stark poverty, and famine. The King, surprised at his own reaction, would listen to such news with a smile. So pleased was he with the messenger that he appointed him his official spokesman. Acting in this important capacity, the messenger soon won the support and the affection of the public. Concomitantly, hatred for the monarch started to grow until he was finally deposed by the people, who had risen in rebellion, and the former messenger was crowned King. The first thing he did upon assuming office was to order the execution of all candidates for the position of messenger. Starting with those that had mastered the art of imparting bad news.

Unpublished Works

THE OWNER OF A PRINT SHOP-CUM-PUBLISHING HOUSE greets the lady that has just walked in. The owner, a mustachioed man going prematurely bald, is still young; he is negligently dressed in checkered pants and a flowery shirt that affords a glimpse of his hairy belly. By contrast, the lady looks cheerful and discreet in her gray suit. In a beautiful morocco briefcase she carries a manuscript: poems. She would like to have them published, she says, and it is at this moment (but only at this moment, not thereafter) that her voice trembles in an almost imperceptible way.

The owner of the print shop doesn't find her request surprising. His father, from whom he has inherited the business, used to publish books of poetry—deluxe limited editions, aimed at a small, select readership. He charged a lot for this kind of work, which he did, he used to say, not for the money but for the pleasure he felt in disseminating culture.

A pleasure which his son and successor does not feel. He knows nothing about poetry or literature; as a matter of fact, he hardly knows anything about printing itself; so much so, in fact, that business has been steadily going downhill. However, he thinks of himself as being shrewd; a while ago, when this lady walked in, he had a hunch: *today's my day.* And now as he leafs through the manuscript (beautifully handwritten, incidentally) he is indeed convinced: here is his lucky break, his opportunity to hit the jackpot, to come out on top of the heap. Because in these poems the woman speaks of a hopeless passion; besides, she is obviously rich. A rich widow or divorcee, maybe a rich heiress. A middle-aged woman who writes passionate poems and who desires to see them in print: She'll pay any price.

No problem, says the owner of the print shop, we'll print them, sure; we'll design a beautiful edition, a real work of art. That's exactly what I have in mind, says the lady. A work of art, if possible with illustrations. Certainly, the owner of the print shop hastens to say, with illustrations, yes, beautiful illustrations, and I have the right man to illustrate the poems. He proceeds to give her further details: He will do the typesetting with special typefaces, the paper will be of the highest quality available. Of course, this kind of work, he forewarns her warily, unable to contain a certain anxiety, doesn't come cheap. Oh yes, I know it doesn't, the lady is quick to say, but it doesn't matter, money isn't a problem. The owner of the print shop can barely contain a smile. A handshake (how soft her hand is) seals the deal, and a moment later he is already asking for an advance payment: It would be a good idea to buy the paper right away, prices are soon going up again. Without any vacillation, she writes out a check and then leaves.

This money, he invests. And from then on, he keeps investing: the money for the illustrator; the money for the typesetting expenses; the money for the invitations to the launching of the book. He invests and invests. Every time the woman makes a payment, she inquires about her book. It's coming on nicely, he replies, don't worry.

He gets a good return on his investments; he pays off a few debts and he can even afford to buy new clothes. But he is in a state of restlessness. The fact is . . . he has fallen in love with the woman. There is no denying that he is really in love. He, of all people, he, a seasoned man who has lost count of the number of lovers in his life. What on earth possessed him to fall in love? And with a lady to boot, a woman far above his social class, and to make matters worse, a woman whom he merely intended to take advantage of.

Apparently, she has not noticed anything. She phones him, but only to inquire about the book. Then one afternoon she comes to the print shop to have a look at the work in progress. There is nobody else there besides him; the two old typesetters who work for him have already left. He lays a few rough sketches for the book cover on the desk in his office, and while she is examining them, he approaches her from behind. He embraces her. She offers no resistance, and merely asks him to be gentle. Right then and there, on the tattered couch in his office, he possesses her. Afterward, they lie there, she smoking in silence. He would like to talk, to tell her things about himself, to describe his unhappy childhood and tormented adolescence to her. But she, claiming that she has things to do, says good-bye and leaves.

They continue to meet, but now in a discreet motel. Yes, they have become lovers; however, all she is interested in is her book: how is the printing coming on, when will the book come out? He finds her dogged insistence somewhat irritating: Why always talk about the book? Why not talk about love? She claims that she is in a hurry, she is leaving for Europe soon, she wants to see her book launched before her departure. One night they have an argument. She gives him an ultimatum: She wants her book ready on the next day. Otherwise, she will go to the police.

He leaves the motel furious and hurt. So, she wants her book; well, she will have it. He makes for the print shop; he himself will do the typesetting. There's nothing to it, really, just a few little poems. However, the job turns out to be extraordinarily difficult. There are things that he does not even understand; what the hell does this word here mean? And this one, why did she divide it like this? Laboriously he toils away until suddenly—the day is already dawning—a revelation: In a flash, everything makes sense, he now understands what she is saying with these strange words. Yes, it's of love that she speaks, and she does so beautifully; so beautifully that tears of joy begin to run down his face. Yes, he, a boor of a man, is touched, deeply touched by the beauty of these poems. On a scrap of paper, he starts to scribble a few lines of poetry; they strike him as pretty good; nothing fancy, but quite good. He revises a word here, a word there, another word here. And then an idea occurs to him: He will add his own poems to the book, he will be the co-author. Something symbolic and timely, too, for he has already decided that he is going to propose to her.

In the morning he goes to her house. A servant shows him into her study, saying that the lady won't be long. Impatient, he starts pacing the room back and forth.

The telephone rings. With the confidence of someone feeling very much at home, he answers the phone.

A man's voice. Asking for the lady of the house. She isn't home, he says with brazenness (from now on she won't be home for anyone). Would you please, says the caller, tell her that the contract is ready. What contract? asks the owner of the print shop, surprised. The contract with our publishing house, the man replies; we think that her book is very good and we're going to publish it.

Mechanically, he puts the receiver down; in his amazement, he stands there motionless. But then she appears, dressed in a beautiful flowery tunic, looking more elegant than ever.

With an effort, he recovers himself. She, too, smiles. Who was it? she asks in a casual tone of voice.

Wrong number, he replies. Wrong number.

Wrong number, she murmurs. She stands there motionless, a faraway look in her eyes, her face lit up by a smile. He knows what she is thinking: It'll make a good title for a poem. *Wrong number*.

A Minute of Silence

THE KING DIED, and the government issued a decree: at ten o'clock in the morning of the day after the funeral, the entire population was to observe one minute of silence. Everybody complied with the order, and at the appointed time, a heavy silence fell upon the whole country.

People who happened to be out on the street saw other people standing silent and absolutely immobile. Supposedly, they were all thinking of the dead monarch, and indeed, many were; in fact, almost everybody was, with the exception of a professor of mathematics who, as soon as he fell silent, started to do some calculations. He found out that the total sum of the minutes of silence of twenty-six million and eight hundred thousand citizens amounted to fifty years—exactly the age of the King at the time of his death. One life lost, the professor was thinking, and now another life is being lost in this silence. And later: No, not being lost, not entirely, for I've discovered something—but what is it?

At that very moment in a maternity hospital, his wife was giving birth to a baby who, suffering from multiple congenital lesions, was unable to cling to life: He lived for only one minute. Long enough for his mother to name him after the King so sadly missed by everybody.

The Prince

SHE WAS ALONE IN A BAR, drinking beer, when he came up to her. He said nothing, and didn't even introduce himself, but immediately she knew for sure: He was a prince. A handsome young man, dressed in austere but elegant clothes, his straight chestnut-brown hair carefully combed. A prince, yes. And the great adventure that she had always hoped to have was finally about to become a reality.

Smiling, the prince gave her an imperceptible nod. She got up and followed him out of the bar. They got into a big silver-gray car that had been waiting for him. Without a word, and as if by prior arrangement, the chauffeur started the engine. They drove across the city for a while before reaching the suburbs; and not a word passed between them—between her and the prince. At times they would exchange glances, and as they did so, they would smile, but without saying anything, for words didn't seem necessary. They arrived at a country house, which was just as she had imagined it. A big house in the middle of a stretch of well-kept lawn. At the door, a butler was waiting for them; they immediately went upstairs to the second floor. The prince opened the door to a bedroom, and just as she had imagined it, there it was, the large double bed with its muslin canopy and richly embroidered counterpane. With a sigh, she fell into his arms, and without further delay, they engaged in foreplay, which a few minutes later culminated in the sex act. Afterward, he opened the champagne bottle kept in a silver bucket; always smiling, and never saying anything.

And there the two of them remained in silence, drinking champagne. Then all of a sudden, she couldn't contain herself any longer; all of a sudden, her eyes glittering, she blurted out:

"Have you noticed, Your Excellency, that we haven't said a word since we met?"

The man still tried to detain her, but it was too late, the spell was broken, and he burst into tears, for he was irremediably transformed into—what?

Into a prince, certainly.

The Problem

THE PROBLEM IS INITIALLY ENUNCIATED LIKE THIS: Our grandmother loves her husband Isaias very much. Which seemingly doesn't constitute a problem at all; however, the fact is that Grandfather Isaias is very old and sick, and there is every indication that he will die soon.

The enunciation of the problem continues in this manner: Our grandmother will never consent to a separation from someone who has been her lifelong companion. She will probably have his body embalmed, which is not unusual. However, we have every reason to believe that our grandmother intends to keep the embalmed body of her deceased husband in the large closet in her bedroom.

The problem then reaches an almost crucial stage. The question that is bound to arise is: How to get rid of the corpse, whose presence in the house we cannot obviously tolerate. In this regard the grandchildren propose a variety of solutions. Some suggest setting the body on fire—an idea that seems quite feasible, but it stirs up a controversy. It is not a mere matter of finding out if an embalmed grandfather is combustible; the crucial factor is that the risk of a widespread fire should not be taken lightly. For this reason, others suggest that we cut our grandfather into tiny bits, which could then be disposed of; if done gradually, his widow would not notice a thing; however, this could go on for years. The best suggestion comes from a granddaughter who works for a research laboratory. By means of a conditioning process, she intends to train a rat, which will then nibble at the body of our grandfather until it is gone. Of course, our grandmother might come across the rat, but this won't matter. The problem will be formulated in a complete, definitive, and relentless way at the time when our grandmother starts calling the rat Isaias.

In the World of Letters

HE COMES TO THE BOOKSTORE during peak hours, but it is already common knowledge that he does so on purpose: It makes his job so much easier.

He steals books. Something he has been doing for years, practically ever since his childhood. He started by stealing a textbook that he needed for his school work; it was so easy that he got hooked on it, and he was soon stealing adventure and science-fiction novels, as well as books about art, politics, science, economy. He perfected his technique to such an extent that he was able to steal four or five books at one go. He shoplifted in the bookstores of every city he visited. At one time in London, he was almost caught red-handed—an incident that he now recalls with a feeling of amusement.

At first, he always read the books that he stole. Later, reading lost its appeal for him. The whole thing became theft for theft's sake—he stole just for kicks. He would give the books away as gifts, or simply discard them. But he had less and less time to frequent bookstores; his commercial enterprises required his full attention. Besides, as an entrepreneur, he couldn't afford to run the risk of being caught in flagrante delicto. A problem that he solved, as he solves all his problems, with acumen, audacity, imagination.

Bingo! He has just pilfered another one. Nothing spectacular in this action: He merely took a small book and stuffed it into his pocket. He glances around him; apparently, nobody has noticed anything. He greets me and leaves the store.

A minute later he returns. How did I do? he asks, not without anxiety. Great, I reply, and he smiles, grateful. Which makes me happy, too, for praising him is not just an act of compassion but also a certain measure of prudence. He is, after all, the owner of the bookstore.

Sensitive Skin

A MAN IS ON THE BEACH, lying under an umbrella. A pleasant day. A soft breeze. The man looks at his watch, and much to his surprise, it is almost two o'clock in the afternoon. He has been there since eleven in the morning; he simply wasn't aware of the passage of time. That's the way it is, he concludes: when you feel fine, you don't notice time go by.

Such a realization leaves the man worried. He is no longer young; he is fifty years old. By ignoring the passage of time he is in fact speeding up a process that inexorably leads him to death. What's the use of feeling fine (and he does feel fine; he is rich and well known; and the beautiful woman lying beside him is his present wife), when in fact he is dying? And dying without giving much thought to it.

His hearts sinks; he has the impression that the day has darkened. However, being an energetic and courageous man, he won't let defeatist moods descend upon him. If this painful sensation of the inevitable end originated in a peculiar way of thinking about a sunny day, all he has to do in order to counteract this sensation is to find a different way of thinking. A trick, as a last resource. A trick of reasoning. He soon devises one. It goes like this: Well-being and happiness speed up the march of time; ergo, discomfort and suffering must slow it down. An undeniable truth, for in this present brooding—a painful and, it seemed to him, awfully slow process—he has spent no more than two minutes, as indicated by the watch of an excellent make that he wears on his wrist. Which goes to prove that *slow* and *painful*, the two words that have occurred to him to describe the crisis he is going through at the moment, are closely connected. As a matter of fact, he can't think of a single painful thing that does not also slow down time. For example, a small operation (without anesthesia) that he had as a child was the most unbearably prolonged thing in his entire life; and yet, it took the smiling surgeon no more than a few minutes to perform that operation.

Therefore, he will have to inflict some imaginary suffering upon himself. Suffering that could become quite potent. How? By imbuing it with a sense of uselessness. In the case of that childhood operation, the pain was allayed by the idea that it was necessary. So, what he will do now is to picture himself in a situation in which suffering will result in nothing, absolutely nothing.

He imagines himself as being a guerrilla in a country that is a dictatorship, in a country under a strong and unassailable military government. He imagines himself being captured and subjected to horrible tortures: a red-hot branding iron on his genitals, pincers pulling out his fingernails, and so on. For what he has in mind, this kind of imagining should do the trick; in one of these torture sessions life will *have to* stop because the victim has voluntarily repudiated any moral support and given up all hope for the future. By renouncing the future, he acquires an eternal present time.

The idea about the guerrilla and the subsequent torture is good but difficult to implement. A series of measures will have to be taken to put it into practice: the man will have to sell out his businesses, travel to a distant country, contact the leaders of the guerrilla movement, etc.—all of this requiring, for starters, that he leave the beach. No, it just won't do. He then starts thinking of something else, of something more within his reach. If I move away from this place under the umbrella, he ponders, and expose myself directly to the powerful sun, I'll feel at first discomfort, and then pain; soon afterward, the excruciating pain that I will have to endure will, by increasing exponentially, turn every second into a year, and every minute into a millennium: time will lean toward eternity.

But eternity will never be reached. Not only because the sun keeps marching toward its own decline, but also because this unbearable suffering, as it approaches the moment of breaking the barrier of time, will gradually yield to the joy that results from having overcome time; such joy will then promptly actuate the mechanism of the invisible clock, thus once more making existence measurable and finite, inevitably finite. There is no solution, the man groans softly. His wife, lying beside him, opens her eyes: "What do you want, honey?" The suntan oil, he replies, and when his wife passes him the plastic bottle, he gets up, squeezes a few drops of the dark, viscous liquid onto the palm of his right hand, and slowly begins to spread the oil over his face. As the advertisement says, when it comes to sensitive skin, you can't be too careful.

The Surprise

ON THE LARGE DOUBLE BED that has been in our family for several generations, a man lies dying. His cancer has spread to such an extent that the doctors have virtually stopped treating him. He has asked his doctors to let him die at home, on the same double bed on which his ancestors slept, made love, and died.

His wife, tearful, is at his bedside. The man asks her to cheer up: They have to discuss how his final minutes will be spent. I want my son here with me, he says. But he's just a child, the woman moans. I know he's a child, and it's for this very reason that I want him with me now, contends the man, who happens to be my father. I want my son to retain in his mind a positive image of myself—an encouraging image that will guide and sustain him throughout his life.

He is already gasping for breath. It is with a tremendous effort that he continues to talk.

"I'll tell him that, yes, man's life on earth does make sense. That kindness and tolerance are appreciated. That dignity must be maintained at any cost. And that love . . . "

He interrupts himself, his face contorted with pain. What is it, darling? asks the wife, in despair. What is it?

"Nothing," he says, controlling himself with difficulty. "Where was I?"

"That love—" She is in tears. "You were talking about love."

"Ah, yes. That love is everything. That love is *indeed* everything. It's important that he know this. That he believe in love."

She is now crying softly. And then, like a jack-in-the-box, I suddenly spring up from under the bed, open my arms wide, and

"Surprise!" I shout.

The Winner: An Alternative View

IN THE FIRST SEVEN ROUNDS, Raul was soundly trounced. Which didn't come as a surprise: He was badly out of shape. Months of indolence and even debauchery had taken their toll. The combative pugilist of the old days, the man whom many had considered a world-class boxer, a star, was now reduced to a limp dishrag. The crowd was not at all in the mood to show any complaisance. There was a succession of boos and abusive jeers hurled at him.

Suddenly, something happened. While lying on the canvas, floored by a devastating hook, Raul raised his head and saw his niece Doris, the daughter of his deceased brother Alberto, sitting in the front row. The girl was looking at him, her eyes brimming with tears. It was a look that pierced Raul like a dagger. Something inside him burst apart. He then felt the rebirth of that energy that in the old days used to turn him into the wild beast of the boxing ring. Leaping to his feet, he advanced upon his opponent like an enraged bull. At first the crowd did not realize what was happening. But when the fans noticed that a real resurrection had taken place, they started to root for him. With a barrage of well-aimed punches delivered with great violence, Raul sent his opponent to the canvas. The referee started counting the regulatory ten, and then declared Raul the winner.

Everybody was applauding. Everybody was delirious with joy. Everybody except the person telling the story. The person telling the story was the one that was floored. The person telling the story was the one that was defeated. Oh, God!

Memoirs of an Anorexic

IN THE BEGINNING OF WHAT the doctors had dubbed "her disease" (adding its name: anorexia nervosa), Rosa would refuse to eat the food that was served to her and her family at the table, and she did the same in the hospital where she had been admitted for treatment. Before long, however, she began to realize that what she was doing wasn't enough: She couldn't limit herself to merely refusing to eat the rice and beans, or the steak parmiggiana. She would have to go beyond this. But how? For several months she tackled this predicament until finally she hit upon a solution: imaginary foods. A category with no barriers that would hinder her refusal to eat. Slowly, she began this new phase. She would close her eyes, and with hardly any effort, she would find herself in that same elegant restaurant which she and her parents used to frequent when she was a child. She would study the menu at length and then order a really sophisticated dish, like lobster or trout. When the waiter came back with a platter on which small portions of food were artistically arranged, she would rise to her feet, and laughing, throw everything on the floor. Or she would throw the lobster at the face of her astounded father. For a few times such behavior was condoned but afterward, of course, she was barred from this luxury establishment; even imaginary managers were capable of being moved to indignation, which hardly upset her, though: She simply started to go to luncheonettes and other modest restaurants. What she was now throwing on the floor were pizzas, hamburgers, hot dogs. And soft drinks as well, for sure. At first this kind of behavior was condoned because in imagination (as well as in reality), she was rich and could pay for the damages. In the end, however, the restaurant managers became fed up with her; soon she was being thrown out of even the cheapest grease joints. By that time, she had already destroyed an incalculable quantity of food, and her weight was down to a mere forty kilograms (keeping in mind that the young woman was one meter seventy centimeters tall), but she felt that she had not accomplished her mission yet. She would need something big, something that would not only rock the world but also put an end to the very substance of her body—her flesh, her nerves, her blood—in a most definitive manner. In order to carry out this project, she would have to steal all the food available in the country and send it—where?—to Africa, of course, to that place where those poor creatures, incapable of anorexia nervosa, suffered the pangs of hunger. Therefore, she began to visualize huge storehouses chock-full of grain, gigantic cold storage rooms packed with bloody carcasses of beef, large barrels filled with whole milk. In single file, an army of dutiful servants would transport all this food to magnificent ships, which would then sail across the ocean in the direction of Africa, where millions of famished people would be waiting eagerly on the beach. And as soon as the ships were unloaded, the people would scramble for the food.

It is not hard to imagine what happened next. Well nourished, the natives were no longer satisfied with what they called "crumbs" (a semantic incorrectness: none of the food that had been sent to them left any residual matter that could be called "crumbs"). They wanted more, and in order to get what they wanted, they did not hesitate to resort to violence. Hordes upon hordes crossed the ocean in crude boats. They disembarked clamoring for food; and they killed anyone that got in their way. Rosa, bludgeoned with precision on the skull, was the first victim. The death certificate referred to a cerebral hemorrhage; it also mentioned anorexia nervosa, but those in the know do not hesitate to attribute the cause of her death to food. Imaginary victuals are very dangerous, even when not ingested.

 *Epilogue*

In the Tribe of the Short-Story Writers: A Deposition

The year is 1943. The setting is a neighborhood in Porto Alegre, a city in the southernmost part of Brazil. Like many other cities in this area of Latin America, it received a great contingent of European immigrants in the early 1900s. This neighborhood in particular is a neighborhood of immigrants: Jews from Russia and Poland. And perhaps for this reason, it resembles a small village in eastern Europe, with its small houses, tiny shops, grocery stores. During the day the streets are crowded: women gossip, kids play, street vendors cry their wares. But now it's night, a warm summer's night; all the residents are out on the streets, seated on chairs placed on the sidewalks.

In one of those groups, somebody, a woman, tells a story.

The year is 1943. There is a war going on in Europe. Brazilian troops have just landed in Italy, where they joined the Allies' army. Disturbing rumors about death camps just started to circulate—but this is not what the woman talks about: the story that she tells conjures up the first few years of the immigrants in Brazil, their astonishment at the forests, at the vast grasslands, their excitement upon tasting tropical fruits for the very first time. Oranges! There were oranges in Brazil! And to say that in Europe they carefully divided one single orange among the entire family. . . . Oranges, yes, and bananas too, and exotic fruits. And sugar: in Russia they would hold a cube of sugar between their teeth and drink tea through it—in this way, it lasted longer. But in Brazil sugar is plentiful and cheap, so plentiful

471

that they even put it in their maté, this beverage which the gauchos prefer to drink unsweetened in the macho way.

She is a great storyteller, this woman, and everybody listens, fascinated; and more than anyone else, her son, a six-year-old boy who would rather listen to stories than play soccer with his friends. He doesn't know it yet, but he is making a decision: in the future, he will tell stories, like his mother.

More than fifty years later I remember that night in the Bom Fim district in Porto Alegre, and I wonder about this mysterious impulse that makes a person tell stories and transform, as Kafka said, life into fiction. In my case, it's a life that has changed a great deal: life in general is mutable, but far more so in a country so mutable and contradictory like Brazil. In fact, very early on the contradictions of Brazilian life became part of my own way of being, and consequently, of my writing.

I'm thinking, for example, of my name—the result of an interesting combination. Scliar is a very common surname among Jews. Moacyr, however, is an Indian name; it means "he who inflicts pain." I've often wondered about the reasons behind my mother's decision to give me such a name: the traditional masochism of a Jewish mother? Or a desire to make things easier for her son by giving him a very Brazilian name? Being a teacher, my mother knew that Moacyr is a popular name in Brazil because of a fictional character created by José de Alencar, a nineteenth-century writer who, in a romantic way, idealized the Indians—in fact, victims of a genocide that reduced their numbers from millions to a few thousands.

An Indian name has a symbolic meaning. Tribes: I have moved from one tribe to another in the course of my existence. Real tribes, but they have inspired the characters with whom I have peopled the territory of my imagination. The first tribe was the one in my neighborhood. The Jewish tribe: the sounds of Yiddish, the melancholy humor, the rich tradition. Although not a believer, I read the Bible enthralled, and in the parables I discovered a literary form close to perfection.

Time went by, childhood was gone. I went outside the limits of my neighborhood, I discovered other tribes.

I took up medicine. The reasons? Many. The main one: I dreaded illness. Every time someone in my family became ill, I was terrified. I decided to conquer this terror by confronting it. In medical school I became acquainted with corpses, and later, in the public charity hospital, with patients. They came from all parts of the state; mostly, they were poor rural workers, the victims of Brazil's latifundia—the large landed estates with labor often in a state of partial servitude. Thanks to medicine, I plunged deeply into the reality of my country: I got to know the Brazil of sheer wretchedness, the Brazil of the *favelas*—the shanty towns. Like many others, I felt indignation over the appalling gap between the rich and the poor in Latin America. My first short stories translated this indignation; like many young writers, I was influenced by the socially committed literature of which Jorge Amado was the major exponent. In 1964, however, protest gave way to silence. This was the year of the coup d'état that was to keep the military in power for twenty-four years. One scene became engraved in my memory: I was downtown when all of a sudden, army trucks arrived at top speed. Soldiers, dozens of them, jumped out and blocked the door of a building whose mezzanine housed a small left-wing bookstore. From there, books were thrown into the street. The soldiers gathered them up and took them away.

The military dictatorship paralyzed the intellectual life of the country. The repression culminated in 1968, the year when I published my first book of short stories, *The Carnival of the Animals*.

Rereading those stories, I identify in them many influences. There they are: the Biblical parables, the Kafkaesque situations, and also magic realism—the Latin American way of combining political fiction with humor and fantasy. In my case, the experience of Latin America is also the experience of the Jewish immigration itself—the astounded, suspicious, amazed eyes that the Jews cast upon the continent.

Like many other writers, I didn't stick exclusively to the short story. I've written novels, essays, newspaper articles. But I keep returning to the short story. An implacable literary form; like the sphinx, it issues a challenge: decipher me or I'll devour you. That's why the tribe of the short-story writers lives in a permanent state of apprehension, searching in vain for the territory in which it can feel safe.

It is an ancient tribe. Storytelling is an art that goes back a long way. We can imagine primitive men gathered around a fire in a cave. Outside, wild beasts prowl and a thousand dangers lie in wait, but it is not of dangers that they are thinking because someone is telling a story, and the story has the magic power of performing tricks with reality, of transporting listeners, or readers, to another world, at times wonderful, at times frightening, but always different.

Short-story writers. Like poets, they start young; like poets, they die, or used to die, young: Poe at forty, Kafka at forty-one, Maupassant at forty-three, Chekhov at forty-four, O. Henry at forty-six. By contrast, Dostoievsky at sixty, Faulkner at sixty-five, Mann at eighty, Tolstoy at eighty-two: novelists last longer, their text doesn't have the dramatic urgency of the short story.

Nor does the novel have the challenge of the short story. The physiological law—the all-or-nothing law—applies to it. If we apply an electric stimulus of growing intensity to a lone muscle, we won't get a response at first; however, once the muscle contracts itself, it will do so with all its energy. A short story is like this; it results from a sudden revelation, from an epiphany. It either succeeds or fails; and when it fails, it fails completely, irremediably. A novel can have passages that are better or worse, more interesting or less interesting;

it will be judged as a whole. But the short story, a brief form, does not consent to such a possibility. Thus, the permanent state of anxiety in which the short-story writers live. An anxiety that is irreversible. Whoever is admitted to the tribe of the short-story writers cannot leave it. For better or worse, you are imprisoned for good. That's what happened to me. But I'm not complaining. I'm just telling. Which is what short-story writers are good at.